Sebastian

The Saga of Sebastian Edwards and his rise as a Liberal Democrat politician in 2015-2017

By Julian Hamilton

November 2015

Published by Julian Hamilton

I am indebted to my wife Hilary Hamilton and my former secretary Mrs Marion Hawley for their tireless work in checking the proofs. As the writer is always the backstop any errors are mine and mine alone.

ISBN 9780993281716

Table of Contents

This story is to be continued and is yet to be written for years 2017-2020

PART ONE – A Safe House

CHAPTER ONE

"There you are!" he said, "It looks perfect! Just perfect! Exactly what we wanted! Exactly what we are looking for?" It was a summer's day in Cultra, Northern Ireland in the year 1994.

Sebastian Edwards stood in the gateway of the house and was obviously delighted. "Do you know we could easily convert it to five or even six letting rooms? And what a view!"

"Don't you think it's a bit large dear?" murmured Sarah "I am not at all sure that I could cope with that number of people! Are they double or single rooms?"

"From the estate agents' details, four double and one single I should think!" He replied mechanically for he could already see his project coming to life.

"But that could be nine people plus ourselves, plus Alexander and Rupert, that would be thirteen!"

"Well" he said "Rupert and Alexander are only likely to be back for the holidays and we are basically looking for business people not married couples. No! I should think that we'll have to cope with seven a day at most. That's not much is it?"

"No I suppose not" she admitted" but I don't think that I would be very good at doing the evening meals!"

"No, no!" he said repeatedly "just bed and breakfast to begin with, you'll soon get the hang of it. There are plenty of restaurants in Holywood and the centre of Belfast is only ten minutes away. Come on let's go in!" and without waiting for Sarah's assent he opened the black metal gates and swung them back on their hinges.

"Look!" he said "The area to the right of the house where there is a rough lawn, we could cover that with gravel and it would make an ideal parking place for what, seven cars I would think? Take that old wooden garage away, that's an eyesore isn't it? Yes this really has got the makings of what we want!"

As usual Sarah remained silent, Sebastian knew she was used to ideas like these being floated around. They knew if she protested too loudly at each plan that he would become angry and would accuse her of being negative. However he relied on her to counterbalance his optimism so he expected her to weigh up the situation. There was really no point in arguing, they knew that! He knew she would bide her time and if she thought it would not work she would choose her ground carefully and pick on one or two of the most obvious points. So she said nothing as he knew she would but she inspected the old wooden garage and opened the rotting door.

Sebastian turned abruptly left down the path alongside the front of the house and climbing the three steps to the front door, suddenly turned around as if he had just emerged from the place.

"Just look at that view!" he insisted and it was indeed a beautiful scene. The house was situated on the south shore of Belfast loch. It stood in about an acre of grounds. The lawn in front of the house was laid out like a tennis court although it was obvious that it had not been well kept for many years. The lawn was bounded by a white painted stone wall beyond which there was a narrow road, a grass verge and then not sixty feet away from this was the loch itself; a flat millpond stretch of water although it was a tidal loch, and in the distance he could just pick out a church or two on the northern side perhaps two or three miles away. To his right he could follow the loch towards the sea, the spreading industrial city of Belfast was over to his left but it was hidden from view by a rocky outcrop. A few hundred yards to his left in an inlet was a yacht club whose second floor observation room he could just see. The masts of the smaller boats were just visible and twenty or so large ones rode sleepily at moorings along a pontoon structure pointed into the loch.

"There you are!" he said "I told you so that beats the best view you could ever find in Liverpool! My! What a panorama! I could sit and snooze on a sunny Sunday evening wakened only by the hooting of the ferry as it passed by."

Sarah said nothing but she seemed to nod her head in assent indicating it was a great deal better than she thought it would be. When he had first suggested to her that they should live in Northern Ireland she had been horrified. She had told him that she did not like the thought of living in a land where the only things that seemed to make the news were bombs, terrorists and a dozen or so politicians whom frankly she could not understand at all. But there it was, she had had little option. Sebastian had suddenly been made redundant and in his late thirties he hadn't had many job offers. In fact he hadn't had any at all in Liverpool where they lived due to the poor state of the local economy. The only alternative seemed to be to move to London but that, she agreed, would mean a severe drop in their standard of living and she really couldn't stand being in a massive conurbation. It's true that there were cultural activities by the score but they had discussed it, neither of them could stand the choking mass of humanity that London presented.

Sebastian had been out of work for three months when the Northern Ireland Communications Company had written to him from Belfast. They had heard through the agency grapevine that he was available, would he work in Northern Ireland? Would he come over for an interview? The position was as a Financial Director and a salary increase of over £7000 more. They had spent hours weighing the pros and cons. "Was not Northern Ireland" asked Sarah "just as shown on TV, a round of perpetual riots and fights?" The agency had flown them over and they had both spent a weekend at the Bristol Hotel, a very expensive place and it was clear that she was amazed that life appeared to be very normal. They visited the shopping centre in Belfast and even discussed the possibilities of Alexander their elder son obtaining a place at one of the schools.

Then they had had to wait and wait. The lines of contact had gone dead and they heard nothing from the company for the whole of July. They made allowances for summer holidays and still had no word.

By mid-August Sebastian had decided that London really was the only option. Then suddenly on the 18th August without warning a letter came from Belfast '.. apologises for the delay... beyond our control .. most anxious that you should start as soon as possible.. no later than 15th September ... allowance of two house hunting trips....agreed your use of company flat until house acquired..... please confirm acceptance by return!'

That night they went through it all again. Sebastian was emphatic "There is no doubt that it is a good company and a good job as well. Don't forget that I am part Irish too and I don't feel that I will be a stranger there." At times his wife reminded Sebastian of his mother in her looks, by all accounts she had been a beautiful Irish red-head, who had died tragically in a car crash. He had nothing left of her but a small faded sepia photo.

Sebastian knew that Sarah felt uneasy, she was after all losing not only her home of ten years in Liverpool but also several close friends and moreover a job. He knew it represented her individuality, her independence and she had on more than one occasion over the last few months pointed out that her part-time job had tided them over when the redundancy pay had run out. They both knew that chances of a job for her in Belfast with the higher unemployment there would be negligible.

The idea as always had been Sebastian's and it was sparked off by that weekend they had spent house hunting in Belfast from the Hotel Bristol. "My God!" he had said "look at those hotel prices!" At first he had thought that the hotel had charged for the weekly instead of the daily rates and he had double checked them. No! He was assured the prices were correct.

During that weekend he had made casual enquiries of the Tourist Board of suitable temporary accommodation just in case. In truth he discovered that there was little recommended accommodation near Belfast other than hotels which appeared to charge exorbitantly.

"Do you know" Sarah, he had said "I think that there must be a very great demand for a good, high quality guest house here!" During the night of 18th August Sebastian had explained his plan. "Look Sarah! I've been thinking if we sold our house for £140,000, net of mortgage costs and added the £40,000 that Aunt Maude left you last year we could start up our own business, a small hotel or something for business men. I am sure that for £180,000 we ought to be able to buy something suitable. House prices have risen recently, ten years ago in the mid 1980's they held steady but I am sure they will catch up with the mainland!"

"But I cannot cook commercially, I have had no training!" said Sarah.

"Oh come on now Sarah you know that's not true after all you have been demonstrating electric cookers for the past five years!" "Yes" protested Sarah "but that's not cooking! I mean it's just demonstration work."

Sebastian would have none of it, cooking was all cooking to him and in any case his wife really was an excellent cook, their friends had always said so! Sarah had conceded that she would at least look at suitable properties. After all he was quite right she did like the cooking bit much more than the bit of trying to sell the cookers and ovens. She had always said she found it easier to demonstrate what the cookers could do rather than actually get the buyer to sign up for one. She smiled as she looked at the views over Belfast Loch. She told Sebastian maybe he was right, it could be quite pretty with a few more roses and hollyhocks and yes it would be quite pretty.

"Sarah! Look at this! Sarah where are you Sarah?" She turned startled; Sebastian had gone into the house and was inspecting each room excitedly.

He rushed past her into the kitchen "The kitchen seems fine just what you would expect, er only superficial problems!"

Sarah commented that the kitchen was an enormous room and had an old-fashioned range cooker; that the place seemed very dirty and the lino on the floor was cracked to reveal square red unpolished tiles, worn down unevenly. The cupboards were poorly painted white but had become yellowed with age and the surrounding woodwork was covered with layers of brown paint. Some of the sharpness of the edges of the wooden doors and cabinets were smoothed and did not fit properly. The Belfast sink was cracked in two places and an old fashioned plunger lay beside it, as if ready for use. She patted the walls "These are sound enough and most of the original Victorian sash windows appear to be workable!"

"Sarah! Sarah!" Sebastian called again and she went through to the left hand front room and there indeed she was impressed by what she saw.

"What on earth is it?" she asked.

"It's a billiard room or that's what the estate agents blurb says" replied Sebastian. "Yes, yes here we are, 'Exceptional Home built in 1906 by Alexander Manners – Shipbuilder, contains two large front rooms, a kitchen of extensive proportions' and yes here it is 'a substantial addition built on in 1910 of a full sized billiard room with a full width sliding door leading from a delightful lounge of considerable proportions 18ft by 18ft, complete with original oak flooring and affording a magnificent view over the loch, recently used as an old people's home - in need of some modernisation'. Huh you can say that again!" murmured Sebastian. "Just imagine", Sebastian mused "we could put back a billiard table and that would be an added attraction!"

"Wouldn't it be better with a snooker table dear?"

"It's the same thing!" replied Sebastian impatiently. "That's useful" he said continuing his survey. Across the hallway the dining room had a large bay window facing the loch, and, no doubt when the house servants had been dispensed with, probably between the wars, a new serving hatch had been knocked through into the kitchen but the plaster-work around it was cracked and in one or two places had come away revealing the brickwork beneath. The glass in one of the big bay windows at the front was cracked and another of the sash windows was nailed to the casement.

Sebastian was apparently oblivious to these various faults and had raced upstairs to view the first floor. He was reading out loud from the 'blurb'. "One large master bedroom over the dining room and across the spacious landing, another bedroom over the lounge from which a small corridor had been stolen to provide access to another room over the billiard room. This was originally said to have been used as an observation room where the shipbuilder could view the traffic coming up and down the loch. Two smaller bedrooms at the rear and a flight of stairs leading to the second floor where there were a further four attic rooms to complete the.." his voice trailed off and he scrambled up the last flight of stairs to the upper storey.

He looked at himself in a broken mirror which was hanging by a nail on the wall at the top of the stairs. Well he thought he was in pretty good shape really. Although he had been athletic in his youth, he was, he admitted, past his prime and was, in fact, several stone overweight. He was 5ft 10" and 'compact' as he liked to call it, though his family suggested 'fat' was more appropriate. He had a thin precise moustache and crinkly slightly greying hair which always looked as if it had been carefully combed. He spoke with a distinctive Oxbridge accent and his voice when raised could be heard, so he had been told, from several offices away. He had a full plump face and deep set eyes. He adjusted his tie and continued.

He had to admit that there were one or two deficiencies on the top floor. These, he concluded, were obviously the servants' quarters. It seemed the place had not been lived in for, well, at least twenty-five years the wiring up here was of the old two pin sort, one or two of the floorboards were worn almost through and an odd piece of hardboard had been nailed over one corner, the panes on one of the front windows which formed part of the dormer windows had broken and a generation of birds had made their nest and deposited droppings inside. The rooms were smaller than those on the first floor as the attics were built into the roof space. The rooms at the back had small roof lights, one of which had decayed so that the incoming water had trickled down the wall leaving channels of brown stain.

There was, he thought, no need to worry Sarah about such faults. It might, he thought, put her off the whole project. Nevertheless after fifteen years he couldn't lie to her either.

"How's the top floor" she shouted up from below.

"Oh, Ah well one or two things to put right, the roof seems OK though - the estate agent's particulars indicate that it has been regularly inspected."

Sarah fell silent and Sebastian knew she only half believed him as to what the state of the place was likely to be, but she made no further enquiries.

"Look! dear, I know there's a lot of work to be done but look at the price £140,000 and I am sure that for a quick sale, cash in hand, we could knock it down for £130,000 and that would leave £40,000 for repairs but we will have £10,000 over and could either save it or open up this top floor". "It should be enough you know?"

"But do you think you can make it pay?"

"Yes I am sure so – look you know what's happening here Loyalists and Republicans fighting for supremacy? Well here's an ideal opportunity! We should be able to take people possibly businessmen from both sides as guests. We will offer a sort of safe place – we could start off by recommendations, so we needn't pay advertising and we could build up prudently as we made improvements and bring more rooms into use."

"I see you mean by taking only those known to us we could ensure that we don't get involved in all the troubles. You mean a sort of safe haven?"

"That's it!" he exclaimed "that's it exactly! And it's a project we can both work on together!"

CHAPTER TWO

Sebastian had carried out some research into his future employer

Northern Ireland Communications Ltd was a substantial employer in the province of Northern Ireland and the Managing Director was very conscious of his commitment to the area. The company was one of several regional operations in the same London based group, the UK General Communications Co PLC. Andrew Steel, the local Managing Director, was an Ulsterman born and bred and moreover he had started with the company as an electrical engineering apprentice when it was still part of a nationalised concern.

He had pushed himself upwards not only by the force of his personality but also his intellect. His father, who had been a welder in the shipyards, had advised him to go into 'electrics' as he put it. He had started work at seventeen at the end of the war. There were scarcely a dozen of the 1000 employees, that he did not know by name and he had worked in almost all departments in his time. He was a loyalist in political terms and had only been dissuaded from active involvement in the loyalist parades when he had become a director of the company.

All this Andrew Steel had explained to Sebastian over the months after he joined the company; he had invited Sebastian and Sarah back to his house for several evening meals and he had talked long into the night about 'The Troubles' and how it affected them.

Of course he recognised that there were two communities in Northern Ireland, Protestants like himself who recognised the authority of the British Government and Catholics, who were mostly Republicans who would prefer to be ruled from Dublin.

Andrew Steel was clear in his mind how the position stood and had stood for generations, it's not that he disliked Catholics at all he just distrusted Republicans. After all he was running a key British enterprise where security was important, as he had often argued with British civil servants. What was the point of having elaborate security procedures if some IRA group infiltrated my workers and then tapped civil service and police phones? Would the civil servant mind if his phone was tapped in that way? That line of argument normally carried the day and so various key sections of the company needed security clearance. As a result those sections had almost no Catholics employed at all and those that were, were "Castle Catholics" - those Catholics with long service to the Province either serving in the British Army or in the Royal Ulster Constabulary.

Andrew Steel was big and bluff and knew his trade; he valued two characteristics above all others, respect and loyalty. So far he had managed to run the Northern Ireland Company the way he wanted, his monthly trips to London to report to the parent board were to him a pain and a bore! How could he explain to those effete liberal Englishmen what the situation was like in Northern Ireland? Half the Board called him 'Paddy' simply because they called all Irishmen 'Paddy' being unable to distinguish the different regional accents, even though Paddy was short for Patrick and Patrick meant Catholic and Catholic meant Republican. After ten years he had given up trying to explain the difference he was merely thankful that they never called him 'Paddy' to his face!

Sebastian soon learned to appreciate some of the difficulties of running a large organisation in the Province. The delay in offering him the position for example had been due to security clearance carried out by English police and the same applied to all senior and often some quite junior positions classified as 'sensitive'. There had to be a very careful selection of repair crews. Certain specialist crews would only work with police protection for fear of attacks by various Republican groups. In the past there had been reports of phone lines down which later proved to be an elaborate trap for the repair crews.

The problem was compounded as several of the Northern Ireland Communications Ltd employees had been actual RUC reservists or part-time members of the Ulster Defence Regiment which were, for obvious reasons, mainly Protestant in composition. The company had leased out repair work in certain areas to avoid conflict in this way and in other areas had handed over work to a new operation The Telephone and Wireless Company.

Sebastian Edwards appreciated Andrew Steel's knowledge of the area and of the business and was amazed to learn that most of the senior managers were English like himself; most personnel were on three year assignments from London, but the Operations Director Roy Brooks had lived in Northern Ireland some fifteen years and admitted to Sebastian he felt quite vulnerable, a 'suitably soft target' for the IRA as he put it. He was large and plump with a down to earth attitude to problems and often indulged himself in his favourite pastime of telling endless jokes. There's no saying if his subordinates understood them all but over the years they had become attuned to waiting for the catch phrase or punchline and laughing appropriately. Only rarely did they miscue, no one knew where his fund of jokes came from, certainly not from within the senior executives of the company since any attempt by the others to tell a joke would lead to a torrent of them which it was impossible to avoid. The stream was endless and once buttonholed it often took Sebastian five minutes at least to extract himself.

Sebastian as Financial Director held a key function in the company and he soon found out that he had plenty of work on hand as the accounting systems the company used were outdated and the method of storing, holding and sharing data was much behind that used by other regional companies of UK General Communications PLC. He soon had a list of tasks and priorities and although Andrew Steel was somewhat taken aback by the extent of the changes, he reluctantly gave them his consent.

Sebastian's subordinates within his own department were less satisfied with the proposed changes and resented the implication that in past years accounts had not been up to standard. Soon the matter was brought to the attention of the Trades Union whose local shop steward one day burst into Sebastian's office.

Sebastian was taken aback by this intrusion. Recovering his poise he started "Oh ah glad to meet you.. Mr William Bartlet isn't it? Can I help in some way?"

"Too right you can!" he protested with his rough Northern Irish accent. "My members are concerned at the direction you are taking! They think that these are major changes and they are concerned by the effect on their jobs. I can tell you that the way this company has been hiring all sorts of accounting staff really, really worries me Mr Edwards!"

"I suppose, Bill, I ought to have explained the position as I see it" and Sebastian launched into an enthusiastic forecast of the improvements to the system but long before he had got through the list, he saw Bill's eyes glaze over. Sebastian knew that he had lost him somewhere along the way and it was clear his mind was on other things. He abruptly rose whilst Sebastian was in mid-flight and slammed his notebook on the desk between them.

"I understand all that but what about the effect on my members?" he shouted "You will hear more of this!" he warned "You must stop, this will go no further!" and with no further ado he turned on his heel, wrenched open the door of the office and stormed out leaving the door open. His steps could be heard tramping down the corridor that ran through the finance department and every so often there was a slap and a muttering as he tapped his notebook on the walls as he went.

Sebastian was alarmed and completely stunned by the turn of events; he had risen from his desk and muttered "I say...." and slowly slumped back into his executive chair. He remained motionless and deep in thought.

His secretary knocked from an adjoining office, opened the door and peeped round "Tea, Mr Edwards?"

"Er yes thanks, tea, yes tea thanks"

To be frank, he thought, he hadn't really noticed his secretary. On joining the company he had been introduced left and right, Mr Mc-so-and-so and Mrs Billy this, he's in charge of that and she's so-and-so's sister in law; not much of it had stuck.

It was after all very difficult to even catch the names of sixty people, never mind connect them to jobs and faces! During the six weeks he had been there he had gone through what he considered was the rather mechanical side of finding out how the accounting was done and that had not really left time to get to know any of his staff. He had had barely half a day with his secretary and scarcely remembered her name.. 'what the hell was it now? Janette, yes that's right'.

"Er Janette" he called "do we have a file on the unions?"

"Just a minute, Mr Edwards, I am making the tea!"

A few minutes later and Jeanette came in bearing a tray and a teapot all carefully balanced on a large file. "Here you are Mr Edwards, it's all a bit old, I am afraid!"

"Perhaps you can help me then? Is there any procedure on union discussions at all?"

"No I don't think so, we've not had that before, but don't you worry about Billy, Mr Edwards, he has his good and bad bits, he'll calm down you'll see!"

Nevertheless Sebastian was concerned that he had made an apparent enemy so soon after taking over as Director. That lunch time he walked down to the MD's office on the floor below.

"Andrew, sorry to bother you" he said, "could you spare a moment? There seems to be some sort of a problem with the unions over the plan of system changes that I gave you last week."

"Well what exactly do you expect?" Came the reply. "Within weeks of arriving here you are telling us this and that whereas in practice operations have always run here very smoothly, I agreed with your plan but it's up to you to put it through."

And with that the meeting was over. Sebastian recoiled and he sat for a long time at his desk that evening with his head propped on his hand. Up to then it had all been plain sailing but now he was not so sure. It was clear that his boss was not going to back something in which he himself did not believe – his support could not be assumed – even worse it seems that either his boss or his staff had talked to Billy without consulting him. However he knew he could rely on London confirming it because he was put in for that purpose. It was a hiccup nothing more. He was, after all, now deeply committed to his own Project. He had no other option, so far no great damage done he would call Billy and try to talk him through it. He laid his plans carefully and discussed the details of the new system with each of his senior managers and finally by December he was ready to meet with the Unions.

He asked for Billy but was told in a nonchalant way that he would not be available immediately. Finally the following day Billy appeared and asked if Sebastian could 'make it quick' because he had masses of Union business to attend to.

"I would like to explain, Billy, what the plans are all about."

"I don't want to know about plans" came the swift reply "What about my members? How are you affecting my members?"

"Well here it is Billy, here is the plan. I see no reason why, with natural wastage at the current rate that we shall not be down to the number of people that we really need in fifteen months' time. So no-one need be concerned for their job and furthermore due to the change in structure there could well be a re-grading of three or four positions and a clear promotion to a new management group that I am planning."

Billy grinned, "Well that's good news, my members hoped you might say that" and then he leaned over confidentially, "That big lady in Payroll, you know Betty, she has been niggling me about a re-grading all week; now I tend to agree that there's nothing wrong with her current grade indeed if she were increased in grade that would mean that another five similar jobs might have to be re-graded which would punch a hole through the system, but as a union representative I feel I have to support her case. Of course as a member of a grading committee that's a different point. Do you see Mr Edwards, I think between us we should be able to dispose of it, if you follow my meaning?"

"Right Oh Billy – I'll do what I can!"

With that he got up and moved to the door, half turned and winked nodding "Thanks Mr Edwards" and quietly closed the door.

Sebastian sighed with relief he seemed to have achieved a breakthrough and without help from higher management after all!

CHAPTER THREE

The 'Safe House Project', as Sebastian now began to call it, had taken somewhat longer to organise than he imagined and yet by December he was well pleased with its progress.

Sebastian had created a plan and from this he prepared his CPA chart. This linked in tasks with objectives and gave the actions and activities that he needed to complete on a daily or weekly basis to achieve the post-Christmas opening of the premises. Sebastian and his wife stayed in the small but serviceable company flat used by visiting foreign experts, it was in the University area of Belfast not ten minutes' walk from his work. They had left all their own furniture in store in Liverpool. He did not like living in someone else's flat and more importantly he disliked the idea of the company paying expensive bills for visitors who couldn't stay there. It was, he realised, inevitable that they would be there for several months to which Andrew Steel had reluctantly agreed, provided Sebastian pay a normal rental after eight weeks.

He had first approached an architect recommended to him by the agent through whom he was buying the house. Sebastian had explained the nature of the project to him and slowly the total cost of it dawned on them. The architect pointed out numerous deficiencies. He noted that there were at least five sash windows in need or urgent repair, the loft roof needed attention and the flat roof over the billiard room extension would have to be totally replaced, water had apparently seeped into the first floor bedroom and down into the billiard room itself behind the wood panelling. The kitchen would require total stripping and replacement, the outhouse and the large porch enclosing the rear door were in danger of collapse, the bathroom on the first floor at the rear would have to be gutted, and the number of guests necessitated the addition of a new shower and WC to the second floor. "My guess" he said is that it will cost £55,000".

For Sebastian this was bad news indeed, he had imagined that the project would provide him with a useful second income, after all, he had said that the £40,000 from Aunt Maude would give at best £2,000 income if invested and even just a few people staying in the 'Safe House' per night would equal that. Now however the calculations had changed. In order to complete the project as he had envisaged, it would be necessary to extend his existing mortgage of £35,000 to £70,000. Regrettably too the building society had refused to contemplate a mortgage as a residential property and as a result Sebastian had had to agree to a commercial interest rate which would cost a lot more!

The overall effect was that it was no longer a hobby, it had grown to become a business and if he was not able to fill the rooms to the 50% level he could not make a profit. He cursed his optimistic estimates and he realised it would put the whole project in doubt unless he watched every penny, it could easily send him bust before he even had the first guest.

He had discussed the problem with Sarah and he was convinced that his project would be viable, he had talked with some of his colleagues at work and they too bemoaned the lack of suitable guest accommodation. Sebastian was convinced that there was a gap in the market and there was an opportunity to 'satisfy the market need' as he explained it to Sarah. He carried out more detailed research and found out that the 'Troubles' had been responsible for the closure of all the small seaside hotels which used to attract holidaymakers from Scotland in the 1960's. The sea front at Bangor had been pepper-potted with them, so he had been told, and after their failure the knock on effect on the tourist trade had been emphatic and with that ended the era of cheap holidays in the Province. Generally however, those whom he met were enthusiastic and encouraged him.

Both his colleagues and the architect had queried how he could ensure that the house would be 'safe'. "You can't just say that it is 'safe' I think that what you mean is that you will welcome both Protestant and Catholic or anyone else so that visitors can be assured of a welcoming and friendly atmosphere. You are, I think, counting on the fact that visitors from outside the province don't want to have to think about the Troubles, they just want a peaceful and safe place to stay and that's the same for nationalists and loyalists from within the Province too."

"But that's not the end of the matter" his architect had emphasised "here in Northern Ireland all visitors expect some sort of screening and checking. To ensure that within the hotel area they are also protected from bombs and so on and I strongly recommend that you visit your local Royal Ulster Constabulary station for advice."

Sebastian was now concerned at the seemingly endless additional costs and yet he knew that the advice he was given was well founded. After telephoning the RUC station at Holywood, just a few miles away, he had briefly explained his plan and was instructed to see Sergeant Jim Hannah on the following evening at 6.00pm.

Sebastian liked Holywood, a pleasant little village near Belfast, its main street had previously doubled as the main road to Bangor, a wealthy seaside town, ten miles distant along the south shore of the loch. Its older whitewashed buildings were interspersed with the glass and block Co-op style architecture typical of the early 1960's which blighted hundreds of villages throughout the length and breadth of the UK. Holywood is built around a cross roads with the minor road leading down to the water's edge and on the other side upwards from there to the hills overlooking the loch.

Down the road towards the sea Sebastian found the RUC Station. Even Sebastian, only being in the Province a few weeks, could tell that the area must have been relatively quiet since the building was not completely enmeshed in barbed wire nor was the roof totally covered by wire netting and camouflage sheeting which he had seen in other areas of the Province on his house search visits. Nevertheless the white painted head-high wall was half covered in moss and topped by a rusted coil of wire laid on top of coloured broken glass stuck into concrete. It hardly looked, Sebastian thought, as if it would withstand a normal victory parade of Liverpool football fans returning home, never mind the IRA. Perhaps, he thought, it indicated that this was, after all, a peaceful enclave.

However at the far left of the building was a concrete block which had been recently added, it was about ten ft. square to which was attached a gate made of steel and covered with more netting allowing vehicle access. There was a smaller pedestrian entrance built into the main gate – a wicket gate. It was here that Sebastian paused and, pressing the button as directed, was questioned from a small metal box at eye level. "Who is it?"...

"Sebastian Edwards for Sergeant Hannah."

"OK come through the gate and take the first door on your right please" came a metallic voice.

He heard a buzzing sound and the latch was pulled back and he pushed the gate open. Moving to the right he passed a blacked out window and arrived at an old door whose brown paint must have been applied many years ago, chipped and scratched areas showed it had been green originally. There were sounds of a steel bar being swivelled on its bolt and there was a clang as the door was pulled inwards. There was a smell of sweat and carbolic.

"Hello Mr Edwards, please come this way!" and a policeman in uniform lead the visitor down a cramped passageway into a dark office where the wooden furniture was clean but old and worn. Sergeant Jim Hannah indicated him to sit and he introduced himself. "Now Mr Edwards what can I do for you?"

"Well" started Sebastian clearing his throat feeling somewhat embarrassed by the poor furniture – how could he mention that the furnishing costs of his project alone would amount to several thousands of pounds whereas the furniture of this office would not even fetch a 'fiver', indeed they should probably have been scrapped and put on the loyalists July 12 bonfire celebrating the Battle of the Boyne. "I had an idea of setting myself up, or rather my wife and I, up in a small bed and breakfast overnight accommodation just down the way at Cultra. It's on the shore road between the Transport Museum and the Yacht Club. It's an old house 'Bryansburn', unoccupied for many years. I would really like your advice on measures that I need in order to make the place secure."

Sebastian paused – perhaps he had not been well advised? It seemed remarkable that the station was so ill-equipped, perhaps he should visit the crime prevention headquarters that they would be sure to have in Belfast? The sergeant said nothing for a moment or two. He seemed to Sebastian to be quite young perhaps only thirty or so but he sat motionless at the desk, his face was glum and serious, already lined and his protruding eyes were strangely remote as if stuck there like a teddy-bear's button eyes. There was a depression in the skin of his forehead where the cap which he must just been wearing had been removed. It lay on the desk. Sebastian had not yet got used to the strange dark green colour of the uniforms worn by the RUC - it reminded him of Bus ticket Inspectors back in England; he had not yet got used to appreciating that here was real power, but the revolver in its holster on the wall behind him was a grim reminder of that.

Sebastian started again "Perhaps you would let me know who I can talk to, if you yourself are too busy? It's perhaps not a very important matter."

"No! No!" Mr Edwards you have come to the right place I assure you." He turned his penetrating stare onto Sebastian who felt embarrassed now to have raised the matter at all. "I must apologise we have been very busy lately, the new initiative of the Government you know? There have been a lot of marches and so on", his voice trailed off as if reliving the incidents he had witnessed. "A guest house you say? Bryansburn House! Yes I know it, that seems a good idea but are you sure you can cope? Is the time right for this sort of venture do you think? Of course it's true that one of these days the troubles will be over and visitors will return. I suppose you have talked to the Tourist Department?"

Sebastian explained at length how he had thought of the idea, how he had obtained detailed estimates of costs, the surveys that he had carried out on the property and the marketing which indicated a 'gap' in the market for a good, safe, cheap, homely accommodation. His English heritage, he felt, would be important asset to show that he himself was uncommitted on political issues; that he had raised the money and was assured that planning permission concerning the premises would be a mere formality, and that there were no near neighbours anyhow to object.

The sergeant looked at him intensely but said nothing occasionally losing focus as if he was somewhere else. Sebastian was a bit uneasy thinking perhaps that Sergeant Hannah was a bit depressed. He continued talking mentioning the detailed of the number of rooms, views over the loch but eventually his voice tailed off as he realised that perhaps much of it was not being listened to. He stopped speaking and waited.

There was, thought Sebastian, an awkward silence.

"So what you wanted me to do is to advise on security matters, is that right?"

"Yes" confirmed Sebastian "that's it exactly"; he was glad at least they seemed to be at last on the same wavelength.

"Well I would advise that to take careful precautions, Mr Edwards; remember that this is Northern Ireland and I am glad that you approached us first. I think that what you need is a package: steel lined ground floor doors, video cameras at key points, a couple of security devises and good outside lighting. That should do the trick! Of course if you really want to go to town like the big hotels you can get detector systems to vet the guests. I am not sure they are much practical use because of course you will then need staff to monitor them, but the IRA are wary and will not bother entering where they see such systems installed. Good security, you see Mr Edwards, is a positive advantage for guests, every indicator that we have is that visitors don't like being subjected to those sorts of searches but on the other hand they like to know that all the other guests are! But in your case..." his voice trailed off and he said nothing more and then suddenly, "Bryansburn you say?"

Sebastian was feeling uncomfortable again, was he listening? Sebastian was unnerved and tried to extract himself from the situation.

"Well thank you, Sergeant, I am sorry to have bothered you. I'll get the architect to make some changes along the lines you suggest, I hardly think that I shall be able to afford the whole package though."

The Sergeant seemed to come alive again. "Perhaps I can help you there. There's a small builder trader in Holywood, I can personally recommend him to you; unlike other tradesmen around here he is prompt and gives very competitive quotes. Here's his card. Call him please; I am sure that he can help you. Good Luck with your project Mr Edwards I do hope it goes well. Constable William Stewart will show you out!" "Billy" he called without moving. The door opened and a young lad came in, hardly out of school Sebastian murmured to himself.

"Oh Sure! Mr Edwards is it? So it is!" And he engaged in pleasantries. "Northern Ireland Communications Ltd! Oh! That's a good company – Financial Director that must be an interesting job? Bryansburn House, yes I know it, so I do! Yes it's a good view. How do you find house prices here? Please call me if you need anything – you are on my round, so you are!"

Sebastian stepped out of the gate with relief as he was never happy in dark, enclosed places and soon became claustrophobic. The sergeant had seemed shell shocked and he clearly thought him mad to come here. He didn't think it necessary to call at the station again but he did call the builder who had been recommended and noted with satisfaction that, despite bringing in a few more of the security features, the quotation was the lowest of the three his architect had chosen.

In the end the final negotiation on the purchase of the house went more successfully than he anticipated and as he gave the instructions to start work he realised that at least he was within the planned budget. That was, he thought, a very good omen. The builder proved to be a godsend but even he was unable to control the subcontractors and there were frustrating weeks spent waiting on plumbers, electricians or kitchen fitters. Each night Sebastian and Sarah would review the work done and he would carefully mark off the tasks on the chart which he kept in his briefcase. Sarah frantically darted around the shops buying beds and quilts and soft furnishings and spent each weekend busily measuring and making up the curtains and pelmets.

Sebastian's plan had worked perfectly, the place was completed a week prior to Christmas and on the 20th, crack on the date, the van arrived carrying their own belongings from the Liverpool store and they were glad to be moving from their company flat in the University area. The weekend was spent in the hectic arranging and reorganising of their old furniture amongst the new.

"Sebastian?" Sarah had questioned "do you really think that we need all this stuff of your father's?" Sebastian was touchy about that topic as about none other. He had scarcely known either of his parents. His father had been a civil servant in the Colonial Office in some high ranking post in Nigeria. Sebastian had been brought up at boarding school and, except for a few long summer holidays, rarely saw his parents. Even when he did his father was often away for weeks adjudicating cases and when he returned spent every other evening at official receptions of one kind or another. His father had stopped on after independence, long after his normal retirement age, at the insistence of the new Nigerian Government. He had learnt later whilst at University that both parents had died during a riot, their car had been overturned by accident it seemed.

Sometime later their belongings were sent in one of those large black metal trunks. When he opened it he found almost nothing, his father's uniform, some of his old law books, his hat and camp washing kit and a collection of masks, spears, shields and war clubs which his father had made a special study of for several years, plus an old swivel chair which was in pieces, but not a note, a letter, a will, a photograph or anything else remained – presumably all stolen en route – except in a pouch an old signet ring which he immediately recognised. Now several years later he began to have difficulty remembering their faces and voices but he could still just imagine his father sitting in that chair working.

These became the symbols of the parents he never really had. Sebastian now reverently placed the spears, clubs and shields up the walls of the stairs and on each of the landings. The chair went into his study. The signet ring he had thereafter always worn on the little finger of his right hand.

At last all seemed ready, the refurbishment was completed and Sebastian and Sarah carried out a tour of inspection.

"We shall have to get more crockery, I think" Sarah said "we still only have a dozen place settings and we could need more. We also need gravel for the parking area, that hard-core doesn't look very nice." All the same it seemed to please Sarah, he could see that and he too was surprised. He went out of the house and looked at it from the gateway as a visitor would. Yes the sign was there, the newly painted post awaiting the 'Vacancies' attachment and the house looked good with its freshly painted woodwork.

He walked up to the door, turned and looked out over the loch. He could imagine the Titanic coming out for its maiden fitting out run from the shipyards a mile or so away and the hustle and bustle of accompanying tugs and supply boats. He regretted that all those skills had simply vanished, but those days were long gone.

It was a cold day but it was not windy and he could quite clearly see the opposite shore. 'Let me see' he thought 'I should be able to see Carrickfergus Castle built by the Normans in 1100 something or other and the Technical College or Poly or whatever they called it now'. He would have to be able to point them out to his guests – still there would be time enough later to identify points of interest more precisely.

He turned and went into the house. For the first time Sebastian felt this was home. He was going to make something of this and if successful who knows, maybe he would end up as an hotelier? Why not! He had to take opportunities as they came!

He moved right to the dining room, yes it really was a nice room now, with the white table cloths nobody would notice that all five tables were well worn; the new carpets and curtains looked good. He wandered into the side room. He had managed to buy an old billiard table from a club that had closed down. It was worn but serviceable, and he hoped it would provide some evening entertainment; there was also a large TV, later maybe he could install a small bar in the corner. Well that was for the future! Yes that was fine! He turned back to the entrance and checked the inside porch behind the door. Yes what a good builder he had had, he had been persuaded that as the door had to be rehung anyhow, a steel backing plate could be added for a little extra cost of £20 and that, together with the large bolts and double turn locks, made it look very secure.

He limited his tour to the ground floor. Sebastian knew he still had much to do. The top floor was still 'work in progress' and lacked the finishing touches, so although the plumbing was in for their personal bathroom the walls were still unpainted. He planned to do these himself over the Christmas break. His study on the top floor was a clutter of books and he had yet to fit in there the coiled fire escape ladder which the Fire Service had insisted upon. This led onto the flat roof of the first floor billiard room extension.

He turned around, went back to the hallway and into the little cupboard under the stairs from here he could control the security system; what a prize he thought; there were two video cameras outside, one located at the front corner by the car parking area and one above the door by the rear entrance. This way he could, if necessary, scan the whole area except the rear of the billiard room extension. He had considered that blind spot but felt the additional £300 or so cost to cover it was not warranted. The builder had also managed to get hold of a metal detector walk-through scanner which he had obtained cheaply when one of the Government buildings was being refurbished and it had been installed inside the porch. It looked a bit ungainly there but Sebastian thought they could try it out and see what the reaction of the guests was. He had also bought a couple of foot pressure pads and an alarm system connected the metal filaments in the windows with the door locking system. In this way the alarm would automatically go off if, once the system was set, anyone broke in anywhere downstairs.

The young policeman, Billy, had called by several times and also suggested one further change; for the sake of a few pounds, he had said you can wire your system live to the police station, which Sebastian had declined, or he could also buy a few hand held flares, these he was told were like very bright lights and if everything else failed Billy said, they would see them from the station and come within a few seconds. So he had paid for them and positioned these on the top floor in a cupboard near their bathroom.

"Believe me, Mr Edwards, I think that you have done a fine job. If only some of our politicians here took the same trouble as you have done there may now be one or two more left alive to tell the tale! I am sure that all your guests will be well pleased with the arrangements and sleep safer in their beds. By the way when is the opening day?"

"January 10th" said Sebastian. "I am really waiting now for the children to arrive back for Christmas. We're going back 'across the water' as you put it, to pick them up. They will be our first guests. We will send them back in January but it should be a good practice run!"

Before he left he called his oldest friend Douglas Finlay. They had boarded together at school years previously and he had always kept his friend abreast of events. Douglas was noticeably noncommittal about this venture and his friend reminded him that as he was associated with the Ministry of Defence in England it would be out of the question for him to visit Belfast.

'Hum' thought Sebastian he knew that he was shutting himself off from his friends and he wondered what reception awaited him in LIverpool at his in-laws where his two lads had been staying in the holidays whilst all this refurbishment was taking place. It would be good to see them again and tell them his plans.

CHAPTER FOUR

He had really tried hard to get on with his father in law Will Jefferies but always found it hard work. Sarah was an only child and her mother, Jenny, had always been very protective of her. So Sebastian quickly learned that the way to have a peaceful time was to work on the mother who would in turn pacify the father. That however would not be easy.

His idea had been to call in, stay the night and then bring the two lads with them to Belfast before Christmas returning them for a few days before term started and before they were delivered by the Grandparents to the same prep boarding school he had attended.

Of course this schooling came at a price and following his redundancy his father in law had offered to continue to pay the school fees until Sebastian had become settled again financially. At his wife's insistence Sebastian had reluctantly accepted, anyhow it was all too complex to work out how to get them educated in Northern Ireland. He knew that the state schools in the Province had generally a higher educational attainment than in England, but he felt that the day school attendance would not mix with the Safe House project. He himself did not have funds to send them to his old boarding school right now nor would he until his project was proved and yielding a profit. He had even used Aunt Maud's bequest to Sarah for his project which he would have to repay.

He had used his parents' small legacy to pay for most of the cost of their first house and to provide the school fees for his children for the first years at a point which he had hoped his earnings would rise to cover them. They were both still at a prep boarding school but he planned that they should follow in his footsteps and go on to his old senior school as well.

The meeting with the in laws was frosty from the start. After dinner Sebastian had explained the logic behind the scheme and showed them the plans and photos of the place. He talked of his new job and that he felt he was now settled in the company.

His father in law however subjected him to some severe questioning "So how do you know there's a market for this?", "What makes you think that either one side or the other would see your place as a 'safe house'?", "How on earth are you going to market your place?" and, more closely "What's your occupancy rate and what are your charge rates?", "Are you sure you can make a profit? I remember in my business it took me years to work things out and get the right staff and turn in a reasonable profit from the five local stores that I owned – didn't it Mother?"

This allowed Jenny to intervene and Sebastian thought she was about to deflect the questions but it made matters worse "Well dear, I hope you will be able to get enough staff to help you?"

"Well, Mum, to begin with we are going to have to do everything ourselves! Until it takes off that is", Sarah replied.

"But what does that entail dear?" and Sebastian dreaded the next reply, he knew that Jenny Jefferies had not worked for thirty years and even had a 'cleaner' in one day a week, how would she take to her daughter's doing menial tasks?

"Well we will have up to four double rooms with a possible fifth single added later – but these should mostly be business people for breakfast and evening meal – maybe four on average – not much more really than I would do when the lads are home from school."

"Well good on you! Sarah!" Sebastian muttered under his breath, that should stop the inquisition – he made a mental note to thank her later for backing him up in that way.

"So Mum I am now going to become the MasterChef of the Ulster Fry, that's the standard breakfast the locals enjoy and comes with sausages, bread, bacon, tomatoes, the famed Irish Soda bread and potato farls — I am really looking forward to that, it's are very, very tasty — I have got the recipes and, whilst I am here, I am just dying to try cooking one which I hope you'll enjoy!"

"That's lovely dear" said Jenny and Sebastian was taken aback and a bit shamefaced — he had not thought that far ahead just assuming that food was, well, just food. So maybe his hope that Sarah would actually engage with the whole business was beginning to work out. Anyhow it had distracted discussion from the finances. Sebastian was worried if he could fill the place which he would have to do to pay off the money his wife had put into the venture.

"And" his wife continued "for evening meal it will be a simple choice steak, or fish, with chips and peas — and for afters a pre-prepared sweet changed every day, like lemon meringue pie or a crumble."

Alexander wanted to know more about the place. "Do they play cricket there and rugby?" and more intellectually "How do people live in a divided society?".

Sebastian was on surer ground and explained. "Well, in 1929 the schools were allowed to remain in or opt out of the state scheme and all the Catholic ones remained out, although subsidised they are technically independent and so schooling is in the main segregated on religious lines. Voting is almost entirely on religious allegiances too; there is a small cross divide party called the Alliance Party but it has never managed more than 10% or so of the vote. It's possible to live one's life almost entirely amongst people of the same religious background. Of course this might change and we hope that it will and one day there may be peace here but the divisions are deep and it may not be for some time – meanwhile unrest and violence continue." Sebastian spoke with sincerity and clarity.

Rupert had listened intently and piped up "So why go there dad, isn't it risky?"

"Well" Sebastian replied, "as you know I was made redundant from my last company and I was left with fewer options than I wanted. Either I would have had to work in London, maybe commuting from home perhaps on a lower salary, or, taking the opportunity of a hefty increase in salary and position, move to Belfast. It's very unlikely that we will be targeted, we may represent the Union but it's the Loyalists who are under threat and Republicans who are fighting to bring the North into Ireland. Strangely we are not regarded as enemies by them although British troops are – I would not have accepted the position if I thought that your Mum or I were at real risk!"

This seemed to satisfy Will Jefferies who for the first time managed some sort of smile and said "Well I hope you two make it alright – it's just that we are worried about you, you know, and we don't really know what's going on. Please call us regularly to tell us how things are going, and you lads can report back to us when you get back here after Christmas."

"And look", Sebastian added "I am so grateful to both you, Will, and Jenny helping us out with the lads in particular."

So Sebastian was relieved, that had gone off much better than he feared.

"One final thing all the people that I have met have been helpful, straightforward, and honest to a fault –they're nice people we shall not want for friends!"

Rupert piped up again "Dad you mean they are friendly but still kill each other?"

"Yes that's right they are lovely people but just stay away from discussing religion or the border!"

CHAPTER FIVE

Christmas was, Sebastian recalled, the happiest they had ever had as a family. Together they decorated the house and got in all the food and drink. He showed the lads around Belfast and the Transport Museum along the way. On Boxing Day they all took the train to Bangor and walked back right along the coastal path – it was a beautiful sunny day.

There was a lot to show the two boys and it was evident that they were impressed by the house and its location. One day Sebastian found Rupert alone on the shoreline sitting looking out over the loch.

"Dad, it really is lovely here, I hope everything goes well for you and Mum, you know Granddad isn't always too kind about your venture but I suppose he's just worried about his only child. How soon before this takes off so we can holiday here from school?"

"I just don't know, it'll be as soon as we can; maybe July, but come along now! We have got some painting to do you and I. That spare bedroom right at the top – remember? Then I can put each of you into a separate room which you can call your own."

All too soon Christmas was over and they were gone. That just left time for Sebastian to finish off and put the final touches to the bathroom on the top floor. There was just one room left, his study, which was still a mess – it had a desk and filing cabinet and bookcase and amongst all that the golf clubs and a bag of fifty used balls which he allowed guests to use on the local municipal golf course. Pride of place in this little room was given to his father's old swivel chair.

The weekend after Christmas he started putting together his Marketing Plan which he already had thought about in some detail. He realised there were three target markets – he listed these down on a piece of paper.

1) <u>Businessmen,</u> visiting from 'across the water' England or the 'South' as the republic was called – he imagined these would be single males from Monday to Friday.

2) <u>Tourists,</u> again from England or Ireland these would be more likely to be couples and possible spread over the week but staying a couple of nights.

3) <u>Locals,</u> either coming from across the province for Weddings and Funerals or other family get-togethers.

He worked out how each of his target markets could be reached, for example the Tourist Board and by getting inserts into travel books, so he wrote a number of articles with photos and these were taken up by the local press because such a 'safe house' was something rather new. He didn't actually use the words 'safe house' but just highlighted that it had 'modern security systems' and the extensive views over the loch which earned him praise from local editors. He then created a list of the top 100 firms in Belfast and wrote to them enclosing an attractive brochure offering 'exclusive cumulative discounts'. If they introduced more than ten guests then the eleventh would have a night's free stay. He had a small ad in the British Airways magazine offering discounts such as four nights for three and for five nights a free weekend, and he charged by the room so bringing a partner cost just the breakfast. He advertised in the local freebee for the local trade, again offering discounts over the weekend, three nights for two.

He realised all this research might have repercussions at his work but his boss Andrew Steel proved very understanding even offering to put the details of Bryansburn House onto the social noticeboard and, as the firm often had visiting contractors, offering to pass the handouts to the purchasing department as well. Sebastian was relieved that his absence for the odd hour had not been detected and that his subordinates had covered for him. Anyhow all his reports and accounts had been in on time and he had received several compliments about his new systems.

He was sure that once his place was sufficiently well-known, say by June, he would be able to devote more time to reviewing the company management accounts properly and making suggestions for further savings. These he felt would be forthcoming after further investigating particularly the performance of some of the maintenance crews. He had tried discussing 'Section F' performance with the Operations Director, Roy Brooks, who had merely fobbed him off at the last management meeting with a couple of jokes about absentee landlords. Sebastian realised he would have to work on this, he didn't want anyone to feel that the "Safe House" was getting in the way of his real work. At normal daily management lunches he no longer mentioned his project at all!

Although bookings in January proved slow by February things were picking up and they had turned away their first guest as they were full. As a result they reduced the discounted offers and by March it began to look as if it might be a financial success. Sebastian reviewed the first three months' results with Sarah.

"I think you have done really well, Sarah, I think we are about 50% full – I think it's going to be a success." Sarah was enthusiastic too but all this hard physical work was causing her wrists to swell up. Sebastian was a bit concerned and took her to the doctor who had diagnosed nothing serious.

By April it was noticeable that there were a number of 'regulars' using the place on a weekly or monthly basis and these now formed a hard core of the business. Sebastian made notes so that when they next came to stay he could quickly refer to a scrap of information they had shared with him. "Did you have a good holiday in Majorca then?" or "Is you wife better yet?" Most guests tended to be pre booked and Sebastian was in charge so he was always back from work on time and available all weekend. Sebastian plucked out of his pocket these notes about his 'regulars':

Fredrick Mullins – Freddie – cockney accent – contractor in the building trade – educated at teacher training college – 30s bearded – came by casual phone call – married never refers to wife or children – lives London – flies in. Seems to support the current regime but will not be drawn

Roderick Morley – Roddy - suited, wears pork pie hat and military style raincoat – doesn't say much, says visiting Northern Ireland about contracts with British Aerospace – has some local family – an aunt but prefers to stay here based Liverpool – flies in. Recommended by supplier. Aged 50s

Ian Marshall – coloured parents - Jamaican – a cricketer employed by ICC to try to improve cricket in the province – visits schools and clubs and plays during the summer for top league club. Aged 24 - lives London - came via referral from Ministry here in Belfast.

John Rush – from Dublin - deals in engineering products, microchips, electronics, aged 35 believes that the troubles are all too complicated and doesn't hold hard position, doesn't think South could buy the North anyhow – his company owned by Japanese. Arrives by car.

William Whiteside from Derry - arrives by car; actually his driving licence gives him as Liam Whiteside - works with the Transport Ministry surveying roads and bridges currently on a major contract in Belfast. - last holiday Cyprus. - senior manager in his firm - dislikes talking politics. Aged about 40.

As a matter of course he asked all his guests to sign a register and put down the car registration number alongside. Billy Stewart from the local RUC often used to pop around at off peak times, usually around 11 am and chat with Sarah about the business and guests and took an interest in seeing this register.

Sebastian made a good host and passed around the Bushmills whiskey after supper and always offered to play a round of snooker. Sebastian was pleased that he had bought the table and it had proved its worth – although he had not previously appreciated it, snooker was the ideal game because any number could play; two, three, four or even more and could come in for a game without disturbing the other players too much. It had proved the centrepiece of his establishment, so after a matter of minutes 'ah – ing' or 'oh – ing' about the improved security – that was it! But the snooker table made it a real winner. Also he had managed to arrange a deal with a posh golf club to charge just green fees taking him as a Corporate Member giving his guests access to the clubhouse. He had invested in some second hand golf clubs so was happy to entertain his guests at off peak times.

His guests did not chat between themselves much although they shared some experiences such as when Sebastian had had to switch off the security system because the large bags filled with cricket equipment triggered the alarms. There was no time to unpack everything and pick it up again. Similarly, with John Rush's stuff where every piece of his samples set the alarms off. So they had to disengage and re-engage the system each time he left. This caused some mirth between the guests.

Otherwise they spent most of their time in the lounge watching TV. There was a large bookcase in the billiard room and any guest could take any book they wished and replace it with another. Each guest had a door key so they could come and go as they liked and bring in other visitor, but Sebastian told them that at 11pm he would set all the alarm systems as he would then move upstairs preparing for bed. Sometimes of course guests could not make it back in time, if they were delayed they were instructed to press the doorbell at the side of the front door which chimed on the top floor – if, instead, they used their key the whole house would be wakened and all the alarm systems would have to be reset.

Sebastian felt that his approach had worked and he found it easy to engage with the guests without crowding them. Things generally ran smoothly and he found that the businessmen's needs were fairly limited and they were not too difficult to please. By May things seemed to have settled into a routine and apart from the current regulars he had picked up a number of weekend tourists and several funeral 'wakes', where virtually whole families flew in at a weekend. Sebastian could accommodate ten or even eleven if the small room on the top floor was let. No discounts were offered or asked for. Of course it was exhausting work but it made the whole operation very profitable and at that only a few months after opening. It was going well!

So well, indeed, that Sebastian began to enquire into the ownership of the rough land with a shed alongside – maybe he could extend the premises? He would need income from at least another three rooms to cover the costs of a part time cook and cleaner so that he and Sarah could relax a bit. It would mean him extending out over the car park perhaps, a cheap way of adding more rooms. Maybe his father in law would invest? Sebastian realised that he couldn't keep going like this for much longer, it was very difficult to manage two jobs.

For the moment he would have to run it till July and then with several profitable months under his belt, he would prepare a possible business expansion plan.

CHAPTER SIX

Sebastian was shattered by the attack.

He looked at the report he had prepared on the incident. He had called in at the request of the RUC to make a statement at 9am and Billy had been very helpful in guiding him as to how he should write it. He returned by agreement at 1pm in order to sign it. It had been initially handwritten but as Sebastian studied the typed version prepared for his signature he noted one or two changes had been made. So he read it in detail and compared it line by line with the original handwritten version which he had asked for.

Of course by then it was a News item carried on the BBC Radio and the TV channels, who were all still on site.

ROYAL ULSTER CONSTABULARY   -   WITNESS STATEMENT AN REPORT ON INCIDENT

AT.... *Bryansburn House* **ON** *May 28th....*

Witness *Sebastian Edwards of Bryansburn House, Cultra, County Down, Northern Ireland delivered at RUC Cultra Northern Ireland.*

"On the Thursday evening May 27th all five of what I called my 'regulars' were in that week (see list attached that I kept as a memory jogger) we had chatted over Dinner taken at 6 pm so that we could have a quick game of snooker and then watch an international football match at 7 pm.

Freddie Mullins (Bedroom 1) went out soon afterwards saying he would be back before 11 as he was drinking with his friends – he would let himself in.

Ian Marshall (Bedroom 5) said he had a lot of work to prepare for tomorrow's school visits and excused himself. He went upstairs with his large cricket bag which he had left in the dining room.

William Whiteside (Bedroom 2) got up later when 'News at ten' started so I assumed that he had gone to bed.

My wife Sarah came in towards the end of the news before the sports so it must have been about 10.25 saying that she had finished for the day but also that the back door was opened though she did not know why and that she had closed it. She also pointed out to me that the security filaments in the window of the wash/utility room appeared to have been tampered with. (Sebastian noted that the earlier handwritten version had said that Billy Stewart had checked this just the day before on his usual round.) *I walked over with her and checked this and reattached the wire to the cable joint.*

Whilst I was returning in the hall way Ian Marshal came racing downstairs rushed passed me and went into the front dining room sounding agitated "Hey Mr Edwards there's a strange car on the road outside and I think Freddie is there too – two people seem to be getting out, they are hooded" I rushed over and saw 3 balaclava helmeted people race towards the front door.

I slammed the front door closed and raced back and triggered the alarm system in the cubby under the stairs.

As I did so I shouted a warning to Robert Morley and John Rush in the Lounge "Get Upstairs!" Robert Morley raced past me and leapt up the stairs to the first floor but John Rush appeared to think it was some sort of a joke maybe a fire drill, and I shouted again "Get Upstairs!"

At the same time there was a splintering of glass from the back area and that triggered more of the alarm system. My wife Sarah shouted terrified asking what's going on? And I told her to stay where she was upstairs.

A volley of shots hit the front door which was protected by sheet steel behind and this held up the attack. The sound of the alarms was deafening.

We raced upstairs and on the way passed I wrenched the display of clubs and spears off the walls.

The front bay windows were shattered and there were sounds downstairs as if they were searching the place room by room.

I led our people upstairs and pushed Sarah my wife into the study, then went and grabbed two of the flares from the cabinet by the top bathroom.

I noticed William Whiteside was not with us and heard him shouting to the intruders – "It's not me not me I am Liam from Derry – there upstairs!"

I opened the window and yanked the chord sending the flare upwards then hurled the other one down the stairwell just as one of the attackers was coming up. It hit him in the chest and he fell back making a dreadful sound but this was followed by a hail of bullets and then there was a pause. I pushed Sarah, Roddy and John into the study but Ian and I remained on the top floor landing.

Ian went into his room and emerged with his bat and some old cricket balls. Wham Crack he was hitting them downstairs with all his strength. I pushed past the others in the study and grabbed the golf balls and began to hurl then down stairs a head appeared and I caught it smack in the face there was a groan and this was followed by another clip of bullets this time through the floor.

I threw into the stairwell the spears and clubs which formed a tangled mass on the stairs.

We retreated into the study.

Together we pulled the metal filing cabinet across the door and stacked up the books around it as best we could. I remembered that we had fixed the fire escape rope ladder and I opened the window and they began to climb out.

There was the sound of shots outside and I pushed my way to the window and saw a person lying on the ground with what looked like a terrible wound in his stomach and another helping him but with a hand to his own head.

They were then cut down in a hail of bullets from what appeared to be soldiers from across the road. Another hooded man raced across the open ground and jumped into the car that I had first seen which came around the corner from Cultra but it too was hit by a number of shots and slowed to a halt by the loch.

(Sebastian noted that the following bit had also been removed from his initial version - "I then thought I saw an RUC officer walk over to the bodies on the ground which appeared to be still moving and saw him shoot at each with his revolve. He did the same with those in the car. One of them appeared to be Freddie. The soldiers had turned away and were walking back towards an RUC Land Rover.")

By this time the house was on fire from the flare that I had thrown. I found the fire extinguisher and began moving downstairs into the smoke spraying left and right as I went, but I had to retreat due to the heat of the flames and the billowing noxious smoke.

We all escaped through the window onto the flat roof below.

By this time the fire engine was on site racing right up to the front door and managed to put out the fire in a few minutes but the stair well was burnt through.

We met up with William Whiteside later outside.

It was by then about 11pm. We spent the night in the RUC station.

Signed Sebastian Edwards ....

"That looks OK" said Sebastian "just two or three bits to correct".

"Firstly it isn't Robin More but Roderick Morley.   I do think you should get the names right you know!"

"Yes, well, the Sergeant will tell you all about that, you know, we don't usually give out such names!"

"But this is a police report!"

"Ah yes but certain people you know are treated differently, so they are."

At last the penny dropped with Sebastian "you mean he is security forces?"

"Well Mr Edwards, I wouldn't rightly know, so I would not!"

"What about the checking of the rear window – did you not notice that Bill?"

"Ah yes, well you see that was.. er so that.. No I think you should talk with the Sergeant, so you should!"

"And the final shots?"

"Well the Sergeant says that it's all a bit 'graphic', yes that's what he said, 'graphic'! After all you probably couldn't see that much from that angle on the second floor, and the smoke and all upstairs. So they were all armed you know – but again speak with the Sergeant.

If you sign this now I am sure you can discuss it with him tonight, so you can. Shall I book you in for say 6pm here at the station? He's out right now."

He called the his sons from the police station hopefully before they heard of it through the media and Sarah called her parents.

The press was very upbeat Sebastian noted. Generally they described it as a victory and in particular Sebastian was singled out for praise in having such complex security systems and more importantly rescuing all his guests except one who had apparently died in the firefight. Headlines were:-

London Tabloids made it —

Safe House = 0, IRA = minus 4

Local press noted less stridently.

IRA Hit Unit beaten off and killed
– Guests escape over roof.

Together with large photos of the smoking ruin of the house and of Sebastian and Sarah in front

There was a standard service background of "An RUC Sergeant who was quoted as saying:

"It was a successful combined RUC and Army co-operation!"

CHAPTER SEVEN

He wasn't sure how he would be received when he arrived at work.

His boss Andrew Steel called him in immediately and asked "Are you OK? Do you want to return to work yet? Is your wife hurt?"

Sebastian assured him that he was OK "Yes and I am happy to get back to work, I realise that recently this side of my life has taken over more of my attention than I would have liked, so I feel it's about time I repaid you and really got stuck in, it will take months for the building damage to be repaired. Sarah is shaken but she's OK thanks!"

Sebastian had hoped that Andrew would say something like "Oh no that's all right but glad you are back fully with us" but he hadn't. Hmm, maybe his lack of drive at work had been too visible? So he started off again "Perhaps it's time I should really get into the performance of this 'Section F' that seems to be extremely poor, I'll take it up with the Operations Director this afternoon."

"Yes, well, I was meaning to have a word with you about that; in view of what you have been through I should perhaps explain. It will come out soon anyhow I am sure. You understand these installation groups, or sections as they were called, have the responsibility for cabling – this particular unit handles all sensitive work and accordingly has a high security clearance. We were told by the RUC that 'Section F' had been compromised somehow, details of phones and addresses of prison officers had been leaked. You know they are the primary target of the IRA? Your premises were refurbished and connected by 'Section F' although you would not have known that, they looked like ordinary electricians; they also installed your security systems. Of course we don't know what happened after that. But it seems that the IRA were after a high ranking security officer whom they thought was in your 'Safe House' and obtained that information through devices planted by

'Section F'. The Section's performance was poor because we needed an additional two people to check what was going on within the Section. As a result of this operation we were to check the devices and so to pinpoint the person responsible in that section. Unfortunately he disappeared over the weekend, probably to 'border country' that sort of no-man's land just south of the border. Anyhow the IRA unit was cleaned out and their spy in 'Section F' has been eliminated, he's a marked man now, so it's been a complete success!

"The Security services called me this morning and asked to personally thank you on their behalf."

"Andrew, you mean this was a set up job from the start? But my wife could have been killed and the boys perhaps too if it had been in the summer holidays?"

"I am sorry, Sebastian, but once it comes under security provisions there is nothing I could have done; to tell you would have compromised the whole operation. Now take a couple of days off please, to readjust then let's start afresh!"

When Sebastian appeared at the RUC station that evening he was in no mood to play around. "Sergeant Hannah I have since learned that this was a massive set up job. The unmasking of an IRA plant in 'Section F'. So I, my wife and all our guests were put at risk just to provide you with your little project.   And it looks as if you have killed an entire IRA unit. I saw what happened in the end you made no attempt to give medical assistance or revive them: I believe you just killed them in cold blood!"

Sergeant Hannah was quiet for a moment.

"Mr Edwards my father was in the RUC after service in the British Army after the war. Do you want to know how he died? Well I'll tell you anyhow. He was a sergeant same as me and he was in charge of a

Border Patrol in the Crossmaglen area in South Armagh. He was travelling to the 'look out post', a watch tower. He was in an armoured Land Rover crossing a stream; the whole thing went up with an enormous bang that was heard for miles, probably detonated from behind a hedge nearby. The IRA frequently laid a second bomb so the ambulance could not immediately approach them. My father was left out there to die of his wounds.

Do you think the IRA would have offered to take him to hospital? His two brothers were both farmers further up the valley and were killed in the night by attacks on their farms – both of them in the 'B Specials'. Do you think in the second wave of the attack the IRA sent in a number of nurses?" "His father, my grandfather was based in Dublin in the 1920s also as a sergeant in the Royal Irish Constabulary, he was badly wounded in the leg and was maimed for life!"

"Are you aware that over 300 policemen have been killed in Northern Ireland since the Troubles began?"

"Mr Edwards you have no idea! This is an undeclared war and will be so whilst ever the two communities are at each other's throats. But this is OUR war it's not YOURS."

Sebastian could see that he was shaking with rage and was barely able to control himself, his fists pounded the table.

"You have heard about the Troubles so how on earth did you think you had the right to remain immune from everything around you. It's YOU not I that wanted to set up a safe house, indeed I questioned if it was right, if you remember? But YOU were determined to do it! It's YOU who decided to stick your oar into this mess. By what right do you think YOU can call anything here a 'safe house', the only way it's safe is if it's surrounded by soldiers or police and I pity those gullible fools who have paid you over the odds for any such assurance. There is and never will be any guarantee that it is 'safe'. He shouted "DO YOU UNDERSTAND ME!" and he stood up and leant across the desk smashing his fist so hard on it that his whole frame was shaking.

"You understand that if this IRA unit had not been stopped here and now it would have claimed more lives, several of our security personnel have been killed by them, so yes it was a trap and yes it was a success, a great success in the war that's fought out across the province. You played a significant part in this because of its apparent normality. It was because you really believed it was safe that others were convinced so too and that was necessary for the trap to be sprung. It simply would not have been possible to let you in on this, you show your emotions too clearly, but you have proved that you have great courage. Of course we would never have left you on your own, our special agent was always a few feet away from you, he would have used his revolver if he had to, to protect you, but you acted so quickly that it was not necessary."

Sebastian was stunned into silence, he was right, this was not his war, he had no right to expect any favours!

Jim Hannah eased himself back into his chair and recovered his composure.

"Now to practicalities. You have done us a good service and we want to be fair, I realise that this has caused considerable damage and that you have made a significant investment. I have called the Ministry here in Belfast for you. Normally they would insist on having a year's worth of trading before paying you compensation as if it were a business, but they will make an exception in your case. They are going to make you two offers either firstly, repay you everything that you have spent on your project from day one including building, work, furniture, architects fees in one lump sum and you walk away or; secondly, they will carry out the refurbishment for you to replace like with like and give you compensation for profits for that period equal to your best monthly profit since you started. They will be in contact with you shortly but you will have a couple of weeks to decide."

"So thanks you for coming around Mr Edwards. Hello Billy will you see him out please?"

Billy popped his head around "So that's all sorted then, so it is!. He's a good man, Jim Hannah, he tried his best, I am sorry, sure I am, that I couldn't drop the hint, so I was! I hope everything's going OK? Drop around if I can help at any time."

"Just one thing Billy please which the Sergeant did not explain; why did you disable the alarm system to the rear?"

"Well now it's no great secret I suppose, that would probably have been Freddie Mullins disengaging it before he went out!"

"Not you then?"

"Ack, gerraway! No! What would I be doing with it? No! That's a funny notion now! So it is!"

Sebastian was unconvinced.

CHAPTER EIGHT

Sebastian threw himself into his work for the next two weeks. They were back in the same company owned flat from which had they started out. Sarah had become extremely nervous about going to new places she was clearly depressed.

The Compensation Documentation needed a huge amount of paperwork support and they still had not made up their minds what to do next.

They decided to take a short break before the school holidays and booked to stay with the in laws before travelling up to see his old friend Douglas Finlay for a few days in Northumberland.

They booked to do a circular tour taking the car to Dublin, from there to Liverpool, then across to Northumberland returning to Cairnryan and back to Belfast, stopping at 3 star hotels on the way.

He realised he would not get the best of welcomes from Will Jefferies but he was totally unprepared for the onslaught.

"Do you remember what you told me 'It's unlikely we will be targeted, I would not have accepted it if I thought I or Sarah were at real risk'? So what they hell was that? A full attack by a notorious IRA hit gang? In one of the newspapers it was suggested that this was a trap set up to catch them. Is that what you did? Are you in that business as well now? Do you think you are in the secret service or something? What the bloody hell do you think you were doing?"

Sarah jumped up "Now stop Dad that's enough – can't you see that we are both mentally exhausted, the last thing we need is being shouted at, that's enough or we leave here right now!"

Sebastian was taken aback he had never heard her explode in that way before, but she then erupted in a mass of tears and rushed to her mother for consolation. Sebastian was alarmed and confused he had talked about the incident with Sarah and she had always reacted in a practical way. Perhaps he had underestimated the intensity of his wife's feelings? But she was not hurt at all? He had not noticed any change in the relationship between them.

Sebastian started "It was all going so well you know and Sarah was doing brilliantly, we were managing the place well and getting in satisfied customers who kept on coming back to us. It was profitable too, we were really making a success of it; the only major problem was that it was draining away my effort at work and I was at the end completely knackered. I have no doubt one can get used to this sort of life but it has been a very hard few months!"

Will Jefferies interjected "You are surely not going back to do it again? Surely you can get out with your head held high and all your cash – that's one of the options as I understand it?"

Sebastian tried to buy time. "Well we have as yet made no decision and really are taking these days off to reconsider everything and to have some recuperation time together."

"I am really proud of you both!" Jenny Jefferies said with tears welling up again. "I think you have really achieved wonders – I was so worried about whether your confidence would hold up over your cooking but you seem to have mastered that, and you came over very well on the TV Sebastian, they are all talking about you around here... but you two have to be serious about this now! You know you cannot manage this without more help otherwise you'll wear yourselves to the bone. Sarah's wrists seem to be swelling up, probably with all the housework, and you must admit it's given us here a terrible fright, maybe you can choose somewhere else?"

Sebastian acknowledged it was difficult to make it work with just five bedrooms; he did not see that without more rooms he could afford permanent staff which it surely needed. He had of course got this bit of land alongside, perhaps that could be developed?

That caused a pause in conversation which then passed onto other matters; how well both Jefferies looked, where the boys could stay for the vacations as Belfast was now out of the question and how the boys were developing and what their future careers might be.

The following day Sebastian realised that Sarah had begun to relax and she several times just fell asleep whilst reading and was happy just chatting, calling old friends and sleeping. Sebastian decided to leave his wife with her parents, to which she readily agreed, and move on to stay with his old friend on his own.

He and Douglas set themselves a routine of long walks one in Kielder Forest and the other along miles of Hadrian's Wall. They had both done these walks several times before but Sebastian was always astonished by the thought that here was a company of Roman soldiers who suddenly became wall builders – two jobs! They surmised too that somewhere somehow there must be an explanation as to how such a clearly excitable nation like the Romans/Italians could be so organised and logical. Like the mafia being in charge of the USA Army?

Sebastian relished the physical exercise and bit by bit, hill by hill, stile by stile Sebastian entrusted his friend with his innermost thoughts. He had clearly underestimated the cultural divide and could not necessarily guarantee any kind of safety. But it had worked, they had succeeded, but what on earth was he to do now? Douglas listened quietly. Sebastian knew that his friend would let him chatter on and then suddenly pose the relevant questions.

"So what are the options do you think?" asked Douglas.

Sebastian outlined the basic alternatives, he could either continue with his main job or try to get a job elsewhere, although the latter did not look too promising as he had spent less than a year in the current job, not long enough to convince any new employer that he had achieved anything. So it looked as though he would have to stay for another year at least.

The next thing to consider was what to do with the Safe House.

"I can reinstate or take the cash. I cannot manage indefinitely without some part-time staff, but according to my calculations it would not then pay its way. Perhaps Will Jefferies would lend me the money so I could expand and really make a go of it but it would need a further £30,000 to 40,000 to build on out over the car park. If that was not possible then I could take the money and hope that Sarah might get a job locally otherwise there would be no possibility of paying privately for the children's education – but is that really necessary anyhow? The boys are both bright enough to compete in any school, the problem is more to do with me than them. Unless I have a settled job where I can put down my roots, it would be wrong for them to be uprooted by too many changes, but so far I have not found that job that would both pay enough and give me the freedom of management which I feel I need to work at my optimum. I feel that I have no right to drag the boys to new schools every two years. No! Until they were settled the arrangement with Will Jefferies will have to do!"

"Hmm" Douglas mused "maybe you should test out your job a bit more and see how that goes? After all it will take months to get the house back as it was. Are you forgetting Sarah in these plans? You should not underestimate the effect of this trauma on her! I only wish I could come over and see it but you have just highlighted that's impossible!"

"Douglas my old friend you really do help me sort things out."

On Monday after the weekend he drove back to Liverpool to pick up Sarah and after spending a couple of nights at Grasmere with family friends, they made their way back to Cairnryan for the ferry to Larne and so back to Belfast.

CHAPTER NINE

As soon as he arrived back in Belfast he phoned Sergeant Hannah. "Sergeant I having difficulty making up my mind about how to proceed with the Safe House. Can you tell me frankly, do you think if it was refurbished that the IRA would come back in a revenge attack?"

"It's impossible to say Mr Edwards, you know of course we can guarantee nothing we are not in the business of being commercial security guards. It's perhaps unfortunate that the press made out that it was from the start a trap. Repeat attacks are very rare because they achieve very little. Of course we will do all we can to help you."

Sebastian was rather surprised that didn't seem to be much of a payback for having delivered to them an entire IRA hit unit, and it seemed his usefulness to them was now ended!

For the next month Sebastian was never home before 7pm and he worked as hard as he could to improve profitability, get the debtors down and watch the stock write offs. They delayed the decision on the House. He felt that something was not right at work. They could never get a strategy clearance for anything from Head Office in London, all Capital Expenditure had first to be justified under a new corporate code NPV system to cross compare spend here and in other regions and then suddenly no Capital Expenditure was signed off at all. He had frequently disagreed with Head Office priorities and they had not agreed with his new systems. They did however have other strange requests which had to be carried out overnight such as, 'What was the cost per square foot of each of the offices which they had owned and what could these be sold off for?'. As many of the offices had been owned for forty years or more that involved considerable research even to find out exactly where they were and their existing condition. Andrew Steel was the only person to report to London for the regular regional meetings but he could not make sense of it either.

Then the bombshell dropped.

Andrew called him in together with the other Directors.

"Look I have some bad news".

"The parent company has decided to split the company into Hardware and Software lines and they have decided to sell off the Software side to concentrate on developing the Hardware. This they believe is the core business and that they will never do justice to the Software side whilst it's under one management.

In effect that cuts back our turnover by 25% but our profit by 33% so we will have to have a total restructuring and delayering if we are to retain the same net % margin in the Hardware side as on both together.

It's up to us to work out how this should be done and where the redundancies should fall and there's no guarantee at the end of it that any of our own jobs will be saved. So we will meet on Monday to get this done and work out a plan.

So before that, clear all desks for action! All vacations are cancelled unless that would cause financial hardship!"

That evening Sebastian told Sarah about the call to Sergeant Hannah. Sarah had not even thought about a revenge attack, after all the IRA had failed, why would they try again but she willing agreed that it was impossible to proceed. They signed the compensation papers for the full reimbursement.

Sebastian threw himself into his work.

He went over the figures many times, working out different conditions and solutions with Andrew Steel and they went over and over the lists of assets, premises and staff working out how to split everything and what was left over, how many would be made redundant. These were then listed according to time with the firm and age and perceived performance as required by Head Office.

Andrew Steel began a series of weekly trips to London to report but it was clear to Sebastian that the whole process was wearing him down; he had spent years building up and maintaining the operations and these assets were often those he had acquired and was now scrapping and many of those on the redundancy list he had personally interviewed and hired.

He told Sebastian that he found the whole process intensely disagreeable and tiring, worst was that they could say nothing to anyone inside or outside the company, they were sworn to secrecy until the split went 'formal' and the stock exchange was informed.

Andrew Steel was beginning to rely on Sebastian to prepare the details for these meetings and gave him grudging praise for his work. "You should have been here 3 years ago three it might have made all the difference!"

The Human Relations Director was offered another local job which he took immediately and Sebastian took over that role as well. The list of names of those to be made redundant was already agreed but the difficult bit of talking to all the staff still remained. It was not a rewarding job and Sebastian soon became identified with the London HQ who were driving it but who refused, themselves, to attend these sessions.

The only person who offered any sympathy was the Union man William Bartlet who now understood that the systems and organisational changes Sebastian had brought into the finance function had in fact split the divisions and that any reduction in staff had been covered by natural wastage. Seeing the devastation caused to other staff William thanked him warmly for his foresight. In fact three months previously Sebastian had himself split senior accounting responsibilities between his two lieutenants.

At the end of September Andrew collapsed with a heart attack and died over the weekend but that did not stop the remorseless move to split the operation.

Sebastian thought his own position now went from bad to worse, the original Operations Director Roy Brooks took over as temporary MD. He had no time for Sebastian's heroics, he himself thought it had been stupid to get involved in that way and always assumed that Sebastian was part of the trap because he had spent so much time working on it. He knew little about 'Section F'. He was waiting for the redundancy pay-off to buy himself a house in Cornwall.

So Sebastian found himself answering for all the decisions that Andrew Steel had made. His secretary Jeannette was made redundant early on obliging him to work with a temp which merely increased the pressure.

The split between the divisions had to be carried out by December. It was clear they weren't going to offer him a job - he had in effect worked himself out of it! But he was left with all the tail-end bits and was expected to deliver workable systems and accounts by then. He managed to obtain agreement to time off for interviews and a format for a reference letter. His notional London boss had disappeared and no-one even bothered to offer him an exit interview which he knew was standard.

He negotiated the final pieces of the claim and started the business of going for interviews, they had allowed him to take reasonable time off till February.

He felt he had achieved little.

He realised he had failed as they put it 'to manage upward', he knew that he had relied on the quality of his work to speak for itself.

Sarah was distraught by the news that they would be moving once again and spent more time chatting to her father and mother.

GROUND PLAN OF BRYANSBURN HOUSE

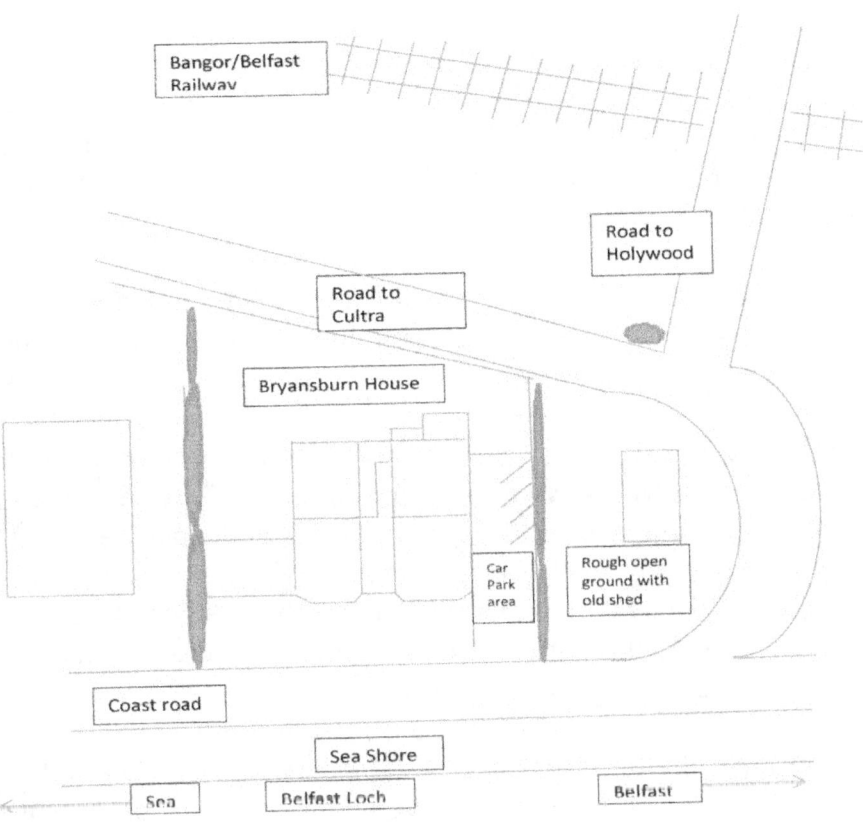

Bangor/Belfast Railway

Road to Holywood

Road to Cultra

Bryansburn House

Car Park area

Rough open ground with old shed

Coast road

Sea Shore

Sea

Belfast Loch

Belfast

PART TWO - A Terrible Place, Terrible Times

CHAPTER ONE

Sebastian rushed home and, avoiding the questions from his wife, went straight upstairs to the small room he used as a study. He wrenched open the filing cabinet and took out the wallet of neatly filed bank statements. He placed the wallet on his desk and crouched over it carefully turning each page.

His wife Sarah rushed up the stairs behind him. "What's wrong? Sebastian! What's wrong? Is there something missing? Have we been burgled? What are you looking for?"

He impatiently waved her away concentrating on the matter in hand muttering "No No! Not now I'll tell you in a minute." He continued his search, rapidly turning over the pages and occasionally referring to another file or a half used cheque book. Sarah knew better than to interrupt. It took several minutes and suddenly he stopped and slumped into the swivel chair, the last relic of his father's furniture, which he used at weekends when working from home.

He turned around and faced his wife. "Thank God thank God! There's nothing there, nothing there at all! Everything seems to be accounted for. No unusual entries!" "Phew!"

"I told you last night when I arrived back late from work that we had a problem but that I hoped I could resolve it! Well, yesterday evening I called the security officer because an employee had been acting strangely. You remember we recruited Elizabeth six months ago and she had shown great promise impressing several line managers. As she was evidently well versed in IT matters having been recently employed by a UK manufacturer of tower PCs, we had entrusted her with an order for twelve very expensive PCs costing with routers etc. well over £30,000."

"We had certainly received six of them, they were in the office next to mine but she had said that all twelve had been delivered and had insisted on payment, but the delivery note was missing for the other six. We were unable to explain that and it was mentioned to the Internal Auditor who happened to be on a regular visit.

The Internal Auditor immediately seized the initiative and instructed that the serial numbers should be checked with the delivery notes and that all those PCs should be collected and checked. The employee, Mrs Elizabeth Trickett, had been phoned in the afternoon and was asked to comply with this check."

"She called me back at 6.pm when I was still in the office, and, in a very aggressive tone, demanded to know what was going on and challenged me to bring into the office the Managing Director, Manuel Diego, on whom she had made a very favourable impression."

"So" said Sarah "did you call him?"

"No! – for by this time security was involved and we decided not to call the MD but to await developments and see if she would relent and agree to the search". "Well, this morning I received a phone message saying that four of the missing six PCs were at the IT agent that we had used to carry out some software changes. I went there with our security officer and collected them but the agent refused to explain what was happening".

"I was by now highly suspicious of the confusion that she had created. If she was attempting to get paid for items never delivered she might also have breached the financial systems in other areas. So, working on a hunch that there might be some sort of fraud going on I immediately instructed staff to carry out an emergency check on any payments that might have been made in her name."

"Within three hours we had found three suspicious payments. One was a payment made out in her name which had been passed through the bank the previous week, another was to company bearing her name made in the previous run of trade creditors at the previous month end. It now seems evident that she was trying to defraud the company in some way and exactly how and why I am not quite sure".

"She was responsible directly to me and I had had a worry that she might have tried to involve me in some way. If, for example, she had transferred over even just £500 into my bank account then I might have been incriminated too and it might have been almost impossible to prove a negative – that I was not involved!"

He paused hoping that she had caught up with the story.

"But what was she trying to do?" Sarah questioned, "Why would she have done something like that? You said all the managers were impressed by her ability and knowledge. There was even some talk of a promotion for her?"

"Yes" he said "that's what is most perplexing, but what on earth did the IT agent have to do with all this I wonder? I better get back to work and find out more – the internal auditors are there right now."

CHAPTER TWO

Four days later Sergeant James Stewart called in at Sebastian's office in the American owned factory in Glasgow. He introduced himself and then proceeded to ask him some leading questions in a relaxed style.

"So Mr Edwards can you tell me what you think is going on?"

"Well I am not sure that I can. I have had some discussions with internal audit and with security and at first it seemed simple enough; she was involved with the IT agent in getting twelve PCs which were specifically excluded from the capital cut backs so that we could use them to offset the huge redundancy we were in the process of finalising. We didn't receive all the PCs but she wanted to be paid for them."

"Well Mr Edwards I have already been over to the IT agent and they say that this was all part of a major IT programme involving a spec for a new BMB 20B computer for which they appear to have an order, signed by your purchasing department."

Sebastian was staggered, a BMB 20B that's impossible! He thought there must be some mistake but how could there be – the police wouldn't say that without some information?

"Well I better check that" he replied rather lamely.

But then Sergeant Stewart continued. "But now what of these other two items which you found, your security officer told me about them? And perhaps we should start from the beginning – tell me what your position is and the relevance of this equipment?"

"I am the Financial Controller and Company Secretary of California Electronics Inc., I came here about eighteen months ago. The company is based in the USA and we make electronic assemblies which go into PCs –

in fact we supply to a range of agents in Europe but most of our trade goes to associated assembly plants in the Far East. We are just installing a $200M new facility here to expand production but this has come at a time of downturn in sales – so on top of all this new work, we had a hold on all staff hiring. To cap it all a directive from HQ in the USA instructed us immediately to take enforced holidays right across the plant, operatives, accounting staff and management!"

"So how did you manage with the installation of the new factory equipment, that would have led to even more work would it not?" asked the Sergeant.

"Yes that's right it did – we desperately needed more staff to do the checking of the suppliers' invoices which was complicated as much of it had to be paid in dollars. However dollar invoices had to be booked in sterling as we draw up our accounts for UK tax purposes in £ not $. We had to use inexperienced staff from the factory production lines as we were not allowed to hire new accounting staff as they said 'No new headcount, make do with the people in the factory'."

Sebastian tried to explain, "The truth is that the existing accounting IT systems are very clunky and, once made, payments appear to simply drop off the statement. Look, here's a statement of what's owing to a supplier. A monthly run is made and cheques are automatically raised for the amount outstanding, they are then signed off by myself. That's how the system works but it makes it very difficult to track through past payments against invoices. If the payment was left on the account we could then check if the following invoices had been paid or not. On this occasion Elizabeth approached me saying that the system was 'down', this happened quite frequently nearly every month or so, and meant that we could not draw automatic pre-signed cheques. So she came to me saying this was an emergency, the supplier had to be paid urgently and asked for my counter signature on a hand written cheque. I remember that quite distinctly."

Sebastian continued, "The second payment appears to be a straight forgery – we are waiting for the cheque to be returned from the local Bank branch but they already acknowledge that it should never have been paid in cash over the counter and that it's a poor copy of my signature. The bank seem to have accepted responsibility for this."

"And the final one?" The sergeant asked. "That payment was made direct to Mrs Elizabeth Trickett and was passed off for payment by the Managing Director against her written invoice."

Sebastian added "But I am still quite confused as to why she did this – she was getting on well with all the managers, one might almost say too well."

The Sergeant interrupted quickly "What do you mean by that?"

"In line with company policy each senior manager was required to designate a successor in case of death, disability or just leaving – so the company could continue to operate efficiently irrespective of the absence of any one individual. The Managing Director had suggested that I might choose her even though she was the most junior of the three accountants at that level. He said that this was also the view of the Facilities Manager, a US national who was in charge of the IT function."

The sergeant said "Elizabeth had only been with you for six months but seems to have been already in a powerful position – why do you think that was?"

Sebastian was irritated. It was clear that the policeman knew quite a lot and must have spoken to many of the managers and staff already, indeed he seemed to know more than Sebastian himself and that made him feel uncomfortable and nervous, he fiddled with the ring on his finger. He was silent for a moment.

"Look, is that all for the moment? I have still some things to check through and I have to sign off today's cheques, can we continue this sometime later? In truth the redundancy hit us very hard, several key staff left and we are now having difficulty even getting the accounts completed on time."

"Of course – perhaps tomorrow afternoon 2.00pm"

The security officer called by and asked how things are going. "You have no need to worry, you know Mr Edwards you are not under suspicion, we have been in contact with the police in Northern Ireland as you were last employed there and we know you have the highest possible clearance."

Sebastian was however in mental turmoil, what the policeman had said suggested was that there had been some sort of underhand game going on. Was it part of a larger fraud, he wondered?

The office was an open plan space and it was impossible to carry out any private discussions; he was unable to confide in his key staff and he knew he had lost the confidence of his immediate staff by agreeing to the 40% redundancy in his department. Up to now there had been four levels of posts with recognised qualified and unqualified positions but all this went out the window; the MD had insisted three months ago that this plant must fall into line with equivalent plants in the USA. There were now mostly two levels between the senior and his staff, so there was no possibility of an internal career path, there were no training posts and no holiday or illness cover. It was all on the American system. There is a position – interview and fill – you get the man for the job, that's it. The payroll department for example for 900 employees consisted of three full time and one part time accounting staff. Due to a commitment to 360 day working of the plant when in full production this posed a huge pressure to maintain a service irrespective of staff available.

Sebastian thought the new manning levels were 'suicidal' and had told the MD as much. One dose of flu and the payroll department would be wiped out and there was still $100M left of the capital plan to spend but with inadequate staff to cope with the currency problem. He had told the MD that it was quite possible a mistake or fraud might occur. It was clear to Sebastian that the MD did not like being put on the spot and he sharply snapped back "Then it's up to you to make sure we are properly insured for that risk!"

Sebastian knew that he would have to cross-train all staff to cover the work or he wouldn't be able to survive.

On the morning after the redundancies were announced, Sebastian remembered the dismay and disappointment amongst the staff. He had at the same time been handed responsibility for the IT department, whose manager had been sent back to the USA. In that department the redundancies were even tougher. Feelings against the company were running high, relations became so bad that he was alerted by one of the continuing IT staff that several leaving staff had planned to sabotage the entire computer system. The idea had been to trigger a memory lapse so destroying the database information. Sebastian remembered how he had had to rush down to the local pub where the IT leaving party was being held to halt the proceedings. He had had to 'read the riot act' warning against such actions and obtaining their individual assurance that no such sabotage would take place before he would agree to handing over their termination cheques.

After the sergeant left he went over in his mind what might have occurred in the way of the fraud.

Sebastian's own relations with the other service department heads were no better. There had been a significant disagreement with the Personnel department over Elizabeth's hiring. Her last employer BMB had sent them a perfectly satisfactory reference letter, however a month after she had joined, a staff member had cornered Sebastian and warned him about Elizabeth's family background. Sebastian had instructed HR to carry out a more detailed review. Calls to BMB revealed that she had also been in dispute with them over her expenses. This didn't make sense to Sebastian. His suspicions were further aroused when HR had tried to track back her previous employment and education in Australia; she said she had obtained a degree, but the institution when called revealed that the premises had been destroyed by fire and nothing could be proved or disproved. Sebastian knew that he didn't have enough to remove her, he could prove nothing and would face a nasty grilling it he tried to sack her in view of her current apparent favourable status within the company.

The following day he needed to check something with the purchasing department, he took the stairs to the identical office on the floor above. The department was overworked in the same way as his being involved in buying the equipment for the large capital programme. He spoke with the manager, "Alex, I wonder if you could help me? Do you know anything about an order for the BMB 20B?"

"Err no! Not really Sebastian!"

But Sebastian had noticed a purchase order was lying neatly in one of the filing pockets on his desk labelled OFFICE PENDING.

"Yes there it is – silly of me" said Sebastian "This is the order. Right?"

"Oh!" Alex replied "that one - so you know about it then? I was told that this was in abeyance pending the recent discovery – yes you will see it was signed off by Mrs Trickett and by the MD Manuel Diego so it's quite OK!"

"But not by me?"

"No it's not – I was told you had had a falling out on the matter with the MD and that some sort of changes were imminent and she would be in charge of its installation – it was apparently copied to the USA IT Director."

Sebastian knew that was not true, he had visited BMB and he himself had agreed the need to upgrade the IT installation but that the full specification was awaiting approval from the USA IT function. It was a company rule that any connection that fed into the USA mainframe had to have USA approval to prevent the risk of corruption and to ensure compatibility. He was alarmed that the Purchasing Manager would accept such an order without even attempting to check it through with him.

He went back to his desk in a state of shock – so there was something going on!

Sebastian's secretary slapped a report on his desk which she said she had picked up by chance. He didn't believe her but read it quickly. It was about the fraud, and there it was: "Significant questions were raised by an employee concerning Elizabeth Trickett, HR made several phone calls but were instructed by Mr Edwards to cease these investigations".

Damn and blast, thought Sebastian, that was a deliberate lie. The HR department were trying to cop out of all responsibility for their own failure. His position did not look good he remembered that the discussion with the MD over the redundancies had been very long drawn out and acrimonious. Manual Diego had obviously been instructed by USA to reduce the number of accountancy employees; he,

Sebastian, had managed to save two of the ten staff which he was asked for but he was clearly going to get no more.

He knew that once the MD had agreed something with his line boss there was simply no way around the situation. Two weeks previously one of the managers had been criticised by the MD for poor operating performance and a confrontation was contrived as the manager in exasperation said 'Well if you can do better...!' and twenty minutes later he was sacked.

Sebastian knew all this because he prepared the termination and P45 tax notification papers but Sebastian already knew that the MD was previously committed to reducing the number of his operational managers. He had no doubt at all that, as far as his own Accountancy Department was concerned, had he refused to accept the redundancies he would also be receiving his own P45.

So this must have been a reserve plan, some kind of Plan 'B' to try make even more severe cuts and replace people with PCs. It was a silly idea because without software there would be no gains and a BMB 20B computer would take months to install!

So the picture was becoming clearer to Sebastian. Elizabeth as designated successor was the only person in the department who knew of the possible redundancies. She knew of Sebastian's disagreement with the MD and she had clearly persuaded the MD to back her installing the new equipment and reducing the staff even further as payback.

There did not seem much point in calling for a meeting with the MD, he was working to instructions and would have cleared this informally with his chief.

However his bargaining position was now somewhat better than before, with his only 'competitor' Elizabeth, under suspicion his position would be inviolable for the moment.

At the meeting later with the sergeant he briefly went through how the system worked but saw no reason to divulge the internal intrigues and pass on his suspicions. As far as the police were concerned it was a fairly open and shut case. Theft and fraud. They had assured Sebastian that it would all be over in six months. She would plead guilty; she had no escape, it wasn't a difficult case.

Nevertheless Sebastian felt betrayed and he immediately began a search for another job; he could not reconcile himself either to the idea that senior managers and the MD had been deliberately duplicitous. He suspected that when all this was over they would move to replace him anyhow because he had questioned the logic of the redundancies here in the UK to fall in line with US based plants. He knew that in the company electronics engineers were the kings but accountants were simply not important. Whilst in the UK accountants were classed as qualified usually by passing exams, or not, in large US corporations such as California Electronics Inc., the accountant was just the one who did the numbers – all thinking work was done by engineering staff who were very much more financially literate than their English equivalents. Allocations of costs to products and provision of accruals were the only skills required of the accountants here – any other financial or accountancy services they would buy in from outside as they needed it.

CHAPTER THREE

Sebastian returned home and began to explain things to Sarah.

It was clear she didn't understand him or maybe she didn't want to. Sebastian knew that it would be hard. He would leave! In the first flush of the decision he felt enormous relief. Bugger the lot of them, the lying bunch of toads! He thought.

But then he had to face the practicalities. Sebastian had only just received the final compensation payment from Northern Ireland. In the nearly two years since they had been in Northern Ireland house prices in England and Scotland had risen alarmingly whilst those in Belfast had hardly changed, so buying a house near Glasgow had been about 15% more expensive for a standard four bed house in good location. Even with Aunt Maude's bequest they still had to carry a sizeable mortgage.

He thought he was in a position that he could get another job within a few months.

Sarah kept on coming back to the same point "But you have done nothing wrong, it's she who has committed the frauds so why should you leave, why don't you sit tight and fight it out?" He tried to explain that he had clearly lost the confidence of the MD and other senior managers. It's clear they would have had him out had he demurred even for a few minutes, it's clear that his staff felt he had failed them.

In short he began to hate every minute of it. He knew that he simply could not work well in circumstances of mutual suspicion and veiled threats. He knew he would lose self-confidence, he found it very difficult just to withdraw and to watch and wait.

Sarah became angrier that he had ever seen her. "Who do you think you are? What entitles you to pick and choose like this? Did I pick and choose in Northern Ireland? No! I just buckled to and did what I had to! What about the family? How can we provide for them and what about the expensive education you promised the children? You will not be able to afford any school fees will you?"

Sebastian agreed to try to negotiate a settlement with the MD which would cover him for say six months to give him time to find another job.

There was one thing nagging him that became an obsession. He vaguely remembered that when the money was taken for one of the cheques there had actually been a warning phone call from the bank. One of the transferred production employees had taken the call 'Mr Edwards the bank wants to speak to you concerning a cheque and Mrs Trickett.' Sebastian was in conversation on the other line at the time which lasted several minutes so the girl called across again, 'Mr Edwards! The bank!' Still mentally dealing with other matters he said 'It's OK I'll talk to her about it later!'

That was it, thought Sebastian, that was the moment that he had missed taking action! Had he taken the call he might have been able to detect what was going on and prevent the whole fraud – trapping her red-handed. He had missed his opportunity. Neither the girl, who was moved back into production two days later, nor the bank had remembered the incident, but he had. He knew that he had failed to come up to his own high standards. He had slipped up.

CHAPTER FOUR

At his level of management employers take no prisoners – they pay well but expect a successful track record. None of the first twenty applications he made for similar posts in other companies even made it to the interview stage. No one was in the slightest bit interested in the internal problems and intrigue. He changed tactics, altering the reasons why he was seeking new employment, using new phrases like 'wanting to return to the Midlands where he was born' or that 'the whole operation was being downgraded from a business to a mere factory unit'. This way he got several interviews in the next batch of applications but, if anything, it made matters worse; it was clear, although the interviewers didn't actually say so, that they thought he had been sacked, that he could not stand the pressure or that his IT systems were a failure, any mention of the fraud brought questions asking if he was involved. All the time he was on the defensive, unable to put forward his real achievements there.

Time was dragging on and his notice period was disappearing month by month. If he didn't act soon he would be out of a job and no money coming in to pay the mortgage.

Eventually one company based near Nottingham made him an offer; it was for a steep drop in salary and the job was below his capabilities, but Sebastian felt he could cope with that. The company was based off the road to Derby making oil drums. At least his marriage was saved and he had money to cover the mortgage and the removal fees were met by the new employer.

He was pleased, it was the first glimmer of something to hold onto, a base from which he would try once again to climb the 'greasy pole.' As his house was already on the market he found it easy to drop the price and he immediately made the sale. The new house in the outskirts of Nottingham was smaller and to reduce costs they downgraded from four beds with large garden, to a much more modest three bed property with a very small garden scarcely bigger than the size of the garage.

There was just one problem and it began to loom ever larger in his mind.

Mrs Elizabeth Trickett had not yet pleaded guilty as the Scottish police had assured him that she would. In the meantime he had read press reports of recent fraud trials and he became more and more alarmed. He had been warned that if she did not plead guilty and the case came to trial Sebastian would have to come and give evidence which could take several days.

From reading the papers he knew that defence barristers were trained for one quite simple task; to totally demolish the credibility of the witness and the more they could tie him up in knots the better they could force him, the witness, into either agreeing that he had permitted the fraud or actively encouraged it and been complicit in it so that he could later enjoy the fruits of his work. The more confusion the barrister could create and the more gullible or involved he could show the witness the better! He read with alarm that bishops were seen to be easily duped by con artists who feigned illness or temporary impoverishment to ask for loans. They were more easily led into handing over money as being more trusting than the average person. Sebastian had been told by the visiting corporate internal auditor that, for the same basic reason, there were more frauds than average in Salt Lake City because Mormons were inclined to be more trusting and known to be more easily defrauded. He felt that defence lawyers might try to suggest that his failure to sack her when he had his suspicions would be taken as assenting to the offence.

Sebastian was worried about being verbally abused in this way in public when it would be reported in the press, but as he was no longer employed by his old company and if the trial came to the notice of his new employer he would be likely to be quizzed all over again by him. He hadn't mentioned the ongoing case on his application form since, had Elizabeth pleaded guilty, he might not even have even been mentioned. Now he felt vulnerable to exposure.

He realised that witnesses are totally unprotected – the injunction to just 'tell the truth' pales into insignificance when faced with a whirlwind of questions designed specifically to entrap.

His fears were well founded. Soon after taking up his job near Nottingham, he was advised of the date of the intended trial. He would be needed for several days and it was being held in Glasgow. He had obtained time off from work but had not given any reason. Elizabeth eventually pleaded guilty but following the hearing giving details of her imprisonment, an article appear in the 'Computer Business Worlds' briefly describing the fraud and naming Sebastian as the Finance Director of the company.

This had been passed to the IT manager of his new employer and came to the attention of the board. Sebastian was interviewed but as far as his new employers were concerned they claimed that it was a breach of trust and they should have been told of the matter at the interview. He argued that the press allegation was untrue and that her confession and imprisonment showed he was not responsible.

Sebastian was sacked on the spot – his company car was taken from him and the contents of his desk were handed over to him in a black plastic bag.

He was devastated; they paid him the three months' notice but after that there would be nothing. There was no higher authority for any appeal and there was clearly not the slightest chance of reinstatement.

Sarah was distraught and immediately called her parents to tell them the news.

For the first time in his life he 'signed on'. He could have avoided that by just not claiming but he didn't see the point of that, he thought this might be a long haul – he had no idea how he could get out of this mess.

He attended one or two short courses run by the employment office; the purpose of the first was to go through claimants' CVs and make them fit for sending out, and the other on positive thinking was to get the person in the right frame of mind. He cursed his parents for giving him such a pretentious name as 'Sebastian' as if he was a permanent member of the upper classes, it certainly didn't sound like a working man's name! It caused quite a stir when the job centre consultants, employed to assist him getting jobs, found that Sebastian had been earning much more than they were. One or two of them asked outright with knowing winks why he was in this mess expecting to find that he himself had been prosecuted but they soon proved helpful when they had heard the full story.

But that didn't help Sebastian. He went for a number of interviews mostly at 50% of his former salary – jobs for which he was well overqualified. It seemed often that the interviewers were just interested in his story and had already made up their minds that he was not employable anyhow. Others were uncomfortable about having someone much better qualified under them, could they handle him? Would he show them up?

Sebastian sunk lower and lower in self-esteem. He took to walking for miles during the day as if literally he had been working then at least when arriving back home, he felt he had done something. Walking, walking, going over and over again in his mind why had he resigned, why hadn't he fought?

At last under pressure from his wife, who was becoming worried about his mental state, he called for a doctor's appointment. He saw Doctor

Singh. He quickly gave a shortened version of the story. Doctor Singh empathised with his predicament and compared it with a similar situation in the medical profession. "But you, Mr Edwards, from what you tell me you have done nothing wrong; you are not disbarred in any way are you? I am not a legal man but I really cannot see why you would be compelled to say that you are required as a witness, that does not seem to be relevant to the job you applied for. Have you tried to sue your last employer?"

Sebastian said "It has crossed my mind in a moment of anger but where would I get the money to mount a legal challenge? Maybe I could take it to a tribunal but the results of the case would be made public and if it were to go against me that would end any prospect of employment as an accountant!"

"Well look Mr Edwards I can only deal with your mind and body I cannot get you back into your career, I wish I could, but what I can do is to give you a prescription. It will make you feel better more able to face the world – but mind do not drink with these – the mix is not good. Then come back and see me in three weeks' time, say after Easter. In fact I have a charity which badly needs financial advice and I really do not have the time to do it myself."

Then the money had finally run out, he had banked on getting a job in a couple of months but his meagre savings were gone – he could see it coming like a giant wave falling over him. He shut off everything he did not need. He cancelled his health insurance which had been part funded by his employers, he stopped magazine subscriptions, he stopped his life assurance and his accident insurance, he stopped the health club which he rarely used and his county cricket club subscription which he knew was a pity as it entitled him to free attendance and he faced the prospect of plenty of idle time.

He was now dependent on state aid. He thought positively 'Well this is what it's like for hundreds of thousands of others why should I feel more privileged than anyone else?'

He knew that his wife Sarah did not quite appreciate how it had all come to this, but she managed to get a part time job as a receptionist in a firm of Quantity Surveyors. However the pay was poor and she was not well treated it was clear that the others regarded her as lady muck, she found it difficult to learn procedures and terminology and could not settle, though Sebastian knew she put a brave face on it.

All this Sebastian endured but he was becoming introverted, the last move had cut him off from all his professional colleagues and he had no sporting or other hobbies to absorb his time. He felt less and less able to cope with situations as they arose. On the rare occasions they went out for a meal Sebastian was withdrawn and said nothing. He sat in front of the TV for days seemingly immersed in it but in reality he felt his mind was in neutral.

One day his father in law, Will Jefferies, called; Sarah had obviously kept him up to date with events and the boys were due back from school for the Easter vacation. "Hello Sebastian how are you? How's the job hunting going? Too bad! Look I wanted to touch base with you, the lads are due home next Friday and I thought I would take them off your hands for a bit; I have talked it through with Sarah and she's happy about that indeed I think she would like to come too. So I thought we would buzz off to a small hotel somewhere. I suppose you want me to continue paying their fees. Well I was expecting it – they are nice lads you know. See you on Sunday then."

Sebastian had just grunted – what else could he do?

He sat in his father's old swivel chair and In his hand he held one of the two remaining African war clubs he had reclaimed after the fire in

Ulster. It was blackened and encrusted with charcoal, he raised it to his nose and yes he could still smell the fire. That thought threw him back to the incident in Belfast and he realised that somehow he must get himself out of this.

He lifted the phone and called his old friend Douglas Finlay. "Douglas are you OK for me coming to see you on Easter Sunday and Monday?"

"Yes" came the cheery reply. "How's it going with you? Not too good I hear!"

Sebastian determined that tonight he was going out to think things through. It was quiz night at the local pub – he had never been before and hadn't a clue of the format. But this was it!

He called to Sarah "I'm going out for a walk. It's 7.30, be back later, don't wait up".

She asked him "Where are you going? Remember the boys are coming back tonight!"

He arrived at the pub about a quarter of a mile from home, right at the start of the quiz night and managed to attach himself to a group that was one person short. He was feeling good. He'd actually DONE something on his own! As he sat down one of his team called, 'What are you on?' He gave an automatic reply, 'Oh just a beer thanks! Sebastian was very good at general knowledge and was masterful on the two rounds dealing with Current Euro Politics and for history with Kings & Queens. His group won both rounds conclusively and Sebastian bought the next round of drinks 'same again' he said.

There was a halfway interval and that led to another half pint. Sebastian was feeling a bit worse for wear but he felt it was nothing he had not felt before; they were clearly winning and although the next round on

Painters saw them way adrift, then came Motorways and he came up with the impossible - naming the motorways in Northern Ireland – he was spot on! A winner again! He got up and walked to the bar but he felt his legs crumble and then, Oh God! He remembered those bloody pills!

He heaved himself up and returning to his table said he had to go home to meet his sons but they were assured of victory anyhow and he began to walk home.

He threw up at the tenth tree and then at the fifteenth but he had not leant over far enough and it caught his sleeve and bottom of his trousers. "I must get home and clean up before the boys arrive" he kept muttering to himself. He arrived in front of his house but couldn't find the keys.

He banged on the door and got no reply and banged again so hard that he broke the pain of glass and cut his hand. Blood dripped over his shirt. Suddenly the door was opened and Sarah shouted at him, "Oh what a frightful mess! Just look at you! Have you been in a fight or something? Boys help your father!"

Sebastian shouted "No! I lost my keys! No! I can do it myself! Get out of my way!"

Then Alexander, his elder son, said "Now Dad cool it, all we want to do it to help."

But for Sebastian his embarrassment was total, all he wanted was to get in and get cleaned up. He roared "Get out of my way!"

A neighbour's door opened and someone asked "Is everything OK?"

"No it's bloody not!" yelled Sebastian

The boys tried to pull him inside but Sebastian shouted "Get off of me, I can do it myself" but missed the step and crashed head first against the opened front door. He caught his ear on the door handle and blood spurted over the boys and Sarah.

Then Rupert grabbed his arm but Sebastian threw him off and the boy fell to the floor. There was a thud and the boy shouted "I think my arm is broken, it hurts like hell."

Sebastian was still shouting "Let me in! Let me in!"

"For God's sake Dad be quiet! Come in and sit down!" Sarah was crying loudly. Sebastian pushed past her and they both fell on the floor. He heard Alexander phone for an ambulance.

Sebastian had to be restrained again and when they attempted to put him in a chair he threw up.

The ambulance crew attended to Rupert and took him off to the hospital not more than a few miles away. Sebastian eventually calmed down and then he tried to explain to his other son Alexander that he had forgotten he should not drink with his pills, he had just gone to a quiz night at the pub. And it was the first time he had had a drink in months. He suddenly understood what he had done and broke down crying. All the tension and humiliation came out in a terrible outburst of uncontrollable sobbing. Eventually Alexander carried Sebastian to his bed and he fell asleep almost immediately.

When he woke next morning initially he remembered little of the events of the night before but slowly it dawned on him that the incident was far from over. When he went downstairs for a late breakfast he saw that his son had his arm in plaster and a sling although the hospital had said it was not broken, it was badly sprained. The mood around the table was suppressed. Sebastian thought that in his absence they had had a family conference about him and what to do next.

Sarah summarised "Sebastian I realised that mixing those drugs and drink was what caused the problem but we cannot continue like this! My father has proposed that for the time being we stay with them in Liverpool. He has already booked to take us on a short holiday. I think the best thing for you to do is to sort yourself out and then we will think what to do next."

Sebastian sat in his chair head bowed facing a plate of cereal. "I am sorry, really sorry; I have not been drunk like this for seven years. It was stupid of me to forget the effect the pills would have – but it was the first time I have been out to the pub for a drink in months. The irony is that our team was doing so well we won the competition!" He stopped and wiped a trickle of a tear that fell from his right eye, he nervously fidgeted with the ring on his figure.

"Look I'll make it up to you, something will crop up, I will sort it out – but there's no need to leave – I am sorry I seem to have messed it all up."

Alexander said "As Grandpa says it's not just this – it's the mess in Belfast and the problems in Scotland you seem to attract trouble wherever you are."

"Well thanks for that!"

"No, no Dad!" said Rupert, "I am sure he didn't mean that but we can't leave Mum here with you alone in case something else happens."

Sebastian tried to retain some self-control. "As you know I have agreed to go and see my old friend Douglas Finlay tomorrow. I assume that I can have the car? I will not be able to get a job without it!"

"Yes yes of course" Sarah replied. "My father is coming later on today to collect us. We will pack a few cases and be on our way as soon as he arrives. We can always come back for more bits and pieces later."

"OK I don't particularly want to be here when he comes, I don't want to go over everything again. So I'll go off for a walk. Sorry lads that I have made such a mess of things. Take care of your mother, I'll be seeing you!"

He went for a long, long walk; he didn't remember where. He knew that he had lost them; in his depression he fought to remember the good times, the last Christmas in Belfast, the walk along the loch!

When he returned they were gone. She had taken all her clothes, all her personal belongings, jewellery, books and mementoes. Everything of hers was gone there were no 'bits and pieces' to collect later.

There was a brief note from Rupert which said "Love you Dad – good luck! Hope to see you again soon."

That was enough to set off another outburst of sobbing and eventually he just sat there completely drained.

CHAPTER FIVE

He arrived on Sunday morning. Douglas asked him how he was but he was evasive and changed the subject to ask where they were going for the walk which he was eager now to complete.

Thus the discussion was of footpaths and views and old listed houses and then in turn another favourite topic, his friend's view of the Church of England from his perspective as a parochial church councillor. Douglas and Sebastian had been following the impact on the Church of the introduction of female clergy. The new vicar in Douglas's local group of churches was the first woman incumbent and her effect had been nothing short of dramatic with church attendances on Easter Sunday doubling from a barely sustainable seven to twenty in her first year and then to thirty-five last year. An astonishing turn around they both agreed!.

Sebastian had made it to his friend's in time for the late morning service and the tea and cakes that followed in the vestry. In fact Sebastian had no particular truck with any religion but one by-product of his own very expensive education had been compulsory church attendance; they had had to sing all the popular hymns, so now this had a reassuring effect on him, in any case he was a good singer! So why not? He felt he was supporting his friend in this.

Douglas seemed to Sebastian to live in a different, parallel, world where the seasons were still important. Douglas's wlfe was a talented artist and the house was always full of her work either ready for sale or in the course of completion. She specialised in miniatures of local flowers, poppies being a great favourite. Some of her pictures had been for sale in the vestry alongside bunches of flowers.

After Church they drove to the drop off point for the walk. As usual his friend made no attempt to lead him in discussion but waited. Sebastian suspected that Douglas was worried since he knew that the conversation usually revolved around his friend's plans, his next move and the floating of another improbable venture.

They had reached Housesteads, an old Roman fort on Hadrian's Wall. It was sleeting and they took shelter in an archway.

"Seems as though I am always ducking for cover recently. Frankly, Douglas, I am in a complete mess. It's a long story but I have no prospect of a job and Sarah and the children have left home. I am at rock bottom right now!"

Douglas did not reply. Sebastian knew his friend couldn't advise him on the details of his career. Slowly in a matter of fact way Sebastian told him briefly of the events of the previous days.

He surprised himself by his ability to look more positively on matters. He spoke without really wanting or expecting any reply from Douglas as if he was summarising out loud. "Perhaps the family break up could have a positive outcome. I no longer have responsibility for providing for my wife or the expensive education I had mapped out for my children, nor indeed the upkeep and mortgage payments on the house". This he could now sell and downsize eliminating the loans completely. Sebastian was convinced Sarah would never return. He felt that after the Belfast fiasco her father had completely lost confidence in his, Sebastian's, ability to take care of his only daughter. He would now have to reform his life but without any baggage or expectation.

Douglas interrupted the verbal reverie, "So what are you going to do next Sebastian? Have you any ideas? I am really worried you know!"

Sebastian was touched. "Well the first thing that I'll do will be to get myself working on something, anything just to prove my worth to myself. When I saw the doctor and he gave me those bloody pills he mentioned that there was a charity that urgently needed financial review and advice, I'll try starting with that; there will be no salary but at least I will be working and as the saying goes its always easier 'to get a job from a job'!"

Sebastian had thus made up his mind what to do and for the remainder of his time with his friend he was able to relax and they reminisced and joked over old times and former school friends.

CHAPTER SIX

Sebastian returned to Nottingham on the Monday and the following day he booked an appointment with Doctor Singh. He was warmly welcomed.

"So Sebastian how has it gone? Did you find those pills of use or more importantly have you got prospects of a job?"

"No" he replied "it resulted in an unfortunate incident as I forgot your warning not to drink when taking them! But I want to take you up on your offer of some unpaid work with a charity that you mentioned last time."

"I'm glad to see you are in positive mode. I had wondered if this sort of work would be beneath you? Well there are in fact two different projects."

"One of these is a refuge for Asian women. It fights against Forced Marriage and Honour Based Abuse. You know one of the problems we have in our Asian culture is that women are supposed to do what they are told by their menfolk? In many cases there's no problem but in some cases something sparks a great deal of anger and lines are drawn and families often try to enforce their will. The daughter may attempt to escape the pressure by leaving home and the family may then take steps to mutilate her in some way to show their anger or even worse try to kll her, the so-called honour killings. They believe that somehow honour is served by such death or mutilation. We have set up a charity to protect those who escape these enforced marriages so that they can be protected and can try to lead a normal life. In this case the accounts are in a mess and they have to apply for grants and funding but have no money and no-one who can help them to prepare a case to the local Council. Would you do that?"

"The other case is a care home. It has thirty-five beds so it's a large place but I hear they are in difficulties. I have some friends who are prepared to invest but we cannot do that until we are convinced that it's a solid operation. The people who run it are very nice but I know from a supplier that they are not paying their bills on time. Frankly we are not prepared to pay for a £25,000 report from a posh firm of accountants only to find the business is dead in the water. I would be very grateful if you could help us and prepare an initial report. From what you have told me you seem to have the competence to do all this."

Sebastian replied "I would be delighted to take on both."

Doctor Singh reached across the table and shook his hand "Good, thank you and perhaps no more pills for the time being!"

Within days Sebastian knew he was really making a difference, of course he still had to apply for jobs and not make it appear that this charity work was a full time which might therefore have meant he was ineligible for the unemployment money.

The battered women's home was saved by the correct preparation of a claim and full report. The council were impressed by the clarity of the figures and commended them warmly for their work.

The care home was more complex and meant that Sebastian had to refer back to the last accounts prepared over a year ago, correct the accounting entries and prepare new accounts and forecasts. He worked out the gross and net margins and worked out that the average occupancy was lower than expected mostly because they always left the rooms vacant for one week between occupants and this often slipped to two weeks. They also agreed to consider having a maintenance agreement with local plumbers and electricians which in the end might cost much less. The existing management agreed that tightening up in places like that would result in a reasonable profit. With this report Dr

Singh and half a dozen medical friends negotiated with the owners and decided to invest £300,000 for a 40% share of the care home. They felt it would form a natural backstop for their own clients in an environment that was doctor reviewed and controlled, whilst still retaining the existing management.

Doctor Singh called Sebastian in at the conclusion of the assignments and handed him two references, one for each project, which lucidly related what had been done, that Sebastian had performed well and was entirely responsible for the success. He handed him a cheque for 'expenses' of £1,000. Of course it was nothing like the fee consultants would have charged but it was an endorsement of his ability and helped paying the mounting bills.

By now he had sold the family home and moved into a much smaller two bed house and he had repaid the £40,000 that his wife had loaned him from a legacy she had received when they moved to Belfast.

Sebastian felt he had at least tried to clear some of the past overhang but he was still in desperate financial straits, he had to weigh spending every penny, he lived on a very tight budget, abandoning Waitrose and familiarising himself with 'own brands' at discount supermarkets. He never went out, he made no new friends and never called former colleagues. In effect he disappeared from view.

The sadness and loneliness remained. At Christmas he filled his time in walking. He donned an old coat, trainers and jeans and set off. He didn't really care where. Often he would take his car into one of the parks in Sherwood Forest and just walk the most circuitous route he could find, he would walk till he was tired and continue until he was exhausted. He read books but could take nothing in.

He wrote a letter to each of his sons, Alexander and Rupert trying to explain what had happened and how his hopes of everything turning out

OK had been shattered. He included a photo of each of the boys taken with him that final Christmas in Belfast. He sealed the envelopes and dated them and left them with his personal belongings in a file in his desk. He didn't want to continue his parents' legacy - they had died without leaving a will, letter or even any personal trail as if literally, they had never even existed; then he had felt forgotten as if somehow he had always been an intrusion into his parents' world. This way his boys would know that he had cared for them. He found the pain at times almost unendurable.

CHAPTER SEVEN

He had, in the end, managed to get a job as an Internal Auditor.

RKW International had not be able to find anyone remotely experienced enough who was prepared to put up with all the travelling. Sebastian had taken the letters of recommendation from Dr Singh in with him to the interview.

The job indicated a salary at 50% of his previous long term appointment.

There were two on the interview panel, an HR specialist and the line manager to whom he would be responsible; sleek self-assured sort of people who knew they had the power to grant a job or not and if they had rejected him then there would be no come back on them, he would just be on a file of 'rejected candidates'. But they knew he was experienced from his CV and from what he told them of the work that he had done, he was if anything overqualified and had passed all necessary exams, he ticked every box they had except one.

The problem at issue clearly was his character and circumstance.

They nodded to each other and the HR man said, "Now look! Taking you on involves a certain risk for us. Would you be prepared to start work on a three months' probation, we need to see how you fit in? We would of course be watching you closely!" The Accountant added " and you understand that initially you will have to spend a considerable time on the road visiting our various plants. At this subsidiary of RKW International we have some twenty quarries and ten cement plants making pre stressed concrete beams to order here, and some five in Ireland North and South so at least that part of your career will be relevant!"; turning with a knowing grin to the HR man alongside him.

"So will you accept?"

"Yes" Sebastian had replied "I thought it might involve travelling and am available as you see!"

"Well you can start next week assuming we can obtain a proper reference. Mr Williams you say? Here you can take these references with you we will not need to keep them." He dismissively thrust the references from Dr Singh back across the table. "Come to the Head Office! You know where it is, I suppose?"

And they had made him work, and work. The programme was two months behind schedule and the company knew that, with the external auditors coming soon, unless the internal audit programme was completed the external auditors would charge for their extra work in assuring themselves that the internal procedures were operating properly. He was reminded constantly, "Remember that the external audit extra fees will be five times your salary!"

Sebastian thought that he had at last the opportunity to make a new beginning.

CHAPTER EIGHT

Several years later and he had just decided to embark on a long awaited and expected holiday to Russia. He liked long train journeys and the previous year had had a similar expedition to Turkey.

He pondered on the transformation since the 'terrible place – terrible times' as he used to call it. Then he thought those bad times would never end. But they had!

Hmm! He remembered those days visiting and checking and questioning and the evenings spent in writing reports.

He had just buried his head in his work and was thankful for the income coming in at last but it took a different toll on his family. Soon after he had called his estranged wife Sarah at her parents' home to say that he now had a regular job, she had returned to his home for an attempted reconciliation, but it had not lasted long. After a week she eventually broke down and began shouting at him and blaming him for the mess they were in. More red letters had arrived for gas and electricity. She said she could not cope anymore and suddenly she was gone and moved back to her parents in Liverpool.

She left a message "Sorry cannot stand it. Nothing has changed!" He later found out what had triggered this. A bailiff came the following day saying he had left a message with his wife about the non-payment of £250 he had owed on the car. She had panicked and fled. Luckily Sebastian had just been paid and was able to make the payment but the damage was done. In reality he knew that his father in law would never permit the children to return. She had had to choose.

She did! It was something he had expected yet dreaded; his family was gone for good.

He didn't really know how he had kept it all together over the following weeks and months but he had just forced himself to drive the work programme and blocked everything else out. Six months later his boss had moved to a new job in another industry and two years later an Area Accountant's job became available. All those who had interviewed him so dismissively were gone. By that time he had established a track record of reliable and good quality work, not the least of which was a complex fraud case which he had satisfactorily resolved, and, since he knew the systems inside out, he stood head and shoulders above the other candidates for the job. So he had been offered the position. From there he was successively promoted twice, he was just now made up to Regional Accountant covering two of the six regions in the UK and it included mineral extraction and distribution. He imagined that his career was at last stabilised.

Everyone thought that he did his job competently, or that's what they told him but in fact he knew he was bored. Several years carrying out the same work year after year, where the greatest drama had been a missing asset of £100,000 on the equipment inventory list which was actually found to have been scrapped years ago, had begun to deaden his brain.

It was several years after his wife left that he was canvassed at home and some chirpy youngster had asked him what party he had voted for.

"Well to tell you the truth I haven't ever voted, never!"

"Never?"

"No! Never, I have always been too busy and always left it to the MPs to run the government, it doesn't seem to matter too much either way surely!"

The youngster was horrified, "You mean you don't care about improving the NHS, or where housing will be built or that OAPs are dying because the ambulances service is so poor and that one in six school children are barely literate when they leave school?!" "Oh dear! Oh dear! What planet have <u>you</u> been living on?"

"Well of course it's important – yes I see what you mean."

"Well there's a Council by election coming up and we have a meeting next Wednesday. Would you like to help us elect a Lib Dem here?"

And so he became involved and decided that it was after all important, not only that but he decided he rather liked it. The work was totally different from his office world and as he had had no family to consider he could carve out time as he chose.

After a year or so he was elected as one of the two delegates to a mini conference in Harrogate, in truth he knew he was the only other person willing to go. He had found it exhilarating to vote on key issues of policy which might eventually change the face of the country. He was drawn into the social events too though these were rather mundane, a 'bring and buy sale' and the garden party hosted by Mrs Leggs the chairwoman. She was a very keen and earnest sort, who had been elected some ten years previously for a few years, only to be swept away in one of the Lib Dems up and down performances as the party votes increased by 10%, dropped by 5% then increased by 10% again. She told everyone 'Look! Mark my words this man Sebastian will succeed – I somehow feel he is the man of his time!'

Later on he had suggested setting up a new branch in Middleton, a suburb in the M1 corridor between Derby and Nottingham. "I am sure we can succeed here" he said and he duly became chairman because everyone acknowledged his organising abilities. When the District Council seats came up for election in 2011 he was selected as one of the candidates for that area and, throwing all his weekends into canvassing, literally door knocking and persuading people to vote for him, he won the seat at his first attempt.

Through all this Sylvia his secretary had helped him at work. If he was scheduled to be busy for a Council meeting due to work commitments she would re-arrange his calendar of meetings, and although it soon became apparent what he was doing at work, he was not considered to be important enough in the hierarchy of the company for this to prevent him doing 'his politics' nor did they think he would ever win a seat, nor indeed would they much care if he did.

Politics however became the abiding interest in his life.

Anyhow he had decided on this holiday over a year ago.

He packed his passport, visa, train tickets and checked his flight tickets to Moscow and back. He parked his car in a pre-booked car park and headed for the terminal.

PART THREE - A Journey too Far?

CHAPTER ONE

How the hell have I got myself into this mess? He thought, cursing himself for his stupidity and naivety.

He wriggled around in the dark pushing his hands out in front of him feeling snow and timbers of some kind – smooth edged but wrinkled as if through burning. He couldn't quite reach further out without standing up as the boards seemed to rise above his head. "Ouch" he exclaimed aloud, something hurt but he didn't know if the fall had broken anything in his body. "I must have fallen somehow!" he muttered.

He wiggled his arms and legs and found that he could move, though his right leg was painful and, reaching down, he could feel that it was bloodied. Ouch! Damn! He thought. Stretching out his hand he touched something still warm and he noted with relief that it appeared to be his camera. Anyhow he shouted for help though he thought that would do little good because he could hear nobody, so who could hear him? And just then the deep throated whistle of the train and pulsating skidding then grinding of the wheels suggested that his only lifeline, the passenger train, was starting and moving away. "Help! Help!" he yelled at the top of his voice.

Damn and blast he thought, but I can't be more than a few feet away from the track. What the hell has happened? Just his bloody luck stuck in the middle of Russia on his own! He nervously twiddled the signet ring on his finger.

He tried to recollect his thoughts. Maybe he had been knocked out or winded on falling? But he had been standing near the edge of the embankment and suddenly found himself here, but where the hell was he and why could he see nothing at all? Was he dead or what? He remembered that he had not re-done his will yet after his wife left him and made a mental note to do it first thing on his return to his home a suburb near Nottingham. Anyhow that seemed to spur him into working out what next to do.

He ventured to stand upright feeling for any walls and brushing aside the snow as he did so. Some sort of roof had collapsed in on him but pushing against this he was eventually able to clamber out of his prison into the light or at least the partial light reflected from the stars and half-moon. He could see now that he was in some sort of cabin and could make out the walls and there appeared to be a doorway a few feet away. He stumbled over the snow and timbers towards it, picking up as he did so the fur hat that he had purchased in Moscow before setting out. How pretentious he had thought at the time! Not exactly the sort of headgear worn by a fifty-five year old accountant on the main street of Middleton, a Nottingham suburb! Much too flashy but when in Rome......? At least he thought he had done something right, he probably wouldn't freeze! But his ankle was hurting, and he had a banging headache.

He managed to get through the door picking up what appeared to be a sizeable pole and using it as a blind man's stick edging forward, feeling his way.

He looked around and could just make out a ridge in the snow a short distance away. Good, he thought, that'll at least get me to the rail tracks. How on earth had he been so foolish as to take the girl's advice? There had been nobody sharing his sleeper compartment, something he had not wanted anyhow. Travel holidays are one thing but to get stuck with an insufferable bore like the one he had on a recent trip to Turkey on the Orient Express was not something he wanted to repeat, so he was happy to pay for the privilege of solitude. Of course he missed casual discussions with another traveller of the scenes as they passed but he had his travel guide for that. No! This was nothing to do with that decision at all! What was the girl doing? She must have known the train would not wait.

He clambered up what appeared to be an embankment slipping several times as his city shoes failed to grip in the snow which seemed to be a foot deep at least.   But at last he regained the track. He looked both ways but could see nothing except the gleaming rails disappearing into the darkness but noticed that the track going in the other direction was also shiny suggesting that recently a train had gone the other way and then he remembered; ah yes it was so! Just before his train had stopped he remembered the whooshing sound as a train came in the opposite direction. Blast! He thought, maybe hours before another train passes and in any case how could he hope to stop it? Luckily he had on his heavy black Gant coat and he knew that it contained his passport, credit cards and wallet. Phew! He thought as he searched his pockets to make sure everything was still there. It was! Well the motive can't have been robbery!

He saw what he thought was an old platform or something, maybe this was a disused halt but there was no other building. Anyhow he sat there and pondered. It had started to snow lightly again.

He had bumped into her as he was going to the bar on the train soon after they had pulled out from Yaroslavski station at 13.50. "Hello?" she had introduced herself in English. "Hello" he had replied "how do you know I am English?", "By your tie!" she replied "look around nobody here wears a tie!" Sebastian sheepishly acknowledged that he had not yet moved from his office garb into tourist mode. She explained her name was Olga Ivanovna she had spent a year at an English language school in London, paid for by her father. Although taller than him, she had an engaging smile and they chatted about London and the local political scene, particularly the Russian reaction to events in the Ukraine and wondered if the same Orange Revolution could happen in Russia. She simply said she supported Putin "as all Russians do 100%". She said she always liked to practice her English. He introduced himself as Sebastian Edwards a Regional Accountant with RKW an international mining and extraction company, he was on vacation, so he said. He had bought her a drink but soon made his excuses as he was feeling tired. He had passed her once or twice in the corridor later on in the afternoon but he just said "Hello" nodded and passed on.

He had retired to his sleeping compartment early ticking off the stations as he went along, Nizhni Novgorod at 20.04 and passing through the Volga region but dozed off without changing, relaxing at last to life on the train The Rossiya! At last he was free of the office, he disliked being cooped up. The Rossiya! Ahead lay thousands of miles of countryside and all he had to do was sit and watch it glide by! He was awoken by the reduction of the speed of the train, which had suddenly started to slow and the brakes squeaked as they were applied. After a time the train came to a complete halt.

He got up and peered into the corridor and noticed that an outside door was open further down his coach. He had grabbed his coat and hat and made his way towards the door. She was outside on the other track clearly arguing with what looked like the Provodnista or assigned carriage attendant. He noticed other train doors opening. "Hey what's happening? What are we stopping? Is it safe to get out?" She shouted back "There's some sort of incident ahead as there's an obstacle on the line at a village crossing point. Really you shouldn't get out and the guard wants you to get back in but I guess you can take some crazy photos of the train, just don't take too long!"

He pulled out his small camera, always in his pocket, leapt down from the train and moved towards the side of the track he took one shot to the rear and another towards the front but to take a perfect picture with the moon at the right angle, he had moved back an extra foot and then a bit more..... then it all went dark.

Damn! Damn! Hell! and Blast! He blamed himself what the hell did he think he was doing? He must have just fallen and knocked himself out. He wondered how long he had been out for, he looked at his watch it was 3.45 am, he remembered that was Moscow time and, squinting at it, thought perhaps the whole episode had taken about an hour. In putting on his hat which had fallen off as he sat down on the platform, he noticed a wet trickle down his neck. He felt it with his hand and it appeared to be blood. He found a lump on his head. Wait a minute! He suddenly became frightened – was he pushed? Had he seen someone out of the corner of his eye and then a gunshot? But with his camera to his eye maybe he noticed nothing. He wasn't sure. Was he a target of some kind? But what on earth could anyone want with a fiftyish accountant from near Nottingham, England? He cast anxious glances left and right and tried to see if there were any footprints in the snow – was there anyone else here? The recent snowfall appeared to be thickening but he could still just see the footprints he had made when falling into the shed and his return to the tracks.

This worried him because he knew that anyone sent to find him would soon not be able to see his footprints in any search if it kept on snowing. Surely Olga would by now have raised the alarm and they would start a search but when and from which direction?

Also if someone wanted to do him harm he had better not shout until he knew who they were?

He decided to take an inventory. It was time for logical thought. He was alive and well though his ankle still hurt but the blood had stopped from the bump on his head; he could move, no bones were broken. He had a camera, wallet and cards, all his travel money, a warm coat and a packet of Russian toffee he had bought before leaving Moscow. Although cold it was not freezing too hard and Olga would surely mount a search for him? There seemed no-one about and he didn't appear under any immediate threat. His hat and coat were serviceable though he had left his gloves on the train as well as his phone, so he could not call anyone .

Anyhow who should he have called? He had told his firm what he had planned, indeed he had left his itinerary with his secretary. Sylvia knew it anyhow and had even helped him plan his trip. He had suffered a very messy divorce partly as a result of his dedication to his work. His 'normal' day was 9am till 7pm with emails and messages during evenings and weekends. He had slowly got used to the life which RKW Plc demanded of him. He was now onto a good salary although of course it had been used to pay off the debts he had amassed when he had been unemployed – but he was just about in the clear now. Sylvia his secretary had been an absolute brick during this time. He committed himself there and then to putting in for a special bonus for her in line with her performance review.

He stood up and pondered for a moment. He had no real idea where he was to within 100 kilometres, there were villages on the map of course but he could neither remember them nor in any case even read the weird Russian hieroglyphics; next stop was Perm he knew and he was told the speed of the train was a regular 50 mph but he was too dazed to work anything out, so the only thing he knew was that there had been an obstacle on the track at a village crossing point up ahead. That seemed to him his only possible direction of travel. He told himself. 'Get to the crossing then find the village and hole up there for the night, well it was at least a plan of sorts!'

He began to walk along the tracks to where he thought he could see a black object by the line.

Yes, he thought, Sylvia would know how to handle things. He had called her from the hotel in Moscow as arranged and she had persuaded him to make an extra stop at Irkutsk for a trip around Lake Baikal and indeed faxed over the changes to his hotel room. She said the company were paying!

What a splendid girl! He was due at Irkutsk in a few days and so he would after all be missed. She would start a search even if Olga did not. Strange though that the company had taken such care of him. He had had their support taking a whole ten days on the trip to Turkey last year and there too there had been a change in plans for him to stop off in Belgrade on the way, but nothing else happened except for him to pick up some legal documents. He had no idea why they were important, some local business perhaps? He was a Regional Accountant responsible for the UK Midlands operations of the gravel extraction company, one of the 20 main operating subsidiaries of RKW. He had been promoted to this position from the Internal Audit function several years ago. He was nicknamed 'the bruiser' because of his ability to drive the operations under him to achieve budget whatever the circumstance. There was 'no messing' with him! So this was the company's grateful acknowledgement of that! 'And about time too' he muttered to himself.

He used the pole that he had picked up to prod his way through the snow in places where it was deepest but he was soon tired of slipping into the gully along the side of the track and was glad when he made the crossing.

He approached it with care, there seemed to be something lying at the side of the track. On closer examination it appeared to be a car which had been pushed out of the way as it was on its side and a door was completely crushed and stove in. He didn't know much Russian but it appeared from its signage and roof mounted lamps to be a police car and he noticed the word 'Meeleetsiah' or at least that was what his basic Russian in the guide book implied! He had decided to commit some twenty Russian words to memory learning them on his flight from London to Moscow. It was now snowing more heavily and the wind was picking up, he stuck one hand in his coat pocket. He peered into the Car but could see no sign of any passengers.

CHAPTER TWO

He looked more closely and saw that the police car appeared to be lying on top of a trailer which had fallen into the gulley at the side of the track. Then he noticed a trail of something coming from the driver's door, showing up in dark spots in the snow and a trail as if something was being dragged. It disappeared across the rail tracks to what might have been a cart track but the snow was so deep there from earlier snowfalls that there was little difference between the endless fields and woods beyond, the edges of the track could only be guessed. He knelt down and touched it and looked at closely, yes it was blood alright. He decided to follow the trace of blood and marks in the snow, because in any case it would seem to lead to a building in the distance that he could vaguely see highlighted by the half-moon. As he passed the car he noticed that there was a hole in the car windscreen with a mosaic of fractured glass around it.

Oh dear! He thought, this was really taking him out of his depth. But these findings changed nothing! Where else was he to go? Maybe the policeman from the car had called his station or an ambulance? Anyhow the tracks in the snow would give some sort of direction.

"Well I only hope that this Jeffrey Pardoe I am supposed to be meeting at Irkutsk will wait." He muttered under his breath. Strange that as the fax said 'You will be met at the hotel by our agent Mr Jeffrey Pardoe whom you will know, who will arrange for your day trip starting at 10 am on the day following which will be fully paid by the company'. Well there we are, to have agents all over the world was part of the stock in trade of his company as they were always on the look-out for suitable acquisitions, but he had to admit he had never heard of Jeffrey Pardoe. "That's odd" he said out loud. "Anyhow that's another person who will be looking for me; Olga, Sylvia and now Jeffrey" and that gave him some comfort.

He continued warily to track the trail and spots which showed up here and there on top of the snow, so he thought the person must be in some pain. It was blood he was sure, it was pooled then sprinkled as if the person had stopped in pain and then continued and done so repeatedly. One side seemed to be scraping along the ground as if something, maybe a leg was pulled along whilst the other foot showed a clear print in the snow. The person, whoever he or indeed she was, appeared to be in a bad shape. The footprints were large as he put his own foot alongside, he deduced that it must be large male. Perhaps he was the policeman from the car?

Then he saw a something lying in the middle of the track on its side but he could see that it was still alive as it was struggling to move ahead and at Sebastian's approach the shape seemed to redouble its efforts as though in fear of his arrival. When Sebastian caught up with it he saw that it was probably a male, he was lying on his back with his fur hat clamped in one hand and a revolver in the other, blood was seeping from a wound to his leg where his trouser was torn.

The moon was behind him and Sebastian was able to see the man's face which was pallid and covered in blood perhaps from his hand which he held to his leg every so often.

He gabbled something in Russian and brandished his revolver at Sebastian.

Sebastian shouted "whoa, whoa, whoa" ,bloody silly thing to shout he thought later as If English was not bad enough that's what you shout to a horse damnit! Then he said "Just a minute —I am friend! **FRIEND**" using his old aunt's trick when addressing foreigners, if they don't understand then simply SHOUT for sooner or later they will either understand or get somebody to come who does! "English" – "ahngleeyskee! Comprennez? Verstehen?" as he was running out of words and languages.

"I - Police — meeleetsiah! - Tahm - I go there" he said pointing to a shadowy building something to the right and 100 metres or so ahead. Sebastian tried to lift him to his feet but it was too difficult to hold him up. He signed to the policeman what he intended to do, he motioned putting the pole he had brought and wedging it into the boot. The policeman nodded assent and undid his belt and used it as a tourniquet to stop the blood and straighten the leg attached to the pole. It was clear to Sebastian that the policeman was in agony and that the leg was probably broken. He shouted in pain several times during the process. "Tahm, tahm" he shouted gesturing to the building. By now the wind was stronger still and eddies of swirling snow were making it difficult to see anything. Sebastian realised that he must keep moving and that those few minutes standing in the snow had made him feel really cold. His feet crunched on the snow. It was clearly now freezing hard and he was unused to such low temperatures.

Sebastian said "You phone! Get help!" "Tee-lee-fon!" — "Niet, Niet" came the reply. He just gestured again to the building.

Leaning on Sebastian they hobbled towards it their feet making deep holes in the snow. Sebastian was wearing ordinary office shoes and the snow forced it way up his trouser legs, he periodically had to halt and shake out the snow. The broken timbers in the roof were banging about in the wind. The policeman produced a torch. Sebastian thought the building was some sort of church although run down. The roof appeared to have mostly collapsed, but Sebastian managed to push a way through an old door and found himself inside a small wayside chapel open to the sky but off this to the rear there was a small vestibule no bigger than his bathroom at home, with a ceiling and with various large cabinets. There was a gap between these and the roof overhead. It looked to Sebastian as if it had been disused for many years. It smelled terrible and there were bones and leaves on the floor and parts of birds' nests.

By this time the policeman was in a state of collapse and Sebastian dragged him into this vestibule since the temperature appeared to be dropping alarmingly but it was the only place which protected them from the winds which were now rocking the structure. The snow fall became heavier, swirling in eddies of white flakes which blotted out the moon completely.

At last the policeman appeared to relax and tried to say something to Sebastian, making a barking sound and picking up his revolver and aiming shots at non-existent enemies. Sebastian thought that this might be a delirium caused by loss of blood and he indicated, by gestures, that the policeman should lie on the table so that Sebastian could look at the wound again. But this was achieved only with difficulty as the policeman fainted attempting to lie down and dropped the revolver onto the floor.

Sebastian pulled him fully onto the table and looked at his leg. Pulling off the boot it seemed clear that a bone had penetrated the skin, it was still leaking blood and he knew that he would have to take this opportunity to try to pull the pieces of the wound together or it would continue to bleed with possible fatal results. In the cabinets he found some ragged old black vestments and in the dim light of the torch he wound these tightly around the wound and then reconstructed a splint system using the pole and vestments twisted around the leg, secured by the policeman's belt. Sebastian paused to take pride in his work. He jammed the boot back on. He realised that he had done as much as he could and began to feel weary and hungry. The exertions of dragging the policeman and the worry made him tired and he knelt on the floor in exhaustion. The policeman had apparently fainted whilst under his treatment but at least the flow of blood was staunched.

He was not aware of how long he had dozed off but was awaken by a fearful scratching at the door and a howling or barking immediately outside. It sounded to him as if there was a pack of animals trying to get in.

"Oh bloody hell that's all I need!" he shouted aloud "what are these fucking wolves or something? Shit" He quickly shut the outer door by its simple wooden clasp, but it was clear to Sebastian that it could give away at any moment. He assumed that it was the smell of blood which had drawn them here wolves or wild dogs, it didn't matter much, either way it was not something he had much experience of in Middleton!

With a burst of energy motivated by sheer fear he opened a large cabinet and seizing the Policeman by the shoulders physically and rammed him into it jamming the door of it shut and forcing against it benches that lay on the floor so that the cabinet door was braced between two cabinets by the bench.

All the while the whining and the noise of the animals was becoming louder and louder. Sebastian was shouting and screaming at them "Fuck off you bastards! Fuck off!" and rattling the doors with a stick which he had torn from a chair. He remembered the revolver which he picked out in the beam of the torch just as its glare was failing; then, using the chair he clambered on top of the cabinets and wedged himself in the gap below the ceiling kicking the seat away as he did so, but that still left his legs dangling over the end.

The growling and scratching became louder and it was clear that the animal break in would happen very soon. Suddenly there was a crash and the outer doors gave way and within seconds what seemed like a mass of animals surged towards them but the torch faded and it was pitch black, he could see nothing.

Sebastian could only just fit into the area above the cabinets and he was only two metres from the ground and immediately the animals began leaping up and lunging at him, one grabbed his ankle but he managed to kick it free though he felt the blood running again. The smell of the blood seemed to affect the animals and they now burst into frenzy, howling and snarling, snapping at anything even each other.

Sebastian had never been in anyone's army he was trained as a chartered accountant and that didn't include weapons fiercer than a biro, so he had this revolver but how did it work? In desperation he took aim towards the noise and pulled the trigger but nothing happened and the animals again seemed to launch another attack moved to a snarling mass. He heard scratching above just inches from his head. Maybe they would fall in on him. He pulled the revolver back and tried feeling various bits to find if there was some kind of safety catch. He took aim again and nothing, more fumbling. He could smell the wet fur of the dogs and feel the scratching at the cabinet door as they could detect more prey there. Again he tried. He realised that if the gun was empty there was no chance of reloading as the bullets would be in the policeman's pocket or even maybe in the car. With increasing panic and desperation he pulled and fumbled with every lever or corner of the gun as well as the trigger which he pulled sharply towards him and held on to. He could smell the dogs' pungent breath.

All of a sudden there was an almighty bang followed by another immediately afterwards which in the enclosed space deafened him momentarily and the recoil spun the gun out of his hands and it dropped to the floor. There was a terrible roar and whine from the dogs and whimpering. It was clear that something had struck home and within seconds they ran out howling, the room seemed to be cleared. Then there was silence.

Sebastian decided to remain where he was. In the struggles his right shoe had been torn off by the animals and his foot was aching again but despite that he fell asleep exhausted.

He was awoken with a start by a furious banging on the doors below him which shook the cabinet on which he was perched. He remembered in a flash where he was and realised it was the policeman trying to get out. By this time dawn was breaking and he could make out the scene below. On the floor were two of the dogs, wolves or Alsatians it was not clear, and these seem to have bled to death. The floor was a tangled mess of blood, the remains of the vestments he had shredded to make the dressings, bones, bird nests and broken furniture.

Slowly he climbed down and first retrieved his shoe and then shouted "OK! OK! I am coming!" and he removed the bench jamming the door and opened the cabinet, he helped the policeman out. He stood for a few moments surveying the scene holding onto the cabinet door for support. "Spahaseebah" he said "Khahroshiy" giving Sebastian a huge bear hug but then spotting the revolver on the floor, quickly recovered it.

CHAPTER THREE

Sebastian was relieved to see the policeman seemingly restored to life; when he had shoved him in the cabinet he only seemed able to grunt and had slumped into the empty space. Sebastian sheepishly pulled his packet of sweets from his pocket and handed them to the policeman "spasibnahk" "thank" he said taking two or three and Sebastian did the same.

"Just a minute" trying out some Russian!" meenootah"" just a minute!" He said and whipped his camera out of his pocket and took several pictures of the scene and a 'selfie' with the smiling Policeman.

As they emerged from the vestibule, the sunlight came streaming through the gaps in the roof and he could now see the building which appeared to be an old wooden church with pictures on the walls but most of the religious symbols appeared to be defaced and it was covered with graffiti.

They passed through the church and out by the opening where the door had been ripped off by the wind.

Instinctively Sebastian wrapped the policeman's arm over his shoulder and in this way, step by step, they reached the track. It took a bit of time to co-ordinate legs, Sebastian thought it was a bit like a kindergarten three legged race!

"Khahroshiy!" he repeated "Good!" and the Policeman stood upright and took a deep breath. It seemed to Sebastian that although he still could not walk properly it was less painful than last evening. He realised he was able to see him clearly for the first time, he was well over 6ft. tall since he knew his own height was 5ft. 10in. and even with the policeman's arm slung over his like a rugby football prop, he still had difficulty clearing the wounded leg over the ground so that the policeman bent it back angled at the knee to prevent it dragging. Sebastian looked him in the face and said "I, Sebastian" the Policeman replied "Ilya Ilyitch Volkov" and held out his other hand to shake. Ilya appeared to be a confident person, Sebastian thought, used to making quick assessments of people. He had jammed back his traditional policeman's fur hat on his head but his black hair hung down around his forehead and there were patches of blood and dirt on his angular face.

Sebastian saw a tractor approaching along the track. Ilya shouted "zdrahstvooyteh!" "mneh nooshehn vrahchah!" "Meeleetsiah" and aside to Sebastian he said "Docktor" – "Police!".

With a wave of the drivers' hand the tractor gathered speed and soon came level, with some difficulty Sebastian and Ilya heaved themselves onto the trailer behind. There was a further discussion which Sebastian could not understand and the tractor proceeded back up to the crossing and the policeman looked for some time at the wreck of the car. At a few words from Ilya the tractor driver scampered to open the doors and bring back the contents to the trailer. A rifle and a bag of food were recovered together with the phone system. He then ordered the tractor driver to move pointing in the direction past the church. He offered Sebastian a lump of black bread saying "Goood".

Sebastian noticed that they passed directly through a large wood with trees 40ft. tall, noting that it must have taken well over thirty minutes to get through it. They came to a cross roads and on either side grouped around a small square were perhaps a dozen of old wooden houses constructed of old rough sawn timber a foot or so thick and laid flat on one another, around these houses was a motley assortment of cars and farm equipment and even some older horse drawn trailers.

They stopped outside one of the houses with wisps of smoke rising from the chimney giving off a smell of pine wood. They climbed down and without knocking on the wooden door, passed into the lobby.

It was clear to Sebastian that this must also be a police house. In the main room were a counter, tables and chairs together with what appeared to be a communication system of some kind. There were maps on the wall and bundles of files in a bookcase. Ilya, still leaning on Sebastian, saluted what appeared to be his senior officer; an oldish man with greying hair and small moustache.

Ilya slumped into a chair and the officer seeing he was injured rushed over to inspect and called to someone in the room next door. Immediately a woman ran out and quickly pulled Ilya's leg onto a bench and began attending to it, unwrapping the dressings. She stopped after a minute or so and indicated that she wished to inspect Sebastian's leg too. She looked at it and washed the wound on his leg. She spoke insistently to the officer then returned to treating Ilya.

All the time Ilya was going through his story quickly between pauses and stifled intakes of breath as the bandages were re-arranged.   It seemed to Sebastian that he was obviously repeating bits again and again under close questioning from the officer. Sebastian nervously felt his ankle; would they fine him for getting off the train? He began to sweat and mopped his brow he felt the lump on his head, no more blood! He twiddled the ring on his finger.

Suddenly Ilya pointed to Sebastian and with a big smile said "gehehroee"... "Hero"! The officer approach Sebastian and gripped him warmly by his hand saying "spasibnahk" and turning to Ilya who said "Thank!". They were both given black tea and bread. A bottle of vodka and little glasses emerged as if from nowhere "meedeetsinnah" the officer said laughingly. He then went to the communication set and made a number of phone calls. Sebastian was shown to the rooms behind and one of these was a bedroom; an assistant appeared who showed him a bed and washing facilities, his wounds were inspected again and his ankle bandaged. He showered and put on the bathrobe provided.

He checked his watch, it was still only 8. 30am. He was dog tired, lay down and immediately fell asleep.

He was awoken it seemed like hours later but was only a matter of minutes by someone who put his nose around the door "please get clothes on and come please". He dressed into a clean police shirt laid out for him and tried to clean up the trousers. He went back into the main room. There he saw a small man with glasses and bushy beard dressed in a jacket and trousers but with snow still on his boots.

"Hello Sir! Hello Sir! I am teacher in English at school. Police asked me translate you. Come please and tell us what happened."

He led Sebastian back to the main room and a chair was placed for him in front of the table with the officer and Ilya behind it. "They have questions for you" said the teacher "we need be quick as he goes to doctor soon."

"Repeat your story from beginning! Please!" Sebastian was able to show them in turn his passport, visa, train tickets together with the fax received in the hotel recording the change in itinerary and additional stop. He told them that he liked long train journeys; it was a time to reflect and be presented with the world in front of you. He had been planning this Trans-Siberian rail trip for over a year. He told them also that he had read bits of Tolstoy and intended to see that museum in Moscow on the return trip.

"Why did you get out of train?" they asked "It is not permitted!" "Who is girl Olga?" "Who was she arguing with?" It was clear to Sebastian that they thought his getting off the train was highly unusual. "Why you get re-entry visa?" He muttered that it was because he had decided to break his journey and didn't know now exactly when he would leave.

He was then asked about the battle with the dogs in the vestibule and he recounted his actions, making a splint for Ilya and jamming him in the cabinet and eventually firing the gun.

The officer came over with the translator and said "Thanks you have save this man his life, he would died, freeze or bleeding or killed by wild dogs."

Sebastian said to the translator "Wait a minute! I have caught the events on my camera!" He went over to the policemen and showed them the pictures of the carnage in the vestibule.

The policeman said something at which they all laughed. "What's that?" he said... and then translated... "and next time you push a policemen into a cabinet please remember to clean it out, it was full of bird and dog shit. It must have been their lair, he smells terrible!."

Sebastian asked "What happens now please? I have this meeting in Irkutsk?"

The translator said "Wait please more questions! Passport please, we must check, have you been to Russia before? Do you have any connection with business in Russia? Are you going to meet anyone for business?" To all these Sebastian said No! No! and No!

"Regional Administration database in Irkutsk say someone called Edwards from London wanted for questioning? Is this you?" Sebastian was a bit unnerved by this. He certainly didn't fancy a few nights in police custody whilst they sorted it out. They spent some minutes discussing the matter. He nervously again rubbed the bump on his head!

"Can we take copies of the photo please?" Of course Sebastian was only too pleased and helped. Much to his surprise a memory stick suddenly appeared and the pictures were downloaded.

"I don't know about this!" said the senior policeman through the translator, "We have no reason keep you here, it's not police matter! OK so they want to see a Mr Edwards in Irkutsk, well if you go there too, then we will send you there!" he laughed. "We fax them immediately and add our report of incident. But be careful Mr Edwards somebody might make matters difficult for you!"

A few moments later a determined looking woman appeared and, after a few muttered words with the officer, walked straight to Sebastian, "Tetanus and Anti Rabies injection! Arm please. Police officer here call me and tell me story." She then took Illya into the side room for treatment.

In the meantime the senior policeman made a few more phone calls and seemed satisfied. "Now you have to go, translator will drive you to Perm and there take plane to Krasnoyarsk or Novosibirsk you get a plane and get back to Rossiya train and so go to Irkutsk. We pay for plane in thanks to you. Good-bye, Good Luck and Thank You!"

And with that Sebastian was bundled out of the door and into a rather a smart four wheel drive police car complete with snow tyres and a large number of diesel cans in the back.

On the way out he picked up his fur hat and outer coat which had both been cleaned but smelled rather strongly of disinfectant.

CHAPTER FOUR

The translator introduced himself as Andrey Andreyevich Petrov and told Sebastian that they were to drive to Perm and they were lucky that today the snow was melting. He said that early snow always caught out invaders and he laughed; visitors too! 'General Winter' was worth several divisions!

He estimated that the journey would take about six and a half hours. There was no other available transport. They had to arrive at Perm by 19.55 in order to catch the plane for Krasnoyarsk but maybe there would be also an opportunity to fly to the nearer airport of Novosibirsk. At either of the two places he should be able to re-join the Rossiya train and get back into his compartment and thence back en route to Irkutsk. They set off at a fast pace.

Andrey insisted on making good for Sebastian's loss of his train tour by recounting the stories about Perm, the area to the north where there was an entire settlement of wooden houses dating from 18th to the 20th century and in particular the Perm-36, the Gulag Museum, where buildings of the repression era had been preserved.

After a while Sebastian fell asleep and was awoken by the driver some three hours later at a wayside petrol station for more diesel, a sandwich, drink and WC.

It was all very confusing he thought! He tried hard to unpick the mysteries. What was the policeman doing to the train? What caused the accident? But the driver was non-committal and said he did not know but "probably accident on crossing!" His mind was now clearing a bit and he wondered if there was no accident but maybe they had orders to stop the train and search for him? But if so why not wait till the next stopping point?

He took out the fax that he had received from Sylvia and re-read it. Apart from the change in travel arrangements there were several lines about updates on several of the jobs he was progressing, arrangements for stock counts, another gravel deposit had been located, the next meeting of auditors, instructions about year-end accounting rules and at the end an update on staff; 'Mrs Smith a junior assistant had a baby and was on leave', another of his staff had passed his exams and 'Mr Lewis from Accounts Receivable had given his notice in again for the third time as several operations depot managers had breached accounting rules yet again'. Sebastian knew they must have delivered to customers on the 'D list' who were supposed to be banned. These companies often went bust but Operations people always ignored the new notices if they could in order to achieve sales targets and gain bonuses.

What on earth did she send him all that stuff for he thought – a fat lot he could do about it in the middle of Siberia? Oh really! But then, stuck in the middle of all that, was a line he could not understand. It read "John Macvicar released, company concerned similar scam could be repeated".

What's going on here? This was a case now several years old where an employee had got into trouble. It wasn't 'John Macvicar' anyhow but 'Joseph McVicar'. Silvia surely knew that! She had noticed on the initial legal papers which they had made out for the police that they got the name wrong in the same way and had to re-copy several pages and get them re-signed. He referred to the fax and read it again. Strangely it said the agent 'whom you will know', but he was quite sure he had neither heard of nor worked with any such person!

Well what's going on he thought? He trusted Sylvia implicitly he had known her for years. So she puts in the fax a load of stuff which was quite unnecessary and in the middle of it there's a sentence which was quite simply wrong, wrong! She knew it and he knew it! Why?

He mused that there were several possibilities, maybe she thought that the fax might be handed to Corporate Directors so she could not openly warn him without drawing attention to herself! Yes he could see now that his immediate line manager the Corporate Finance Director, Mr Noel Chambers, was copied as well as somebody he had known of previously, Bill Williamson of TJD Mining and Exploration. SA. Noel Chambers joined the company after the case against McVicar so it would have meant nothing to him!

So Sylvia had put in a line amongst the dross which she knew would have been of no interest to the others but only to him. So she was sending an open message with a hidden warning of some kind.

He racked his brain about the details of the case; McVicar in every other way a responsible guy, an Accounts Manager, had in fact set up a parallel company with a similar name to his employer's company name and had managed to divert funds from customers telling them that the bank account number had been changed, and asking them to pay into the new account. He even managed to raise an overdraft from a bank. Of course that operation soon collapsed but not before he had managed to inveigle several local businessmen to act as directors. He had hoped to avoid detection because the parent company was selling off several units so McVicar was able to show letters addressed to him from the company which did indeed suggest that that particular unit might be sold. Of course Sebastian uncovered the fraud as part of his internal audit checks. That operation was wound up and the money recovered through anti-fraud insurance.

So Sebastian now concluded that the mistakes in the fax were deliberate and that this was a warning from Sylvia that something odd was going on, probably involving this Agent Pardoe and the stop in Irkutsk. He thought very hard for several minutes going over all possible connections.

He was aware that like most international companies if they chose to operate internationally they most often took a local partner. This was partly done to encourage local funding from prominent businessmen who, in spite of having huge wealth usually from monopoly positions, lacked western expertise to produce efficiently on a consistent basis. These local partners often were able to gain entry to markets which were effectively closed to outsiders and where local money obtained access to important decision makers.

Even reading as he did the monthly in-company newsletter, he was unaware of any direct connection between his company and Russia. Except that he had seen a note of the resignation of a former managing director of the firm. He had heard that this was because of an affair with a competitor's female HR director and that he had subsequently set up a company which he had listed on AIM the junior stock exchange in London a few years ago. It was called, he thought, Siberian Minerals.

This might be the link, but as far as he knew his company had no connection with it whatsoever.

But how could he be involved? He thought about it then said aloud, which startled the driver "Oh dear, Oh dear, Oh dear!" The McVicar fraud had only been possible because Sebastian's signature had been falsified on the Company Registration documents where he had been recorded as the Company Secretary. It had then taken him months to finally prove his innocence to the police, his problems in a previous job had not helped!

Well he had worked out a most likely scenario. But why was this hidden background not mentioned? It seemed to imply that someone up top in his own company RKW was involved.

Relieved that he had made sense of the situation he fell asleep, but awoke again at another stop for necessities.

He now felt much better and talked with the driver Andrey about his perception of Russia and hopes that it could progress to a normal democracy. Andrey stressed he hoped the same but said the "Russia had a long way yet to go".

Then suddenly he was quiet. Then he said "I think you are good man!"

"Well thanks" said Sebastian, slightly embarrassed now.

"Do not repeat what I say?"

"No of course not" said Sebastian, wondering what was coming next.

"The Rossiya train is not permitted to stop for any reason except at recognised stations, sometimes it's just ten minutes late on journey of several days – nobody stops Rossiya. Understand?"

"Well then what really happened?"

"Perm" Andrey continued "has Russian Mafia; it's called here 'Krysha' meaning 'roof' many things here are subject to this 'protection'. This all started in move from old communist to new market economy when individuals seized hold of whole sectors of industries as they were privatised. Better now but it still happens – often police are used to enforce."

"I do not know what happened to train and I do not want to know why they want you in Irkutsk". He paused, "but, my friend, be very careful, very careful indeed! Mafia has big stretch – reach!"

He thanked Andrey for that and both agreed to exchange email addresses and Sebastian said he would send him a progress report.

"Now look" said Andrey "just in case of trouble, we will park car and I will walk you through to departure gate – I have travel warrant. If you are stopped I have Police authority to make sure you continue. Local police very grateful for your courage!"

They arrived at Perm airport on time. As there were no delayed flights to Novosibirsk he took the plane to the further stop of Krasnoyarsk.

 He now had a plan which he would evolve on the flight – he was due to arrive in Krasnoyarsk at 7.15 the following morning. That would leave him several hours free in the city there which he intended to put to good use.

CHAPTER FIVE

He was oblivious to the details of the type of plane, the queues and chatter of the other passengers, the instructions from airline and airport staff and he ate the food mechanically, deep in thought.

Hmmm. He expected a trap of some kind in Irkutsk. The company's agent and the fax from Sylvia suggested that his company was perhaps covertly involved. But there were now others involved too. Was the Russian Mafia connected or were some big power players, the oligarchs behind it all? But how did he fit into all that?

He preferred the window seat - he could always escape a bore simply by looking out of the window and close down any conversation. In the corridor seat alongside him sat a small middle aged, bald headed man with thick glasses. As they were going to share each other's company for several hours he thought he might 'invest' in light chatter.

"Hello" he said "I am from England, do you speak English?"

"Yes I do" came the reply, "I am employed as a Doctor for an international operation associated with a large UK based international Oil Group. You know that company of course?"

They were soon discussing the recent history of that company, the resignation of its driving force and involvement with a Russian deal. Maybe they would form a big joint company? Maybe a share swap perhaps?

He asked the doctor why he had chosen private work. He said it was because the government system lacked funding and some local hospitals were lacking the expensive scanners common in the west. His own son had died last year because of such a lack. "The doctors here are good" he said "very good, very dedicated, but with poor equipment what do you expect?"

Sebastian asked him about Lake Baikal which he wanted to see and asked if it was a protected area. He was assured that it was but that "there is always some mining or quarrying operation or other, careless of whether they pollute or not. See it now for it's a pity but soon it will be polluted".

He asked about the hotels in Krasnoyarsk. The doctor said he was staying at the Hotel Krasnoyarsk which he described as sensible and serviceable though part of the old Soviet built system but it was centrally located being near the main thoroughfare of Karl Marx Street. They agreed to share a taxi and exchanged email addresses.

Sebastian sank into his own thoughts. It was likely then that this AIM company, Siberian Minerals would have required all sorts of licences, to prospect initially then to extract, probably some sort of payment on volumes extracted, then to employ people safely and finally an license to ensure that no damage was done to the environment. In other words, creating what was confusingly called 'sustainable extraction'. He had been through the processes many times and assumed there must be something similar in Russia. But of course it is a different matter tracking owners of a field in say Hoveringham on the banks of the Trent in England which could almost certainly be traced back to the Doomsday Book in 1086, with the much less precise art of tracking ownership in the largest land territory in the world where ownership had oscillated in and out of communism. This had provided lots of opportunities for manipulation by all those in the vast military complex whose careers suddenly came to an end with the fall of the Soviet Union.

Hmmm he was already getting the feel of a problem. Maybe 'Krysha' protection was at the root of it? Was it about paying off local power brokers?

He decided he could do no more and dozed off. Occasionally he awoke and slightly adjusted his plan; he would have to act quickly if he was to get everything done in time.

On arrival at Krasnoyask, the doctor hailed a taxi and they went straight to the hotel. The doctor commented that it was strange that he had no luggage at all.

"No that's right!" he replied "and I am not even staying the night either as I have to catch the Trans-Siberian train the Rossiya, at 23.03 tonight. But before then I have to make some important contacts. I wonder could you tell me how I can contact the local press or media agencies."

The doctor said that he would call a colleague and within minutes Sebastian had several contact firms' names and addresses.

Sebastian checked into the hotel at the cheapest room rate and asked if he could use the internet system in the lobby. After several attempts he got through and was able to print out the information he was looking for. Then, feeling famished, he had what was left of breakfast at the hotel. He started on his visits to the agencies and soon after returning to the hotel he showered and slept with instructions to be called at midnight.

He called a taxi then went to the Station. Although the Rossiya was the best known train in Russia he was well aware that it was not by any stretch an 'express' indeed its average speed was only 50 mph or around 40 mph if all the stops were taken into account – whereas a plane would travel at around 500 mph.

There he re-boarded the same train that he had left explaining to the amazed train staff at the station that he mistakenly missed the train at an earlier stop near Perm but now regained it and wanted readmission. This took some time as his details were checked and he was able to board the train on arrival though he had to endure a distinctly aggressive telling off by the Provodnista carriage attendant who was quietened only by a substantial tip. He was shown to his old compartment where his entire luggage was neatly piled up. He was at last able to change into more suitable clothing.

He dozed as he concocted a plan which he hoped would get him out of the mess he was in!

CHAPTER SIX

He awoke refreshed as the train rolled along.

He realised that it was the first time for several days that he was able to relax and actually see the countryside. He let it drift over him. As it was October still, there were patches of snow on the hills and in other places it was obviously quite deep, so that passing by small settlements gave a Christmas card effect and at least softened the sometimes terrible Soviet architecture or crude exposure of industrial operations with a blanket of snow. The trees were either green firs or deciduous where the leaves had already turned brown.

He thought of his own family life, the dreadful deal that he had done with his father in law so that on the breakdown of his marriage to Sarah he, Sebastian, had been forced to agree never to make contact with the children again on threat of legal proceedings. If Sebastian agreed then his father in law would pay for their private education. He had kept to the bargain but not a Christmas went by without him imagining what each of them would be doing. He could only hope that his sons, Alexander and Rupert, would understand and that he would somehow be able to explain it all to them. He realised now that it had been a dreadful mistake; with hindsight the private education had been a red herring. All his father in law wanted was him out of the way and in effect to have the sons that he had never had himself!

The train arrived at 15. 57 Moscow Time at Irkutsk but later due to the time zones. So it was 20.57 local time.

He took a taxi to the Baikal Business Centre, a hotel to international standards which had been pre-booked for him. The concierge passed him a pile of emails he noticed one from the agent which he read immediately.

It was from Jeffrey Pardoe himself suggesting a meeting at 23.00 and telling him he was bringing along some local businessmen for lunch at 1.pm the following day. The rest he rolled in a bundle and put in his pocket.

Then he went upstairs threw his luggage on the floor and had a quick shower.

He got dressed and started to read.

The first was from the Sever Press Agency in Krasnoyarsk recording his visit and discussions.

The second was from his Accountancy functional boss Mr Noel Chambers, the Director of Corporate Finance, asking him to remember that the agent Jeffrey Pardoe had his full understanding and authority in any local business matters which he, Sebastian might be brought into. Interestingly he saw that it was addressed unusually to Director Sebastian Edwards also copied was Bill Williamson of TJD Mining and Exploration.

The third was from Sylvia asking about his whereabouts as they had been alerted by the Moscow police of his disappearance from the Trans-Siberian Rossiya.

The fourth was a mass of papers received connected with Siberian Minerals Co and on TJD Mining, these he scrutinised in detail, noting that several of its directors and investors of over 5% shareholding were known to him as being existing or former employees of RKW International, the large mining and extraction conglomerate for whom he worked. He saw that Bill Williamson was a director and shareholder of Siberian Minerals.

He went downstairs to the Business Centre to find a translator which the centre offered as one of its services and asked him to Google in Russian the names of those who appeared to be the Russian shareholders and large equity holders. This he did and gave Sebastian a brief summary in English of the key items on the background of those individuals.

He logged in and sent an email message to Sylvia saying he was OK and thanking her for the item about McVicar adding that it was strange how the most plausible of people turn out to be so devious and that he would be 'interested to meet Jeffery Pardoe once and again!' hoping she would get the hint.

He took his now increasing bundle of papers to the large lounge and waited.

Jeffrey Pardoe walked in on time, wearing an expensive Barbour and a regimental tie. With a ramrod straight back and bushy black hair Sebastian thought he looked the epitome of a middle ranking officer, probably initially deployed in a small intelligence unit with a watching brief over Russian army movements, no doubt he had become either bored with lack of promotion or was seeking more lucrative or exciting employment.

He introduced himself and said "Look we had better get straight to the point as there are people we would like you to see tomorrow and I need to call them to say that the meeting is on for lunchtime."

"Fine" said Sebastian "but it must be really important to pull me away from my holiday – are you sure it cannot wait till I get back?"

"No! 'fraid not, listen I have the run down on you from your boss, Noel Chambers, you are a first class man, excellent accountant and loyal long serving company man, and Regional Accountant of many quarries and other units, you also uncovered a scam I believe several years ago!"

"Now, not to put too fine a point on it we're in a mess! I'll be frank it's a dreadful mess! We need your help."

Sebastian interrupted "Who is WE?"

"Well, actually it's Siberian Minerals."

"But," Sebastian said "that's formally speaking nothing to do with my company is it?"

"Ah but you see it is! After your Accounting Year End in June, the RKW accounts were passed off by the auditors in September. In October several of your directors decided to invest in Siberian Minerals which was then short of money, at the same time as a convertible loan was arranged in London. This gave Siberian Minerals another £90M plus a stronger board representation and enabled Siberian Minerals to replace some UK Funds Investors who were threatening to sell shares in Siberian Minerals Plc at virtually any price. That would so depress the price making it vulnerable to take over! But the individual directors' investments were guaranteed by your company and this amounted to £20M."

Sebastian said "Yes I can see all this from the paperwork I have managed to extract since my arrival here. So how does Bill Williamson fit into all this and why did nobody brief me on this to start with? I might have guessed there was something. I initially asked for a Tourist Visa but Sylvia was told a multi entry visa would be best as it was more flexible, incidentally also allowing for business? So you must have known about this for a month?"

"Well, Bill Williamson set up TJD Mining and Exploration having worked for your operation and managed to get the first concessions for extraction in this area. It was a long shot but he did it in conjunction with a rich local contact who had made his money in coal mines."

Sebastian interrupted him, "Don't be silly! The communists ruled for seventy years, nobody had any money and the only way of getting it was to grab it at the time of privatisation. I understand that's what he did eh? His name is Gennady Ivanovich Badurin is that correct? Maybe, just maybe, he got wind of my visit and tried to also get me out of the way?"

Jeffrey was open mouthed, "Get you out of the way!" he repeated astonished. "Well how did you get all that information and how would he have known of your trip?"

Sebastian replied "I just found out the names of the Russian investors and directors and do you know who Bill Williamson is? Well at the time of the McVicar problem I was aware that there had to be some insider involved because it was difficult to forge some of the signatures. I could never prove anything and everything was under wraps so nothing got out but a few months later he left. It's his operation that has a shareholding in Siberian Minerals and he is also a director! He knew of my visit and this suggests that he and Gennady are in this together."

Jeffrey listened, open mouthed. Sebastian went on "But there is also in place as a shareholder a Regional Development Bank and I suppose you want me to meet them and reassure them of RKW's involvement and support? Is that so? So what were your plans?"

"Well yes! The idea has been that you would become Finance Director here; there would of course be a sizeable increase in pay and extensive travel allowance and indeed some share options that you could take up at a discount. In this way it would give the Development Bank confidence in the operation. You see Badurin is telling that Bank that the prospects are now very poor based, as you can see, on the last year's poor turnover. He has now made a press statement and, as the shares on the London Stock Exchange have slumped, he has threatened to buy further shares, kick out the board and drive the operation through his other company. This would in effect suck out the trade and reduce the profit as he does favourable deals with his own company at low prices. This would leave Siberian Minerals as a worthless empty shell."

"And you really think that merely my being director will stop all that? It seems unlikely!" "Well it's all we could come up with in the short term. We would then hope that the situation would change as the profits increase!"

Sebastian thought a minute. "Well, in fact, if the operations do yield the volumes that your mineral report suggests, then there is something to aim at."

"Hmmm" Sebastian hesitated for a second. "Well I'll do it!"

Jeffrey was taken aback "Really? Are you sure? I mean I'd wanted to explain this in detail but they would not agree to it. I do apologise for dragging you out here like this!"

"But" Sebastian said "under certain specific conditions! I suggest that we list these down then jointly email over to RKW the entire agreement for public release and for the assent of the board and each of the UK shareholders. And tomorrow, instead of a trip around Lake Baikal which is what I came here for, you will take me to some of their local operations and introduce me to all the staff. Do you agree?"

"Why yes! Yes of course! Wow, Yes terrific. Well done!" Jeffrey seemed to Sebastian to now be fully 'on side'.

"OK but you just wait till you see the conditions that I intend to impose!" Sebastian murmured.

"OK let's get on right now and hammer out these terms and get them over to London so they can reply for tomorrow's meeting."

CHAPTER SEVEN

They met the bankers in the hotel at lunchtime as arranged although discussions were a bit delayed due to the difficulties in getting email replies; they wanted an agreement in outline before Sebastian put the proposal to the Bank. The guests introduced themselves as local directors of the Siberian Development Bank.

Jeffrey mopped his brow; Sebastian thought he was shocked by his list of demands.

There were three bankers and Sebastian was greeted by them with huge smiles. "Gehehroee" and immediately called for vodka for toasts. Sebastian thought 'this isn't going to be an easy session!'

"What's happened?" asked Jeffrey in English and Russian. The bankers produced the local newspaper with huge headlines in Russian which Jeffrey read 'English Tourist Saves Police' with a detailed account of the incident near Perm and photos of the Rossiya train, the dead dogs and the very much alive but dirty policeman.

Sebastian told them of his background, the company and his involvement and then outlined his proposal for which, as he indicated, he was still awaiting confirmation and acceptance.

Sebastian explained the conditions. Bill Williamson was to be told to leave and his investment frozen on the basis that he might have been the insider in the McVicar affair and might have been the leak leading to Sebastian's possible mugging. Using information from the Siberian Development Bank, Siberian Minerals would formally block Gennady Badurin's intention to buy out cheaply and increase his shareholding by applying to the London Stock Exchange that this increase was undesirable due to the danger of undisclosed manipulations. Sebastian was to become the Finance Director and Deputy Managing Director of Siberian Minerals visiting every six months and Jeffrey would fly to

Moscow for local board meetings on a monthly basis and report to him. Sebastian would be given share options based on future profit targets being achieved. Sebastian's employer, RKW, would invest a further £40M convertible loan notes into Siberian Minerals (a small sum in relationship to the massive assets of that company) and in return the development bank would lend a further £20M. The individual shareholdings of RKW directors in Siberian Minerals would be taken over by RKW itself. Gennady Badurin will be told that only arm's length business deals would be allowed with his own company. There would be no special deals, no discounts.

He added that Siberian Minerals would comply with all environmental guidelines and would set up a charitable fund to buy equipment for a local hospital for treatment of youth cancers.

Sebastian explained that he had put all this to the chairman and board of RKW and offered them the very simple alternative of? Well, Sebastian returning home immediately, leaving Jeffrey to sort it all out!

The bankers were much relieved and agreed to put this proposal to their board without delay. Of course they still had to raise the new £20M as their part of the deal but they were otherwise faced with the possibility of Gennady Badurin leaving it as a worthless shell but now, with a well-funded operation and in professional hands, it would have a much better chance of success.

At this point an email was received from the chairman of RKW in London agreeing to all the terms.

They then agreed that their next job was to confront the errant Russian investor Gennady Badurin together and tell him of the new plans.

Sebastian was now convinced that Badurin had ordered somebody to mug him on the track near Perm. All Gennady Badurin had had to do was delay Sebastian; then the bankers who had been told of Sebastian's impending arrival would take his absence as a sign that there was no further financial support forthcoming. Sebastian said "I think we have enough to implicate him in all this, we should call in lawyers and the police, let's start by taking away his Directorship and then passing a resolution that no dividend would be paid for two years. I suspect that will show him how we mean to proceed and that this is a long term investment not a smash and grab raid."

The Bank directors members nodded in agreement and departed.

"Maybe one day I'll make the trip around Lake Baikal", said Sebastian "apparently at this time of the year it's a remarkable sight! All that I can gather from this is that somehow prominent members of the RKW board decided to take a 'flyer' on this operation probably believing tales supplied by Bill Williamson of an imminent turnaround in profits. The guarantees would have come to light in months."

"So it seems you have actually saved their bacon!" said Jeffrey.

PART FOUR - Power, Chances, Secrets and Lies

CHAPTER ONE

In August 2014 Sebastian thought for a moment as he studied the form which he had to complete to be considered as Parliamentary Candidate. He knew it would be perused by several people but he felt they would surely only really go into the last ten years in any great detail. He felt safe that he had proved himself within the constituency.

The mere thought of that terrible earlier period of his life gave him a shudder and he felt that he didn't need to go through all that publicly nor did he wish in any way to harm Sylvia, his wife. She had done nothing to deserve any interrogation. "It's best to keep all that to myself" he muttered out loud "nothing to be ashamed of, but nothing the outside world has a right to know!" After all, he thought, it's not as though I have a real chance of being elected as an MP, much less become a government minister if I was elected, since at Head Office they scarcely even know me and I'm not on the short list of winnable seats yet.

He thought back over the 'terrible place – terrible times'. Was it time to come out of the shadows at last?.

At home Sebastian sat back in his chair and sipped the tea which Sylvia had made for him. So was this the right course of action for him now? Forget the form. Did he really want to stand for Parliament? And why?

When he had become the Regional Financial Manager his relationship with his secretary had been exposed and she had transferred to another position before leaving the company in 2013 soon after the Russian trip had ended.

The company promoted engineers and operations staff, accountants were well 'just bean counters weren't they?' He had recently been passed over for promotion that would have meant moving to the corporate board HQ in London. He knew he was always regarded as too matter of fact and to the point to mix with the smoother characters there!

Maybe as a result he had resolved to ensure he kept his area well, he became known as 'the bruiser', woe betide any unit not delivering its branch accounts to him on time, woe betide the manager of any unit being unable to justify his results or falling behind in his profit forecasts! After the Russian deal he was often flung into difficult tasks and effected a profit turnaround on other units often abroad. They considered his recommendations always went 'over the top' or as he put it 'they really hadn't the balls to do a proper job!' but he knew they regarded him as someone to hold things together and deliver results.

Then came the Russian trip. It was clear to him that if he had failed to dig RKW out of the hole they were in they wouldn't worry about *his* career – indeed he would know too much about their weaknesses and the board, he felt, would manage to find a way of 'letting him go'. That's why he did it, there had been no turning back!

As he expected the board had approved the Siberian deal and were appreciative. He was allowed to take on a deputy so that he could supervise the Russian units regularly from the UK and report direct to the corporate board. He was also to be paid bonuses based on the Siberian Mineral Co's profit performance. On every trip to Siberia he managed to acquire new rights for cement and gravel plants for that company and they also took over mining of rare minerals where these became available. This extended the range of operations. He was helped by Jeffrey Pardoe, an English local director of the Russian company who he knew from his Trans-Siberian railway escapade. Sebastian enjoyed good relations with the Siberian Development Bank, the company's commercial bank, and even the major private investor, Gennady

Badurin, began to appreciate that the increasing profits were also making him wealthy.

He was phoned one day by Jeffery Pardoe and asked on his next trip to Russia to stop over one night in Moscow as the interior Ministry wanted to make a presentation to him for his bravery the previous year and he had agreed to do this during the trip scheduled for November 2014.

His thoughts went back to the form as he sat by the window in his father's old wooden swivel chair with the bit of paper about applying to being considered as a candidate. He had researched the matter extensively. The blurb said 'the process is designed to ensure clarity and transparency'   and concentrated on the 'six competencies', communication skills, leadership, strategic thinking and leadership, representing people, resilience and a rather mysterious one 'values in action', he had no idea what that was but as to the rest he felt he could pass the test.

"Hell" he said out loud "I'll go for it." He thought, 'if I leave it I might never get another chance, it looks as though I'll retire from my UK company job in a few years and that will only leave me with the Russian directorship, that should give me enough time to do it!'

So he completed the form as it was with no further changes and posted it off. He hoped he would not regret it!

By the end of October he had gone through training sessions and several selection board interviews chaired by the East Midlands Candidates Chair. The last hurdle was the constituency members election but there he was regarded as a star performer and easily won against a candidate from another constituency. Then he was finally installed as the Prospective Parliamentary Candidate for Middleton and this fact was duly recorded on various media sites. He knew he could not have achieved this without the support of Mrs Leggs, the constituency chairman, who was truly a motherly sort of person and had spoken up for him strongly, giving him a written reference of high praise, 'He's a real go getter' she had said 'he may just win the seat for us'.

CHAPTER TWO

As the most recently elected and so most junior of a small group of Lib Dems elected to the District Council in 2011, Sebastian had been proposed for a seat on the Planning Committee.

This involved daytime meetings and site visits so he had managed to negotiate with his employers a 50/50 split of time as this was 'public service'. His MD told him 'So 50% of the fourteen days a year that you need will come from your holiday allowance of four weeks, which we agree that you have rarely used recently, and the other 50% will be allowed as additional by RKW', that this was done without any argument by the company, Sebastian realised, was not caused by their generous nature but rather it would be used as a marker that he was no longer suitable for promotion because of his outside interest.

The Managing Director once pulled him aside and said 'Why do you do this? You always offer us unpalatable opinions on how to run the company raising uncomfortable issues in your reports'. In fact he thought the company would be happy to lose him, they preferred an easy life and would never delegate power to those below them, like Sebastian, to make the operation more effective!

However he knew that these opinions were just what was required in the political world where new ways of doing things were often given a hearing. Indeed he was required on the doorstep to have opinions on everything from illegal parking, evictions of travellers, the current stock market and whether and if the coalition would last.

As Lib Dems in this District Council held only five of the forty-plus seats, they were not represented on the important Policy committees, however under Sebastian's leadership they soon made an impression disproportionate to their numbers.

He quickly began to tangle with the Tory chairman of the Planning Committee who, although a fair minded person and not given to bias under normal conditions, appeared to him to try to push some decisions in a certain way, of course quite legally. Under the coalition agreement there was to be a significant increase in renewable energy to combat climate change. The Planning Committee were supposed to act as a tribunal as independent members with no party whip and generally this was the case; but the Tories were hostile to both wind turbines and photovoltaic 'sun farms'.

Sebastian responded by defending their installation for example in one case saying: "If we don't do this we will anyhow use up all our energy supplies of coal and gas further heating up the planet! We may already have gone too far. We have spent years using up energy resources which cannot be replenished; we cannot continue to do that".

On one occasion when the council turned down a wind turbine application and it went to appeal, Sebastian spoke in favour representing one of the parishes adjoining the main town. This drew praise from the only Green councillor, Tim Dabbs, and, although the planning consent was not given, he acknowledged Sebastian as a kindred spirit.

Sebastian was determined to put this relationship to good use and suggested a meeting. "Tim, I was doing some research with colleagues. They mentioned to me the so called 'Merton Clause'. Have you heard of it?" Tim confessed that he had not. "Well it's like this; a Council officer in Merton decided that although they had few opportunities for wind farms or photovoltaic set ups they could still actually do something, and that was to ensure that every large housing development and large commercial building when set up HAD to agree as a planning condition that it would try to introduce other energy saving measures like a common heat grid, ground heat source pumps or thermal heating units. Well Tim, according to my calculations we have actually recently agreed to building 400 houses, far more than the energy saving from alternative energy installations like Solar panels and wind farms which we have approved of just 320, so we are in green terms worse off than when we started – that's our own 'district energy deficit' if you like."

"So" said Tim, "What do you suggest?"

"That we put up a motion to the Council saying something like 'This council endorses the Merton Rule and that it be used as a condition on all large residential and commercial planning approvals'."

Tim was quickly won over and if Sebastian put up the motion Tim agreed to second it. Tim had tried to put forward motions before but they had all failed because, as the sole Green councillor he couldn't find a seconder.

Sebastian led off the motion, "The members will be aware that dinosaurs were probably killed off by climate change. It's interesting to follow some voting patterns here of members who consistently voted against the granting of turbine applications but who are also against the Merton Clauses, thus voting against any and all sustainable energy use. Are we, because of this, to also end up as dinosaur fossils to be dug up from under a layer of burnt earth in a million years' time with a placard saying 'there is no climate change'? "

The chairman of course struggled to intervene and remind members not to trade insults but as far as the Tories were concerned the damage was done and the local papers picked up on the 'Dinosaur Tories'. The Lib Dem party's own In-house Focus magazine made a feast of it picturing a huge Tyrannosaurus Rex standing over a little lady saying "There's no climate change!" It caught the imagination and interest of the residents though some thought he had gone too far.

A vote was called and hands were raised along party lines. That is except for the fifteen Labour Councillors who said nothing at all; it was a standing agreement in their group that a Lib Dem motion of any kind would always be opposed. As their leader John Clark said "We do the opposition and we are not going to have Lib Dem upstarts beginning to think they are relevant here."

But that's not what the local press thought, they warmly welcomed such a new approach. Within days it had set off a whole debate about climate change, renewable energy and the developers' responsibility to initiate measures. The local paper began to see Sebastian as a very credible and quotable source. Increasingly, after full Council meetings his comments were regularly reported.

In a similar way he was able to ridicule the District Council's weakly enforced policies on affordable housing, the guidelines which all developers should follow regarding the size of the buildings in terms of number of bedrooms. The idea of successive Governments had been to ensure that the houses were built to match local housing need not just to maximise the developers' profit. Planning officers knew the local area needed mostly one, two and some three bed houses to accommodate the average family size of 2.5 persons. They had done a needs assessment. However Developers could increase their profit by £50,000 to £100,000 by the addition of extra bedrooms at very little additional cost, so they wanted to build four and five bed houses. Sebastian saw that, unless the guidelines were followed taking in account 'needs', first time buyers would be unable to get on the housing ladder. They would be, in Sebastian's view, condemned to living with their parents or in rented accommodation which they could often not afford. Affordable Housing was meant to ensure a steady supply of low rent housing.

Sebastian formulated a motion for the full Council: "In future all development must conform to policy 9b on house sizes, mix and affordability without exception".

When the motion was put this caused huge embarrassment to the officers and the Tories. The Tory Deputy Leader, Chris Walmsley, tried to damn the proposer by undermining his credibility "So the Liberal Democrat is now an expert in planning matters, maybe we should have hired him rather than our officer here who has had over twenty-five years in planning compared with his two years on the committee. I consider this to insult the very credibility of our officers."

There was uproar as the Tories voiced support for this and Sebastian shouted above the din "Then why do you persist in setting policies which you know you cannot achieve or is it that you are easy queasy when it comes to discussion with developers and you run away and cave in to their proposals frightened of appeal costs if you turn it down?"

CHAPTER THREE

At the same time as Sebastian was elected in 2011 a young Lib Dem called Tim Holland was also elected in a neighbouring ward in Middleton. Although having the necessary qualifications to go to university he had decided not to follow that path but had become involved in politics at a local level.

He had bags of enthusiasm and was in his element on the doorstep canvassing, delivering, answering questions or picking up and noting local issues, such as getting potholes filled, ensuring timely bin collections and that small planning issues were dealt with promptly.

He and Sebastian had forged an alliance despite their differences in age and outlook. Sebastian arranged a quiet meeting and put the gist of a deal to him.

"Tim, in view of my work commitments I cannot stand in the County elections but I will happily support you; I think I can make a difference locally and regionally but I cannot do it without your support!"

So Tim supported Sebastian as leader of their five District councillors whilst Sebastian gave Tim support for the County Council elections in 2013. Tim had stood in a division which covered both of their district wards and they were able to build on their earlier 2011 success. He was duly elected to the County Council which at last gave him a permanent income. Tim later supported Sebastian's nomination for Parliamentary Candidate.

Together they worked out a plan for the constituency based on their earlier successes. They determined that the key to their success would be increasing the membership. They reckoned that they should try to raise it from the current 130 to 400 members.

Sebastian guessed but didn't know for certain that Tim was gay, Sebastian didn't care he was extremely good at his job.

They agreed to slowly increase the area covered by Focus newsletter. For 'hot topics' a street Focus would be produced no matter how trivial the issue and delivered to that specific area. In this way local issues and more positive constituency level matters were brought together also covering the coalition scene. The writing and editing of the Focus was understood to be Tim's area of expertise.

The essence of Focus was simple as Sebastian explained to the unpaid deliverers "1, See the problem; 2, Do something about it; 3, Tell people what you have done; 4, If the residents see you getting small things done they will trust you with bigger problems."

Sebastian's role was to run the strategy and special projects.

Supporting this machine was the social affairs section whose mission was to draw all members into some pleasurable fundraising.

Sometimes there were disagreements over priorities. There was a series of redundancies in local government resulting from cut backs following the recession. Some of these Sebastian found inevitable and indeed welcomed. He recalled his father saying some twenty or more years ago, 'Don't worry about government cutbacks; you see unless cropped government departments will continue to grow without any instruction from anyone. Look at it like this and, mimicking a Devon accent, 'You just look at that climbing rose! It's grown all o't place and there's wild suckers around it too! Now you just take a good pair of secateurs and cut it all right back – don't be a'feared 'twill grow right back in a couple of years! And better and stronger!'

He had been right and Sebastian concluded that there were reserves of fat in Council management that could be eliminated; many private companies had shown that slimmer operations often became more efficient not less so.

But Sebastian looked on social issues as a priority. When a local family were threatened with eviction from their rented house, he visited them and prepared a report. He presented this to the next monthly executive meeting saying "We must look into this case, the Williams, who are in danger of eviction because their landlord wants the place for his daughter who is returning to the UK. He is legally entitled to do that. However, the Williams family are low earners, the husband works in the social services sector on little more than the minimum wage but with some overtime payments, but the problem is that the family have a daughter with special needs who requires attention and daytime care. There is, as you may know a fall back situation, District Councils are bound to provide for homeless people. In this case the accommodation offered is several miles away and the father is unable to drive and so will have to give up his work, it will also mean taking the child away from school where she is settled. The alternative is for him to find digs locally and for the family to move away. But that may well lead to a family break-up."

"So at the moment – I do not know what to do – I am in contact with the local council house providers but so far nothing at all has emerged." He was disappointed that the executive members seemed not to be listening. He tried to emphasise the point "Look this is likely to lead to family break-down, does anyone have any ideas please?" but there was no response.

Other cases met with greater success.

Sebastian saw that Tim was taking like a duck to water to his role as County Councillor and when he brought back news of further cuts, together they decided on how they could formulate a response. There were three issues which particularly impacted the area: cut backs to the day care centre, cuts to the youth centre and cuts to the library.

Sebastian agreed that it was difficult to do anything about the day care centre which had been run down over successive Council administrations. Sebastian had a quick look at the details and reported back that according to the attendance figures, as presently run, it was simply uneconomic. Five people was the average attendance, cared for by five staff - a manager, two assistants, a cook and a driver, an uneconomic ratio. Only medical and social care staff could recommend new admittances so there was no way to increase numbers with referrals from voluntary or community organisations. There was clearly a need but this one 'fell down a crack right in the middle' and the care policy needed fixing at national level.

Next was the Youth Centre; Sebastian was well aware that it had had a poor reputation from the complaints he had received of youths pouring out of the centre, some worse for wear and becoming rowdy in the nearby park later on.

At Sebastian's urging, Tim immediately went to work canvassing all local youth organisations to see if they could take the place over and if not to see whether it would be possible to find an individual prepared to take it on. Sebastian could see that Tim was working hard at it, if enough interest could be raised and volunteers could be persuaded to come forward there was a distinct possibility of making a success of it!

A more immediately challenging matter was the threat of closure of the library which had recently been refurbished and was well used. The manageress was a dynamic, outgoing personality with a crusading spirit determined to make the library the 'cultural hub' of Middleton. Sebastian proposed that Tim should set up a 'Friends of the Library' and by the following year it would be staffed predominantly by volunteers at a substantially reduced cost.

Sebastian was impressed by Tim's work and maturity in meeting and motivating people and commented so to Mrs Leggs who had replied "Yes, Sebastian, he is doing very well, I see him eventually as your replacement", but seeing a frown come over Sebastian's face she quickly added "... not now of course but possibly in time. I meant I see him as your successor eventually! I am going to recommend that he becomes an approved candidate in case we are short of good candidates for nearby seats for the General Election."

Sebastian nodded. He wondered if there was another suitable project for Tim to show these skills.

CHAPTER FOUR

Sebastian thought that the outcome of the April 2014 TV debates between Nick Clegg, the Lib Dem leader, and Nigel Farage, UKIP leader, had come as a nasty shock to all Liberal Democrats. He called a branch meeting at his home to get feedback from those who had listened and to discuss the matter in depth.

Tim was strangely noncommittal. Sebastian tried to pull the discussion together and asked about which powers they thought should be brought back to the UK and what should be done about immigration. The worst aspect of the debate was that Nick gave no vision of the future within the EC, just more of the same which didn't really tick any boxes for anyone! Sebastian saw this poor showing might impact on the format of the leader's future TV debates.

"Let me just test you further. Imagine that both Ukraine and Turkey have now joined the EC with between them some 100 million plus people – what would be your reaction?"

There was a general "Ugh!" in response and they were all negative: "If we think we have problems now that would be much worse! There's only so many immigrants any country could be expected to carry", and "Our real problem is low efficiency and an influx of cheap labour does not encourage employers to invest in capital equipment to improve efficiency."

No-one offered much in the way of taking back powers except to say that they thought that there must be a way to get rid of those who abuse our hospitality.

Sylvia came in to collect the empty cups and said quietly, "Remember that my family are immigrants too!" The others did not know that and Sebastian saw no reason to tell them that her family had tried to force her into an arranged marriage which she had resisted and had been savagely been beaten by her father before escaping.

He mulled over the points raised and studied current Lib Dem policy, he somehow felt that HQ had missed a trick.

Sebastian decided he had to lead locally and stir the media, so he threw out a challenge to a similar debate on local radio between Lib Dems and UKIP, but UKIP refused to offer a spokesman so the idea was dropped. Sebastian then wrote a letter to the local paper briefly noting the case for Britain in Europe. This sparked a letters discussion and Sebastian was challenged to explain what additional changes he would make and what he would do about immigration. He replied:-

"I am hugely supportive of the EC but I would propose that there should be no new countries joining for a period of ten years; that means no! to Ukraine and no! to Turkey. Some localities feel swamped and at local government level they feel overwhelmed and powerless. If we are to continue to allow free immigration we must insist on greatly increased EU funding to cover the increased infrastructure costs to provide more schools, more hospitals, more housing in the areas most affected."

Although his stance didn't lead to any immediate positive changes, it did have one very significant result.

In the week that followed the largest business club in the area asked if he would speak on behalf of the EU at their AGM where up to a hundred members were likely to be present. It appeared that the local Conservative MP, Andrew Laws, had declined to speak due, some said, to his uncertain political position. Sebastian accepted the invitation with alacrity and his photo and small article appeared in the local press. The business community had apparently noted his willingness to state his case in contrast with the serving MP's reluctance.

The whole Lib Dem organisation was shocked by the dismal performance at the Euro Elections in May 2014 although they were able to muster over 1 million voters, this was a miserable 6.61% of the total votes cast.

The turnout was desperately low at 34% perhaps only half of that for a normal General Election.. Lib Dems were crushed falling from ten to just one MEP.

Sebastian mused that although Lib Dems had been constantly and deliberately supportive of the EC, indeed it was one of their flagship policies, they had failed to convert that into votes. They knew that support for the EC was at least 50% Sebastian assumed that the floating voters had split either flocking to UKIP to 'teach 'em a lesson' in frustration or supporting Conservatives and Labour against UKIP. Sebastian concluded that Lib Dems had failed to seize any initiative and that the available political oxygen had been sucked out of them. As few local members were directly impacted because no local canvassing was carried out and the only work done was ensuring that the official free mail leaflet was distributed; Sebastian noted that locally it had been fairly easy to shrug off this failure.

CHAPTER FIVE

Sebastian sat in one of the two comfortable chairs in Edna Leggs' office. It was the only office not filled with copying equipment, boxes of paper, leaflets for every ward and the general detritus of a constituency office. Helpers were doing another print run downstairs supervised by Madge O'Connor, an enthusiastic media student in her final year. A supporter James Smith, who owned a carpet shop, had offered the Lib Dems two rooms at the back and they had leapt at the opportunity. He was retiring anyway and as there were other empty shops on the row he had thought that it was at least occupied and paying council tax so he wasn't losing anything!

Mrs Leggs was by now in effect Sebastian's closest confidante and at the tail end of a regular monthly briefing she handed him a brief article that had appeared the national press, "Have you seen this?"

He read it quickly. "Hmm, it's not entirely surprising is it?" he paused and read it again. "It's the story that's being 'going the rounds'! So let's analyse it a bit. It says that *'Andrew Laws our conservative MP is now fighting attempts to unseat him as a party candidate amid fears he could switch to UKIP'.* Well that ties in with what I heard at the business club."

Sebastian continued, "It seems clear that the Tories are all at sixes and sevens over Europe, the older generation seem to think back to the Europe decades ago and are prepared to put up with minor indignities that we seem to suffer but the younger ones want 'their say' which often means OUT!"

"But then it says *'... a long standing affair with his secretary by whom apparently he has had another family, boys aged 3 and 4'.* It says *'... he has been using her house as his second home for his expenses and thereby obtaining some tax benefit'.* It seems his long suffering wife has now finally got fed up and pushed him out of her house!"

"Oh dear what a mess! but there's more" Sebastian continued to read, "it seems *the Conservative constituency association have received a motion calling for him to quit but a friend of his, Chris Walmsley the Councillor from Ogthorpe, said yesterday 'whatever the outcome of the vote he's not stepping down and if other councillors try to move for his deselection then he would advise Andrew Laws to demand a secret ballot of local party members on the issue to which the party rules entitled him'*. He also denied that his friend, although a Eurosceptic, was about to join UKIP."

"Well" said Mrs Leggs "Isn't this an opportunity to openly question the morality and loyalty of the man?"

"I'm not sure Edna", he paused and looked thoughtful "but I shouldn't like to be in his shoes and I'm not sure there would be any merit in adopting a high moral tone and increasing his discomfiture. No I'm not going to make political capital out of it!"

"That's a surprise! You struggle to make media headlines, then when you have an opportunity to get in there and strike hard, you turn it down. If I didn't know you better I'd've thought you had something to hide! Anyway I leave it up to you, here our rule is that personal attacks are only carried out by the candidate, no other person on our committee has the right to launch an attack but would Andrew Laws be as gentlemanly to you? I don't think so, I think you are missing a trick you might regret!"

She paused, she could tell something had touched a nerve. "By the way how is Sylvia? It's a long time since we have seen her."

Sebastian responded without enthusiasm, "Oh OK as you know she has a part time charity job, she doesn't like the limelight and tends to avoid public appearances. She always checks my diary and sees I go to the right meetings though, she was my secretary for some years as you know. I am sure she will be more visible nearer the election."

That seemed to satisfy Mrs Leggs but Sebastian knew that it was not the whole truth. His agreement with Sylvia was that her photo would never appear in the press, nor would she be seen in public with him. He twiddled the ring on his finger.

The prospective Labour parliamentary candidate, Councillor John Clark was not so pleasant about the Andrew Laws matter, he was a brash and in-your-face sort of person. He walked around the council committee rooms not caring who overheard him saying "He can't control his dick, can't do his expenses and doesn't know which party he belongs to! My God! Where, oh where do the Tories get them from?" In truth the Tories were asking themselves the same question and Tim Holland had repeated the comment. Sebastian realised that there was contempt amongst all political foot-soldiers that ran across all parties for louche behaviour of senior elected representatives and MPs.

John Clark was buoyed up because, following the death of an Independent Councillor with a substantial personal following who had earlier defected from Labour, there had been a by-election and the party had regained the seat.

Sebastian studied the results. It was a Labour heartland seat previously Independent 522, Conservative 403, Lib Dem 380, Labour 110, but this time with UKIP in the fight the result was Labour 450, UKIP 400, Lib Dems 200, Conservative 180. This gave no one much to shout about.

Labour, who being in opposition might have expected a big win, had lost votes; the big gainer was UKIP but to capitalise on this they would either have to stand again in an area where they had no party structure nor policies or just walk away, unable to build on their successes. The Tories had reason to fear because their vote had halved from 28.4% to 14.6%. As for Lib Dems Sebastian knew they could have done better. They had been caught out. However he saw Lib Dems had been reduced from 26.8% to 16.2%, not good but not bad when compared with the national opinion poll of 8%!

The Labour campaign, as always, was based on just three key issues, failure of economic policies, cost of living increases and, defending the NHS.

Sebastian concluded he would need something of a scoop to achieve a break through.

CHAPTER SIX

In Moscow the snow was deep that autumn and the Russian company, Siberian Minerals, of which Sebastian was director, decided to hold the six monthly review meeting at one of the large hotels there. The previous meeting had been in Volgograd following the acquisition of a large mineral extraction company there. So recently the company's operation had become countrywide not just Siberian based, Moscow was the natural focal point for all communications.

Sebastian's flight was delayed. He eventually left at 9.40 and arrived at Terminal A of Moscow Domodedovo airport at 16.00. In contrast to the usual long wait going through immigration and customs he was met at baggage collection by someone in a smart black fur coat and hat with silver badges who was clearly a senior police officer. He held placard at chest level 'Mr Edwards RKW'; Sebastian had expected the company to send a car for him but this seemed a step up.

He remembered about the presentation by a ministry official and he assumed that this was the reason for his reception. The officer showed his police card. "Mr Sebastian Edwards? Please I have duty to take you to Minister – please come – baggages will go to hotel!"

"Can I just get changed please?" Sebastian said indicating his cases, he didn't want to be received by a Minister in jeans, polo-necked shirt and jacket for any photographed presentation.

"No! Please come quickly we are late!" With that he was ushered out of the concourse by a side entrance, deposited in a large black car and driven hurriedly away from the airport. He could not see the road signs as it was now dark and there was swirling snow, but it seemed they were on the main highway heading towards Moscow.

It must have been a twenty minutes later and Sebastian noticed that they were turning onto the Moscow Ring Road (MKAD) and he was getting increasingly worried. He turned to the official. "Where are we going please? I have to prepare for the meetings tomorrow and need to check the meetings room". They were clearly not going into Moscow itself as he had expected!

"Mr Edwards, no problem, everything in hotel OK, please we finish journey soon!" and it seemed plain that he would get nothing more out of him.

Sebastian dozed and then wondered what it could all be about. It's unlikely they would travel outside Moscow for a presentation. Hmm, but the official seemed pleasant enough, there didn't seem any reason to be alarmed.

The official occasionally muttered to the driver who was clearly under pressure to deliver Sebastian somewhere to time. Soon they turned off the ring road and eventually they arrived at an entrance gate giving access through a high wall. The car was stopped by a military guard, papers and his passport were asked for and checked against a list then it was waved through.

He tried again, "Where are we?" and this time he got a direct reply "Gorki-9 does that mean anything to you?"

"What is it?" Sebastian asked becoming more worried by the minute as he looked back at the imposing gates closing behind him. He nervously fidgeted with his papers for tomorrow's meeting, he really needed to go through what he was going to say. Wherever he was, he was certainly trapped now!

"This area has Government dachas, sometimes ministers work from here not Moscow – no problem, don't worry!"

The car stopped in the circular driveway in front of an imposing building, but as it was now quite dark he could only see the vague outline which looked rather like a smaller version of the White House. They were guided round to a side building where a face that was vaguely familiar stood on the steps to greet him.

"Hello Mr Sebastian Edwards! I am Andrey Andreyevich Petrov your driver from Perm, remember me? Have you had good trip?"

He thought for a second and then it clicked, he knew the voice as he had spent hours on the back seat of the police 4 X 4 two years before. This was the driver, a small bearded man with a jacket and unmatched trousers, a nice intelligent chap, the translator, a school teacher as he remembered. He had seen him only briefly since when he had used him to drive the UK board directors around the Russian operations.

"I want thank you Mr Sebastian Edwards for good things you say about me! Since then Government ask me to check on what you do, everything, they ask me here as you know me but my translation not always correct – I am sorry!"

"You mean you have looked at all the work I do here?"

"Yes",

"And seen all the contracts, all the financial results, all the licences?"

"Yes."

Sebastian was startled. "Well at least thank you for being so honest and straightforward!" Sebastian was getting increasingly agitated and twiddled the ring on his finger trying to control his nerves. It seemed he was getting into something which he was neither able to control nor dodge out of. He was trapped!

"Does this mean I am going to be interrogated?"

"No sir! Certainly not! Come now sit and eat" and he was taken into an enormous room with a huge fire and mantelpiece over it. The furniture was solid dark wood with soft brown leather furnishings. The floors were of large planks of wood covered in part by animal skins; the walls were huge squared logs lying flat one on top of the other like a huge log cabin. The air was pungent with the smell of applewood logs which he remembered from his youth. In front of a large sofa was a low table covered with food in large dishes. To the side there was a table covered with what looked like old maps.

Suddenly a door opened and three men came in. The first was a smallish man with blond hair, he offered his hand and began to speak in perfect English. "Hello, good evening, I am Dmitry Tatov. You know this person?" pointing at Andrey, "we asked him to come as you know him. He thinks you are a good person. He will translate!"

They spoke in Russian then Andrey turned to Sebastian and explained. "He is First Deputy Minister of Foreign Affairs and behind him are Mikhail Fadrov and Alexander Bartnokov."

Sebastian knew that it was the common practice in Russia, although senior executives and officials spoke perfect English, they often preferred to use a translator even though, as in this case, they knew that the former schoolmaster's English was inferior to theirs. However, as Sebastian was aware, this was making Andrey increasingly embarrassed as he saw the others grimace at his lack of fluency. Nevertheless Andrey continued to translate.

"It's not my role to give you award – Minister of Interior will do that later" Andrey translated. "I check everyone – they tell me you are good person, and you hope Russia will be bigger and richer?"

"Yes" said Sebastian, "many years ago I took a course on Russia and am well aware of its past problems and the immense wealth that it holds. Historically England has been your ally and I would like to see that again."

"Eat while I speak, it may be some time before you get to hotel" and Sebastian turned his attention to the food on the table.

"I should tell you that I am gravely concerned by events in Ukraine" Andrey continued as translator. "I had hoped that former president would remain in control, while he had rejected EU & NATO approaches he was about to sign agreement with us, but then 'Maidan' occurred."

Dmitrov he blew his cheeks out in exasperation. He interjected "The Police were fools and opened fire, some died and they lost control of the situation and he flew away! Yes the President just flew away!" Dmitrov continued becoming more involved, "The Maidan people were pushing the government towards NATO and the EU we could not have that."

One of the others, Mikhail Fadrov, interjected, "So what is NATO? The cold war has ended YES? So who does NATO fight? Are we Russians still the enemy? It seems that we are. So why would we like the enemy right on our front door? Who was it that saved Ukraine from Hitler, was it NATO, was it England? It was Russia – the Soviet Union! Come look at this table!" and he brought Sebastian to the table covered with old maps. "These are here historic maps; we keep them to remind us!"

Sebastian looked at them but it seems a jumble of arrows and saw-edge curves in red and black covered at intervals with large Russian characters.

He asked Andrey, "What is this?" who in turn studied the map for a short time and talked in Russian with the others.

"It's plan of Battle of Kursk – July 1943. These are attack lines, Germans try to squeeze here and here and cut off Soviet Armies, but it's big victory for Russia!"

They studied the other plan clearly covering a larger area. "This seems to be battle of Dnieper?" Andrey muttered he was clearly at a loss to understand what the relevance of this was to RKW. He was asked to leave by Dmitrov and immediately did so.

Dmitrov Tatov explained in faultless English. "These two battles go to the core of the Russian memory, at Kursk for the first time whilst perhaps in a trap we were able to repel Nazi forces equipped with their latest weapons and turn it into a German defeat. In Kursk we lost 254,000 men and 608,000 wounded do you understand Mr Edwards? How many people live in your place? Derby and county?"

Sebastian was caught by surprise, "Well I suppose about a million."

"So imagine all dead or wounded!" Sebastian was shocked he knew the fighting on the eastern front had been savage but this lecture was not what he expected!

Dmitrov asked, "Now see this, the battle of Dnieper ranged through all this area and liberated Donbas and Eastern Ukraine, all this area flat open area of the Steppes. We paid for this victory with 348,000 dead and 900,000 wounded. All this land is the land of the Rus! We can never again allow enemy to hold this ground. It's impossible for us, Mr Edwards, impossible! Do you understand?"

Sebastian had recovered his composure "I can see your point, but I simply do not understand what this has to do with me."

The second man whom he thought was Mikhail Fradov explained. "We know you are in the Liberal Democratic Party right, and that you have the chance to meet up with Head of your party. He is in coalition with the government? We here do not wish to be forced into a war nor do we wish to allow NATO access to our Russian Steppes, sanction is no matter but it is not good. We wish you to take a personal message from Excellency Medvedev to UK Foreign Minister to suggest new ways of ending the problems. We think you are a friend of Russia."

"Our proposal is this: In return for immediately ceding Crimea to Russia – it has Russian cultural majority - then we propose the following solution. The three main oblasts or provinces nearest Russia including Lukhansk and Donestsk be offered a referendum supervised by the UN and given three options a) to remain in Ukraine equal with other oblasts elsewhere, b) to transfer now to Russia and c) if Ukraine move to NATO or EU association or remove Russian as the main language, than a further referendum will be held. Also UN forces to patrol all three oblasts and so called Rebel forces to be under Russian control. 150 officers from Russia control all these units and be responsible for them and finally Russia will find those responsible for the air crash if in this area and hand them over for trial. Will you take this message please Mr Sebastian Edwards."

By this time Sebastian had recovered some of his composure and he simply stated "There's no way they will accept you just walking into another country and taking a chunk of it. Would you be prepared to hold a similar referendum in Crimea?"

"Maybe but we cannot allow Ukrainian Soldiers in!"

Sebastian thought there really was no way of getting out of doing what they wanted; if he refused then it might reflect on his Russian operations – come to think of it the last contract they were awarded had NO competitors; he wondered now whether he was not already trapped; it was getting later and later and by quickly agreeing he could get back to his hotel and prepare for tomorrow's presentation.

"Ok I will do what I can but the coalition is about to fall apart and I may not be able to get into the Foreign Office."

"Thank you!" came the reply and he was asked to go over the points until he had the message off word perfect.

With that they all shook his hand and departed; Sebastian was shaken and nervously twisted the ring on his finger.

Andrey returned somewhat shamefaced. "I am sorry, Mr Edwards, I am not international translator!"

"Don't worry Andrey, let's just get out of here and to the hotel and you can tell me who these people were and where we are."

Within minutes the car arrived and they were whisked to the Marriott Grand in central Moscow. Sebastian listened attentively to Andrey. Both of them were exhausted. After going over the papers for the morning with the local director Jeffrey Pardoe and checking out the room, they all retired as it was nearly midnight, but Sebastian had a few minutes to update Jeffrey on the meetings with Russian leaders. Sebastian agreed it would be a good idea to take him along next time to get a better understanding of what was going on.

The meeting the following day went well, each of the units presented their returns and Sebastian noticed that the recently establish units funded out of existing cash flows were doing particularly well. He made the closing speech congratulating the Chairman and workforce in his newly learned faltering Russian.

In the afternoon they packed up and went by taxi to the Interior Ministry for the presentation. Sebastian was booked to fly back the following day and there might just be time to tour the Kremlin, this might be the last chance to take a trip inside the buildings.

First he had to go to the presentation which he had imagined would be an informal occasion; instead he stood in line with perhaps twenty others in a crowded hall in one of the magnificent presentation chambers in the Kremlin. He was obligingly nudged by the person behind to walk the length of a red carpet to be presented. He recognised that it was Dmitry Medvedev, the Prime Minister himself, who presented him with the medal and scroll saying in perfect English "Ah the English hero! Mr Edwards – thank you!"

Immediately afterwards he was taken to a lobby and was besieged by a barrage of Russian and foreign TV and press correspondents. Of course he had to go through the whole scenario. Left behind by the Rossiya train, saving the policeman, being attacked by a pack of feral dogs and re-joining the Trans-Siberian express, finishing by pointing out that he had never yet completed that train journey or visited the Kremlin! In his closing speech the Tourist Ministry representative promised a free ticket to both!

In the afternoon they headed back to the hotel. The early flight from Moscow would get him back to London at 7.05 am and he knew he would be busy! He slept soundly – he had a plan.

CHAPTER SEVEN

On arrival at Heathrow Sebastian sat and had a good strong cup of tea in a café working out what he was going to say. At 8 o'clock he phoned the party office in his constituency and was redirected to the chairman Edna Leggs. She hadn't replied so he left a message on the answerphone.

"Hi Edna just got back from Russia still in London – I've decided to call in at Lib Dem HQ about an interesting contact I made in Russia; may have to go to the Foreign Office, call you later" and with that he was gone. Although he had called his wife at 10pm the night before, it was a longstanding arrangement to call every night at that time, he called again to say "Going to HQ and FCO now, should be back 2 pm – Love you!"

He hoped to speak to someone about the Russian 'proposal'. He took the underground to Westminster and walked to George Street. He introduced himself as the Constituency Candidate and asked for the Head of the Candidates' Office Services. He showed his party card and his passport and in a brief conversation he asked for the Party Foreign Affairs spokesman. He was nervous and twiddled the ring on his figure. Was he about to make a complete fool of himself? Ouch, he felt a twinge in his stomach again and quickly took a pill from the little pot in his jacket pocket. He'd have to see the doctor again when he got home.

Within a few minutes a face he recognised from TV appearances popped his head around the door. "Mr Edwards – I've just got a few minutes, how can I help? We're counting on you in the East Midlands to win a seat there soon and break the duck!" This was Tim Beaumond MP who was formerly Party President, a genuine down to earth sort of person.

Sebastian told his story, explaining his role in the Russian company, his Russian police commendation and then the strange meeting at the dacha.

"Hmm" said Tim "sounds important to me! What I suggest we do is to get you to write it all down. You can use my laptop and while you're doing that I'll call David Liffington who, as Minister responsible for Europe, is the best person to deal with this.

So Sebastian carefully prepared a report on the trip to the dacha. Tim Beaumont returned looking serious "You'd better come with me and bring your luggage and any work papers you've used on the trip. This is going to be difficult; they are caught up on sanctions and think you might have breached them!"

Within minutes they arrived by taxi at the Foreign Office. They were taken into a reception room and soon the door was swept open and a person who introduced himself as 'David' brought in two men and a woman, dark suited individuals with dead pan faces - they were not introduced.

David said, "Would you please repeat what you said to Tim. I understand that you have a report?" Sebastian handed it over and it was passed over for photocopying. David started "I suggest you tell us your background and how you became involved in Russia in the first place. Can we have your passport too, please?"

For the second time that day Sebastian went through the whole episode, occasionally interrupted by the 'dark suits'. They particularly wanted to know exactly why he was in Russia, what the business was, exactly where he was taken and exactly who he spoke to. Fortunately Sebastian had obtained most of this information from Andrey on the way back to the hotel so he was fairly certain of the officials' names. The FO trio then retired and returned a few minutes later.

"Are you aware Mr Edwards that all the people you talked with are on the 'sanctions banned list'?" He then read from a statement:

On 5 September 2014, the EU agreed to build on the existing package of measures in a further Council Decision and Council Regulation. The

extended measures came into force on 12 September 2014. The EU sanctions fall into 3 main areas:
1. Financial sanctions against designated Russian banks, energy companies and defence companies
2. Arms embargo and restrictions on certain dual purpose technologies, which although intended for civilian use, might have military application
3. Restrictions on exports of high tech goods and services in the energy sector.

I now need to ask you a series of questions to ensure that you are not in breach of these sanctions."

Sebastian was interrogated for a further thirty minutes on the exact nature of the Russian company's operations and how it was funded. Sebastian tried to explain that the reason he was there was to pass on the proposals he had brought but he was warned not to interject. "In a few minutes Mr Edwards, we shall be clear in a few moments!" Sebastian showed the presentation papers he used at the meeting the previous day, all of the operations were either profitable or according to budget and Sebastian was clear that as far as he was aware no additional funds had been raised or borrowed which would have triggered a sanctions issue. Eventually they appear to be satisfied and the woman withdrew.

"Now, Mr Edwards, what on earth do you think you were doing, these are dangerous people and dangerous times why on earth did you not simply say that they should contact the British Ambassador?"

"Well I didn't feel I had any option, nobody asked me if I wanted to discuss anything! I was collected and driven to meet these people, none of it was my initiative! I dare guess that I was about as able to say NO to them as I am able now to walk out of this building without your permission!"

"Mr Edwards these are just exploratory questions. If you have broken no law of course you may leave at any time! However I would just like to ask you a further couple of things. So what do you make of their proposals? It seems you were in a room attached to the Prime Minister's dacha and those people are all senior Russian members of the elite in Foreign Policy, Ukraine and Internal Security. You are quite sure of your facts? Why do you think they chose you?"

"Well there's this medal" Sebastian began,

"And what's this about a medal?" one of the 'suits' asked in a rather off hand and superior tone.

"It was presented to me by Prime Minister Medvedev yesterday"; Sebastian bent down and picked the medal box from his brief case, opened it, together with the endorsement in Russian, and presented them to 'David' also showing them the Russian press cutting from the Irkutsk papers.

They all gathered round and read the citation in detail and studied the photo. "Ah I see" one said. Another asked "Did this really happen Mr Edwards?" Sebastian simply rolled up his trouser leg which clearly showed signs of a large scar, "Yes." They looked at the dates on his passport and visa, one pulling out a tiny magnifying glass to check something. They stood in the corner of the room muttering quietly, then 'David' returned.

"Thank you for coming to see us, this is an interesting matter, it's good that you came to see us so promptly, we will consider what you have said. Meanwhile, Mr Edwards, please return to your normal roles and we will be in touch. If there is anything you can remember which you think would be of help please call this number," handing Sebastian a card. "If you are pressed on any matter please use 'Tim' as the go between. If you intend to return to Russia please check with us first and we would be grateful if you would link us in on any email communications. I hope you will be willing to return to Russia if necessary. Thank you, that's all we need for now," and turning to Tim

Beaumond "I suppose it's too much to ask to not to involve the press?" A look from Tim was enough, "OK let's see how we go."

With that they were ushered out of the building but then as if from nowhere several photographers and TV reporters sprang forward.

"Mr Edwards I believe that you have received a special proposal for peace in the Ukraine, is that so? Do you wish to say anything?" "Have you been to Russia?" "What are the proposals?"

They were being jostled and it was becoming uncomfortable, immediately Tim stood up and said "There is so far nothing to disclose, Mr Edwards, one of our Constituency Candidates in the East Midlands, he has business interests in Russia and has simply been asked to deliver a message concerning Ukraine to the Foreign Office; what might interest you however is that he has been awarded a very rare Russian police medal for his bravery in rescuing a Russian policeman."

"Damn" said Tim as they were at last able to extract themselves, "How on earth did they get to hear of that? Just what we didn't want, I had to say something because it was clear they knew your name and where you had come from! Damn! Damn! Who leaked this?"

The Press were not to be stopped and Sebastian had briefly related for the third time that morning his story of the events at Perm and was asked to pose with the medal and for copies of the picture taken by him at the time.

Meanwhile Tim called the FCO and Lib Dem headquarters but no obvious leak from either place that could be detected. "Just a minute" said Sebastian when he had extracted himself from the melee, "there may be another source." He explained that he has told his constituency chairman and had rung her again when they were about to leave for the Foreign Office. He had called Mrs Legg, "Er hello Mrs Legg, Edna, did you get my latest phone message." "Yes of course my dear and a nice man called from the Russian embassy asking where you were and I told him. I hope that was alright?" "Yes of course" Sebastian replied anxious not to cause any further problems.

Tim immediately called the FCO and told them the origin of the leak; there was a muttered discussion; he turned to Sebastian "Well that is apparently what the Russians do – they had to find out if the message was delivered and this is their way of making sure – tipping off the press that there was a scoop at the FCO!"

Within hours the press was in full pursuit and a raft of photos appeared in the evening papers, late editions and on TV. By the time he reached home his face was splattered over front pages throughout the country.

Lib Dem Candidate Foreign office go-between for Peace in Ukraine

No Focus could have achieved greater fame locally. The story made the headlines in the local press and eventually Lib Dem HQ gave out a press release indicating that the story was true but no further details could be revealed. However the press were more interested in the human story and the headlines soon changed to:

Senior Lib Dem saves Russian Policeman and is called a Hero!

Members of the party locally were jubilant, they had no idea what it was all about but they hadn't commanded the front pages for well over ten years.

The Tories were not so happy. At the General Election in 2010 they had held the seat with a healthy 45% of the vote against 30% for Labour and 25% for Lib Dems and they disliked intensely being pushed off the front page, that was where their voters had expected to see their sitting Tory MP Andrew Laws, an heroic Lib Dem was not what they wanted to read about!

CHAPTER EIGHT

Sebastian read the latest news from Lib Dem HQ. The Charlie Hebdo killings and attack on the Jewish supermarket leaving seventeen dead shocked France and Europe too. Deploying all their techniques the authorities had been able to nail down the perpetrators. 'As was so often the case', mused Sebastian, 'when none of the perpetrators was taken alive it wasn't possible to trace back the sources and make sure that the pipeline was clear of terrorists or ascertain whether further attacks were imminent'.

Nick Clegg had spoken for the Party calling it a 'barbaric attack'. "My thoughts are with the victims of today's barbaric attack in Paris, and with their families and friends. Acts of terror like this will never ever shake our commitment to freedom of speech and civil liberties. It will never stop us from being a tolerant and liberal society. We will stick together and defy any attempts by radical extremists to gag or intimidate us. To the people of Paris I say, everyone stands with you in the aftermath of this vile attack!"

But Sebastian was not so sure that the "Je suis Charlie!" was the right sort of response here in his constituency.

He was well aware that part of Muslim culture was sometimes interpreted strictly and he had considerable concerns about treatment of women; his own wife had avoided an arranged marriage; but he was concerned about the line of argument pushed in France. He decided to carry out more research and called one of his committee, a dentist, Mohammed Rahmam. He asked for a quick meeting and Sebastian visited him at home over lunch. It was a pleasant modern house in a well to do area and Sebastian had no doubt that Mohammed had put every hard earned every penny into it and would be nervous of any racial backlash to his family.

"Mohammed what do you make of this whole affair?"

"It's a dreadful atrocity, an appalling waste of lives! I assure you that it's not done in my name!"

"No, no! I understand that, but public perception is fickle." Sebastian stood up and walked to the window choosing his words carefully. "Here we have a case of a newspaper, virtually a comic with a tiny circulation of 60,000 that has been fire-bombed before and because of that had police protection. Their circulation was falling and it has appeared to some that the editors were careless of whether or not they offended."

"Yes I agree" said Mohammed, "it seemed to be almost designed to provoke further attacks."

Sebastian continued "The question is similar to most neighbour disputes, 'What right do I have to jump on the daffodils in your garden?'. Throughout Europe one clearly has a right to jump on one's own daffodils but no right to jump on one's neighbour's, so verbal or written offence could be treated in the same manner. Does someone with a different or no religion have the right to abuse another religion? It must be said that even this picture is confused because we are well aware that almost throughout the Middle East the severest penalties are reserved for those who convert from Islam to Christianity, for apostasy, and those pockets of Christianity that do exist, for example, in Pakistan are under daily threat."

"Well, Sebastian, you should remember that most of us came here by choice and when we did so we acknowledged that there is no practical possibility of converting everyone here to Islam. Most of us are happy here and glad of the opportunities open to us. My father was a railway man from Uganda although he rose to become an inspector, he then opened a store but we were all kicked out and my family devoted everything to my education; I built my practice from nothing."

"But then what does 'Je suis Charlie' mean to you?"

"Well that's a problem if I am Charlie Hebdo, then that presumably means I stand for press freedom and free speech; I am happy with that but does it also mean that I have to insult the Prophet. I cannot go along with that as a practicing Muslim, as you put it Sebastian he, Charlie, would be jumping on my daffodils! I cannot praise him for that can I?"

Sebastian thanked him a left. He returned home and constructed the following press release.

"I am sure that I speak for my whole constituency when I condemn the outrageous attack in France, it was an appalling massacre. I also praise the French police for the diligent manner which they have concluded their dangerous work. If I were in France there's no doubt that I too would be shouting "Je suis Charlie!" but I would not do so here! From a personal point of view I find the French approach defends a magazine whose primary role appears to have been to taunt, tease and infuriate a particular element. It does not inform, it does not carry out rational debate. I fear that a knee jerk reaction will merely prove even more divisive. "Je suis Charlie" obliges France to choose but the ordinary Muslim in France will feel offended; he has no mechanism for saying that the crime was appalling but that the deliberate taunting is also irresponsible and unacceptable. People fail to understand what integration means; it's not just living alongside one another, but the acceptance that every ethnicity has an equal say, is treated the same and enjoys the same respect, opportunities and responsibilities. We still have a long way to go here in the UK to attain these objectives. The French must choose their own road but we should follow our principles.

Terrorists hope to achieve two things, firstly to frighten the general public and bring their attention to the perceived injustice and secondly to gain supporters. This they try to do by compelling the authorities to react in a manner which makes a particular group feel the need to defend itself. Some members of that group then begin to perceive the terrorists as a means of protection, and the extremists find more recruits."

This was released and printed but immediately there was a chorus of disapproval from readers, comments on radio and indeed from Lib Dem HQ who first of all misread it as anti-French and were on the point of demanding that he withdraw it. The local Labour party was hostile and the Tories reacted by arguing for a firmer approach and screening of all immigrants to try to drown out the UKIP's 'I told you so' and warning of further extremism unless immigration were controlled.

He received guarded praise from the local Imam Abdur Afzal which seeped back to him through the letters to the editor in the local paper and Mohammed Rahmam, a Lib Dem committee member, stood up at the next meeting and called it a 'masterful piece' and it then received grudging acceptance by the members. A few were worried about Sebastian's increasing tendency to rush off and do his 'own thing' and then to publish without consent or agreement and he was perhaps increasingly seen as a bit of a maverick.

Mrs Leggs pulled him up sharply. "Sebastian we went along with you on Russia, green policies and affordable homes but please, I need to know what is going on! I was called this morning at 9 am by one of our members concerned that you were supporting terrorists! I do plead with you, Sebastian, you could win this seat but not by offending our voters."

"Edna, I do apologise but as you know we only have that one Muslim committee member! We are not, despite what we would like to think, a representative party, we don't have members proportionate to the electorate. Are you aware that there are twenty-four yes twenty-four Mosques in Nottingham alone, some of them have a capacity for over 1,000 people, perhaps 10 to 20% of our voters in certain wards are Muslim here. I feel I also have to speak for them. As you know I spent some time in Northern Ireland and am well aware of how easily tribal differences get out of control.

CHAPTER NINE

Despite the coalition Government at Westminster, at District Council level there was no such co-operation; the Conservative majority did what was normal for them keep every bit of power as closely guarded as they could. Sebastian's response was to challenge this wherever possible. He knew that his up front and confrontational style did not endear him to either the Conservative Leader of the Council or the senior officers of the District Council.

The allocation of seats to committees of the Council was a case in point. Sebastian was not clear to what extent the Chief Officer was complicit with this arrangement, but it was clear that he would do anything to prevent an uncertain position at the top. Several years ago the situation had been so unclear that three versions of the budget had been pre-prepared by the officers to cater for any possible decision in a hung Full Council and this was a scenario that officers feared more than anything else: uncertainty in completing the budget was for them a disaster and Sebastian felt they would do almost anything to prevent its re-occurrence.

He felt too that if the Chief Officer was in doubt he would fall in line with the Leader and vice versa, in other words as Sebastian saw it they ran the Council together. Of course staff had to be designated to carry out the objectives agreed so it was natural they should work closely. But how close should that be?

Sebastian was often in trouble for directly or indirectly attacking the officers. This was generally considered to be taboo because it was said the officers could not adequately defend themselves, so any questioning of their competence or expertise was challenged by the ruling party.

Sebastian crossed swords over the amount of and justification for the huge capital spends which the Tories proposed without any apparent sense of restraint. He repeatedly asked for a proper business plan for a leisure centre designed to last for forty years costing over £10M, but no plan was ever published. He raised this issue in the Lib Dem group but all he evinced was a rather half-hearted comment "Oh go for it then!" but Sebastian was incensed that the technique for assessing Council projects could be so far behind that used in the private sector and he said as much!

He was accused of challenging the professionalism of the Chief Financial Officer, the so called Section 105 officer who, in addition to his responsibilities to his local political masters was also responsible to the Treasury for direct reporting of financial matters to protect the assets of the Council. But did it, he wondered, have the opposite effect of preventing the fluidity of thought that any commercial accountant would need in order to survive in a competitive world?

Sebastian was not impressed and his outspokenness had resulted in another formal complaint being made against him.

A more serious conflict occurred over the persistent failure, as Sebastian saw it, of the ability to deliver new build houses of the type suitable for the area. Again it was a complex matter and one where he admitted he had failed totally to get through to his members. The problem began in 1947 when the Government in effect nationalised all development rights – that is the right to build new or change substantially existing houses. In doing so the government unwittingly interfered with any hope of a free market economy in housing. For forty or so years it didn't matter much as the government of the day encouraged council house building, but then suddenly it did matter: after Margaret Thatcher's 'right to buy' council houses at a significant discount, all monies from the sales went directly to the Treasury, so hardly any new council houses were built to replace the stock sold.

In frustration Sebastian had suggested that the officers of the Council were complicit in under-delivering the houses needed by not negotiating strongly enough with developers. Again he was warned that this might lead to an investigation into his behaviour for questioning the professionalism of the officers.

Sebastian stated openly, "We have a massive problem here in the District and across the UK, there is a yawning gap in the market, the recent demand on all councils to allocate and provide more housing land may be part of the solution but I fear that unless there is direct government intervention in the form of directly building at least 50,000 affordable home these unfulfilled and unsatisfied non-home owners will form an underclass in our society which will linger for a generation!" and he referred to a recent article in 'The Times' stating that only one new council house was built for every twenty-one sold to tenants.

The final contentious issue was the extension of the tram route. There was an alternative proposal for a new light rail line to run on an old BR spur line. After much heated argument it was agreed that a feasibility study should be undertaken. However, even before this report was published planning permission had been rushed through for the new Council office building to replace the one being demolished to make way for the scheme before the route was agreed.

Some of his executive openly questioned whether his confrontation style would get him anywhere – he risked being suspended if he made any further allegations against officers. Sebastian was concerned by an apparent gap emerging between himself and Tim Holland. Tim was very much more inclined to look for compromises. He told Sebastian "if we cannot win it, then let's leave it and concentrate on areas where we can!"

Sebastian thought that the only way was to confront stupidities wherever they emerged and try to change them.

He believed that the pressures for further devolution were so great that it was impossible to create new regional structure on top of counties without reforming those below and that the District Councils were those most likely to disappear, hence to build brand new bespoke council offices and chamber was simply counter intuitive and a complete waste of money – he said as much.

CHAPTER TEN

It was now 100 days to the election and Sebastian asked Mrs Leggs to call a meeting of the executive and other key members, to organise a task force to oversee the elections, work out strategy and plan day by day responsibilities. Everyone was asked to put their ideas in writing, the purpose being to provide a thinking pad for the discussion.

The meeting consisted of Sebastian in the chair; Edna Leggs and the rest of the committee including Tim Holland Focus content; Mohammed Rahmam UKIP watch, ethnic and green issues; Madge O'Connor Focus Production; Sally Jones Focus routes and delivery; Rod James posters and signs; Johnathan Thomas Focus design. Also attending were Will Jenkins, often absent due to illness; Councillor John Laver a businessman; Jim Smithson, aged 70, wanting to retire, and Norman Dodgson the treasurer for fundraising and 50/50 club.

Will Jenkins and John Lavers started the session off as they were interested in winning their own seats. It was quickly agreed that the five District Council seats currently held by Lib Dems would be fought as would the three extra seats that they had identified; two more would be a bonus, for the rest they would put up paper candidates and hope to have a Focus newsletter in the-easy-to-deliver areas. The difficulty was that there had been a referral to the Boundary Commission challenging that the district was over represented in number of seats on the Council so four of the wards were now three member seats.

Sebastian calculated that as Tim and he were in the same new three seat ward they might be able to draw one more Lib Dem councillor in on their coat-tails, but each of the other three Lib Dem Councillors were in multiple wards and it was likely to be an uphill struggle and they needed more candidates. They had no women or ethnic minority candidates and were in danger of being labelled white, male and middle class. They needed a wider spread. Time was running out but if they were to achieve ten district council seats on 7th May 2015 which they needed to have as a springboard to attack the Tory majority. They could target two more County Council seats in 2017 covering these new District seats they would win. There was some UKIP activity and it was expected that they would win one seat. The Labour vote was regarded as soggy, with only a hard core motivated to cast their votes.

The discussion then turned to the parliamentary elections and Sebastian began to make a list which they could then convert to an action plan on a week by week basis. Every member was asked for their comments.

Madge piped up to start with "Well I am the only student here and you have to face it that four years ago maybe 50% of students were for Lib Dems but within days of the coalition Lib Dems lost its entire youth wing and set back youth interest in politics for perhaps a generation". Nobody was prepared to raise that painful issue again.

Edna turned then to Jim Smithson who sat fidgeting in his chair clearly anxious to speak. "Sebastian, I think you have done a really good job to get yourself into the media over the Russian affair and Charlie Hebdo, but you can see these could both backfire on us. You know that the Lib Dem viewpoint is that the Russians grabbed Crimea in contravention of international rules – you're simply not allowed to grab bits of other people's territory, no matter what! Your mission to deliver the new peace route sounds OK from what you say to us, but it could easily seem as though we supported the Russian position. In the same way.." Sebastian tried to intervene, "No! Hear me out please! Even although you have explained why in effect you refuse to say 'I am Charlie', others may use that against us!"

Jonathan Thomas burst in "and why aren't we hitting the Conservative sitting MP where it hurts? He really is a shocker and we are letting him off scot free!"

Unusually Tim Holland disagreed with his leader. "Look we must target these local District and County Council seats as a priority, with all due deference to you Sebastian, you are not going to win the seat at the

General election but we can lose out on locally if we dissipate our efforts." There was a murmur of agreement with this comment and Sebastian could see that it wasn't going to be as easy as he expected.

Madge put her hand up again, "But we haven't mentioned anything about the reduced care of older people, we were unable to stop the day care centre closure but where are those people right now? Collected by bus and driven to another centre where they certainly will know nobody at all! Is that the way to treat people suffering early Alzheimer's? And there's a lack of jobs locally, especially for students. What's the point of educating people to become servers at Macdonald's? Even then jobs are often zero hours contracts, luring them off benefits but failing to provide reliable earnings."

Norman Dodgson interjected "And we don't have much in the kitty. If we are going to commit our main effort into winning those district seats, how much are we going to have left for the parliamentary seat? We're not on the most winnable seats shortlist so we have to fight with what we've got; there will be no financial handouts, a bit of candidate training at District level, discounts on cost of Focuses maybe but nothing more. I question whether we can or should mount any campaign for the Westminster seat, I'm sorry Sebastian, I know you've put your heart and soul into this but there is a limit!"

Heads nodded and for a moment no-one said anything. So Sebastian broke the embarrassed silence. "You all know that the Russian affair came at me – I didn't search it out. It's still likely they will come back to me because the discussions in Minsk are going nowhere; all sides need to break the deadlock. If I can help that I will. I do not endorse what the Russia did but I can tell you as a Director of a Russian business I am a bit aware of how the Russians think – if I can use that to the common good then I will. The Charlie Hebdo response was tied up with my experiences in Northern Ireland and its basically simple, as soon as you stigmatise one segment of the population you begin to alienate it!"

Mohammed interjected "I said then and I say it again – it was a masterful speech, certainly it has given us credibility for the first time in my community."

"Ah but that's the trouble!" John Laver said, it may well have convinced some that playing to ethnic minorities is why UKIP have grown and could pop up here."

Edna Leggs intervened "Now John we are not here to do UKIP's work for them, you know we are fully behind sensible immigration and that on balance it does more economic and cultural gain than loss!"

She then turned to Sebastian "We all acknowledge the work you have to put us on a new level but our first role must be to hold the seats we have and try to increase the numbers. Many of us feel that we cannot stretch resources into your Westminster campaign. Whilst many of us feel that you are a good candidate and will go far, we cannot sacrifice our efforts at district for your political career. I am sorry to put it so bluntly but that's it in a nutshell."

Sebastian looked around the table and realised that foolishly he had not taken soundings before the meeting. He had not managed to convince Edna and he realised she was crucial to his success Damn! he thought but responded quickly.

"Well I would like to make a proposal to you and hope that you will agree. You all know that after the Russian episode I was approached by a business club to speak on Europe and afterwards a couple of businessmen, who I would prefer not to mention by name, hinted that they were fed up with Andrew Laws messing about with UKIP and felt their businesses would be severely impacted by leaving the EC. They indicated that if I had any money concerns they would be prepared to consider sponsoring me. If I can persuade them to fund an extra £3,000, would that then enable you to fully support me to win this seat?" He added rather lamely, "I was meaning to mention this today but of course as the EC debate carries little importance at District level, I would have no doubt that they would be looking to a convincing level of support at constituency level for continuing EC membership!"

Edna Leggs appeared embarrassed; Sebastian surmised that if had he told her about the possible funding she would probably have not have treated him so harshly. "Well, OK Sebastian when you have had a chat with them please give me a call and we will go through it. Meanwhile I think we have our priorities, District first, then Westminster second, if we can raise the money, OK everyone? Can you now please look at the action plans and we will meet again next week, OK? There are lots of other points raised which we can bring into Focus or the action plan."

Deliberately avoiding Edna Leggs' eye, Sebastian hurried away back home.

He twiddled the ring on his finger. 'Only just got out of that one alive!' he thought but realised he was taking a risk; although he had been welcomed by the business club, nobody so far had offered him anything, the truth was that he had mentioned sponsorship to them and not the other way around.

Nobody had said yes, but then nobody had said no either, so he would have to try to pin that down within a week. Businesses do not very often sponsor candidates locally, larger sums given to HQ could sometimes earn the donor a peerage, something not within his gift!

CHAPTER ELEVEN

That evening Sebastian slumped into his armchair and expected that Sylvia would guess that something was wrong – he was twiddling with the gold signet ring on his finger. Sebastian felt exhausted, trips to the loo were more frequent, most nights now were interrupted by attacks of stomach cramps, with the heavy work load ahead that was the last thing that he wanted.

Since the days of despair in his 'terrible period' he had always been reluctant to share his fears, but he felt that Sylvia understood him and that it was time to share his problems with her, for if he was to move ahead he would be taking a risk which would clearly involve her.

He reminded her of the problems in his 'terrible period', his road to hell and back. He then told her a bit more about the Russian trip; was he already drawn into a trap? The fact that the last contracts for mining there had been awarded to his company seemingly without any competition, that was strange! It could mean nothing, just that Siberian Minerals was the only company willing to take the risk, but could it be a put up job? If so could the contract be taken away just as easily? In practice as he was a paid employee director it would not necessarily affect him. Sure he was due to get a big bonus if it was successful but they were now comfortably off, they had a small house with a pleasant garden and now worth several times the price they'd paid, he had savings and the earnings from the Russian company were on top of his normal company job. He had a car provided, a pension scheme and was well into the top tax bracket and yet he worried. His earlier problems made him nervous about any thought of a loss of a job, but now this peacemaker role, where the hell would that lead?

He went over with her that form he had completed in August 2014 to become a Lib Dem candidate; he went through why he had filled it in as he did. He explained that the 'errors in completion' would be hard to justify if he was called before a disbelieving jury, for instance his own executive committee! Would they appreciate why he had short circuited the process, he knew that it was no good to excuse himself with a throw away phrase: 'it's all private and nothing to do with you!'

And now he was faced with a further problem; he explained that the sitting MP's misbehaviour and his possible defection to UKIP meant that his supporters might swing over in their hundreds to the Lib Dems so that for the first time he thought he might actually win the seat. His luck with the TV exposure of the Russian affair had given him exactly the visibility he had previously lacked.

But now the 'game' was getting out of his control. He had to convince someone to sponsor him and any backtracking or withdrawal might have nasty consequences. His sponsors had a right to expect a certain type of behaviour over EC and the referendum; he was getting sucked into a more complex world and had no idea if he had the substance to maintain his position, but he did not think he would ever get such an opportunity again!

Sylvia sat beside him on the floor and held his hand. "I know that what motivates you is helping other people, but it's OK with me if you want to withdraw, do so. We were happy before Russia came on the scene and we can be again, if necessary I'll take a full time job but I feel that you have to do this to earn your own self-respect. This is your opportunity! What do we say to each other? 'Carpe diem', seize the day! But promise me you will see the doctor, those stomach cramps are not right."

Sebastian felt relieved he had cleared the air with his soulmate. She would accept him opting out and would support him, but what did he really want to do, and how could he square some of the problems and then he would have to come clean?

CHAPTER TWELVE

The following day he received a call from Lib Dem HQ.

"Hello Sebastian Edwards, Tim here, I had a call yesterday from the FCO, and they want you down here for discussions like yesterday. They didn't tell me everything, I'm sure, but they've studied all the stuff you told them and it does check out. Apparently you almost certainly went to Medvedev's dacha and the people were a mix of their Foreign Office staff, security staff, probably under Putin, and one of Medvedev's appointees. The Foreign Minister there, Sergey Lavrov, is not considered to be in the Putin or Medvedev inner circle, he's like an extraordinarily powerful ambassador and career diplomat. That shows us this isn't just a diplomatic ploy, this is an initiative straight from Putin - Medvedev.

Recently the Minsk talks have slowed to a crawl and are likely to go nowhere and yet separatists, or Russians we are not sure which, are shelling a seaside town and if that fell the whole of the coastline up to Crimea would fall meaning Russia would have direct access there and be able to push in whatever troops she wanted. We know that the low oil prices are affecting growth in Russia but they cannot bankrupt her because of her immense natural wealth, but it's uncomfortable, but there is another reason too. The FCO chaps don't think Putin is after an aggressive takeover, they think he's merely telling NATO and EC that they cannot expect to deploy their economic and military power right up to the gates of Moscow. The view now is that Russia wants to get onto a long term safe relationship with NATO and the EC.

Anyhow that's what they are telling me! – you can never tell with these FCO types – one minute you are a hero and the next you have broken a basic diplomatic rule, so Sebastian be wary of these guys, they will use you in the interests of furthering UK diplomacy, and remember Sebastian, don't ever make it look as though you are changing Lib Dem policy on your own say so, will you? If you do, we would have to disown you! Understand?"

Sebastian agreed, "OK thanks for that advice; this looks positive do you think you could make an appearance in my constituency and by the way I need some advice on the devolution question – I hope I can call you on that?"

"Sure, I'll come if I can! Now look sharp 9.30 am tomorrow at the FCO – and by the way they had a word with your employers who have agreed to give you leave of absence for the duration whatever that means! Bring all the stuff with you and passport for identification! Don't forget to keep me in the loop old chap? Cheerio!" and with that he was gone.

Blast! No time then for him to book an appointment with his doctor, he would have to be on the 7.30 am train at the latest, and what a fuss that appointment system was, according to the medical centre receptionist you had to phone up at 8.15 am when the surgery opened to book an appointment for that day and all slots were gone by 8.30 am, or you could sit and wait all morning to get in at the end of the session, but you couldn't book in the afternoon for the following day. Sebastian could not work out how anyone working regular office hours could ever get to see a doctor. Maybe he thought jokingly it was some sort of a rationing system, women and children only, anyhow he would have to leave it to Sylvia to book an appointment for him.

Later that day he was in his office completing the quarterly accounts when his MD phoned. "I've just heard from Head Office that they are prepared to give you days off for some sort of special work for the FCO, so let me know how things are going – and by the way the Chairman says he's expecting some more excellent contracts in the Russian operation, thinks you are playing a blinder, keep it up! Mind you the whole thing could be in trouble if these sanctions carry on, the company won't carry a loss you know just close the operation down I expect! Have you completed the last quarter's accounts yet? Email them today if you can OK?"

He collected in his briefcase all the papers he'd had with him on the first visit, Sylvia drove into the station, he caught the London train and then took an underground to the Foreign Office.

He was met at the door by a young staff member and, handing in his passport as identification, was taken directly to a small side office. He sat and waited, finished the cup of tea he had been offered and went through all his papers.

In a few minutes David Liffington walked in with a well-dressed man he recognised from the previous meeting. "Sebastian, this is Roland Smith the British Ambassador and this is Keith Williams who is the permanent Under Secretary at the Foreign Office, I will let him explain."

Keith Williams was every inch a diplomat smartly but not flashily turned out, above average height with a lined tanned face that looked as if it cost 'thousands to go to the place where he got it', his a black grey hair had a cut yesterday look, and he had a faintly quizzical expression, as if he still didn't know what to make of Sebastian.

"Sebastian, may I call you that? Please call me Keith, since you have been to the Russian leaders' dacha the least we can do is to show you the FCO as we go to my room on the first floor OK?"

"Sure!" said Sebastian.

"Well we are now in the entrance hall, there's a picture of George Gilbert Scott who designed a lot of the interior, over there is a statue of a Gurkha soldier - this used to be part of the old India Office. This is the grand staircase." Sebastian was amazed, awestruck - the red carpets, huge marble balustrades on either side and a cavernous building like a Victorian church, marble columns on the first floor and in and around the barrel vaulted upper-ceiling there were immense frescos. "Yes these were made to impress visiting dignitaries; they are said to depict the origin, education, development, expansion and triumph of the

British Empire. There are two great ormolu and bronze chandeliers. It's really quite magnificent! My office is at the end of this corridor; look at the azure blue rounded ceiling with stars and look there it's a painting of a sibyl adjuring 'Silence' above my door – to remind me every morning to watch what I say!"

They went into the most impressive office Sebastian had ever seen with elegant Victorian chairs around a mahogany table set apart from an imposing desk with a pile of red boxes alongside. They all sat around the table. "Oh by the way we have at last got hold of a file from Belfast – you didn't tell us anything about that."

Sebastian replied noncommittally, "Well you didn't ask!"

"Now I think that Tim has updated you with our preliminary findings? But from this point on everything we discuss is confidential – do you understand and accept that?"

Sebastian nodded but he was not sure he knew what this meant – he decided to keep mum until his position became clearer.

"We are going into unchartered territory – the purpose of using an intermediary like yourself is that both parties can simply deny involvement and just say that it was all a figment of your imagination. Both the Russians and ourselves will say the same thing; Tim will deny he was told of any discussions; anything that you say will be denied; no serious paper will give credence because they will be cut out of any future press briefings, so you see we don't need you to sign any forms, that's how the system works!"

"We now wish to proceed to the next stage and see if there is really anything new. It could be that this is just a feint to make believe that there is an alternative – it's really like a game of chess but with more far reaching consequences. So here we are at present, the Russians or their surrogates, it does not matter which, are shelling Mariupol and threatening to break through, if that coastline falls they will have direct access to Crimea and that puts the problem into a new level. The Russians know this, they will hesitate but they do not know what to do next, they need to resolve the situation somehow otherwise they will never be able to claim legitimately what they hold. Putin's game is to restore Russian primacy in the area but not to permanently cut himself off and leave Russia isolated.

So what he has offered through you is a possible basis for a deal offering more than before but still not enough. The purpose of the next meeting is to test how far we can push the deal.

First we accept the three tier referendum: a straight in to Ukraine; or out to Russia; but which puts in place a backstop that for the three oblasts, if the regime changes such that in the whole country there is a move to take away the use of the Russian language or involves having NATO troops of any kind stationed in those oblasts or any direct relationship with the EC such that EC is preferred over the Russian link, then another referendum will be automatically deployed in those three oblasts.

The last point in your discussions was whether they would be prepared also to include the Crimea. They hinted this might be on offer.

We now want to put the flesh on that and move forward by one pace. To move forward -

Crimea must be included
All Russian forces must be withdrawn and replaced by Swedish and Irish troops on permanent patrol
150 Russian officers to be planted onto the rebel units, the Russian army will take direct responsibility for any cease fire enforcement; all long range rockets are to be withdrawn
Those responsible for bringing down the Malaysian aircraft are to be arrested and handed over for trial in a neutral country
Russia must agree to a settlement of Ukraine's gas debt repayment and agree not to cut off the pipeline

The British Government will give an undertaking that it will not agree to Ukraine's accession to the EC for 10 years
The British Government to propose Russia as a NATO associate after five years of the ending of the civil war in Syria.

Now do you understand these new initiatives? Will you repeat them word for word please?"

This took around thirty minutes but Sebastian was able to make rough notes.

"If the Russians agree then it would be up to us, the UK government, to sell this idea to our EC and NATO partners. It's likely your involvement will come to an end soon but we cannot be sure."

"Now briefly tell me did it all happen as you reported?"

"Oh the visit to the dacha, yes, yes exactly!"

"No I meant the business about rescuing the policeman. Why did you do that?"

"Well," said Sebastian "there I was, on my own, in freezing cold, not having a clue where I was and not being able to speak the language, I didn't think I had much of an option, then I saw this guy lying in the snow who was clearly injured, I could hardly walk on by, could I? So where exactly would I walk too? I dragged him into the church, I had no idea there were feral dogs about and when it came to it, I just pulled the bloody trigger, bloody dog bit me here!" showing his ankle.

"But then how did you manage to sort out the financial mess and secure the company?"

"Well" continued Sebastian "I was instructed by my company to call off at Irkutsk, I thought something was funny and my faithful secretary ..."

"Who is now your wife it seems?"

"Why yes, sent what I thought was a coded message. In retrospect I believe that my company were prepared to drop me into a mess, make me a director, get me to sign up with some rogues and blame me if anything went wrong, they could use it to sack me, so I had to do some quick thinking!"

All the while Keith Williams appeared to study him carefully hanging on every word.

"Now tell me frankly Sebastian do these Russians have any hold over you at all?" Sebastian replied "To tell you the truth I don't know and it worries me, why on earth was I selected?" Keith Williams' eyebrows shot up. Sebastian explained "Well we did seem to be able to buy another operation very cheaply which now makes good money but there seemed to be no rival bids" he paused "but this was months ago and I figured in any case maybe we were just lucky or maybe they wanted to encourage British involvement in the sector."

"Hmm or just maybe you have impressed them with your honesty and integrity and they wanted to make sure you were still involved. I can see now why they did it. So thank you for coming to see us. Now it's time to do your bit again!"

An official car was called and Sebastian was driven directly to the Russian Embassy which formed a part of a sort of Russian enclave occupying several premises in Kensington Palace Gardens. There he was met by an official who introduced himself as the Minister-Counsellor of the Russian Embassy, Sergey Kramrenko.

His British FCO experts had described him well, aged in his early sixties with thinning grey hair he had been in the diplomatic service since 1974 with various tours of duty interspersed with periods in Ministry of Foreign Affairs college – he had carried out a full a review of the so-called Foreign Policy Concept, which was personally approved by the then President Medvedev in 2008. He was smallish and rather rotund but had a cheery personality which allowed him to get along at most diplomatic functions. As usual with such diplomats his English was adequate and workable even if it was somewhat stilted.

"Hello! Mr Edwards. Our people in Russia have sent me dossier on you and their discussions with you so there is no need to go through that again. As you know there are many things reported about us which are not true.   Where are those mysterious Russian troops attacking Ukrainian military? You know we have made strong plea for immediate withdrawal of both sides' heavy weapons from line of contact. Russia stands for immediate cessation of bloodshed. Russia believes in conflict settlement based on preservation of Ukraine's national integrity and ensuring rights of those people living in south east part of Ukraine state. Crimea is of course different there was already referendum, but we need long overdue constitutional reform process within Ukraine as part of settlement."

Every so often he emphasised his point by bringing his fist down hard on the large solid desk between them.

Sebastian repeated how he had become involved in the Russian business but that he was not aware of the details of the Ukraine problems, all that he could say was that he was aware of the sensitivity of the whole of the Donbass area and the sacrifices in Russian lives that it had cost to win the area back. That seemed to reassure Sergey Kramrenko so Sebastian began speaking from crumpled notes and explaining the policies put forward by the FCO. Sergey listened intently sometimes screwing his eyes up but he noticeably brightened when it came to the points that the British Government would do. "Hahrahsho Good, good!" he said, then paused for several minutes his head resting on his arms planted on the desk, then said quietly "You know Mr Edwards we do not want enemies at gates of Moscow but if they are friends of course they are welcomed, you understand Mr Edwards, British Empire was difficult to give up – how do they say to readjust? So it is with us here and our former empire Bulgaria, Rumania, Ukraine, Belarus – losing an empire is difficult. Thank you Mr Edwards for your services I wish you well with your Russian business, the latest acquisition was good no?"

Sebastian got back into the official black car and returned to the FCO, this time meeting in a side room. There he repeated his discussion in detail. Keith Williams seemed to be relieved and thanked Sebastian warmly for his efforts. "Please do not disappear on vacation or anything in case there's a need for a rapid response, though I think it unlikely. It will be reported to the Kremlin and we will expect to get a sign from them if it is positively received and then we shall have to work on our partners. All this diplomacy is a long and complicated game requiring the utmost patience!"

He called Tim at Lib Dem HQ on the train back home, updated him in brief without mentioning any names or details of the new proposals and, because Tim had had a cancellation, managed to extract from him a visit date for Saturday lunchtime in three days' time; Sebastian assured him that there were a number of very keen Europhiles waiting to be convinced to support Lib Dems and he could meet them.

"Hmmm" he thought so far so good – now he had to turn advantage into money!

CHAPTER THIRTEEN

At lunchtime the following day Sebastian called the secretary of the local business group and told him that he had arranged for Tim Beaumond to visit and speak to them in two days' time. They appeared to be much impressed by Sebastian's ability to obtain a 'Big Beast' at such short notice, believing that his potential to actually win the seat had somehow been recognised by the Lib Dem Party HQ.

Tim Beaumond gave a rousing speech about the need to remain in Europe, pointing out that the Liberal Democrats were the only party to commit wholeheartedly to the EC but that there could still be improvements in EC management and control of projects and accepting there had been weakness in the accession policy regarding new entrants. He said "The result was that there was a huge difference between the new members' GDP and the UK's GDP, not surprisingly this has led to movements of workers to the UK, particularly those who were keenest to better themselves. Somehow this flow would have to be controlled to manageable levels." He suggested that UK had a lot of work to do to convince the EC that the UK could act positively, accordingly the votes given to Lib Dem MPs were important on order to register UK commitment. Several Euro Polls suggested that Britain would remain in the UK if properly led. He linked the commitment to winning this seat ending, ".... sponsorship of or contributing money to Sebastian Edwards will allow him to increase his spend budget to prove that the EU was a winning ticket, particularly in the light of the wobbly situation of the sitting MP. This seat", he reminded them, "might otherwise go to UKIP giving the very worst result for this area!"

After he left, Sebastian cornered the director of the largest firm represented who warmly congratulated him on Tim Beaumond's speech. He bluntly suggested "that additional funding might win the seat and I am doing my best to unseat the existing MP. Just a few hundred more posters and another Focus issue" he said "could make all the difference." He was looking for an additional £3,000 and would also guarantee he would be available for any later Euro referendum canvassing and speaking!

He did obtain £1,500 from one company that was heavily involved in exporting to the EC and a further £750 from a company involved with export insurance, but that was the sum total, not sufficient to have a realistic chance of winning the Parliamentary seat.

He returned home disappointed, but by chance Mohammed phoned that evening and asked how it was going. Sebastian replied gloomily "I got their interest OK but not enough of their money, I'm still £1,750 short and unless I get further funds we will have to fight on local issues prioritising the District elections and leaving the parliamentary as a side issue." Mohammed was silent for a moment "Sebastian, I have a few friends who would like to talk to you, could you drop by tomorrow at about 7 pm – I think it would be of interest to you."

"Well yes OK, frankly you were the only one to fully support me at the last policy meeting, so thanks for that, yes I'll come and listen. Can I make it instead Easter Monday say at 5 pm I think we have an executive at 7 pm? Your house, OK!" As Sebastian wearily put the phone down he imagined that there was some sort of a problem they needed help with. Could he somehow shift it to fundraising? He had found asking for money much more difficult than he expected. He had missed a District Council planning meeting and went back to the party offices.

There he was buttonholed by Sally and Madge. "Look" Sally started off "We are very glad you have achieved a breakthrough on this Russian thing, it's given us a much higher profile than we have ever had but we think you are missing local issues. You know that old-age care is already facing huge pressures, but Cameron's decision to protect school funding as well as health and overseas aid meant the impact is now going to be 'massive'." Madge added "I'm quite sure they won't be ring-fencing councils which control social care spending, against deficit reduction and so the impact on services for frail elderly people could be very great and the knock on effect for the NHS could be quite significant. We will have a real problem here unless something is done. We need a campaign to expose these issues. "Sebastian, we must speak out on this."

Sebastian realised that although the members went along with his higher media profile in the area, they still really did not believe that he would win. Accordingly they saw it as more important to work hard at the local level, even although they knew that as they had only one Councillor on the County Council for their area, their actual ability to change things was, in practical terms, almost non-existent! They were motivated however by their fears for the residents which he could not deny. He would have to think through how he was going to relate local and national issues in his election.

Edna Leggs called. "Sebastian, I hope things went well for you in London, Madge told me that there's quite a lot in your in tray, several minor problems – somebody worried about trees, roots from the park undermining a wall, another potential homeless case, some potholes need reporting and the usual gripes about car parking from retailers and individuals. You know six months ago we made a big feature about getting things done! Can you have a look at those please and get some action?"

Sebastian went to find Madge and was told she had gone upstairs; he nipped up and found her quietly sitting in a corner. "What's the problem?" he started. Madge was normally a feisty girl not afraid to make her presence felt so this was not normal behaviour for her. She said suddenly "It's about Tim Holland!"

"So what's the problem then, you look worried; has he upset you? I know that getting these Focuses out can be a bit nerve wracking, is it that?" She was silent. "He hasn't been harassing you, has he?" Sebastian asked.

 "No, not at all, that's not the problem – it's that, well lately, he has seemed strange and I wondered what I have done wrong, but then I heard..." her voice tailed off. "Oh not to worry – forget I said anything!"

"OK replied Sebastian but you know you can talk to me any time – just give me a call – why don't you do that!" Sebastian wondered how on earth he could sort out that problem, he badly needed Madge on the production side but he didn't want to see her hurt. During the campaign it was vital that in such a small team that everyone worked together.

Sebastian picked up the paperwork and tucked it into his brief case; he would have to call everyone who had raised a problem and go and see them.

CHAPTER FOURTEEN

He then turned his attention to a next Focus newsletter. It was up to him to write a lead item. They had identified that the weak spot for both Tories and Labour was devolution; it was all tangled up with the additional powers to be given to Scotland which would inevitably lead to more powers for Wales. Then within the UK there was this determination that Scots and Welsh, having been given more powers, must not expect to have a say in English affairs.

Constitutionally, this was a nonsense; as it stood all MPs had equal powers to vote on whatever they chose, this was the so called Midlothian question: to what extent ought MPs in Scotland to vote on matters in England or Wales or even Northern Ireland? If Scotland did a 'special deal' why shouldn't London, the wealthiest of all regions by far and with much the most pressing need for more spend on housing and roads and a new airport, not claim additional powers as well

He looked at the extensive Lib Dem policy hand out but was more baffled at the end than he had been at the start.

Some years back Lib Dems had had a clear cut policy, 'Divide the UK into Regions' and devolve powers to them. It was attempted in the north east, there was a referendum which ended disastrously three to one against.

He considered devolution would depend on the composition of the next national government, the rest was speculation. During the current parliament Lib Dems had been severely damaged by their attempts to change the voting system and to democratise the House of Lords. So, not surprisingly, nobody at Lib Dem HQ was sticking their neck out any constitutional reform

"Damn hell and blast" he muttered.

He went home in some despair – things were really not going to plan at all. The hardest bit he seemed to have achieved but then he was dragged down again by things he couldn't control. He wearily sank into his chair.

He opened his PC and tried to make sense of the bewildering options a coalition might face, maybe he then could work out what sort of devolution might be sensible. He opened a spreadsheet and putting down existing MPs by party. He then carried out his own 'what-if', in this way he constructed what he thought were the Optimistic, Pessimistic and Median, most likely outcomes of the numbers of MPs of each party in the next Parliament

Under Optimistic he had Lib Dems on 45, Tory on 294, and Labour on 255, with SNPs on21
On Pessimistic he had Lib Dems on 24, Tory on 278, and Labour on 272 with SNPs on 31

Then he had to work out what this actually meant, the Speaker of course didn't vote that gave 649, the 5 Sinn Fein never attended, that gave 644, so the 50% needed for a majority was 322.

He then tried to work out the various combinations. In the Optimistic plan neither Labour nor Conservative had an overall majority but the Tories could continue with Lib Dems or, Labour could do a deal with Lib Dems but they would need say SNP, Greens and others to succeed.

Everyone knew that all SNP wanted was more powers to Scotland and that they were capable of destructive voting if they didn't get their way, so exactly what would that offer be? If it was full taxing powers which they wanted, then why would they vote at all, and yet they would still be able to disrupt deals with anyone else once their appetite was sated. More importantly if they held the majority north of the border they might simply declare a 'Provisional Government for Scotland', mimicking a devolved parliament, appointing ministers and to all intents and purposes operating as if they were the government.

What would the Greens want, he wondered, to shut down all nuclear power stations like Germany? Would the Unionists in Northern Ireland want more powers, would they work as a group, if not would they bother to vote? Maybe they just wouldn't turn up.

Sebastian didn't see how UKIP could do a deal with the Tories, Cameron's view was to return powers to Westminster in order to make the UK in the EC workable, UKIP's was just to get out, so they were diametrically opposed.

If Labour were thrashed in Scotland losing say 13 to 20 seats how could Labour do a deal with SNP? After campaigning so vigorously for a 'No' vote in the referendum, Labour were hardly likely to wish to dangle in an SNP noose.

UKIP and SNP did not get on – Farage had been 'duffed up' in a visit to Scotland.

What a mess! Maybe the largest party would stick out its tongue at the rest and try to work with no overall majority but that would be unstable, any party could demand a vote of 'no confidence' and the government could be pulled apart in minutes!

Perhaps a loose arrangement like the Lib/Lab pact when years ago Liberals agreed to support the Labour government on key issues but not on confidence motions, but the danger was that the minority party would be dragged down with the government's unpopularity. The FDP (the German Liberal Party) was a classic example of a tiny party dodging about in coalitions but eventually Sebastian noted it was discarded by both major parties in favour of a Grand Coalition, thereafter failing to gain enough votes even to enter the German Parliament.

Nevertheless it could be a replacement coalition but the junior party would insist that it was for a specific time – but that robs the majority party of its greatest single asset which is the ability to choose a surprise date for any election!

So all that was as clear as mud!

Sebastian studied the polls in mid-March. The latest YouGov gave a May prediction of
Conservatives 36% = 297 seats,
Labour 31% = 262 seats,
UKIP 12% = 4 seats,
Lib Dems 10% = 30 seats,
Green 5% = 1 seat,
SNP 4% = 35 seats,
Others 2% = 21 seats.

The Lib Dem votes were not spread evenly across the country, in percentage of turnout terms they should have had 65 seats. Lib Dems also acknowledged they had to fight the other parties as well as the referee – the electoral system - and it was the vagaries of the system that simply would not deliver an understandable result.

In previous campaigns the Lib Dem vote had risen by as much as 50% in the final weeks before an election so Sebastian was reasonably confident that the party should achieve at least 17% of the vote. The increase would come because Lib Dems were treated as the 'nice party', so if in doubt vote for the nice guys. This was where he expected the coalition bonus to appear, 'Well they played a junior but essential role in the recovery, they made the most of their opportunities and got on with the job, five years of stable government in tough times was the result. The uncertain factor was what would happen with UKIP vote. There no doubt some of the UKIP vote had shuffled across direct from Lib Dems – a sort of 'protest about everything' vote, but if, Sebastian argued with anyone who would listen, Lib Dem votes in the polls once exceeded UKIP, then Sebastian expected a shift of those votes back to Lib Dems. So he concluded it was *possible* Lib Dems could still get 20% in the final surge or yes it could be well, just 10%!

He decided further speculation was quite pointless and turned his attention to preparing the next Focus. He referred again to the latest Lib Dem policy statement:

The Liberal Democrats have called for a process of 'Devolution on Demand'.

"We would deliver this through an 'English Devolution Enabling Act' and Liberal Democrats would introduce legislation in the next Parliament which would empower local areas within England. The Act would allow areas to be able to demand from Westminster and Whitehall the powers that they want from a menu of options. The exact details of the powers available would be subject to cross-government confirmation and the UK Government would retain a list of reserved powers. In order to successfully claim the powers they wished, a given area would need to demonstrate it met tests around geography / population, competence, local democratic mandate, a fair electoral system and a transparent and accountable governance structure.."

Then he read elsewhere

Manchester City Council *confirmed ten local authorities, twelve clinical commissioning groups, fourteen NHS partners, NHS England and the government are in discussions on a 'ground-breaking agreement for health and social care'.*

It seemed to him like a bit of unfinished business. He decided the only course of action was to scrap the bit on Devolution in his next Focus newsletter and try something different. Maybe just keep it short like the latest policy,

"A Constitutional Convention is of crucial importance not only in seeking public consent for major change, but also in ensuring that such change is coherent and properly thought through and does not inadvertently unravel our United Kingdom".

Well that would have to do! He wearily sank into his chair, twiddling the ring on his finger.

He had managed to get an appointment with Dr Singh who asked him to drop by soon to take a blood test.

This he did and a few days later was told to book an appointment to see the doctor again.

CHAPTER FIFTEEN

He emerged somewhat shaken from the doctor's consultation where he had listed what he thought were his symptoms as stomach cramps, loo visits, frequent indigestion and fatigue. He was told that he urgently required an endoscopy and should go as soon as it could be arranged. Dr Singh and he used to meet regularly on other matters but on this occasion he refused to comment and Sebastian suspected that was a medical nod for 'this might not be good!'

After spending the rest of the day at RKW, his regular day-time job, he returned home early. Slumped into his chair he sat with his head in his hands.

"Sylvia, I really do not think I can make it, we are fighting basically a Tory constituency with a long serving MP who has a full time political agent, twenty District Councillors to our five, and five County Councillors to our one and their election budget probably five times ours!" he paused, "I just don't think I can make it, and I seem so tired."

"Seb, don't get so worried, I am sure you will make out OK and if we do lose it's not the end of the world is it? We have each other, a good house and income to cover what we need, just do your best that's all you can do! If the Dr Singh wants you to go for an endoscopy it should be within two weeks. I am sure it's better to get to the bottom of the problem."

Politically Sebastian felt he was going around in circles, the only thing he knew was that if he could win this seat he might keep help keep Lib Dems in power – so much was the result poised on a knife edge.

After supper he received an unexpected call. The phone rang, "Is that Mr Edwards? Sebastian Edwards?"

"Yes" Sebastian replied uncertainly, "Who's calling?" he thought he recognised the voice but he could not be certain.

"Dad! It's me your son Rupert." Sebastian was too stunned to reply immediately and he had an urge just to replace the phone; surely that was past, he had managed in the end to blot out that bit of his life that he knew he could never recover, but here it was coming back to him, what was he to do?

"Hello Rupert."

"Yes it's me! Look I am doing a PHD thesis at Oxford - I got a first in PPE a couple of years ago. I've been trying to find you for ages but you'd moved and Mum didn't know where you were, and then I saw this article in one of the national papers 'Lib Dem possible Dark Horse winner' and your name and eventually I tracked you down!"

"Oh! Rupert!" his mind flashed back to the last really happy times they had all had together - over fifteen years ago?

"Dad, Dad, are you there?"

Then a tidal wave of remorse overcame him and he couldn't speak, he had spent years suppressing his memories of his family, it was almost another world, a world he had successfully buried, did he want to relive all that? Then he recovered, "Rupert! Oh yes how good to hear from you! I didn't immediately recognise your voice – I do apologise. How is Alexander?"

"Well he was at Oxford too and is now a city banker with a pad in London – earning sheds of money!"

"Well that's good I suppose and your Mother?"

"She's well but Grandad Jefferies died a few years ago; she still lives in the same place though, with Grandma Jefferies."

"We should meet up some time; you could come and see us perhaps? It's been a long time, a long time and we didn't part very well did we? But I suppose you know about the agreement? That William Jefferies agreed to continue your education only under the strict understanding that I made no kind of contact with you boys or your Mother until you were twenty-one and that you both would then inherit any money he left after his wife died."

"Yes Dad I'm sorry about that!"

Sebastian thought for a moment, he says he understands, 'yes... sorry!' but does he know how terrible a sentence that was? But that was not the lad's fault, he's not to blame.

"Look, as I am doing a thesis on 'Why voter turnout at local elections is so poor' I thought it might be a good idea to come and help you for a couple of weeks after Easter so I could gain experience at the coalface so to speak. Would that be possible? It would help me get the feel of things. I mean, I won't be any trouble, I'll mess in. I have an old school friend living nearby so I could stay there, I'll do whatever you want!"

Sebastian noticed that Rupert had overlooked the 'us'. He assumed that he was not aware of Sylvia's existence but he hadn't asked?

By this time Sylvia had guessed what was going on. She recognised the name 'Rupert'. At the start of their relationship he had told her of the 'devil's agreement' cutting him off from the boys he loved. She understood, one of the key factors in her father's physical abuse was that she too had had to shut herself off from the whole family, otherwise he would certainly have tried to kill her if he could. She dared not even tell her sisters where she was, she could not be sure that they would not give way under pressure. It was something that had bound them so closely together, they both had to cope with the sadness of missing family who were alive but beyond reach.

"Well that could be an idea. I'll have to check the programme; we are, as you can appreciate, really busy right now. Tell you what, why don't you go and stay with your friend, I'll call you on Tuesday after Easter and we'll try to sort something out."

"OK. Dad you aren't angry with us or anything?"

"No, no! Give me your mobile number and I'll call you on Tuesday, anyhow why not go there direct, the office is on the main street in Middleton, you can't miss it, it's splattered all over with Lib Dem posters!"

If he was to work in the office of course he would have some explaining to do to Edna Leggs; he had disclosed no earlier marriage on the candidate's form, never mind a couple of sons, and how was he to introduce him to Sylvia? How would he fit in with the team? Would he be of any use? Would it just disrupt things?

Then he recalled something else that he had suppressed for years, what William Jefferies had actually said was "Surely you know Rupert's arm is broken – you understand what that means **DON'T YOU**?" By that time he had been shouting "If you don't agree NOW! Right NOW! that you will never ever again make contact with the boys, then I promise you that I will myself go to the police and accuse you of GBH" he was shouting again, "**grievous bodily harm.** If the police accept that then, at the very least you will get a written caution at worse you'll go to court and could even go to prison. **DO YOU UNDERSTAND**?" he was shouting and screaming again! That conversation of a decade before was burned into his brain.

At the time Sebastian had had no recollection of what he had actually done the previous day when he had arrived home worse for wear. He was on prescription medication and was drunk, he had no means of verifying whether the arm was bruised or broken as his son was in Liverpool. He knew he was in a mess; a prosecution would have ruined any chance of a job. What else could he do? He had never told anyone of that threat made by his father in law, but if his son should now even casually mention that Sebastian had once broken his arm, that would throw a different light on matters. A push and a sprain was, well, not a disaster, but a break, well, that's a whole different matter!

But now he didn't know what to do. Should he try to speak to his son again before Tuesday to find out the truth about that terrible day and avoid any possibility of the event becoming public or would that just prejudice his integrity? That's what he had held most important throughout his life. He hadn't told Sylvia the full details either, he had held back from plumbing the depths of his own despair.

CHAPTER SIXTEEN

On the Thursday prior to Easter or, as Sebastian reminded everyone, Maundy Thursday, they were due to hold a pre-election planning meeting to get the real electioneering underway. They decided to start early so that they could finish in time to watch the seven way TV debate. All committee members were emailed a reminder earlier in the day.

Sebastian called the HR department of RKW International to tell them that he would, as arranged, be away from 24th April to 8th May. He was surprised when he received a call back from the HR director himself, John Avis. "Sebastian I should warn you, be careful! Apparently the sitting Tory MP for your constituency, Andrew Laws, is a great friend of one of the non-executive Directors, the peer, you know who I mean! He is saying you are spreading nasty rumours about Mr Laws and that his lawyers are already onto your case!"

The meeting start at 6 pm with all members present: Sebastian Edwards – chairman, Edna Leggs – decision taking, Tim Holland Political Tactics and strategy, Mohammed Rahmam – UKIP watch, ethnic and Green, Madge O'Connor- Focus production, Sally Jones – Focus delivery, Rod James in charge of posters and signs, Jonathan Thomas – Focus content and design, plus Will Jenkins a councillor not often available due to illness, another Councillor John Laver who had managed to get away from his business, Jim Smithson aged 75 previously a candidate 10 years ago and Norman Dodgson the treasurer.

Although some pre-election work had started, Sebastian asked everyone to prepare a plan for the key period after Easter.

He handed out the schedule and they discussed the key essentials. "We have a massive fight on our hands – I have no idea what's going to happen but I want each one of you just to do your best then we can all be satisfied that whatever happens we have done our bit in the democratic process! Let's get on with it!"

From this schedule he asked everyone to complete their own responsibility areas on a day by day basis and email these over to him on Sunday. They would meet again on Monday at 7 pm. The details would be agreed, published and posted on the noticeboard on Tuesday next. Each key person would have to calculate the quantity of materials needed - paper, ink etc. and the number of hours required to complete each of task - canvassing, delivering, letter writing, booking halls, getting photos ready and standard forms completed for all candidates, checking and preparing posters and boards and identifying regular Lib Dem voters for poster placement. In total some 30 – 40 people would be involved.

Sebastian reported that they had had an approach from the Greens about a sharing arrangement. Tim Dabbs, the Green District Councillor, had called saying that he was not standing in this constituency but he had been asked to stand in another seat where there was a problem. A waste recycling plant had been proposed, the technology was apparently unproven and the area was already surrounded by wind turbines; Green HQ had asked him to investigate and if necessary stand to draw attention to the associated ecological problems. However Tim still wished to stand in his current District seat and therefore proposed that in his new three seat ward Lib Dems field only two candidates so that the third vote might go to the Greens. They would field only one candidate so that their second and third votes might go to the Lib Dems. Whilst there would be no endorsement of each other's policies, he suggested both sides' handouts would show a photo of Lib Dem and Green candidates side by side and a comment about on joint work on the Merton rule application. Mohammed Rahmam who had the local Green issues watching brief agreed. Sebastian recommended acceptance. The Greens also intended to fight two more seats but in areas where Lib Dems were either not standing or had no prospect of success. In those cases Sebastian argued there was no direct conflict.

Sebastian stuffed the latest budget together with the Lib Dem budget and the latest Labour Conference targets into his briefcase.

One of the team had brought a TV from home and although some drifted off most stayed behind to watch the pre-election debate. At times there was excited chatter from the group when Nick Clegg landed a good point but at others they were silent as if a boxer had landed a good punch on them.

At the end they had a brief discussion. It was obvious that Nick Clegg lacked the freshness of five years before. Then his style had been an eye opener on how a young new face could take centre stage. Now they had all learned from his style and it was much more difficult to hold the middle ground when seven people were competing for the last word.

The problem was the number of parties making brief statements crowded out discussion on many issues. It was going to be very difficult to work out who won and what the repercussions of it were. For example the SNP and Plyd doing well suggested that Labour might do badly even though Milliband put in a reasonable performance. Similarly if Farage did well that could take votes off Cameron. The Greens doing well might take votes off Labour and Lib Dems.

Although in practical terms Nick Clegg had handled things well according to the pundits, he seemed to have done 'least well' and confusingly 'least badly'. But that was not surprising, he was selling moderation, fairness and co-operation and that's not a position that calls for exciting phrases or challenging words. They agreed that he had done a reasonable job but that it was not likely to have changed the Lib Dem rating much.

Before he left Sebastian called Edna and asked her to work on Sally Jones and Madge O'Connor, "We need more women representing us on the District Council and these are good people – I spoke to them last week, can you try again please?"

He left for his long awaited trip to Northumberland for the Easter holiday with his oldest friend Douglas Finlay. He realised that he had to do some deep thinking and needed space and distance to do so. Sylvia was not concerned as he had visited his friend every year at this time for twenty years — it was she told him 'a ritual which she would not dare to interrupt'.

PART FIVE - To thine own self be true

CHAPTER ONE – Easter Sunday April 4th 2015 - 32 days to go

Sebastian had known his friend for decades - forty years or more. Every year he would return to see him and his wife. Douglas owned a cottage in Northumberland, Sebastian always thought of that area as the most under-valued part of England. Even at Easter you could stroll for miles and see no one and the rolling countryside was excellent for walking. Some 'early Easters' it was quite cold and could be snowing whilst a 'late Easter' could be very sunny and quite warm.

The routine didn't change much; a walk to the pub a mile or so away - when it was still open, he thought, pity it was now closed again and awaiting yet another owner to try to make a go of it; an evening at home and dinner prepared by Douglas's wife Lisa-Anna followed by a favourite TV programme and general update on the country life up there.

On Sunday they went to Church, his friend was a Parochial Church Councillor of many years standing. They sang the hymns robustly whether or not there was an organist. This was a tradition from the time when they were both pushed into the school choir that first term at boarding school; Sebastian found it was a sort of continuity that was relaxing.

Then the walks; since Douglas was a countryman he had literally dozens of routes off pat. Where they went depended on the weather and how fit they all felt – sometimes their wanderings would take them into Scotland or towards the sea and Holy Island; along Hadrian's wall or to the Kielder Forest Park and a trip on the reservoir.

Sebastian always arrived in Northumberland with what he regarded as his 'full walking kit'. After years of experimentation he had settled on a 'Berghaus Bowscale' Gortex Jacket and 'Regatta' Overtrousers and 'Contour Track' shoes and Berghaus back pack together with thick socks and warm fleece, these had always seen him through the worst the weather had to throw at them.

On this occasion when they had returned from their walk and Douglas and Lisa-Anna were doing some household chores, Sebastian sat outside in the garden overlooking the valley.

The main Newcastle to Scotland trunk route passed straight through the valley from left to right just below him, no doubt following tracks used for centuries before. As this was 'border country' cattle rustling would have been rife plodding along the same route. A stream ran parallel to the road, and in the fields beyond sheep were grazing. Right across the valleys and on the lower hills the lambs were visible. In the field adjacent stretching to the road new born lambs were prancing and bleating. Although the weather was windy and broken clouds were racing across the sky, shafts of sunlight broke through here and there illuminating patches on the hills across the valley. Further away clumps of trees were visible on the hills; he could see they were mostly plantations because of the regularity of the lines, just like soldiers in parade, he thought. Here and there were small clouds of smoke blown horizontal by the wind – these he knew were caused by the famers burning off the bracken to allow the young growth. Although there were a few stone walls the majority of the boundaries were made of post and wire, sheep-netting strung between wooden posts, giving the whole area an open aspect. The stone built houses of the village could be seen on the left. Over to his right the sun was setting.

All was as it should be! All was as he remembered it for the last twenty years.

Sebastian wondered how he had got himself wound up into such hyperactivity over the 'Politics game'. He didn't actually need an extra job or an extra career. His own career, after some tricky and terrible times, had at last come good, he had built up some cash and investment reserves and although his house was a modest one, that was of little concern to him. Apart from a rail trip to Russia and an earlier one to Turkey he had had no great inclination to travel far. The sole exception was a visit to southern India several years before. What's the point when you can have views like this, he thought?

So why on earth was he pushing himself now? He knew, he knew! In his darkest days he had sworn to himself that if he survived he would try and do his best for the community; he knew he had been a 'taker' and when matters and people had not come up to his expectations he had simply walked away. He was pushing himself and demanded as much from his Lib Dem people; but he could not, would not, walk away. This time he was going to face up, he was not going to cut and run.

The greatest pain he had endured was the loss of his first family. When he was at his lowest he had allowed his father in law to take his two boys from him and inveigle his wife to desert him. His father in law, Will Jefferies had been very rich and could have easily lent him the £40,000 that would have seen him clear; instead he had threatened legal action against Sebastian when he was in no condition to protect himself so he had concluded that pact. The boys would have a public school education paid by his father in law provided that Sebastian promised never to make contact ever again.

He knew now that it was the biggest of all the many mistakes he had made in his life. He thought back to his own childhood; his parents lived abroad permanently. He had been 'interned' as he put it, in a minor public school and was often left to the care of the housemaster over the shorter holidays. At other times he was left with his Grandfather, a man of Victorian morals and upbringing who seemed to be pathologically incapable of talking with a child. He hardly remembered his father; his only photograph of his parents was of them standing beside an official car with a native driver, that, his Father's chair and signet ring were effectively the only reminders he had of his childhood.

He knew now that he had repeated the mistakes of his parents, he had sent the boys to prep school to be followed by boarding school so that he could advance his career and move jobs without the encumbrance of finding them new schools. When that didn't work out because his career didn't give him the income he needed to pay for the fees, the system had collapsed. The result was he had hardly known his sons; he knew now that his boys were bright enough to have survived without needing private education and it might have been possible to keep them at home. Instead he had condemned his boys to the same loneliness that he had endured.

It was that pain and guilt that drove him on and gave him the determination that he was simply not going to walk away this time.

He knew that what allowed him to follow his goal was the love and deep friendship of his wife, Sylvia. They had met many years before at the time when he was at his lowest ebb. Through Doctor Singh he had been invited to help prepare a business plan to raise funds for an organisation that helped Asian women escape from arranged marriages. At the time Sebastian had had no job but the Doctor proposed he get involved, he had told Sebastian he could not manage his career for him but he could help him earn back his self-respect through work.

Later when he at last found a job he realised that Sylvia, one of the women working in the office, was somebody he remembered from that charity; part of their work was to find suitable employment for the women they helped so that they could become independent. Later, after promotion, he had been able to offer her the position as his secretary.

Whilst he was in Russia she had played a significant role in his being able to sort out the problems there. He asked her out dinner to thank her for her help. He had told her of his dreadful pact and the pain and isolation of losing his family. This was something she understood only too well because she herself had been totally cut off from her entire family when she refused an arranged marriage and she believed her father would still try to kill her if he could, to him it was a matter of honour. She still had the reminder of an 8 inch scar on her left arm which she always kept covered.

They were drawn together by this common bond and slowly the relationship grew. Sebastian was averse to getting involved permanently fearing that, what he saw as his jinx, would follow anyone associated with him. Sylvia had told Sebastian that she still feared being entrapped. One year they went on holiday together and decided to stay together afterwards. As they were both earning they quickly put away considerable savings. Although they had managed to conceal their relationship for a year, when the company realised they were 'an item' Sylvia had left her job with Sebastian's company and taken a part time job at the charity. Sylvia proved to be a devoted wife and they were happy.

Sebastian shook himself from his reverie; it was getting cold on the patio. 'Well' Sebastian mused to himself 'there's surely only one way to go, except for one problem'.

Douglas called him inside for dinner and they had the usual lively debate about politics; Douglas was a natural Tory but was well able to withstand Sebastian's occasional political jabs.

After dinner and when Lisa-Anna had gone to bed Sebastian sought Douglas's advice. He knew his friend was not as au faite in politics, but he had something on his mind which he badly needed to discuss!

Sebastian started "I seem to have got myself into a bit of a problem and wonder if I could use you as a sounding board my old friend? It's a sort of moral dilemma!

It's all to do with a form which I signed on applying for becoming a Parliamentary Candidate for the Lib Dems. I realise now that I should have taken more trouble in completing it but I saw no reason frankly to expose a very sensitive period in my life to outside examination, the more so because a part of it relates to my wife and I frankly think it's wrong to cause her any harm. Whatever I might have done she is not responsible. When I filled the form in I didn't think for one moment that I would possibly win, do well perhaps, but not win!"

Douglas popped in "Yes I remember you saying that you didn't think you would win! If you remember I asked 'So why stand then?'"

"Well, that's easy, if candidates only stood if they thought they would win, then you'd never get anyone to stand in a safe seat except for the winner! Nor would the public ever be given the opportunity to reject anyone that's not enhancing but degrading democracy!"

"But now, first the Russia thing and then various other bits and pieces of projects have been successful in gaining media attention, including the Charlie Hebdo affair. I've been lucky with the anti EC leanings of the current MP and for the Green planning. Finally I seem to have made it onto someone's 'winnable seat list'. If I do get official listing that will mean I get in even more funding from Lib Dem HQ. They have these matched funding schemes so that any money raised locally will be doubled by an outside donor."

"Sebastian, that sounds like a good scheme! So what did you do on this form? Tell porky-pies then? That's not like you?"

"I suppose there are four main issues".

"Four! Was anything you wrote OK?"

"As they say 'noralot!"

"Oh blimey come on let's have it all Sebastian! It sounds serious."

"There's the matter of my basic CV, you know the typical one where you are supposed to give a list of jobs and dates. If you have ever been unemployed I can tell you that most people, and I am one, use the start and finish years. Thus if you leave a job in January say 2010 and get another job in June 2011 you can just put in say "X Job Start 2006 finish 2010" and the following "Y Job start 2011 finish 2014" looks fairly OK except that in the middle you can have a period of, say 18 months unemployed. As I was unemployed twice for periods of time, the CV looks better than it actually was."

"The next thing was that on one particular job I was in fact sacked but I put in 'disagreement with employer' as the reason."

"The form asked for family details and I simply gave there 'Wife, Sylvia married 7 years'. As you know I actually have two sons from my former marriage which I didn't disclose and also, as you know, Sylvia and I were never married and what's more her name is not Sylvia."

"Finally I was asked in one block on the form to identify anything that might come out about me that might damage the party. Well I left the Belfast incident and trouble with the IRA out altogether -I could be portrayed as some sort of private ant-terrorist crank! Also the problem about maybe having broken my son's arm, so if my ex family took against me they could expose me as a-less-than-caring individual or worse!"

"In short Douglas I am in a bit of a mess. Coming fourth or fifth at a General Election no one would have cared a jot, but in the full flash of the media my position might be open to misinterpretation; certainly not what the party would be looking for as headline news in say the 'Mail on Sunday': 'Sebastian Edwards the prospective MP for Middletown is not what he appears to be' -, they would have a field day."

Douglas thought for a moment and then said "I agree that the cumulative effect sounds pretty awful; why don't we take these one by one and see where we get?"

"Now the gaps between years of jobs doesn't seem to be wrong as such. If they asked for months and you gave them years then that would be wrong of you but if they didn't specify then I think you could pass on that one. It's a CV of jobs, so if they wanted a detailed career record it might be different. In any case why are you ashamed of being unemployed? I would have thought that it gives the exactly the right feel 'here is someone who has, like many of us, tasted defeat at some time in our careers'. So I'd totally ignore these items."

"If the form asked you to state the reason for the change of job, it may not matter if you were sacked or left after a disagreement. Fundamental disagreements usually lead to some breakdown and since the employer has the power it's always more likely to be the employee that gets turfed out. My understanding though is that you were fired not because of any work problems but because of a failure to notify them of a court case for which there was no legal necessity for you to do. Again I think you are being unnecessarily pernickety, you are not applying for a job but changing your role within an existing operation from Branch Chairman to Constituency PPC where they have had ample time to see you operating. If you were applying for a job 'off the street' as it were, then I think your concerns might be well founded, but not in this case."

"I think the problem with the non-disclosure of an earlier marriage might not be important but the failure to acknowledge your sons is! You should take this seriously. I think it suggests a wish to cut yourself off from the family ties which is not a trait that either encourages the family as a unit or your wider responsibility. That you chose this course makes it worse even if the alternative was likely to cause more difficulties. The episode of breaking the arm, if that's what it was, then frankly that is not good, but it was an isolated event and you clearly did not know what you were doing, but that doesn't cut it as an excuse and I think you should own up to this!"

"Concerning Sylvia, if you were to clarify this with your constituency officials on a confidential basis, then once people understand the reasons she needs protection, then your wishes in this would surely be respected."

"As far as the IRA incident is concerned, I can see nothing that should worry you, indeed it should enhance people's view of you, after all even though you were duped you did save all the guests, except the one, didn't you?"

Sebastian was silent for a full minute considering all these points. "So you think I should make a declaration or something?"

"Sebastian, that's up to you. You know you're a hard taskmaster and demand dedication to the work on hand. Look at it another way, how would you deal with someone coming to you with the stories you have told me; then you will have an idea what you should say. How would you judge that person? It's not in your nature to avoid the issue but don't be too hard on yourself."

"Another sherry?"

Sebastian knew that his friend was right. He thought for a few minutes, then excused himself and called Edna Leggs.

"Edna sorry to call you so late but I would like to discuss something. You remember when we discussed Andrew Laws' predicament with his family and expenses problems? You thought I was wrong to not chase it up and you said something like 'If I didn't know you better I would have thought there was something wrong'? Well there are a few periods in my life when I have been really down and frankly I would not wish to knock someone in those circumstances any more than I deserved that treatment." He then began to explain his background, the hiccups in his career and finally the family problems.

Edna listened but did not quite react as he had hoped. "Well if, as it sounds, you are saying that there are chunks of your application form that are incorrect then it follows I will have to consult with the approvals committee that appointed you. I understand what you have said but the whole purpose of the approvals committee is to prise out those problems, expose and deal with them. GBH is a very serious matter even if it was ten years or more ago! First, of course, I will have to consult our executive. In view of what you have said I am prepared to allow you a ten minute presentation period at the meeting on Monday and allow them to decide if the matter should be referred elsewhere. In practice the last day for receipt of nomination papers is 4pm on Thursday 9th April, so there is still time to deselect you if the members wish and Tim Holland, you know, is now an approved candidate. We could have an emergency executive meeting if necessary to install him in your place."

"To be honest Sebastian these last few months have been rather hectic and I do rather feel that you have run away with this one a bit, we used to have regular chats, but these ended and several members feel you have got above yourself and we should be trying to double the number of Councillors as a priority and, well, not encouraging your ego trip, I am sorry but that's what is being said. See you tomorrow. Ten minutes, remember, no more!"

"Well", Sebastian muttered "now the die is cast!"

In a sense he was relieved, he had got it out of his system, and there was no going back. He called Sylvia and explained what he had done, she wasn't surprised, and he asked her to come with him on Monday. He started to prepare the ten minute speech then began to analyse the strategy to use. He decided to draw up a rough list of issues and problems and their impact on the local campaign.

Sebastian excused himself saying he had a lot of work to catch up on and went to his room.

He knew he had to integrate all his key points into a coherent political plan and identify clear cut strategies which he could 'sell' to the voters. He realised that most people didn't want to be talked at in some sort of political polemic but that it was very difficult to reduce complex issues to soundbites and even more difficult to relate these issues to people sitting at home on a comfortable sofa; all the while competing with a TV which gave instant news and views.

He had to prioritise key issues. He analysed on a spreadsheet the responses to the questionnaire that he had given to the committee members on Thursday. He picked up the responses and put them into a spreadsheet. He had indicated a range of topics and had asked the members to rank each topic's in importance: 1 for low and 10 for high. The information would be used to weight the Focus content towards the topics of greatest importance to the voter. The results were by and large what he expected but he had been right to have the questionnaires completed anonymously!

Top with 86 points was the need for economic stability. They were well aware that this had been important as far as the coalition was concerned. Next was the need for affordable housing with 60 points, it was seen as important, mirroring the gap of those unable to buy. Then followed NHS funding with 59 points, still seen as a serious problem into the future The Library was seen as a success with 51,

His own pet project of "Unnecessary foreign wars" got ZERO. Ah Well! Local issues like neighbourhood planning and car parking were low on the list but Sebastian saw these as matters he could perhaps directly affect.

He had a rational base for prioritising issues and would follow this for the first Focus and gauge the reaction. He had a check list but would need to refine it as he went along.

He emailed the results to all the members who had taken part and asked Jonathan Thomas to come up with some wording and photos, hopefully incorporating the candidates and linking them in with the text. He also emailed Tim Holland because it would be his job to think up some material for some press releases.

Somehow he had to pull all this together. The Focus people would be using the computer programme to work out routes for Focus delivery, he had already indicated his availability for canvassing and meetings. Other thoughts intruded. He wondered what his stomach problem might be. He tried googling Indigestion, Cramps, Fatigue and Weight Loss but this all seemed to point to stomach cancer and that frightened him - going for an endoscopy seemed the best thing to do!

He turned his attention to tomorrow's presentation on his own personal exposure which he completed on his laptop and as a courtesy he emailed it to both Edna Leggs and Tim Holland, so that they would have time to consider it before the meeting. He also sent off check list of tasks to Tim asking for an early response as he would be 'on the road' back for several hours tomorrow.

Worries continued to nag him. How his son would react to all this, a son that he hardly knew? Would he even recognise him? It would be a tense moment for both of them. He worried about Sylvia, she didn't do well under the spotlight, it was not her scene to be involved in a crowd, but if he continued there was be bound to be some publicity, he could protect her from some of it but not everything; it was the norm for wives to attend the count, but of course he could not tell how his Executive would react to the public baring of his soul.

He fell asleep dog tired.

CHAPTER THREE – Easter Monday – 31 days to go

They had a late breakfast and then there was a chance for a final walk with Douglas and Lisa-Anna. They walked alongside the rushing stream down to the village to collect the papers from the shop that sold everything then back up the hill to the music of the bleating sheep.

He had received an email reply from Tim Holland and agreed to meet him briefly for a beer at 6 pm on Tuesday, but as that was the day after the Executive meeting Sebastian had tried to gain an impression of his views on his personal disclosures but Tim would not be drawn. He checked his diary and remembered that he had promised to call on Mohammed Rahmam who had asked for his help on a problem or something and Sebastian had agreed to meet him at 5 pm that afternoon. So he needed to leave at around 11 am to get in all the meetings!

It's been lovely getting off the treadmill for a couple of days and many thanks for your good advice, but I'm sorry Douglas I'll have to go, I have a huge amount to do."

"Good luck my friend! Good luck! Give us a call to say how things turned out and if you don't make it then why not come here for a longer break, and give my love to Sylvia!"

Sebastian switched on the 'Classic FM – Classic Countdown of the most popular' as he did every year and settled down to relax on his journey south. He had never guessed the No 1 correctly and he realised he'd be back home long before this years' was announced.

Apart from the slow traffic around the A1/M62 interchange he had no problems. He had to watch the road signs though; somehow he had got swept into the wrong lane twice in the past and ended up near Newark.

He arrived home at 4 pm just in time to update Sylvia with everything, ask her to come to the executive at 7 pm then change and have a cup of tea. Sylvia was clearly worried about such exposure but he assured her that she would only be called if necessary. Sebastian didn't like doing that, but if his credibility was challenged he realised that it would mean fronting this out.

However he could see that she was worried and possibly frightened too and he changed his mind. "Sylvia if they won't accept my word why should I ask you to face the music? I'll go on my own. Don't worry! They can't eat me!"

Sebastian rushed off to see Mohamed Rahmam. Mohamed met him at his front door and showed him into the lounge. Sebastian was amazed by the number of people there. He was introduced to everyone, a small clothes manufacturer; several shop owners, some university students, a solicitor and an accountant. He guessed there were at least twelve people. He gave a standard presentation about the coming General Election and then was starting to give his own view of integration and what it meant when Mohamed intervened.

"Yes, Sebastian, I think we all here understand that and appreciate what you are trying to do. It seems that you are looking for three things, money, members and local candidates. Am I right?

"Yes!" said Sebastian thoroughly relieved that he didn't have to bring out his 'begging-bowl speech.'

"Well then we have discussed the matter fully between us and we think you are right in what you say, but there's no point in us just thinking that! We have agreed that to support you - we need to do something practical. This means firstly a donation of. ..."

Sebastian interrupted "Mohamed thank you, but there is something that I must explain as I would not want to take your money and support only for you later to find out that I have misled you. No! No please hear me out it's important to me as well as you".

"You have, I think, never met my wife Sylvia? She was brought up a Muslim but was being forced into an arranged marriage from which she tried to escape with terrible consequences and she was injured. She went into hostel accommodation arranged by the charity and she has been unable to meet any of her family since, fearing retribution. We are happy now and have been together for many years, but you can tell what my view of arranged marriage is. I wanted you to understand this, but I do sincerely welcome the support from you all!"

Mohamed asked Sebastian to wait outside in the hall while they conferred. There were a few minutes of discussion in a language that he did not understand then very soon he was asked in and was warmly greeted by each of them in turn.

"Thank you Mr Edwards we quite understand and appreciate your openness, we all know that arranged marriages are a cause for concern. You know that parental influence is deeply embedded in Asian culture but we also know that it is a real dividing line between our cultures and across the generations; we know that many English born girls want to choose their own husbands; we believe that things will change. So thank you for that."

"But now let me explain how we think we can support you. First, we have a cheque for £1,000 collected from those present as you said I believe that you are short of funds in order to get onto the 'winners' list or something. Second, I have a list of those present and a few more totalling twenty of us willing to join Lib Dems because we heard that you have a target of increased members to achieve. Finally, in addition to myself, I have also here two of us who want to stand with you at the District Elections."

 He introduced the accountant and the solicitor who both nodded agreement, "They both attended English universities".

Sebastian was overwhelmed by all this, he had imagined that the purpose of the meeting was to lodge some sort of complaint; the about turn was almost too great to take in. He looked at the cheque as if it was the first he had ever seen!

"But the special motion tonight have you seen it? I might even be suspended."

"I have seen it" Mohamed replied "but God Willing you come through that! In sha'Allah."

"My grateful thanks for this! I suggest that you report it to the executive tonight and may I ask you to bring your potential candidates with you so they can be introduced to the team and be approved at the next executive and candidates meeting which I am planning for Wednesday.

Sebastian left, delighted but somewhat shocked, and went to the Special Executive meeting.

CHAPTER FOUR - Easter Monday evening - 31 days

The meeting began promptly at 7 pm. Sebastian trudged upstairs and sat towards the edge of the circle – the small room was packed. There was a motley collection of chairs, not even a pair the same let alone a set and even so there weren't enough and people were sitting on stacks of paper, the window ledge and on top of a small filing cabinet.

Although it was termed as a 'Special Executive', Edna Leggs had invited everyone involved; Executive Committee, helpers, canvasses, Focus people and candidates, mostly she said because after the special business they had immediately to go into details of the campaign, so everybody was needed and anyway she didn't want to hide anything.

Edna Leggs explained that as Sebastian had, in principle, breeched the rules on candidate's information that he was therefore automatically temporarily suspended. This is a serious matter she said, "We rely upon the integrity of our system to prevent us later being embarrassed by surprises".

The procedure was that Sebastian be asked to make a ten minute presentation. He would then be asked to withdraw and a twenty minute discussion would take place followed by a vote (a) to accept that no harm had been done and recommend that he be re-instated (b) to state that further information be obtained before a decision could be made or, (c) to recommend his suspension be confirmed.

She continued that in all cases the matter had to be referred for a final decision to the Regional Candidates Approvals Board whose decision would be immediate. That decision could be appealed but in view of the timescale for publication of candidates by 9th April, any decision would stand through the election period and, if it went against him, would prevent Sebastian standing in this election.

She concluded by saying that, "The case has been brought by the candidate himself, but that did not mean that he was not guilt free. He has admitted that he abused the rules which were set up to protect the party and voters from being misled. The Executive members amongst you will then vote and, because we are a small organisation, I intend to open this to all our candidates as well."

"You should all have received a copy by email but I'll ask Sebastian to go through the details quickly."

Sebastian went through his employment as briefly as he could:-
He explained setting up a Guest House in Belfast with his first wife whilst employed with a major group there and that after discussions with the RUC, the police there, he had introduced certain safety measures and marketed it as a 'safe' place and seemingly it was prospering financially. Unknown to him the security services were monitoring the phones installed to entrap and catch an IRA hit squad. That had been successful and the IRA unit had all been killed during an ambush at the house. During the ambush Sebastian and other guests had fought off the IRA, but the house had been 30% destroyed. He showed them the cuttings he had kept. He had not mentioned this event on the form as might be seized on the opponents to discredit the Lib Dem although it would almost certainly be picked up by the national press once this became a winnable seat.

He briefly described his next position where a fraud was committed by someone under him but where it was clear that several of his management colleagues had been inveigled by her lies to undermine his position and that as a consequence he had resigned. It had proven difficult after that to get a job because the case was not yet brought to court and when it was, on learning that Sebastian was due to appear as a witness, the MD of his new company would not accept that Sebastian was not involved even though the woman had eventually pleaded guilty. Also he had marked this as reason for leaving as 'disagreement' but actually he was sacked unjustly!

Then he described the long period of unemployment. It had spanned almost two years from February to the November in the following year but the form merely asked for years of start and finish and so this didn't show. This might be picked up by the media.

Worst of all was that during this period his family life had collapsed, they ran out of money, his father in law paid for his children's expensive education because he could no longer afford to, he couldn't get a job, he became very depressed and was on medication. One night, not having drunk for months, he went to a quiz night at the local pub, had a three drinks that reacted adversely with the pills, he remembered then that he should not drink. He returned home covered in vomit and nearly unconscious, he lost his key pushed at the door and accidentally pushed his younger son who fell over and had to go to A & E where is arm was described as 'sprained'. His wife had walked out taking the children. His father in law accused him of breaking his son's arm and warned him that he would continue the children's education only provided Sebastian never ever contacted them again. He accused Sebastian of Grievous Bodily Harm, GBH, a criminal offence. He stated that if he, Sebastian, didn't agree he would call the police to begin proceedings. Sebastian was in the depths of despair and felt unable to defend himself.

So he had an entire family that was not recorded on the form. If he was successful here, in this seat, the media might well pick this up.

He explained that he had been living with Sylvia whom he had met many years ago, they had never married and that for reasons which were entirely her own she had an aversion being seen in public; he was not prepared to go into this further.

He finished off "When I became a candidate just a matter of months ago I didn't believe that we could win here, but events unfolding have made this possible and I have now felt bound to share this with you. The last thing I wanted was for you to believe in me and then to learn that I was really someone different and to warn you that the press might pick up on the last item - my son's omission from the details and particularly the incident. They might start a witch-hunt".

Sebastian asked the chairman Edna Leggs if he could briefly answer questions. "Five minutes!" She replied.

"Did you break his arm?"

"I don't know, the next morning I was told it was sprained. The father in law said 'surely it's broken!'"

"Do you mean to say you never had any contact at all for what is it, over fifteen years?"

"Yes that was the agreement that I kept to; I had intended to pay for the boys education, the father in law agreed to pay, I had no money, no job, I was broke."

"What did you do while unemployed?"

"I worked for two charities, prepared reports for investors and applied for grants. I was introduced by Dr Singh."

"What were they?"

"One was a refuge for battered Asian women suffering arranged marriages, the other a retirement home".

Sebastian then left the room and stood waiting downstairs. He nervously twiddled the signet ring on his finger.

A minute later Madge popped her head around the corner, "We need to know if the arm was broken".

Sebastian replied "Well you can ask him yourself – I got a call from him out of the blue last Thursday; he'd heard about the possibility of winning, he's doing a PHD at university and he's asked to come and help at the same time contributing to his thesis, so I suggested he come here tomorrow!"

Madge popped her head around again and said "Come up please!"

Edna Leggs started off. "In addition to the discussion here we have an email from Tim which is very supportive but another one from HQ whom we contacted because of your foreign work – that talks of an "incredible story in Russia which Lib Dem HQ are unable to verify and strange statements regarding the Ukraine which seems beyond his competence" and urging us "if there is any doubt to continue the suspension until the stories can be verified".

Edna said "Happily, we can counter that challenge provided, Sebastian, that you assure us that you will not lead on the Russia connection in this election. Though it's up to the Region Office to clarify matters on this. There is then the issue which of real importance, the matter of the broken arm. If nothing comes of that we shall recommend removal of suspension, it's true then we shall have to reconsider and seek legal advice. You say your son is coming tomorrow? If you would ask him to meet me tomorrow I hope we can resolve this and get clearance by the following day. What will he say do you think Sebastian?"

"I have no idea I haven't seen him in over a decade and spoke with him for just four minutes last week."

"Do you accept that Sebastian?"

He nodded. "I told him to report to you when he arrived and that you will introduce him to the people here – I still have my day job remember."

Enda Leggs then brusquely brought that part of the meeting to a close, it had lasted forty-five minutes.

"OK now let's get on with the main items. We have an election battle on our hands like no other I have ever witnessed; we will need every ounce of effort, every small piece of luck.

Mohamed Rahmam has asked to move item on funding up the agenda to item 2 does anyone object?"

Mohamed then began a brief account of how he and colleagues had been motivated by Sebastian's Charlie Hebdo response and realised that integration meant more than just living alongside each other, "It must mean us taking our full part in the political process".

He outlined his contribution of £1,000, plus three willing District Candidates candidates, subject of course to acceptance and verification, plus the new member list of twenty names. This was greeted with applause by those around the room and Mohamed asked permission to introduce the solicitor and accountant in person who, it turned out, had been waiting in the car downstairs.

Edna Leggs said immediately "Yes yes! Bring them up please don't let them wait!" and, as two more seating places were hurriedly found, and aside to Sebastian "When did you hear of this?"

He replied in a whisper "Thirty minutes ago, I have just got back from a meeting at his house!"

Sebastian intervened "Edna I propose that we introduce these two as prospective candidates and allocate them to the wards where we hope to be successful, so they can work alongside the two established members – we don't have time for extensive training. I would also ask the two new candidates to present themselves to Mrs Leggs tomorrow night so that their background and suitability can be checked and, if so, their positions as candidates can be confirmed by an executive on Wednesday. Sorry to push people but I think there's still unfinished business from tonight's meeting and it seems unlikely we can conclude everything tonight. If that is acceptable Madam Chairman? In any case I hope to bring forward some other candidates – no surprises there!"

Edna Leggs called for a vote and, although one or two suggested they would not be available, it was passed.

It was 9.30 pm when the meeting finished. Sebastian hurried away briefly acknowledging the offers of support and encouragement. He reached home soon after and Sylvia put a beef salad in front of him. He motioned to her that he was busy and immediately called Tim Beaumond's mobile number, his agreed contact in Lib Dem HQ concerning the 'Russian affair'. He got no reply but left a very urgent and desperate plea on voicemail. Within a few minutes Tim called back, it sounded as if he were in a meeting; there was a hubbub of voices in the background.

"Hi Sebastian how's it going? Are you 'winning here' as the Lib Dem saying goes?"

"No it's b***** not! Apparently some **** head in London is saying to my Constituency Chairman that my meetings with the Russians are all rubbish and that I should be removed as candidate! What's going on? Have you s*** on me or something!"

"Sebastian, calm down, don't get at me, I've done nothing. All existing MPs are now back in their constituencies fighting like hell, why on earth would I try to screw you up? Wait a minute and I'll try to find out what is going on!"

He called back in twenty minutes. "Look it's late and there's only a skeleton crew there now in HQ but they remembered your case. It appears that when we were all told to get back to constituencies each of the areas of Committee Responsibility like Foreign Affairs, Finance, Military, and Health were disbanded and in its place as a stop gap several Lib Dem peers have agreed to take over temporarily.   I understand in the case of foreign affairs it was Lord Chislethwaite.   It can only have come from his office. I've got his number and will try it immediately and then get back to you."

The phone rang again. "Well I have made contact, happily he had not gone to bed and they've all been advised to be available round the clock so it's OK even at this hour.

He says that he was buttonholed by a Tory Peer, Lord Bridgeford, whom he knows vaguely as a reasonable sort as they are on the same administration committee. Lord Bridgeford made some rather startling accusations, first of all to the effect that you have been libelling Andrew Laws the sitting MP for your constituency and that unless you stood down they intended to issue writs forthwith. Secondly that he was aware of your involvement with Russia and he pointed out to Lord Chislethwaite that Lib Dem policy was surely to condemn the Russian incursions into the Ukraine in the strongest possible terms. He even quoted from the party leader's short response to a question on Radio London. Lord Bridgeford apparently accused you of being a UKIP in disguise since your stance he thought was similar to their line. Lord Chislethwaite had the file that I left but could not made head or tail of it, tried and failed to make contact with me. I was canvassing all day! - and when called by the Regional Candidates approvals office to verify you, Sebastian, he responded as he thought he had to do, that is cautiously."

Sebastian replied "Well It may sound strange but I am much relieved by all that. Now I have to tell you that Lord Bridgeford is the non–executive Director of my employers, RKW, and that when applying to the HR department there for leave I was warned that he was telling other directors that he was threatening some sort of action against me, he is apparently friends with Andrew Laws the sitting MP against whom several allegations have been made in the national press. You can google them if you like!"

"Ah I see "said Tim Beaumond "sounds like there's more to this than meets the eye. I'll try to resolve this tomorrow and get back to you. You say it's the Regional Candidates Application Panel chair? Yes I know her. I'm on to this" and he was gone.

Sylvia had by this time gone to bed. Sebastian felt cramps and pains in his stomach again and went to the loo though that didn't help much. He sat in his chair and started to make notes but pushed them aside and instead he finished off the beef salad and, exhausted, fell fast asleep in his chair.

CHAPTER FIVE - Tuesday – 30 days to go

Sebastian went to work at RKW as usual the following day, Tuesday.

He called the HR director and confirmed that Lord Bridgeford had made a complaint and was planning to take legal action. "Look!" said Sebastian" I know that it's none of your affair directly, all I am asking, to prevent things going viral in the media, is that you ask him in common decency to 'put up or shut up'. After all it's going to do the associated company, Siberian Minerals no good either is it?" He agreed to follow that up and get back to Sebastian as soon as he could.

Sebastian then went to meet Tim Holland at 6 pm. Tim explained that Sebastian's email amplified part of Sebastian's life which Tim had not even considered. "So this was the reason why you decided not to chase the sitting MP Andrew Laws and why you were concerned about the potential homeless case which the rest of us treated as merely an administrative matter- we thought that's what the homeless section of the District council was paid to do surely."

"I know we have very different views but they say two heads are better than one and that you get a real widening of the perspective when you have differing mind-sets; that's good provided you can see when to bury your differences."

"That's good advice and I was going to take it - in short I am happy where I am and I think we make a good team and I had made up my mind to stay. But..."

"But what?" asked Sebastian standing up and offering his hand to shake. Tim took it limply but then motioned him to sit.

"But there's more! This morning I heard that the very guy who advised me has been suspended and resigned as Lib Dem candidate. I know him well as I was his deputy for a time on the County Council. He had apparently been arrested and bailed for some supposed offence ten years ago. His whole team were shocked. We don't know the full details but he is certainly not standing and they are looking for a replacement candidate. I got a call yesterday asking if I wanted to be on the short list. The interview is tonight at 7.00pm. So I agreed! That's why I could say very little yesterday about the ongoing work for the campaign– I didn't want to commit publically to something then let you down. I'm sorry if this mucks it up for you!"

"No!" said Sebastian immediately "I wish you the best of luck; you are a very capable politician a 'natural' as they say. Every politician has to want to have they keys to number 10 in his pocket and before that has to want to become an MP to try and improve the world in however small a way, so good luck!"

"This is going to be an instantaneous decision in view of the timescale. It will be decided tonight. The top candidate is expected to sign up tonight, a reserve will be on standby and the others will be immediately released. So I will call you later on and also hope to hear your good news!"

When Sebastian arrived home there was a message for him to call Tim Beaumond.

"Hi Sebastian! I understand that after your chat the Tory peer has resigned from your company RKW's board, and as a consequence he has withdrawn the complaint, apparently he only wanted to help his friend by trying to frighten you; he's admitted he has absolutely no evidence. So this matter is officially closed and I have told your Regional Approvals chairman as well. Now good luck Sebastian, get on and win!"

And he was gone without waiting for even an acknowledgement.

It was after 10.30 pm when Tim Holland phoned Sebastian. Immediately it was clear to him that things had not gone well by the tone of Tim's voice.

"I haven't got it! They mentioned that they had sought updated references from Edna Leggs yesterday and she had reported back that you might also be on suspension if the vote went against you on the executive and in that eventuality she was looking for me to replace you. That may have counted, maybe not. Anyhow they said I was third so I am immediately released. They thanked me for applying and said that, as this was a winnable seat, they had preferred a candidate who was more mature and had been tested out at this level before! They selected a former Lib Dem MEP of which as you know there are several around since our rout at the Euro elections. Not surprising, though, it has to be said that the EC is not a burning issue in that constituency! Anyhow, mustn't complain that's what democracy is all about!"

"How did you get on?"

Sebastian answered "I am now in the clear about the Russia matter; I am just holding on for the personal thing, I don't know how my son got on so I think it will be Thursday before I get a reply from the Approvals Committee."

He still had not heard from Edna Leggs about the meeting which would determine his future career. He decided not to call her this late. He imagined that if she had something to say she would call. He felt very tired.

CHAPTER SIX – Wednesday Midday – 29 days to go

He was at work in RKW offices again the following morning and by lunchtime he had heard nothing from Edna.

He started to believe that his case was lost and began to prepare his next line of action.

At 1pm he could stand it no longer and called Edna who was in the small Lib Dem office over a converted shop.

"Hello Edna – I was just wondering what was happening?"

"Well" she replied "it's a little bit more complex than I had imagined."

"What did he say? Can you tell me that?"

"I suppose so – it will be made public very soon anyhow!" she paused

"Well?"

"Initially he was a bit put out that you hadn't told him what was coming and that he was being asked such direct personal questions, but I explained the situation, that you had decided to clear the past and that it was important that he was not briefed in advance, but I apologised for being so direct."

"This is what he said, 'You were quite right, at the A & E in Nottingham they said it was sprained but didn't even bother to do an X-ray. You probably were not aware because of your state at that time, but back home in Liverpool he went to a private hospital paid for by your father in law and they concluded that there was a hairline fracture."

"Oh dear that counts as a break does it?" Sebastian anxiously twiddled the signet ring on his figure.

"Well, apparently it does but a hairline fracture is a minor crack to the bone that only shows up faintly on an X-ray. It seems that the symptoms are similar for sprains, that is swelling and tenderness around the injured area. Apparently Rupert was playing rugby the previous day and went off then saying that his arm felt peculiar, so it's impossible from this distance to say exactly what occurred and which incident was the cause of the injury. Happily there were no long term problems as far as the injury was concerned."

"Initially Rupert didn't understand that a 'break' would be important enough to warrant it becoming a police matter leading to further action, nor the potentially serious position you were in now. So with this conundrum your lad came up with a good idea and suggested that he complete and sign an affidavit concerning the events of that day. That's what we have been doing today. Through his friend who lives nearby, he located a solicitor and for a £500 fee, which he paid for, the affidavit was completed. An affidavit is a verified statement meaning it is under oath on penalty of perjury, and this serves as evidence to its veracity and is required for court proceedings. In this case it was taken as a witness affidavit. It relates the events in brief, connects with the game the previous day but states categorically that he didn't believe that your actions were deliberate and that you just tripped over the doorstep, fell over and pushed him to the ground. He confirms that he has no intention of bringing any action against you for this accident."

She paused as Sebastian was following every word.

"So armed with this statement I contacted the Regional Approvals Chairman and in fact went over to see her. By that time she had also received news from the Lib Dem HQ that any complaint against you has been lifted. The narrative on the Russia affair has been changed so that it in no way impairs your ability to raise that issue or to stand as a candidate. So you have a clean record; thanks, I would say, to your own work with Tim Beaumond and your son's knowledge of the law.

The Approvals Committee is satisfied that they have a document which shows the matter has been properly investigated and resolved. However they do ask that perhaps you would now complete the application form, accurately this time! In the meantime they have accepted a copy of the presentation you made plus a minute of our Executive considering the matter. I am awaiting the email confirmation but I will be formally asking the committee to lift your suspension tonight. This incident is now closed! So well done Sebastian but can we now get back to fighting this election please? Shall we be seeing you tonight at the completion of the Executive?"

Sebastian returned to work that afternoon and managed to compose himself. Everything had been resolved.

He now had to shake himself in that realisation and get on to build the campaign. He called Sylvia to give her the good news and she told him that in the morning's post they had received a cheque from Dr Singh of £500 payable to Lib Dems; it just said 'Good Luck – thanks for your help in the past.'

He rang Tim to remind him that the deadline for submission of nomination papers was Thursday 9th April at 4pm; theirs and the agent's had been completed, but somebody had to ensure the new candidates had collected signatures of eligible voters and they were cutting this pretty fine!" Tim replied that they had sufficient people in the office to sign the forms when Edna had checked their CVs and that he would take them to the District Council offices himself... Aware that he had been a bit lax in keeping her informed before, Sebastian also called Edna to keep her in the loop.

CHAPTER SEVEN – Wednesday Evening – 29 days to go

Edna called Sebastian at 6.30 pm and who told him that she had had a meeting with the two new candidates and gone through Lib Dem policy in broad terms, just to ensure that they were aware of national policy and to be clear that they did not disagree with the core principles.

"That's good, thank you Edna, but I have just had a call from our existing Lib Dem District Councillor John Laver. If you remember we discussed the Charlie Hebdo affair and he said then that he believed if we did show 'ethnic' tendencies it might embolden and encourage UKIP support in the area. He said as much just now with regard to the two new candidates. I told him that we would not be limited in whom we took in as District Councillors because of what UKIP might or might not think, that both of them were highly qualified and would broaden our expertise to enable us to be more effectively represented on the Council, but that I hoped he would be fair minded and give them a fair chance. I asked him to think about that, but it might mean, Edna, that we have to reconsider who will stand in which ward, but I hope it won't come to that!

Before the meeting he had a quick word with the Treasurer, Norman Dodgson. They added up the likely finances that had been agreed or committed to the fighting fund.

Tim Holland had spent the day chasing potential wealthy donors in the East Midlands and had achieved promises of £500 on the basis that this seat might be winnable. Donations in response to the latest Focus appeal amounted to: £250, from individual donors: Dr Singh £500, Mohamed Rahmam and group £1,000, James Smith the Landlord had paid for the shop Insurance £500, Euro Group firms £1,500 and another £750, that gave a grand total of £5000 - well above the target of £3,000. Furthermore Lib Dem HQ was running a scheme whereby all additional funds received would be doubled by an anonymous donor. Norman thought it would be too difficult to explain the 'forgiveness' of the shop insurance so they would be in line for an additional £4,500. Together with their current meagre cash reserves the addition of £9,000 cash would be enough to fight the national campaign. If they could make a case to get "winnable seat status' that would give them further funding. Norman declared himself willing to support the national campaign as well as the local District Council elections!

They lodged an immediate claim for matched funding and although the deadline was two days ago they had taken the precaution of advising Head Office that their claim would be delayed and had received approval for late submission. With Edna Leggs in the chair, the meeting started later than planned and they got to work on a shortened agenda.

Sebastian now issued a suggested councillor allocation, in practice he found that due to the Boundary Commission redrafting into three seat wards this allowed him greater flexibility. Instead of him and Tim sharing one ward, he suggested Tim for an adjacent ward the one containing the Library which had been one of his successful projects. The 'Green deal' would also be in a three seat ward. Finally Edna was asked to stand yet again and had agreed to do so.

The others were paper candidates allocated to single seat wards where Lib Dems had not been active on the fringes of home territory around Middleton. Although not expected to win, these seats would be contested and any latest support could be gauged.

With fourteen candidates plus the 'Green Deal'" Sebastian hoped to win eleven seats, up from the current five. Then there would be no overall control on the District Council if, as expected, Labour made inroads elsewhere. That would put Lib Dems in a powerful position to claim or influence committee chairmanships.

Some of the district councillor candidates agreed to stand for Middleton Town Council and the number was made up by family members and close friends. It was hoped they could gain control in order to press for the introduction of a neighbourhood plan for the area, this would give them rights to development land tax allowing them to spend on local roadways improvements like better access or car parking arrangements. They put up eight candidates for the fifteen seat Town Council.

Sebastian was called out of the meeting on an urgent phone call. The discussion on the topics to use in the Focus and on the doorstep was continued without him.

"Hello? Is that Mr Edwards?" Sebastian confirmed, "I have some news for you! You know that there was some rumour earlier that the sitting MP might defect to UKIP?"

"Yes I had heard that, there was a report in the national press I believe?"

"Let me introduce myself I am one of your Focus deliverers, not quite a member of Lib Dems but a supporter, I live in Ogthorpe Ward. It's mostly Tory. Well I was approached earlier in the week by someone I play golf with and he asked me if I would mind putting a signature to something. I agreed and he called around at my home later on with some papers which he needed to complete to stand as a candidate. I said it was strange him coming to me and he then explained that only the proposer and seconder would be mentioned in the press. I hope that's right by the way Mr Edwards?"

"No that's not right" said Sebastian. "Although the other signatures, eight I think, really just confirm that he is who he says. However all ten names will be published on the handbill attached to every polling station in that ward – I am sorry but that's the rule! Who was it anyway?"

"Chris Walmsley."

"Ah you mean the person who spoke on Andrew Laws' behalf at their executive meeting when they were considering deselecting him?"

"Yes that's him!"

"Well I am not surprised. Don't worry there's no harm done to us."

"Well that's a relief because having said I would sign I could hardly go back on my word; he saw me hesitating and out poured out the whole story. It was really about how Chris Walmsley felt nearer to UKIP Policy than Tory policy, how he saw both Cameron and Clegg as professional politicians, how Europe was a disaster and finally was very annoyed by the Tory Committee locally hounding the MP. Finally he had just 'had it' and decided to leap before he himself was pushed out, so he was standing as a district councillor and was coming to me as a fair minded person as his own circle of political friends had mostly turned their backs on him! I tried to find out how many other defectors there might be, but he immediately clammed up, thanked me and left with my signature!"

Sebastian thanked him for this information and asked him to call back if he could remember anything else of interest. He re-joined the meeting and immediately asked to speak and gave a brief summary of the phone call.

There was a stir of interest. Several members questioned whether Chris Walmsley and colleague would do this on their own and wondered how many more candidates there might be. Tim suggested that possibly it was a 'pilot,' that is a couple of known councillors breaking away to UKIP to test the electoral water. If they were elected then the MP would have a ready base from which to launch his own switch. All agreed to try to pick up more information. Lists of persons nominated were due to be published on Friday 10th April.

Sebastian explained that new candidates would be asked to work within a team because he felt they would not be able to handle questions from the public. The target was to canvass about 40 homes per person per night and the meeting ended with each person quickly going through their own key tasks so that everything would be co-ordinated.

Sebastian announced, "So from here on it it's canvassing all the way; you'll mostly go in groups of three, organise your exact areas, get the computer sheets every two days and hand in the completed sheets then. No one can canvass every night but please make sure that there are always two of your group there. Do left and right sides of the street together it's far the quickest way. Stakeboard team please main roads first this weekend? Lesser sites after that! Report back any offers of help such as putting up a poster or telling on the day and identify anyone needing a postal vote-; last day for that is 21st April.

I know we are being hammered in the Polls but let's hope there will be a bounce back in support for us soon! Good Luck I'll be dropping round when I can until I can work at it full time, you'll appreciate that till then its evenings only for me, but many of you have the same problem. Do your best that's all I ask!"

Again Sebastian reached home exhausted.

CHAPTER EIGHT – Thursday – 28 days to go

Sebastian had arranged for his son Rupert to help out in the office and then later come out canvassing with him. He was not going to be available from Friday through to Monday lunchtime, so Sebastian left a message with Edna suggesting he drop by for supper at Sebastian's house that night. Edna called Sylvia to confirm the arrangements for 7.30pm that evening.

Sebastian worked all day to complete the Area Management Accounts and deal with emails from the Russian company. He had only been able to get off two weeks off and, like most other candidates he had to work at his regular job, coming alive to his 'second job' in the evenings, at weekends and during the last two weeks. From now on he would canvass for two hours daily increased to three hours at the weekend. The canvass returns, in effect bar coded historical canvassing records would be input into the database at HQ. This would update the latest voting profile and identify those houses where people were out which would have to be revisited. So before his son arrived he had slipped out of the house and had visited some thirty houses and just making it back home by 7.30 pm.

He was apprehensive about meeting his son again; he wasn't sure how he would take to Sylvia. He didn't want to rush things or dwell on the missed years which he was sometimes prone to do, nor did he wish to overstate his successes or underrate his failures.

He had suggested that his wife cook her favourite curry, in fact two curries, one mild and the other spicier. In case Rupert didn't like curry at all they also had a beef pie. Sebastian arrived back just as a Jaguar XF Type was pulling up...

Sebastian was shocked, it could have been his wife's brother standing before him, and the similarity was uncanny. It could only be Rupert, but he was far taller than Sebastian around 6ft. 4in. and athletically built.

He got out of the car and immediately held out his hand, "Hello Dad, long time no see eh? Well I did leave a note saying 'Hope to see you again soon'! Remember that?"

"Yes I do remember! Indeed I still have that note! Sorry about landing you in it with Enda but we can go through that later. Come along in and meet Sylvia, she's Indian and has prepared a special dinner for you! I hope you like curry?"

"Yes of course, that will be fine thanks."

It was a modest house with two bedrooms, outside the small lawn and a flower bed were immaculately kept, the hollyhocks beside the bay window were just starting to appear. They went in and Sylvia met them inside dressed in her best sari.

"Nice to meet you – Sebastian told something about you in the time before the..." and her voice tailed off.

There was a moment's pause and Sebastian steered the conversation by asking what Rupert was hoping to learn from helping the Lib Dems here in Middleton.

Before he answered his father's question, Rupert gave his account of how they had lost contact and although when he was eighteen he had first tried to track him down he had been unable to do so, his mother had even forgotten the details of the company where he worked. He had then seen the headlines about the Russian trip and Ukraine peace talks, indicating that he was a Liberal Democrat prospective MP. It was then easy to get the information he needed from the constituency details on the website.

"So as I am writing the thesis on 'Why voter turnout at local elections is so poor!' I thought perhaps I should gain some experience at the 'coal face' as they call it. I thought at the same time to make contact with you!"

Sylvia interjected, "Now come on Sebastian, offer your guest a drink" and then disappeared into the kitchen.

"Yes, yes what would you like a beer or a whisky perhaps?

"Beer's fine thanks!"

"Well that's good. I am very glad that you did look us up" Sebastian continued.   "Well do you want me to give you some background information?. We do know however that it is partly connected to four key factors: first is the historical pattern – people get used to voting in the area, so it becomes the 'norm'; second is the socio-economic background, wealthier people tend to be more interested and involved; third is related to the age group, it's known that older people tend to be more likely to vote - but only a third of 18-30 year olds will vote in May!"

Sylvia came in with the food, twenty or so dishes, curry, rice, sauces and side dishes, mild to hot. "Now let's have a break from all that, Rupert tell us all about yourself."

"Well nothing much to say really, since we went back to live with Grandpa we have been living in Liverpool in the same house. I continued at the prep school and then went on to Dad's old boarding school; I obtained good results and for a gap year I worked my way around the world but with stop offs in Egypt and India. I then got a place at Oxford to read PPE Politics Philosophy and Economics. I got a First and decided after a time to take a master's degree which I am doing now and for this I have to prepare a thesis. That's it really!" He stopped abruptly.

There was silence for a moment. Sebastian asked "..and sports, you were good at sports as I remember that?"

"Let me tell you about the curries" Sylvia said and gave a summary of what was available.

Rupert turned to Sebastian and said "Dad did you ever try to make contact with us, we never received a post card, Christmas card, nothing! Nothing at all, in over fifteen years? Dad, nothing!"

Sebastian did not, could not, reply but they were both looking at him, Sylvia looked apprehensive. Sebastian knew that he had to answer; it was the question that he had dreaded most for all those years. How was he going to explain that the pain was so great all he could do was to blot it out completely?

He got up from the table and went to a cupboard in the corner. He searched for a minute and retrieved an envelope with Rupert's name on it. He handed it to him. "Maybe this will explain. I wrote it in the weeks after you left. Perhaps when you have had time to read it, no, no! Not now!" as Rupert moved to open the envelope, "we can talk about it some more?"

Sylvia got up and walked to the bureau above which was a large printed calendar showing one month at a time. Saying nothing she handed it to Rupert.

"Why what's this?" then Rupert began to turn over the pages, he stopped then turned a few more. "So you had not forgotten our birthdays!"

Sebastian said nothing for a moment, he twiddled the signet ring on his finger and Sylvia knew that was under stress.

Finally he cleared his throat and managed to say "I am very grateful for what you did with Edna signing that affidavit, it made all the difference you know. I felt I had to explain all the matters I had skimmed over in my CV when putting up as a candidate. You understand that politics can be a very vicious place; certain people will delight in dragging you down.

What happened to you all those years ago could even now have gone against me, enough to wipe out my political career. I could have warned you of what Edna was going to ask you but I think they preferred to have it from you before there was any question of us conferring. I'll give you a cheque for the costs."

"No don't worry about that, call it a deposit for helping me with the thesis!" Sebastian nodded eating his curry with a fork, and then Rupert seemed to brighten up. "So how did you two meet?"

Sebastian replied. "Well it was long ago, sometime after your mother" he was going to say 'walked out' but checked himself but left a slight pause, "err left and I was working for this charity. I only saw Sylvia for a few minutes then, but a year later she had joined the same company. One day she saw me looking at a holiday tour guide to India and offered some good advice. Eventually she became my secretary and helped me on one particular project, thereafter we got together and here we are now!"

To Sebastian's surprise Sylvia continued "The charity was set up to look after Asian women who suffer abuse due to arranged marriages. I had to cut myself off from my family, had any of them known where I was – then I would not have been safe. So I took a new name, Sylvia. We've never actually got married because of the publicity; even now I hate being photographed and worry about a picture getting into the local paper."

"Ah I see!" said Rupert "that explains why the people in the Lib Dem office knew nothing about you at all. Edna was the only one to have met you and that for a bare two minutes!"

They all continued eating for a few minutes then Sebastian said casually. "That's a nice car you have!"

"Yes, it's an XF Jaguar; nice car".

"Thought so" said Sebastian. "Well at least Will Jefferies, to his credit, appears to have kept to his side of the bargain!"

"What was that?" asked Rupert.

"That you and Alexander would inherit all his money after his wife and daughter were provided for. I suppose he died a wealthy man!"

"Oh no! Not at all!   Over the years he had transferred the maximum he was allowed under the inheritance tax rules and then just eight years ago he transferred over to us some properties in London, each had a hefty mortgage it must be said, but the mortgage cost was covered by the rental income, so it was very carefully planned. After ten years the mortgage has been paid off and there was no liability to inheritance tax. The values of the London properties have of course since rocketed. So with mortgage all paid off, that gives both of us a sizeable rental income. At the same time he passed on properties to us, the house passed to Grandma Jefferies with just enough capital to provide for the outgoings."

Sebastian interjected; "So that was the deal! He told me that he would tell the police that I had broken your arm in a fight; that he would no longer provide for your fees, nor would you inherit any of his money which he said he intended to give to the Liverpool Racecourse where he was a regular attender! And he was quite clear – the rule was to be strict, absolutely no communication of any kind with you! Nothing, not a phone call, not a card, not a letter."

Sebastian felt relieved that he had been able to tell the whole side of his story. Rupert thought for a bit and said "So you took him at his word did you?"

Sebastian said "Yes I did, and I thought when I wrote that letter to you twenty days later that it was the worst deal I ever made in my life. I was going bust and I traded you in, that's what it comes to."

Sylvia was on the verge of tears.

Rupert said "Grandpa Will Jefferies never spoke of you again, neither good nor bad; he would just change the subject no matter how hard we pressed for an explanation!"

They finished the meal in silence. Soon Rupert made his excuses and left, picking up the envelope on the way.

"I'll drop in the office tomorrow Dad for a bit just to help out, I think the folding machine has broken down so I agreed to fold the next Focus. I have to be off home for the weekend. What say I come back on Monday and you can take me canvassing? Right? See you at the office at 5.30 then! Maybe you can continue with your analysis of the reasons affecting voting intentions? You owe me one more of your four 'key' factors' I think?"

"Bye Sylvia! Thanks for the curry – lovely stuff!"   And he was gone.

Sebastian helped Sylvia tidy away the food and gave her a big hug. "Thanks for your support!"

Sebastian felt that as though he had been to confession! Now at least it was all in the open and up to his son to either accept or reject him. He had no doubt that Rupert would discuss the matter with his mother and Alexander who had always, as far as Sebastian could see, taken a tougher line than Rupert on both the Belfast Safe House matter and his ostensible career failure.

Sebastian was so tired that he had to sit down making an excuse that he wanted to watch the TV news. He felt worn out, he was losing weight and making too many trips to the loo. He knew something was wrong.

CHAPTER NINE - Friday - 27 days to go

Sebastian continued work at his company offices but at lunchtime called Tim Holland.

"Look" Tim, "we have this major problem with car parking and I think we have to link the issues together to make our case better. You know we have agreed to an allocation of 300 more houses near Middleton and I think planning might be granted soon for about 50 of them. That might get the Town Council £25,000 to £50,000 income from this development land tax but this would nearly double if it were within a proper Neighbourhood Plan. You know we have been pushing and failing to get the Town Council to move on this which is why we are putting up party candidates. What I suggest we do is to link this with something concrete.

Also we have this horrendous car parking problem, what I suggest we do is to run our own mini-referendum alongside the elections. Of course such a mini-referendum would not be official but it would test out local interest in the need to review car parking, providing some residential parking zones as well as suggesting that it might be possible to acquire land for further car parking through the CIL portion that the town is entitled to. What do you think Tim? You have gone all silent on me? Hello Tim?"

"Yes, could be done, sort of running in parallel? What collecting votes near the polling booths?"

"Yes that's right, not interfering with that process, but the whole point is that it's a time when people's attention is drawn to making changes. So the idea is that we link Lib Dems aims to improve car parking and possibly increasing capacity, and work this in through a new neighbourhood plan and benefit from the higher rate CIL tax. Could we do that? It would mean a lot more work, extra leaflets getting, all the prospective Town Councillors involved!"

"Hmm, let me think now, I suppose you are going to ask someone like me to get on and do it?"

"Yes that's right! Or somebody very remarkably similar to yourself – intelligent, astute, approachable!"

"OK, OK I get the message. Let me think about it, I can't remember exactly who we decided to ask to stand! I think Edna is on? Let me sound this out and come back to you. You are right in one respect, this is the first time we will have politicised the Town Council and there could well be a reaction against us. On the other hand they have been very slow to even understand the Localism Act which gave them new powers. This would certainly crystalize things!"

"Ok, Tim, see you tonight at the office to discuss. Must go! My sandwich is getting cold."

Sebastian completed his work for the day, then after a snack went to the Lib Dem office at 5.30 pm. Edna and Tim and a couple of others were in deep discussion. Edna paused whilst he joined the group.

"Well!" she said, "This, Sebastian, is much more the sort of initiative we are looking for from you, good thinking! Let's draw up a radical plan of targets for the town and get this on the road as quickly as we can. Could we do a special Focus? Tim, will you get hold of the basic rules on car parking zones. I've asked John Laver to get me the District Council view of the uses of CIL and exactly what has so far been logged against it. I don't believe the Town Council has made a list of expenditure targets as the CIL will mainly affect new housing developments and at present we have no agreed planning consents for our allocation."

"Ok let's go with this – can we get a Focus out for Saturday afternoon please before anyone else grabs the initiative!"

Sebastian left them to it and went to find his canvassing team of Mohammed Rahman and Johnathan Thomas for his two hour stint.

On getting home Sebastian printed off from the District Council's web site the list of 'persons nominated' as candidates which had been published at 4 pm. Sebastian was surprised, the number of UKIP candidates was relatively small at five and these were spread mostly in prime Tory territory with just one in Middleton. In addition to the fifteen seats which they held, Labour had ten more nominees, so were contesting twenty-five seats but, because some of these were in three seat wards, they covered almost 30 seats. Tories had thirty-five candidates and covered everywhere except one core labour three seat ward and they fielded only two candidates in the Lib Dem target seats. There were three Greens and six Independents.

For the General Election there were just the three main party candidates, Tory, Labour and Lib Dem, plus one local independent from the 'Lord Trash Party.' He prepared a spreadsheet of candidates by wards and parties and sent it to all key members.

Sebastian and the team now had to adjust the different ward Focuses to take account of the opposition.

They had already prepared the key ward issues, so within an hour or so dummy proofs were available via email. Sebastian had a late night working with the Focus team checking a rechecking the spelling and presentation.

He reviewed the artwork and text for the free constituency leaflet.

CHAPTER TEN - Saturday and Sunday - 26 & 25 days to go

Sebastian worked through the canvass returns to see whether voters were turning in favour or against the party. In truth they had not much to go on despite appearances.

Although Lib Dems now held five District Council seats and one County Council seat, before 2011 they had had only three District seats and before that just one intermittently, so they couldn't track residents' voting patterns very far back. The County Council elections helped since that seat covered two of the existing District seats so they could build up a coherent voting pattern there, but for apart from those targeted areas, they had almost no voting history.

The rest of the morning Sebastian joined the stake-board crew. It was exhausting work dragging the boards out of the car and firmly affixing them to fences or hammering them into the ground but by mid-afternoon they had put up thirty in prominent positions. He got back just in time for the Grand National and collapsed into a chair.

Then back at 5 pm to the Lib Dem office to look through the canvass returns and work on press releases with Tim.

At 6 pm the office was called by the Tory Agent. He made two complaints in a very gentlemanly way. Firstly someone in a Lib Dem key ward had been spray painting Tory stake-boards and four were missing altogether. Secondly they had already received copies of the mini referendum on the car parking issue. They pointed out that although it was not strictly speaking electoral material, it did have the Lib Dem Office address on it and therefore, by the rules, it would be included as if it were. Sebastian agreed to look into these points.

He called Edna and they agreed to have a word with the candidates in the ward affected and asked them to cool it and to make that there were no further complaints; Sebastian suspected that this was just over-enthusiasm on the part of new members.

As for the mini-referendum, it was agreed to stop all deliveries immediately, all copies with deliverers were recalled and the print run done again attributed correctly.

Sunday morning was time off but the rest of the day was largely a repeat of Saturday.

CHAPTER ELEVEN - Monday - 24 days to go

Sebastian visited the hospital for the endoscopy which had been booked by his doctor, this included a biopsy. It was unpleasant and meant that afterwards he could hardly speak; the biopsy would take several days to analyse, the consultant would receive a report the following week, that would be reviewed by the 'team' the week after and then he would receive a date for a consultation.

He went back to work and met Rupert as arranged at 5.30 pm together with the two others standing in the same ward, Mohammed Rahman and Jonathan Thomas. This was the canvassing team. Initially Sebastian and Johnathan led off, two taking the left hand side of the street, one on the right. As these were terraced houses if anyone had a question they couldn't answer, Sebastian was within earshot and came running.

So Rupert was kept busy as the junior and they managed to cover three complete streets; leaving a leaflet with the candidates' names and photos prominently shown, at houses where no-one answered the door. After a while they paused, the work was quite tiring and they went into a local pub. It also gave Sebastian the opportunity to introduce his son to the two candidates,

Sebastian summed up their role. To the people we call on we are the only visible representatives of the politicians who claim to be running the country, so we are fair game for any questions relating to Government as a whole!. Rupert jumped in before Sebastian could continue. "Dad you said on Thursday that there were four things that influence the voter turnout. We went through the first three; Historical - the cultural norm to vote regularly as an obligation; Wealth of individuals – richer are more likely to vote; Age older people are more likely to vote if they can! So what's the fourth?"

"The fourth" Sebastian explained "is passion!"

"Whose passion?" Rupert asked clearly confused.

"Either the passion of the candidates or the passionate belief of the residents in some particular matter!"

"This is why it's so important for the candidates themselves to canvass and get out and meet the voters. It's a sort of bond between the candidate and the voter. That explains why we use very few people canvassing who are not themselves candidates. It's like the candidates have the power of 5 to 1 to convert votes compared to somebody canvassing on their behalf! The other passion is where a resident attaches himself to something which he thinks important –keeping open a hospital or a play area or, as in our case the car parking and of course the library. It's our job to connect with the public and to put forward sensible proposals which have the same effect; it could be cheaper housing, lower taxes, more motorways or whatever."

"In other words passion has a lot to do with increasing voter turnout! It may be that all a canvasser says at most houses is 'Are you voting again for us Mrs Smith' but that's what it means! OK? You're the indispensable part of that chain, canvassing brings key issues to the attention of the voters and voters in turn express their views!"

"Alright let's get back to work and see if we can finish the next two streets in an hour, OK everyone! I can't do tomorrow it's the final District Council meeting. See you Wednesday. OK thanks everyone!" Then aside, "Oh Rupert! Just a minute! Are you going to help in the office tomorrow? OK! I'll see you same time same place on Wednesday! Did you have a chance to chat with the family? Maybe we can pick this up on Wednesday?"

CHAPTER TWELVE - Tuesday - 23 days to go

Sebastian still had to carry with his day job so returned to the RKW office.

At lunchtime he phoned through to Tim to find out how the car parking mini-referendum was going.

Tim replied "Terrific it has at last galvanised local thought and is allowing us to promote ourselves for the town council".

Then he had a word with Edna. "Office is fine and all printing is on course but we have had initial feedback that our association with windfarms and suggested links to the Green Party are causing problems in the country wards." Sebastian reminded her that he and Tim and the others would be required at the District Council tonight for the last meeting before the election.

He was at the District Council's Chamber for 5.00 pm and briefly talked through with colleagues the effect of the introduction of a 'Combined Authority', this was indeed devolution on the doorstep. The creation of a new legal body had been proposed combining elements of Derby, Derbyshire, Nottingham and Nottinghamshire to argue for power and resources from the government. The other Lib Dem councillors knew this would be a tricky matter as Sebastian had openly criticised that bit of Lib Dem policy but now here it was.

He said "Hmmm, seems I was caught out here. It's likely to encourage councils to make claims not to support and fund what they were intending to do, but now to do things simply because the money's there I don't see that we should pass over something which might help in the development of this area and at our end of the district there are too few jobs as it stands. So I think we have to support this? Right? All Agree!"

The Lib Dems supported the move. Almost all other government departments were in 'close down' as the District was beginning to move into 'purdah' and would shortly defer all decisions until after the elections.

Sebastian thought he must be missing something but what? Was he getting too old for the job? Was he too immersed in his own little patch that he couldn't see the broader picture? He was getting tired again; was he losing concentration? He nervously twiddled the signet ring on his finger.

CHAPTER THIRTEEN - Wednesday to Friday - 22-20 days to go

As agreed Sebastian met Rupert at 5.30 pm. He asked the others to get on with canvassing and that they would catch them up soon.

"Did you have a chat with Alexander and your mum when you arrived back? How did they take it?"

"Take what Dad?"

"Well the news of my standing in the election and so on!"

"Fine!"

"So they didn't say anything?"

"No! Not much. They both said 'wish him luck' and that was it! In fact I think Grandma Jefferies was more affected, I gather she was always more sympathetic to you than Grandpa but felt she could never say anything; she asked particularly that I give you this! Its soda bread which I think you like, it's after a recipe you brought back from Belfast!"

Sebastian froze for a moment. "Please thank her – I will enjoy this!"

"Now I just wanted to complete some information for you regarding voter turnout, which you will need for your thesis. The turnout figures are in fact much worse than they look. What you have is the percentage of registered voters voting. In some areas up to 40% only are registered to vote, I checked up on this with the officers responsible. There's a whole raft of reasons why people are not registered to vote but sometimes people just switch off and refuse to get involved. Most of this applies to the poorer areas but there's no uniform pattern. So you had better go over any data you use and check out the base lines. I suggest you will need a couple of days' research at a District Council with an officer usually called 'democratic services' or something but don't try to do that until these elections are over of you'll get short shrift and be sent packing!"

"Now let's go and catch up the others. On this round we're going into the ethnic heartland and I want to be there to support our man Mohammed. Ready to go? OK, let's do it!"

Thursday followed the same pattern of canvassing as before. On Friday Sebastian went through the manifesto and drafted suggested canvassing chatter on the doorstep.

By this time Sebastian was using the second bedroom as his study to work from home. He decided to email all canvassers to focus doorstep canvassing on simple issues.

'Firstly nationally Lib Dems are good coalition partners, secondly for District Council lack of affordable houses and saving the library; and thirdly for Middleton Town Council traffic problems and the start of the neighbourhood plan'.

He told them that 'Right now the political spectrum is splintering and party loyalties are collapsing, this mean even if the person says how they might vote nationally you might still press for the local vote, it's very likely now that they will split that vote. Encourage them to do so, if they wish!'

Canvassers were however to build into their 'spiel' any other Lib Dem policies they thought appropriate. He asked for anyone disagreeing with any points to come back immediately and he attached the manifestos summary sheet.

He emailed some suggestions for the next Focus to Tim.

CHAPTER FOURTEEN - Saturday and Sunday - 19/18 days to go

Sebastian started off at home on his PC reviewing his emails. He was relieved to see from an internal Lib Dem press release that there was good news on the employment front. He read

 "New figures show that the rate of employment is at a new record high of 73.4 per cent".

The number of jobs created increased by 248,000 in the last three months and in that period youth unemployment fell by 21,000 (and 151,000 over the whole year).

 Liberal Democrat Business Secretary Vince Cable *said:*
"Employment levels have hit new records today, with almost three quarter of working aged people now in work.

"Youth unemployment has continued to fall over the year and our successful apprenticeship programme, which the Lib Dems have prioritised in government, will help that improve yet further.

"With wages now rising continuously faster than inflation, living standards are rising too.

"The role of the Liberal Democrats in government has been crucial to promoting economic stability and a strong recovery. And the work I have led to deal with abuses in zero hour contracts and strengthening the national minimum wage will help ensure the recovery is also fair."

He emailed this to the Focus team with the suggestion that they use it as a headline with a start of AT LAST! Sebastian could see that it was really six months too late, people were in one particular mind-set now and he doubted much would change. It was anyhow GOOD NEWS and should be used.

He was told that his son had again gone home on Friday but would be back on Monday.

Canvassing continued as before on Saturday and Sunday. As Sebastian was also parliamentary candidate he tried to check off the returns coming in from each of the canvassing groups.

He made a summary for use at later meetings of face to face canvassing feedback under main issues.

Sebastian slammed down his first in the table in frustration as he felt Lib Dems were simply not properly positioned to take advantage of this latest Tory disarray which UKIP seemed not to have noticed, in its attempt to cover all policies he thought it had forgotten its core objective? The only hope was that Lib Dems could achieve a minimum of thirty-five seats. Well no good wasting time he thought, 'let's get out and canvass!'

Sylvia popped her head round the door "Having a tough day then Seb!"

"Yes you could say that – it's just not swinging our way right now!"

Sebastian felt very tired and returned home in the early afternoon. He knew that something was wrong. He rested up on the Sunday morning and only did a couple of hours of canvassing that afternoon, then went into the office for a meeting of key people, Edna, Tim, Johnathon and Madge.

He started reorganising the national election side of things; he had received notification of the matched funding from Lib Dem HQ.

He had to authorise the final proof of his leaflet for the general election. It had been radically changed and the printers had been alerted; it was now linked in to the web site so that further information was directly available and a free CD was available to any resident. This had to be sent out immediately to ensure delivery before the postal vote forms were posted by the District which acted as the returning officer.

New Stakeboards were purchased and a large wall site in the centre of Middleton was rented, suitable for a banner poster. This was to be placed showing Sebastian at the head of his team of potential Councillors and permission was being sought to deploy other banners in conspicuous places in the town. Madge had volunteered to do this and spent the afternoon tracking members' addresses along the main road to gain maximum affect. These might be late but the cumulative effect could be that of momentum. Showing more and more and more sites displaying either the orange diamond with his name and the bird – 'winning here' or posters with his face.

Sebastian knew he should have pushed all this several days ago. He returned home tired.

CHAPTER FIFTEEN - Monday to Thursday - 17-14 days to go

On Monday afternoon Sebastian had to attend a regular monthly financial meeting in London for RKW. He arrived back home tired and late.

On Tuesday he carried out canvassing again with his son and the rest of the team.

On Wednesday at work he received a mysterious phone call from the Russian company Director Jeffrey Pardoe but it was garbled and Sebastian was unable to understand it. It sounded as though he was in some trouble. Sebastian asked him to call back or email but he heard nothing. Jeffrey Pardoe was a resourceful fellow and it would have taken something of major importance for him to call direct, their usual form of communication was email. Sebastian emailed asking Jeffrey to contact him urgently.

When he had not replied in a couple of hours, Sebastian called the company head office and notified the HR department head John Avis whom he knew well, that there might be some trouble. He called the Russian MD Dmitri Davidoff alerting him to the broken call and asked if he could contact other operational staff to find out what might be wrong and if there were any particular ongoing negotiations which might be the cause of a problem.

For the moment it was a worry. When Sebastian had taken over as Financial Director and Deputy MD of Siberian Minerals, part of the deal had been a substantial profit related bonus, any problems with repatriating profits to the UK would put that at risk. Similarly if the actual operation in Russia turned loss making he was unsure how far his employer would go to refinance the company; sanctions would in any case make that more difficult to do. He feared they might just let it sink. That would throw hundreds of employees out of work in Russia.

But there was also the worry about Jeffrey himself, he was Sebastian's eyes and ears over there, he reported back to Sebastian after every monthly meeting with full financial reports. He had become enmeshed with Siberian Minerals on the deal that they had struck a few years ago. Sebastian liked him and trusted him implicitly. Was it a problem of his personal safety?

In the evening he carried on canvassing as before and asked Rupert to drop over for supper 7.30 pm on Thursday as he had done the previous week and he agreed.

Sebastian and Sylvia greeted him warmly at the door. As they sat in the small front room having drinks, Rupert opened the conversation, "Well tell me what happened over these last years! How did you get out of the jam that you were in and how did you get into this political life?"

Sebastian went over his work for the charity, his eventual hiring as internal auditor, his promotion in the company, the Russian episode, further promotion, getting pulled in to the Lib Dems, setting up a branch, becoming elected a district councillor and various campaigns as he called them.

He was midway through the Charlie Hebdo affair when Sylvia called them both to eat.

They sat down and the conversation passed onto the work that Rupert had been doing in the office and the disagreement between Madge and Tim which Rupert frankly did not understand, but apparently they had fallen out over two or three issues, about the deliveries of the latest Focus and also some of the text which Madge had taken exception to for some reason. Rupert then proceeded to comment on Edna Leggs "She's a tremendous person and a very great supporter of yours despite your sometimes rather scary notions which catch them all by surprise!"

Then he suddenly slipped into a different mood. "You know Dad; it was quite a shock to the system on arrival to be interrogated in your office with no warning. Why did you do it?"

Sebastian was caught on this because he had imagined they had put that behind them at the first meeting, he repeated what he thought he had said earlier about wanting to hear his side of the story before there was any charge of conferring between them.

Rupert challenged "Yes I understand all that, but I wasn't just a witness was I? I was your son! Someone you'd not heard of for more than fifteen years and the first thing you can think of is how to clear your name?"

"Well" spluttered Sebastian "that's just how it happened, I dare say had you not said you were coming it wouldn't have been raised at all!"

"But I had, and instead of 'Rupert how are you, nice to see you again', I was put through a seventh degree inquisition about what happened more than a decade ago! All to help you explain something you did years ago! What would you have done if I had blamed you for the accident? Did you think of that? Chances are we would never ever have met?"

"No, no! That's not true I didn't mean that!" Said Sebastian, twiddling the ring on his finger. Sylvia was becoming upset as she vainly tried to interrupt and divert their attention back to their supper.

"But that's how it comes over, it was done for you, the same way as going into that scheme in Northern Ireland was for you, mother never wanted it did she? And when there was that fraud it's you that decided to leave and walk away from a very well paid job. Mother tried to argue against it but no it's You, and You. You and your bloody self-righteous view of the world. I think Mother is right, something got into your mind as a boy, pushed around by an uncaring father, left to your own devices and dreaming of the way things ought to be! How people ought to behave! But they don't work like that, and it's You and You."

Sebastian was shocked by such an unexpected onslaught, but he was in no mood to be walked over.

"You know you are absolutely right!" Sylvia tried to reach out a reassuring hand to him across the table but he didn't take it. "Totally correct!" said Sebastian.

"It's the first principle of life that I learned self-preservation! Your first duty is to preserve yourself because if you can't do that you can't protect or help anyone else and you become a drain on everyone. You are absolutely correct I was totally wrong ever to have thought that I could educate you expensively, but once I had made that decision I had to move ahead with it. That necessitated an additional income that's why we tried to run the guest house in Belfast, it was not for me, it was for us. And your interpretation of the fraud was quite wrong too, it was clear that my reported comments to the USA on the wisdom of their exaggerated redundancies meant that I was labelled as someone who would defy their rules. That's not how they worked, but I argued against those redundancies for the staff not for me! You see you know nothing!"

"But then that doesn't surprise me – the whole purpose of what we did was to give you a leg up in life to protect you from the realities. That's evidently been a success, so you have never had to take any difficult decisions in your life have you apart perhaps choosing the colour of your car? You sit and criticise but you know nothing! You have never felt the depths of despair."

"But of all of the family you were the one to whom I thought I would someday be able to explain it all. I thought there was a glimmer of an understanding, but no matter, nothing that happened was your fault and I made some serious mistakes. But to summarise it as You, You, You is something I will never accept!"

There was a frosty silence as they continued with the meal. Sebastian felt relieved, the first meeting had been too cosy; this time maybe we were really getting to grips with things.

Sebastian asked "How did your rugby playing go, you remember we used to discuss it a lot and later on I always imagined you dashing onto the pitch and scoring tries. Every time I watch the Six Nations cup I used to think of you."

"Well I made the school team but I wasn't of a high enough standard to play for the Varsity. I imagined you on the touch line cheering me on but then, of course, you weren't there!"

Sebastian quietly said "Well maybe you can show me some of those team photos and bring me up to date and perhaps I'll tell you more of my Russian escapade."

"Yes maybe, I'll work out tomorrow with Edna, and then as you suggest do some more research. I'll let you know how things go!" then Rupert made his excuses and left.

Sylvia looked at Sebastian but he seemed relaxed, "Maybe it has all helped to put your demons to rest!" she said.

"Perhaps it has and perhaps I will try to help you to do the same!"

CHAPTER SIXTEEN - Friday - 13 days to go

Sebastian took the evening off from political work. From Monday onwards he would be 'on vacation' and therefore able to spend the whole day based in the Lib Dem office. He was relieved because the effort required to carry two jobs was draining his energy away.

He contemplated his position, he needed to take stock before the final push and made a list of his key worries and objectives.

For the UK as a whole he was rather gloomy. He took the key leader from the Institute of CA's monthly magazine.

It said - **One thing business craves is certainty, The Conservatives promise continuity; however, the looming threat of an EU referendum in itself creates significant insecurity.**

Meanwhile, Labour's pledge of higher taxes on the wealthy, reversing the corporation tax rate and scrapping non-dom status has many sitting uncomfortably in their boardroom chairs

It looked as though there was going to be an increasingly bumpy road ahead. A Conservative win presaged more uncertainty over the EC, there was as yet no clue of exactly what decision making of importance the Conservatives aimed to bring back to the UK, nor was there the slightest evidence that the EC was prepared to negotiate anything. The Conservatives had no allies in Europe, no plan agreed by several members which was essential to making change. The EC didn't respond to a smash and grab principle. Even to think so, based perhaps on Thatcher's budget demand, was to misunderstand how the EC worked. Sebastian thought that the imminent treatment of Greece would prove that point.

The Greek government took power on the basis of a similar smash and grab defending its finances. So far they had got nothing and seemingly the more resistant the EC and troika became, the more they were determined that Greece should not avoid the restructuring demanded. In some ways then the UK would be better off if the Tories failed since the UK would no longer be in direct confrontation with the EC. Cameron had another similar blind spot on the internal devolution to Scotland and the Regions. He had promised to come forward with a plan for in effect "Devolution max" but it was clear that he had no plan at all on to how to 'renegotiate' internally or set up any sort of structure to do so. This had fuelled the SNP advance

It followed a pattern of the "Big Society" a half worked through philosophy which never took wings. Sebastian saw Cameron exactly as shown on TV, superficial and lacking the ability to think conceptually to any depth.

Sebastian, for those reasons, saw a Conservative victory as a potential disaster.

But was the Labour party any better placed? It's weakness lay in those thirty-five Scottish seats it held which were under imminent threat from SNP. If SNP took them then any chance of Labour having a majority on its own would be dashed. The SNP had veered strongly to the left, seemingly further left than the Labour party. Labour support was crumbling and being spread, pulled to the centre as a 'sensible party', but pulled to the left by SNP. That meant an end to the period of austerity, possibly falling back into recession, a fall in confidence in the £, and ultimately measures like higher taxation.

For sound reasons then Sebastian saw a Labour run coalition as a similar disaster.

He had no doubt that unless there was a real moderating influence from the Lib Dems in a future Coalition; the UK craft would lack a keel, without us Sebastian concluded gloomily 'the UK craft would very easily capsize'.

There was no sign of a Lib Dem 'bounce' in the polls for which he had hoped.

Most importantly of all, was he going to win this seat and how would it affect his lifestyle?

He knew it was odds against because his party was starting from a low position, third at the last general election. It was true that locally they had that secret of all ingredients 'momentum' and had increased membership and support dramatically but would it be enough to carry him past Labour and overtake the Tory despite that party's defections and the MP's personal problems?

He needed to get a handle on the expected local results. Sebastian had no idea if he was going to win!

PART SIX - All that glitters is not gold?

CHAPTER ONE - Monday - Countdown to the election continues

On Monday he just sat and relaxed in the bath for an hour as he began his new regime.

He was at last free from doing two jobs at once, he was technically on holiday from RKW his employer.

He had been booked in to see the consultant at 10 am to review the endoscopy and biopsy that were undertaken earlier and took Sylvia with him to Nottingham Hospital.

He was greeted by a Dr Cottee, small fifty something, informal person with bifocals.

"Well Mr Edwards, how are you feeling now, let me just see the parts affected. Hmm you have caused us some analytical problems, you know? Do you not remember me asking if you had been to the equator areas recently?"

"Why yes I do remember but I have not."

"Never?" Insisted Dr Cottee.

"Well only once about 6 or 7 years ago to Southern India just for a week or ten day holiday."

"So it seems that there you have picked up some infection to the abdominal area and that it has lain dormant and has now become a major problem for you. It took us quite some time to work it out. It is called Tropical Sprue. It was not until we matched the blood samples with the biopsy and the endoscopy that we could be sure. There are a whole host of illnesses like Coeliac's disease or even some types of cancer which could have the symptoms that you suggest, tiredness, stomach cramps, diarrhoea, loss of weight. But you will be relieved to hear that, of itself, if we have correctly diagnosed the problem, and we can never be entirely sure of that because one illness might overlay another, then the treatment for Tropical Sprue is relatively simple and the outcome is likely to be good, although you are advised never again to visit similar locations as it could recur. It's thought that it is caused by an infection of the small bowel by toxigenic strains of the coliform bacteria.

It was a common problem in the Second World War when there was an epidemic, which caused a sixth of all Allied casualties in the South East Asia area. Usually it is limited to the natives of that area and it's unusual to catch this in so short a visit there but it's quite possible.

You will need to take an antibiotic Tetracycline and a foliate vitamin B9 and B12 plus Iron Tablets for 6 months at least. Recovery will be quite rapid to begin with but you must maintain the treatment whatever you do! Is that understood Mr Edwards?"

"That's good then? You seem to have done some good work – thanks for that! Are there any side effects? It doesn't sound too serious then?"

"On the contrary Mr Edwards it is very serious, you have malabsorption of the food you eat that's why you have progressively lost weight. Your bowel is unable to take in the nutrients and if left untreated would sooner or later have resulted in your death. I understand that you have been having some discomfort for several months. You must learn to listen to your body more and not to take it for granted. Come and see me in one month's time, meanwhile under no circumstances must you cease taking the pills.

Take them with a glass of water at least one hour before or two hours after meals and make sure you eat plenty of fruit and nuts. There may be some side effects, it can make your skin more sensitive so limit your exposure to sunlight so wear protective clothing if you are in the sun."

Sebastian returned home and hugged Sylvia emotionally. It had been much better news than he had feared. He rushed round to the city centre chemist with the necessary prescription and immediately took the stated dose.

He knew these pills would become his constant travelling companion.

He felt relieved, he had been reluctant to admit it but he was terrified that it might have been cancer.

He returned to work at the political office at 12 o'clock and Sebastian sat there deep in thought - just 10 or so days to go!

After a few minutes he met Edna Leggs and Sebastian outlined to her what he suggested might be his new daily routine.

In the mornings he would go to the Lib Dem office at 10.am and deal with all the pressing issues raised the previous day, he would run through leaflets to be printed and check these off. He would take delivery of the posters and boards coming in and make sure all the outgoing leaflets for delivery were despatched to the helpers.

At 12 noon he would read through the canvassing returns of the previous day, identifying specific notes – like poster wanted here or some complaint picked up about public services and then spend a good thirty minutes inputting the canvass results into the PC. Although individual canvassers used their own interpretation of intensity of support for a political party, it was soon possible to pull out rough percentages of political voting intentions. Day by day this built up into a cumulative picture.

At lunchtime he would sit with Mrs Leggs and any other helpers and discuss any political manoeuvres by any party, how they should react and work out what to do about it.

At 2.30 pm he would begin to canvass in those areas where they did not expect to win District Council seats mostly in country areas or some of the larger villages hoping to pick up key members for the future. Generally he would pick off one village at a time. Day time canvassing resulted in fewer contacts as a good 50% were 'outs' but they were higher in quality, as those that were 'in' had generally more time available to discuss matters. For canvassing he usually wore his 'Contour Track ' shoes which were dark and his Berghaus jacket which whilst grey was, he felt, reasonably smart and so he could endure most changes in weather without returning to base. He worked straight through minor showers.

At 4.30 pm he was back in the office for tea and a rest or maybe visit important voters nearby or respond to specific residents' questions logged by canvassers.

At 5.00 pm he would start again in the winnable district seats usually with the other candidates. The key canvassing time was when the family was at home together. This finished usually at 7.00 or shortly after. Generally they finished canvassing when the residents took their supper!

Then back home for his own supper.

He would maintain this routine every single day. The target was to canvass every single household in these winnable seats that they had identified and as further afield as was possible.

Edna readily assented to this format which allowed her to stand down from manning the office in the mornings which she had done for weeks and it provided a structure for everyone else to link into as well.

So Sebastian started the process by clearing his desk for action. He entered the previous day's canvassing returns and looked at the backlog of queries left. The regime would start tomorrow.

He then considered the overall position of the campaign.

Sebastian felt that in many ways today, when, for the first time, he was able to work full time at getting elected and had taken time off from RKW to do this, was an anti-climax. He realised that most of the difficult decisions locally were already taken. The names, number and placing of candidates, the canvassing strategy and leaflet deliveries, siting of posters and even which key political themes to use were all being implemented. The political ship was on course and there was little he felt that could be done in dramatic terms to change direction either nationally or here in Middleton.

The national candidates were all declared and the national parties' policies were known. Of course stars like Nicola Sturgeon could hold their position because she had a coherent story to tell. This was anti Tory and anti-austerity and they had simply outflanked the Labour party. In doing so they had even claimed the Labour left wing heredity in Scotland.

Whilst the Natalie Bennett's Green message had faded; instead of their coherent Green policy they had simply turned sharply left but their story didn't resonate. It was clear that their brand could not stretch that far, their entry into mainstream politics looked likely to be a complete disaster.

UKIP's position was simple but, although it had gained momentum, its public discussions were inevitably weakened when its spokesmen were drawn out over other policies in which it had no interest. Sometimes it did make good points, such as SNP's gap in rhetoric between demanding more freedom to take over taxing income from oil which would, if applied at the referendum, have greatly reduced their budget and would have needed even tougher austerity. But none of the other parties gave UKIP the credit for raising an important point.

Sebastian was concerned that between the three main parties the NHS had become a sort of toy, each in turn making the wildest possible claims of billions in support. No-one seemed concerned as to how to make it more efficient. The root cause was a much higher expectation from the public about how each person should be treated. There was evidence that we, the public, were trying to see a doctor 50% more frequently than 10 years ago. Our expectation was that we would be treated for serious illnesses within weeks not months. But most people seemed to think that the latest re-organisation had not worked. It was a solution that in effect put the groups of medical GPs as customers of the hospitals. This meant them notionally 'paying' for the hospital services and this was the hospital's income. Perhaps it was logical and perhaps it had 'saved' numbers of non-medical administrators but no-one knew if it had actually made the savings suggested for it in financial terms nor if it was a better health service in medical clinical terms. Frankly no-one had a clue, so the easy way out was just to shower it with money. Sebastian thought that the NHS deserved a more rational approach, perhaps breaking it down into regions and making it politically answerable at that level might work.

The same thing had happened over the benefits system. For so many it had become a natural way of life, then it had become a right, then it was a norm and finally it had become a necessity around which the entire family depended for its primary income. From that point on it had become almost impossible to adjust it significantly. The spend had become totally out of balance with the money needed to cover it, there simply was no counterbalance to offset the need for spending! But it was almost impossible to launch any sort of debate on the issues without going into detail, which caused everyone to switch off. Nobody had much idea how the Universal Credit System would work, nor why such a complicated system would make any savings. Either the basic elements of the existing benefits allowances would be reduced or duplications in claims would be reduced. Everything was dependent on a system and if it failed the savings expected would disappear.

And about housing – Sebastian thought that the number of houses each party would build was rubbish. According to the Times on Tuesday (page 40) Cons would build 200,000 (starter homes) with a 20% discount for first time buyers under 40 who would also be able to buy housing association houses at discount. Labour would also build 200,000, LD 300,000 and UKIP 1,000,000 in 5 years. But 67% of housebuilders surveyed by Knight Frank said the maximum sustainable was 180,000. The idea seemed to be that CIL might be abolished and planning departments would be beefed up.

However brickies were earning £1000 per week, that's twice as much as the previous year, with 62% of companies waiting 2 months for bricks, and 25% waiting up to four months, with 10% waiting 6 to 8 months. The TV debates failed totally to get into any depth and it simply became a bidding exercise on who could say they would build more houses! Even if there was planning approval there was not enough land and not enough builders to build and not enough bricks in stock to supply the industry. The superficiality of the TV debates horrified Sebastian.

What Sebastian thought was needed was a National Housebuilding Corporation tasked with building 200,000 houses per annum with powers to buy land and develop it and, if necessary, override Local Planning Authorities.

Anyhow Sebastian thought there was little he could do about it from this position, it was, he thought, like watching a car accident in slow motion. He felt he was just a passenger, he could do nothing. But he knew it was steadily moving away from Lib Dems.

So whilst key issues remained untouched the TV channels became obsessed with who was going to form a Government with whom since, from the polls, there seemed no chance of any party having an overall majority.

In Sebastian's mind the TV rattled on about red lines and who would or would not share power with whom but, down at this level, it was just a problem of getting through the relevance of Lib Dems to the electorate here in Middleton, often using simple examples of what they did locally to support the national utterances.

By and large Sebastian realised that they had done pretty well locally He thought that generally, the district candidates had done well in selling the simple messages. They found that a large number of voters were more receptive to hearing what Lib Dems had done and might yet again do.

But then Sebastian looked at the canvassing returns in detail. To date they had visited 60% of houses in the targeted wards. Of course 30%-40% were 'outs' as it was never ever possible to have canvassers call when all the voters were in. From his returns Sebastian was reasonably sure that, if they were indicative of the actual vote, then most of those District seats would be won. They had, he felt, 30% to 45% of the vote in those wards. This was very encouraging.

But the Westminster seat was a different kettle of fish. There were whole blank areas where they hadn't managed to do any canvassing at all and where they had no District Council candidates. Here he felt that the voters might be as low as 10% to 15%, but that was higher than the national average of 9%. The canvas returns were full of 'possible Lib Dem' but very few clear cut 'Lib Dem' voter marks on the canvassing returns. Whilst the Lib Dems being in the Coalition had meant that many were willing to talk, few people were actually committing to vote. Feedback suggested he was quite well known, he assumed that was because of his high profile media coverage. However things were not running anything like as well as he had hoped.

He had counted on there being a UKIP Westminster candidate which he felt might reduce the Tory numbers and split their vote but that had not happened.

So he now did the total sums. Sebastian reckoned that in 33% of the constituency he held a high 40% to 45% of the vote around Middleton town. That gave him 13.2% to 14.85% of the vote but in the rest his vote was way behind with no more than 10% to 15% or so for 66% of the area mostly in country areas. That gave him a mere additional 6.6% to 9.9%, a grand total of just 19.80 to 25.75%. He knew that was never going to be enough to win the seat. Last time the Tory had polled 45% he was still way off achieving that.

Sebastian knew there were always other factors affecting results, for example rainy days are supposed to favour Tories, as Labour voters are less inclined to get wet voting. But in this election there was a double pull, the local and national elections at the same time gave voters two reasons to turn out and Sebastian thought the turnout was going to be high and that this would favour the major parties. There was the expected Lib Dem 'bounce', the last minute acceleration of the vote for moderate radicals always appearing in prior years, but this had so far failed to materialise, nor could he count on anything from the 'incumbent' bonus which all sitting Lib Dem MPs counted on. In effect, the MPs so well known in the locality for their personality and local service to the residents tended to mean a lesser reliance on party and more on being a good MP and so more protected.

These were all clutching at straws.

There was nothing like that for him and he saw nothing in the ongoing campaign from Lib Dem HQ that convinced him that they had shifted the dimensions of the battleground to cover those more favourable to Lib Dems. Foreign Policy was an example where Tory policy was revealed time after time as a shambles. Getting into Iraq had ended in a humiliating holding position and in Afghanistan, where high hopes of cutting out opiates and reforming the culture, had proved how ridiculous those hopes had been. Labour was no better.

Sebastian decided that the national campaign was not getting through and that he must therefore do what he could himself. It was, he decided, almost a position of sauve qui peut.

At 4 pm he called Edna and Tim and asked for a quick meeting tomorrow, Tuesday, at 10 am.

There was a flurry in the office as Edna realised that they had not much time left to get in their lists of supporters to attend the count, the briefing for which would take place only as the polls closed.

He continued canvassing and then went home, deep in thought. He had somehow to reconstruct a better reason for voting Lib Dem.

CHAPTER TWO - Tuesday

They all met in the office on the top floor surrounded by packages of printing materials and paper.

With minimal introductions Sebastian launched into his theme.

Sebastian showed them the figures he had calculated. He reminded that that currently there was no 'bounce' in the polls for Lib Dems. He proposed a more hard hitting and dramatic final 'Focus' to be delivered throughout the constituency centring on

a) Failure of the Tory to engage meaningfully with the EC and mounting concern that he would return with nothing from Brussels and, having decried the existing relationship, in effect be obliged to turn his back on Europe

b) Failure to provide any sort of leadership on Regional Government or on Scottish Governance. The idea of many different elected mayors forming an uneven patchwork quilt of variable powers seemed laughable to Sebastian

c) Failure to provide any ongoing improvements to the Health Service. Just throwing money at was not any kind of solution

d) Failure to provide those on the housing lists with any realistic opportunity of owning or renting, Tories were not 10s but 100s of thousands of houses short.

e) To be against HS2 or 3 as money could be better used on local communication infrastructure.

These were not mainly constrained by the austerity measures it was, Sebastian insisted, Just rank bad government. A similar problem was in the development of HS2 or 3. Somehow someone had the notion that faster trains to London would reap benefits. Sebastian maintained that the same money thrown at improving intercity services (road and rail) in the Midlands East and West would yield far bigger dividends. The route to London would, he suggested, just drain good staff to London with no comparable gain the other way.

Also for balance and continuity

f) There was a need for Balanced economy. This job was not yet done and needed Lid Dem common sense to hold the middle ground.
g) The need to signal that if Labour got in they would in effect be a junior partner alongside SNP; that mean constitutional chaos.

Both Edna and Tim appeared to Sebastian somewhat shell shocked by all this as he came to a sudden halt with

"Well what do you think of all this?"

There was silence for a few seconds. Edna cleared her throat and began rather cautiously. "Sebastian, this is getting back to your old games. I don't think you can, or should, set a number of hares running that are not in keeping with central policy. It's true that these points are not against them but we would certainly do better following the party line. Most of us think that the Lib Dem poll results will improve and there's simply no need to take extreme measures now."

Tim added, "Yes, I think Edna is quite right. Why don't we just stick to local issues? The ideas you came up with in regard to parking and the mini referendum and politicising the Town Council to get things done at last are examples of you at your best locally. My advice to you is to forget the national scene, there's nothing you can do there just help us drive things."

"You mean " interrupted Sebastian rather roughly "trying to get more people elected to a District Council in which I no longer believe. They are an utter waste of time; for 90% of it we act as Tribunal and this uses just 10% of our energy but 10% at the political end absorbs 90% of our attention. The outcome is, for example, a failure to deliver affordable houses even when this is proscribed by law. And just because the Tories have run out of ideas they think that somehow electing one person as a super-area boss, grabbing powers from Central Government makes sense. I am convinced it's a recipe for long term chaos with uneven services being delivered to variable standards."

"I am sorry, we have to act now. There's just time to get out a final leaflet. Both of you know well that the agreement was, following the fund raising, that those additional funds would be used for the General Election."

There was another pause and Madge popped her head around the door and teased "Ho Ho Ho! what deep plans have we got here, you all look like conspirators. Anyhow anyone for tea? No? Ok I see you are busy."

Tim reacted quickly "and I feel just as sure that with more effort we can take more District Council seats! And look, your list is nothing like the so called Red Lines just publish for Lib Dems, these are

'Protecting education funding, introduce a 'stability budget' in the first 50 days, increasing the personal tax allowance to £12,500, investing £8bn a year by 2020 in the NHS, pay rises for public sector workers, fighting climate change and protecting nature'.

Sebastian was silent then said sadly, "Well, it's clear to me that these will not win us the Election! For some reason which I cannot explain, the goodwill that we have built up will not convert to votes."

Edna spoke quite slowly and was clearly weighing every word. "Sebastian I do see this very much through Tim's eyes but, whilst I had occasional vision of you winning the seat, the problem with that is, it's here and then gone on a 'puff of smoke'. If you fail then nothing remains except memories of a good try but if we put in all our energies into the District then we could double our political presence. It's true it could be halved but it's likely we will not be eliminated – there will be something that remains. You therefore pose us with a high risk option with little probable gain, unless you win when there's a huge gain, whereas Tim poses a low risk option with probable incremental gains in the short term which can be built on.

But I also judge that you have lifted the political profile of this constituency and indeed that's what we asked you to do. In that sense you have already achieved far more than I thought you would, awakening the EU supporters, raising awareness in the Ethnic Asian based sector, doing a deal with Greens, bringing out issues like affordable housing. It would be wrong to try to curtail you now. You raised far more money than we have ever had before and much more, Tim it must be said, than any other candidate simply driving local issues would have done.

I now propose the following. That in the three, three-seat wards where we hope to win, Tim you prepare and have delivered a focus and in the rest of the constituency Sebastian you write what you think are the key issues in your focus and we get those delivered as widely as we can.

Well, do you both agree to my proposal? If so then we need to agree that we will have no further argument. I don't want separate camps emerging, so I hope Sebastian that you will stick as far as you can to your canvassing programme minus perhaps more hours to deliver your leaflet. Let's get to it, then we will need to bring out 10,000 more Focuses if we are to make any impact on the voters here!"

Sebastian asked them both to stay as he had another point to discuss.

"You may have noticed that recently I seemed to be getting tired very easily and have had to drop off a couple of afternoons. I hoped you didn't think it was for a lack of willingness because I know how much effort both of you have been putting into this whilst I have been at work?"

Tim and Edna both nodded, Tim offered, "Yes, we had noticed but then it's difficult to do two jobs and we appreciate your normal energy levels were starting to flag" Edna enquired "Well I hope there's nothing wrong?"

Sebastian identified the rather unpleasant side effects and that he had grown steadily weaker but at last he had gone to a specialist who had identified it as 'Tropical Sprue'.

"It's OK you cannot catch it"' he explained; the cure was already working and he was beginning to feel much better. He apologised if he had been grumpier as a result. His weight had fallen by 25% over the past few weeks and it was, he said, "quite a relief to learn that it was not after all the stomach cancer which I had feared".

Sebastian quickly prepared his country and aggressive leaflet version which he headed "Tory Failures"

Tim prepared the local Middleton only version which he headed "What Lib Dems could do for you here!"

CHAPTER THREE - Wednesday to Friday

Generally day followed day with little change, the routines continued.

However the first thing that Sebastian noticed was that he really did feel much better. He had felt it was an almost intolerable burden to try to do two jobs at once. He had in effect being working an eleven hour day for weeks and weeks but now it was down to a more manageable 8 hours and he felt at once more rational. The medication was certainly working and his trips to the loo were less frequent.

He used his 10 o'clock slot to take an overview of what was happening.

Over time he had noticed that the canvassing was becoming more and more difficult.

In the first week many of the voters had been in turns horrified and confused by the leadership TV debates. How had SNP got themselves on the podium when no-one in England could vote for them and why were Northern Ireland parties excluded? So many voices shouting out over each other seemed to drown out common sense; that was the voter feedback to Sebastian. At least that was the initial position. People were reluctant to decide on local issues until they had made the decision on the national scene. This uncertainty offered the opportunity for canvassers to convert voters to Lib Dems, using as support their local activity. It seemed to Sebastian to have worked.

Over the past two weeks that attitude had changed and the crucial decisions were being made. This had still allowed the canvassers to discuss the benefits of Lib Dem moves at local level.

But it was noticeable that many hadn't yet decided and positions were expected to harden over the weekend. So it was more likely that canvassers would be met either with smiles, thanking the canvasser for taking the trouble to visit, or a stare usually ending up in a refusal to discuss matters. An added complication was that postal voters had to make an earlier decision in order to get their votes back to the Returning Officer days before the election date.

The final Focus leaflets were ready by Friday evening. Someone was appointed to carry out the changes to their voter database. Candidates were each sent the changes from the Returning Officer, these were deductions, alterations and additions to the voters lists. In practical terms it was too late to amend the deliveries, which tended to be to every house, but it might be of help in the call up system on the Polling night.

This was the final push.

CHAPTER FOUR - Saturday and Sunday May 2nd and 3rd 2015

By Friday evening they had visited 100% of the houses in the target wards and perhaps 25% of the other wards and it was here that Sebastian called on even more volunteers' time to hand-deliver some 10,000 leaflets to the non-target area wards. This was the major work over the weekend in what Sebastian conceded was a last desperate attempt to break through.

In all some 50 volunteers and members helped. Sebastian thought that it was a 'magnificent' effort and said a thank you to each deliverer as he handed out the wodge of 100 leaflets per helper, many taking a double lot. Sebastian and Tim gave out the wodges as they drove around to each volunteer's house.

All those volunteers were also called on to act as tellers. That is to sit outside the polling booth and collect the numbers of those going to vote. These were the numbers on the voters' lists supplied by the District Council. There was a separate list for tellers to offer, usually, a two-hour slot.

On the Sunday Tim, Edna and Sebastian held a brief session going through the lists of tellers and reassigning them so that the key polling stations could be fully manned, whilst the fringe outlying polling stations would be done for effect and manned at key voting times only. As Sebastian said to one teller in his request as to how it works "Well you list down the numbers and one of us collects the pages of completed numbers from you – that's it!"

"So what happens then?"

"Well we coordinate this at our HQ, tick off those who voted and then give a nudge to our supporters who do not seem to have voted yet – hoping in that way to increase our vote! OK?"

Final touches were made to the "Good Morning – it's time to Vote!" leaflets which were then in production for the run on the morning of May 7th.

Late on Sunday night he was called by one of his Lib Dem members in a state of agitation and remorse.

"Look! It concerns the planning application for the building of the new Council Offices. It seems incestuous that the Council can grant its own permission? Of course I am telling you this in confidence so please you must not use that otherwise they will recognise me immediately. We know that it's probably a 'con' as the MP's letter falls far short of justification laid down, but frankly we were willing to grasp at anything."

The member continued nervously "You'll remember that at the last planning meeting before the General Election the demolition of the old District Council offices had been passed by the Planning Committee at the request of the Leader of the Council. Well we were all very angry and decided to gang together with most of the other retailers and demanded to see the MP two days later and all we stated that unless it was stopped until their own compensation position was clear they would all vote Lib Dem".

He described under terms of strict confidentiality, what happened then. "The Leader of the District Council and the MP Andrew Laws got together and discussed how to calm the near riot on their hands. One of them suggested 'calling' it in, that means referring the matter directly to the Minister of State. They said they would do this using the fact that a section 106 condition was not completed so technically it was still undecided. A letter was sent out by the MP to that effect, this was sent to us. For the moment we were satisfied that he was doing his best. We only noticed it later. We had not noticed that the letter was dated two days before our meeting and by the time of our discussion Parliament had been dissolved and MPs were by then away in their constituencies. Then we also learned that the justification the MP used was nothing like the government criteria needed. I am sorry we ought to have brought you into this, we were made fools of by them.

But you cannot please use this as they will identify that's it's me!"

Sebastian knew that the calling in procedure could only be used when the case was live not when it was already decided. He had checked with the Planning Department; all they could offer was that the application was not yet agreed as completed, although the committee had decided it in favour, because certain section 106 clauses had not yet been agreed laying down the timescale of the operation.

Sebastian could see that this was an elaborate cover up, he knew the Tories had regretted that decision as soon as it was made and when they were nearly physically assaulted by many traders they had felt the need for the subterfuge, to try and make it look as though they could undo their own vote. Otherwise it might cost them hundreds of votes!

'Typical Tory trick' thought Sebastian. – However he quickly concluded that he had no proof that the letter had been deliberately back dated incorrectly, if he broke the confidence it might destroy his relations with the other retailers, but what could he do with this information anyhow? Even if he made the accusation would it be believed? Would voters not simply think of it as 'sour grapes'.

He decided he could do nothing and did not even report it to his committee!

CHAPTER FIVE - Monday to Wednesday May 4th to 6th

Sebastian noticed that the feedback from canvassing was different. Voters were becoming either more generous in their praise of Lib Dems or more snappy as they were turned away at the door. Added to this about 10% of voters had already used the postal vote system, which they had posted back, their work done. Most of these did not appreciate being recanvassed as they had already made their decision. Sebastian knew that most voters seemed to have made up their minds.

Gradually the canvassing ground to a halt. A few streets were revisited with a large number of 'outs' recorded the first time around.

The last run for the early working call out message was complete and the printers in the office fell silent at last.

However after 8 pm on Wednesday evening Sebastian began to relax. He knew that by then he had done everything that he could to pursue his case.

That night he was not as optimistic as Tim and Edna, who both told him that they would make big gains.

CHAPTER SIX - Thursday May 7th 2015 Election Day

Sebastian was up early delivering his share of the last leaflets, wearing his 'delivery kit' of his 'Berghaus' jacket and 'Contour Track' shoes. It was cloudy and likely to rain.

He returned to the office to compare notes with other deliverers and offer to help if anyone wanted a lift anywhere.

He took his turn 'telling' and did the 3 pm to 5 pm shift in a polling station in his Middleton Ward. It was pouring with rain and he felt miserable. He was sitting outside the polling booth on a wet chair with rain intermittently dribbling down his neck. As the hood of his coat wasn't that effective, he was trying to mark the voter's number on his little score card whilst protecting it from the water which would make the list of numbers disintegrate.

Then he did a tour of the outlying village polling booths, hopefully being as visible as possible with Lib Dem stickers all over him. He went into the booths and asked for the number of voters recorded so far. He was thus able to work out that the turnout was high in the villages.

 He recognised many of his supporters and waved to them. He chatted amiably with the other tellers. Only the Conservatives had attempted to match the total coverage of the Lib Dems at the Middleton polling stations. He was aware that the turnout was likely to be high in this Ward as this particular polling station had recorded 50% voter turn-out already by 5 pm. He thought that would bring out a higher proportion of the Tory voters and wondered if that would be good for Lib Dems as their poll rating still had not budged.

He then went back to Lib Dem office to see how the database check off was going. Tim Holland was in charge and everything was going smoothly.

He had a quick chat with Tim and confided in him those revised projections which he had done of 27% overall.

They discussed the count process. They had been informed that it was being arranged in four stages:
 1) Verification - making sure that no slips issued to voters had gone missing
2) The General Election Count, which would take place immediately afterwards and
3) the District Council count, which would take place on the following day, and finally
4) the Parish or Town Council which would take place last of all.

Sebastian dropped in at home it was 8 pm and his vote-getting job was now done. He sat in the small lounge and switched on the TV opened a beer and just flopped for an hour. The various TV stations were already advertising their all-night election programmes.

He idly switched on the PC and read the incoming emails. One from his son wishing him luck and another from RKW head office in London it was from the HR Director, John Avis, it read:

"We fully appreciate you are very busy and on vacation too but we are seriously concerned by the disappearance of Jeffrey Pardoe who acts as your assistant director in Russia. We have been informed by the MD at our Moscow Office that he was on some sort of a mission to assist the Company we have just acquired in Volgograd, who have a problem with their main customer who are constructing a huge chemical complex. We are seriously concerned that he is possibly being held or detained. The Board of RKW is most concerned and asks you to go to Moscow to sort this out as soon as possible when your holiday period end. Please respond."

Sebastian replied *"Sorry to hear about Jeffrey – the next few hours will tell me if I will be busy or if I can assist. Let's talk again 9 am tomorrow.*

My Russia Visa is still intact so I could move quickly if necessary! Please keep me up to date!"

John Avis replied;

"Thanks Sebastian and Good Luck!"

Hmm thought Sebastian 'I had better warn Sylvia, it seems its either the London Bag if I win because I could not reasonably let down my supporters here, or the Russian Bag if I lose because I still have to take responsibility for Jeffrey Pardoe. In the latter case I will take my normal 'full walking kit' that I used in Northumberland, a 'Berghaus Bowscale' Gortex Jacket and 'Regatta' Overtrousers and 'Contour Track' shoes and Berghaus back pack together with thick socks and warm fleece, and I'll travel in my jacket and casual clothes'.

He discussed the matter with Sylvia and reminded her that he would need his passport, credit cards, shaving kit and his medication. He had to be prepared to move either way.

If he was elected then he would have to get away to Russia as quickly as he could maybe at the end of the following week.

He dozed for a further hour then asked Sylvia to keep the TV on BBC1 and call him on his mobile every so often with the election news as it came through.

He ate a healthy supper and went to meet the others at the Leisure Centre in Middleton where the votes were being counted. Initially he was nervous and constantly twiddled the ring on his finger.

It was in the large hall which was the size of four badminton courts. The floor was coated with layer upon layer of resin, the competing markings for the many games played there gave a surreal feel to the battle that was going on above. It smelled vaguely of sweat.

At 10 pm those Lib Dems attending the count met briefly with Sebastian, Tim and Edna who, as Agent, took them through the procedure. They went into a private huddle.

They agreed which were the key objectives. One of those was making sure that the actual count was correct and that votes for one person were not mistakenly put into a rival's bundle and, even more importantly, that bundles were put in the correct basket and that baskets were put on the correct table, ensuring total separation for as long as possible.

But that was only the official reason for them being there.

The most important objectives were to get valuable information about the result by polling booth as quickly as possible. This was done by taking samples as the boxes were opened. Each of the team agreed to take samples.

There were probably 200 people in the hall and there was a constant mumble coming from them.

The count tables were arranged in a square with military precision. Counters strictly on the in-side; the political checkers and verifiers equally strictly on the outside.

The paid counters counted and amateur political checkers checked.

Counters used their hands and were forbidden to discuss the merits of the votes, checkers used only their eyes and were forbidden to touch anything.

Many of the counters had done the work before and some had worked all day supervising in the polling booths.

Many of the checkers were experienced political canvassers. They had sat telling all day outside those booths recording the voters' individual numbers, for checking with the database, and trying to pull out the later voters.

The counters sat in teams in a long line and were allocated boxes. The number or area covered by each box was announced by the supervisor of the team.

The checkers milled around in their political groups usually with Agents and candidates conferring together. Sebastian stood with his group of ten close helpers and candidates and Edna as chief Agent.

The first work that the counters did was the 'verification;' checking that the total votes cast, ensuring that the stub of polling slip, that is the number of slips issued, was the same at the quantity of slips coming out of the voting box.

The tin boxes were upended on the table and the counters then grabbed them, turned then upright and separated the voting slips into two or three piles, if there was more than one election going on at the time (as here where the Westminster seat, the District seats and the Town Council seats were being fought).

A sharp eyed checker could, if he knew the area, quickly take a sample of say 50 or 100 votes and see what the results were spread over candidates. With the General Election that was quite easy as there were only three candidates plus the 'independent'. So within minutes samples could be taken by each of the checkers.

All ten of Sebastian's helpers doing the same could, within twenty to thirty minutes, predict the election results by using such samples, though the more candidates there were the more complex this became.

Sebastian sensed early on that he had not won; the sample returns for Middleton town were, as expected, fairly good but not in the country areas.

The Lib Dem helpers crowded around in order to get their first view of the likely voting pattern. It meant that they had to identify boxes that were upturned, to the relevant ward, and as there were some multi-ward seats with several Xs often split across parties, so keeping track was quite difficult and not necessarily accurate.

Once the verification part was completed they started on the count proper. The piles of mixed slips for the General Election were then re-sorted to each candidate.

Slips were separated then, once counted, were placed in wire net baskets in batches of 25.   The number of batches in each basket assigned each candidate grew and then filled other baskets. So it was possible to see which of the baskets were filling up more quickly

All the parties' checkers jostled for a view.

Most often contact between parties was minimal but on occasions it was simply not possible to avoid meeting face to face as the viewing area narrowed at each corner of the square and, if two parties wanted to cross, they virtually had to acknowledge the other. This happened to Sebastian and Andrew Laws the Conservative.

Andrew Laws held out his hand and said "I wish you luck and by the way I want to thank you for keeping the fight so clean in two respects – first that you never laboured my own family problems as others did and also you didn't denigrate the UKIP people, which would have been easy to do and treat them like some right wing idiots. So thanks for this Sebastian. How do you think you are going?"

"Badly" Sebastian replied "but I ruled that there were to be no personal attacks of any kind. We can, after all, each have our low points and I wouldn't like salt rubbing into my wounds if I were in the same boat. As far as UKIP is concerned I have no problem with much of what they say although I do believe it to be wrong. There's no way I would denigrate them. Fully a third of your voters came from us anyhow and frankly we would like them back! Any time you want a public duel over the EU just give me a call, I'd be happy to oblige!"

Andrew nodded in appreciation "Well I might just take you up on that!"

Sebastian laughed and said "But I'll still have to be on my guard with you. I know full well what you did over calling in the Town Hall development!"

"So you know about that?"

"Yes, sure I do" retorted Sebastian "Unfortunately I could not use the information, as a member told me in confidence, you must be pretty worried if you could stoop to that sort of trick!"

"Hmm yes that wasn't what we wanted to do – in fact you'll have to believe me it was more of a muddle than a plan."

And they moved on. Sebastian acknowledged both the UKIP candidates and shook hands with the leader Chris Walmsley, although it was he who had perpetually criticised him in the Council chamber when sitting as a Tory and reported him for criticising the officers. As Sebastian expected, as they were now out of the protective cloak of a large party, they looked strangely vulnerable, even speaking to those they would normally have ignored! Sebastian passed them with a friendly wave.

The process of the election of someone who was a nobody now but who might, after all, soon be a senior Cabinet Minister and the high octane discussions of who would take which District Council Committee Chairman if they were returned, was, Sebastian felt, rather like an advanced game of deadly Ludo contrasted with the chatter of the counters.

The counters teams were randomly selected but to relieve their boredom of moving bits of paper, opening or unfolding, turning the right way up and putting into piles, they began tentative chatter but none of it was related to politics. Films, Sports and TV programmes were frequent topics.

Sebastian noticed the paradox, power politics one side of the table and necessarily mundane gossip on the other.

All this together amounted to a buzz of the sound of low key voices, a perpetual murmur.

Tense groups of people were quietly chatting in huddles. Some were sitting carefully watching the counters.

Occasionally there would be a minor disturbance as a checker noted the counter putting a slip in the wrong pile or the miscounting of a batch where the supervisor was called and the batch was re-run and the excitement was over.

Sebastian received a call from Sylvia shortly after 11 pm. The exit polls suggested a dreadful result; giving LD 10 and Cons 316, just short of an overall majority. Initially the TV experts themselves had denied it. It could not be right! Paddy Ashdown, the former Lib Dem leader, threatened to eat his hat if turned out it was true. But then the real declarations came in.

Sylvia can back with some more figures. The result became a pattern and a pattern became a blur. After another hour the number of Lib Dem seats falling became a torrent, by 2 am in the morning all that was of concern was the extent of the collapse.

Still the Conservatives seemed short of a working majority. Then came the double crushing blows, as SNP wiped out 50 years and more of imbedded Socialism in Scotland and almost simultaneously the Tories ripped through the heartland of Lib Dems in the Southwest. Two seismic changes which so shocked Sebastian that he had to sit down to absorb the impact of news coming to him via his mobile phone in bits and pieces.

He just had to go home and see what was happening on the TV. Sebastian felt time standing still, it was as if it was all in slow motion as the count moved to its conclusion in the hall.

The returning officer called him over.

Out of sight of the cameras the candidates of the three parties, and the independent, were grouped with their agents in a little huddle and the ritual of the oddities had to be gone through. The convention being that any voting slips where the voter' intention is not clear has to be agreed by the candidates on the advice of the returning officer.

All the weird and strange things which voters have time for in the polling booth are revealed. One by one the returning officer plucked these out and stated clearly "These I am rejecting because the voter's intention is not clear" at least one looks like a picture of a house? A HOUSE? For God's sake, thought Sebastian, let's get on with it. Another was a flower or, what wait a minute, no it could not be, yes, it's a penis erupting. Then "These I am accepting" one was a dot alongside the name, one was a double tick, another the candidate's name is just circled. "Do you all agree?" There were nods all around the group. Get on with it for heaven's sake! thought Sebastian, one vote is not going to be crucial here.

At last that ritual was over - it accounted for only seven more votes. Sebastian nervously twiddled the ring on his finger.

The candidates were then told the results and asked if they were happy, or if a recount was requested but here there were no close decisions. No one spoke. The Leisure Centre tannoy system was turned on and the announcement is made.

Sebastian was still reeling from the National disaster. Here the candidates were all lined up.

The Returning Officer read out the results one by one Andrew Laws the Conservative candidate had won with 44% of the vote, The Independent had 1.5%, Lib Dems Sebastian Edwards 29.5% and Labour, John Clark 25%. And "I declare that Andrew Laws is duly elected for this constituency".

There was a pause then Andrew Laws was speaking and thanking everyone Sebastian also had the microphone stuck in his hands and mumbled something which he could never later recall.

Lib Dems nationally at 10% how could that be? Sebastian at first refused to believe it! His worst estimate was what 20 or 30 Lib Dem MPs?

After a brief chat and with many commiserations from his team, Sebastian left with the intention of meeting later on that day to carry out the District and Parish Council Elections, the count for those was to start at 2 pm.

Sebastian returned home and let himself in, the TV was still on, it was 3 am.

He reached for a beer and collapsed into the chair in front of the TV.

The results were as bad as he has been told. Time would not stand still. Reality hit him hard in the head, In the stomach and in the heart.

Sylvia came downstairs and simply walked over and hugged him as he got up. They remained like that for a minute or so. Sebastian was overcome and drew back, he struggled to speak coherently "It's a disaster – all those good people gone. All that we have done here these last 5 years has been washed away in an single night. Not just by hundreds but by thousands. It's as if the voters deliberately targeted us and only us here in England. Even the Greens with their cockeyed interpretation of global warming equals austerity got a reasonable vote elsewhere!"

"I know, I know, I watched it all on the TV but there's still the District elections tomorrow maybe you will gain seats there" said Sylvia encouragingly. "Anyhow it's time for bed – tomorrow, or rather today, it will all look different."

Sebastian just sat on the edge of the bed with his head in his hands and scarcely moved, then he slid sideways onto the bed and he wept silently into his pillow. He remembered all those years ago at boarding school. His first term he had been bullied to begin with and he knew then that crying out loud would just make matters worse it, would be taken as a sign of weakness. He had then no friends then, so he had cried into his pillow.

But this time is was different, he felt Sylvia put her arms around him, she pulled him close. "It's not me" he said "it's the whole Party – there's 175 years of history destroyed in a single night, a tradition of reform covering for example pensions, and whose thinkers gave birth to the health service and modern economics. Policies which formed the bedrock of the present state. We have, at one swoop, been eliminated from the political scene! Is there some method to this madness?"

He felt her cradle him in her arms as he fell asleep exhausted.

CHAPTER SEVEN - Friday May 8th

Sebastian awoke at 8 am and after a quick breakfast checked his emails.

There was an inbox email from John Avis HR Director of RKW in London timed at 9 am.

"Hi Sebastian, sorry about the political news for you. As you know in politics things can change quickly, so you never can tell?

Re Jeffrey Pardoe, our Board asks that you go to Moscow as quickly as you can, sort it out and go down to where he was last heard of, see if you can track him down and get him out. We don't need any bad publicity, just get him out. You have the closest contact with the Russians. We are counting on you!

I suggest that you get the driver you use there and get some money from the Russian MD who is aware of the problem but, frankly, does not seem too concerned about it. I would book tickets for you from here but it's likely to be easier for you to do it directly. How soon can you get there?"

Sebastian replied at 9.15 am *"I'll check up and get back to you with any other requirements"*.

He called Sylvia over, "Look it's the Russian kit; likely I'll be off over the weekend. Don't forget those special pills and I'll wear my casual stuff, there aren't going to be any posh meetings this time. Ah, and just in case, please pack my Russian Police Certificate that I got with the Medal – it may come in handy!

Sylvia hesitantly replied "OK but do you think you should go, you have always told me that you thought he was a man that could take care of himself; it's not your job. It could be dangerous!"

"I have to go, he was working to my instructions down there, where we recently acquired the materials company in Volgograd. It is my responsibility. Anyhow my vacation is over I am back at work and have to respond to the board; I really have no option."

Sebastian knew she would let him go; he had to work out in his mind what had happened on May 7th a different task might well help him to move forward. She put her hand on his arm, he knew that she understood.

Sebastian quickly checked some flight times. He was in luck, it would be possible to meet up with the driver at Moscow airport and both travel down on the same flight to Volgograd, where they had last heard from Jeffrey Pardoe. He drew up a plan and emailed it to the Russian MD Dmitri Davidoff, and copied it to the HR director, the Russian driver, Andrey Andreyevich Petrov and, just in case he was receiving but unable to reply, Jeffrey Pardoe.

Sebastian knew the urgency of this, it was timed at 10.15 UK time to ensure that suitable bookings etc. could be carried out in Russia, which was 5 hours ahead.

Sent Mail

"Dmitri

I am returning to Russia at the request of the Board of RKW to track down Jeffrey Pardoe and bring him out.

So I will be on the flight from London Heathrow (LHR) leaving Sunday at 8.55 am arriving Moscow Airport Domodedovo (DME) 14.35 (Moscow Time) for onward progress to Volgograd (VOG) at 18.45 (local time) arriving 20.30. I will book this from the UK this afternoon. (return flights Wednesday)

Andrey will fly from Perm (PEE) probably 7.25 Sunday (Perm Time) arriving DME 7.45. (Moscow Time) for onward progress to VOG at 18.45 and arrival there at 20.30 (local Time) . Russian MD to authorise and book immediately. (return flights Wednesday).

I will meet with Andrey at check in for flight to VOG.

Dmitri to meet Andrey at DME with an envelope containing $3K, to be authorised by RKW to be used in obtaining Jeffrey's release . Dmitri to hire for collection at VOG a small car from Avis Hyundai Solaris or similar, price approx. £174, for immediate late collection and return Wednesday to VOG. Dmitri to book from Sunday to Wednesday 2 rooms at Hotel Intourist on Ulitsa Mira or similar in centre of town.

This is at the directive of the Board of RKW as Requested by John Avis – please implement immediately.

Each party confirm bookings in place by 60 minutes from receipt

HR director please email immediate authorisation, confirmation.

Sebastian Edwards- Deputy Managing Director- Siberian Minerals"

Inbox

Forty minutes later email confirmation was received from each party.

At 12.00 noon UK time an email was received from Dmitri, copied to all parties.

"Information received from Interior Ministry that Jeffrey Pardoe is being held in police custody in Kotelnikovo, 190 kilometres southwest of Volgograd. He is claiming he is a director of Siberian Minerals and claims as reference either myself or Sebastian Edwards. Police are awaiting some personal verification on site before they will release him"

Sebastian email back immediately "Well that seems to simplify our search, we will continue with the plans as previously set out – thank you! Please confirm to police that I will be there on Monday morning for verification."

Sebastian smiled, he had had so many such trips and meetings to organise that it had become second nature to him; he knew the systems and the web sites that were in English and exactly what to do. He carried as back up the European Train Timetable, he knew he was robust enough for this work and, since taking the pills, he found his energy returning but he had to keep eating to build his strength back up.

So now he had to rescue the man who always looked as though he could take care of himself! 'Hmmm!'

He returned to the count at 2 pm as agreed. The format was much the same but the huddles were thinner and some were made up of different people. Many of those were independent residents come to hear the Parish Council results.

The first job was to separate all those who voted right down the party ticket, so if in a 3 seat District Council seat there were 9 candidates from 3 parties then, where a person had voted for all three from the same party, these sheets would be separated on the first run and the others, the 'mixed' one, would be put in a separate pile. All these voting slips were laid 'edge on' and a batch of 20 would be laid in that way and the number then added together. This was called a grass skirt by the count staff. These sheets had a total at the end and each of these totals were copied onto a further summary sheet. In cases where there were single parish wards of 10 councillors counting could take a very long time.

Because of the cross voting and the variety of volume and candidates in each box it was much more difficult to assess the winners and losers. Although it was possible to get an understanding by referring to the straight ticket party lines votes, which were stacked up in the same way as for a General Election. Slowly the apparent confusion was unscrambled as areas were taken in turn. When the results were announced there was sometimes an outburst of muffled clapping, then that group or huddle would drift away.

Sebastian remained with his huddle but managed to have a quiet word with Madge O'Connor. He knew that there was something she was holding back and he was determined to get to the bottom on it. He thought that there was something between her and Tim Holland. Sebastian had assumed that perhaps the problem was that maybe Madge was keen on him but was getting rebuffed. He thought, but did not know for certain, the Tim Holland was a homosexual. This had not been raised by Tim but although Sebastian had known him for several years he was not a close friend by any means. It was, well, just the way he expressed himself and how he had never ever mentioned his home life at all and had never attended any social gatherings with anybody either. Sebastian thought that perhaps Madge wanted to discuss that with him privately . Of course, if Tim were a homosexual, then he was still quite entitled to declare it or keep it to himself – that was his private business.

So Sebastian started gently "Well, Madge you have been on the point a couple of times of mentioning that something was worrying you about Tim and then you pulled back and would not explain. Is there anything I can do to help?"

He was surprised by Madge's immediate response "I am grateful you picked up on that, I thought you had forgotten and I want to get it out right now!

Several weeks ago I overheard Tim on the phone talking with some of our candidates standing for the Middleton Town Council. As you know that includes several of our district councillors and friends. The words 'political leadership' and 'next council' came up and then he saw me and stopped dead and put the phone down. That was the first time, but I heard from someone else that something is going on. I am sure that Edna Leggs is also involved as I came on them both in keen discussions and, when I came in, they both looked very embarrassed. I think they mean to unseat you as Leader of Lib Dems on the District Council. I suspect that what they will do is to first decide that the new Lib Dem leader is to be elected by all elected councillors, that is, by District and Middleton Town Councillors, not just the District Councillors. In a way that makes sense because it gives commitment and support in both directions."

She paused. Sebastian hesitated "Well no-one has mentioned this idea to me!"

"Hmm that's what I thought" said Madge "but there might be enough District and Town councillors to outvote you. John Laver was never keen on your idea of integration and Johnathan Thomas is open to ideas, whilst Norman Dodgson believes that putting all the money locally could win us all the district seats we stood for. Edna Leggs is also standing for the Town and the new Muslim members will listen to her. Both Tim and Edna will make much of your outspoken hostility to the Council on various issues. I think they will put forward Tim as the new leader based on his quieter manner and working with, rather than against, people. Sebastian, if I am right we have a major mutiny on our hands!"

Sebastian thought for a few moments as they both watched the count in progress.

"Madge, I have to be frank with you. I have taken a very heavy blow over the General Election results here and nationally. Of course many here will say I told you so – told you he will never do it! I am so pickled off at the moment that I am drifting in and out of calling it a day and walking away from politics.

I have to go away tomorrow for an urgent trip to Russia one of our directors is missing and I have to get him back. I cannot get out that job! So this is what I would like you to do. I think there's a meeting on Monday night of all elected Councillors? Isn't that right?" Madge nodded.

"Tomorrow I would like you to make contact with Mohamed Rahman and Dallat Ahmed, Will Jenkins and Shakil Ali. I will email all these tonight and say you will be contacting them on my behalf. I want you to tell them that I am 'bushed' politically at present and need some time to restore my batteries and that, accordingly, I will propose Tim as leader. And I would like you to propose me as Deputy.

The reasoning is simple, Tim and Edna will imagine that I will oppose Tim's election as leader and thus imagine that there are two 'camps', but in practice many will be loath to split the team. My support for Tim will wrong foot him and there will be mutterings to keep me in. Also you could add on my behalf, please, those many dozen quotes from Edna Leggs saying what a fine candidate I am. I will send you these by email too.

Also I suggest you imply that I will not be prepared to stand for the Planning Committee because of the number of days that I have to commit to it and instead propose Tim for that committee.

This will give me time and space to reconsider what I want to do here. If anyone should be inclined to stand against me as Deputy then please just mention that I will personally view it as a grave disloyalty for the work and effort that I have put in!"

Sebastian looked at her keenly, he knew that she was the one person now that he trusted to do this, all the new councillors would be completely confused by rivalries.

"But let's not make it easy for them. Wait for the actual meeting before mentioning any of this and ask the other members you contact to keep quiet as well? OK"

Madge said "Well it sounds like a reasonable plan to me but what are you going to do?"

"First of all I have to work out how the hell we got into this mess and then how we can climb out of it!"

Madge replied "That will be interesting Sebastian, is there anything I can do?"

"Yes I think so Madge, I am already toying with some ideas and I may well need someone to help me carry out research. Could you do that?"

She offered her hand and Sebastian shook it warmly. "So we have a deal!" he said "now let's get back to this count. Let's face it, I have no idea if I or Tim will actually survive anyhow!!! I can see several people eyeing us, I will tell them that I was just explaining that I will be off to Russia tomorrow!"

Soon after, the District Council seats were declared.

As all the Lib Dem supporters had hoped, they were successful in Middleton South and East, winning 3 seats in each ward but the majorities were very slim, by between 100 and 200 votes. So Madge was elected, as was Mohammed Rahman Dallat Ahmed and Tim Holland. There was nearly a recount. But, in Middleton West the seat where there was a deal with the Greens, none of the Lib Dems were successful, although the Green Councillor himself Tim Dabbs survived. The same applied to the East Lowes seat and the other seats where paper candidates were put up; there they were heavily beaten but still getting 15% of the vote.

The Green Councillor Tim Dabbs came over to apologise and accepted that, without Lib Dems help and support by bringing in extra votes, he would probably have been overwhelmed.

So all that effort for one extra seat!

The two UKIP candidates, one of whom was Chris Walmsley, were each elected with handsome majorities.

As the session drew to a close Sebastian moved over to Edna to congratulate her on winning the Town Council seat. There, 5 Lib Dems were elected. Sebastian made his excuses as he was tired and told Edna about the problems in Russia and said he would be away for a few days and asked if there was anything particularly important she wished to update him on? "No" She replied "there's nothing that cannot wait but we do have a Councillors meeting when you are away"

Sebastian replied "Well I am sure you can manage for one meeting without me?" Edna smiled in reply.

He returned home and immediately sent off the emails that he had promised.

The following day he completed packing his bag and added a couple of books. Like many Lib Dems he had been swamped by technical briefings from HQ during the election on all sorts of policy issues, which he tried to read but, like most active candidates, he had little time for background reading. He thought here was an opportunity, with little distraction, for him to work things out. He was resigned to spend most of the next few days at airports and police stations waiting and waiting.

He noticed that there was no email from his son! 'So maybe this is the end of the relationship' he thought.

CHAPTER EIGHT

Sebastian took the train to London and proceeded by Underground to Heathrow where he had booked a room in a cheap hotel.

He boarded the budget airline flight for Moscow and arrived at the airport. He moved to a different terminal for internal flights and waited at the Check In for the 18.45 flight to Volgograd. He occupied himself in reading the books he had packed; he had also brought along the Times and Telegraph for Saturday May 9th 2015.

Sebastian pondered. What appeared to have happened was a double seismic shift. Labour lost 35 seats in Scotland to SNP and in England the rise in the Conservative seats was due almost completely to the destruction of their partners the Lib Dems.

Neither newspaper paper had more than a few words to say about the Lib Dems.

The Times stated :

'He (Nick Clegg) is right that fear of the break-up of the UK may have played a central key role in driving voters to the polls to prevent the formation of a Labour Government supported by the SNP '.

The Telegraph almost apologised :

'The former Deputy Prime Minister took his party into government for the first time since the Second World War and saw it destroyed, which is a high price to have paid for providing the stability the country needed to recover from the economic crisis the Coalition inherited. '

The local consensus meanwhile was that on joining the coalition the Lib Dems had lost a far higher proportion of their voters than any of them had imagined, maybe as much as one third of their 20% vote. These were the left of centre anti Tories but also pro left wing. They had just never returned during the 5 years of the coalition and whenever Lib Dems made clear, for fairness as much as anything else, that they would listen first to the largest party after the next election which might be Labour they had immediately lost the third that were Conservatives with a small 'c'. The result was the rump of core Lib Dem voters roughly one third of their 2010 base..

Where they had gone to was also pretty clear. Green and UKIP had taken over 17% of the vote in England fully a third of that would likely have come from Lib Dems with the remainder of the Lib Dem diaspora returning to Tory and Labour from whence that had originally come.

The result was a Conservative Party with a popular vote of 36.9% not much more than one third of the total vote, but given a majority of MPs in parliament by the voting system.

What had been brutally exposed was that Lib Dem voters in 2010 were made up of a higher percentage of floating voters than either Tories or Labour. The squeeze exerted by an increasingly dominant and left wing SNP on a threatened Tory collapse shook that party to its timbers and jettisoned any Lib Dems in their path. So Sebastian had no doubt that the trigger was the SNPs switch to the left.

What it did not explain was why there was no incumbency benefit, why constituencies which had elected Lib Dem MPs for decades had just abruptly thrown them over. That was the insult and injury, a personal relationship built up over decades gone in a trice.

Was this the end of Liberalism? Or was it more simply the end of a coalition partner who simply got in-between the Tories and the real enemy and paid the price? Was it ideological or simply positional? Was it obliteration of the notion of Liberalism or just a one off hit, getting caught in a position which was unlikely to be repeated?

Sebastian knew he would have to work it through; few other commentators, or the party itself, seemed willing to do so. The local

Regional Lib Dem organisation for example was all for shouting about an immediate 'fight back' but more of the same did not seem to Sebastian to be the answer.

He ditched the newspapers.

He dozed a bit and was nudged awake by Andrey.

Sebastian greeted him warmly. "Sorry to get you here on a Sunday but it's by order of the board I am afraid. We have to get Jeffrey out. Now tell me did Dmitri give you any more news? Does he know how it started? All I remember is vaguely responding to Jeffrey's request to go to Volgograd to sort out a problem? Did Dmitri explain matters to you?"

"No he did not! He say to Dmitri there is problem and must go! He tell me he call head of new company, he say there is problem with one contract, big client, if we lose that it's critical but he changes his design for plant. Also there is customer fight with competitor but our director say there is no problem yet!"

Sebastian said "So who asked Jeffrey to visit? It does not sound as if it was Dmitri or our new director down there."

Andrey replied emphatically "No I know nothing" and passing the envelope with the money said "Here is money, sign please!"

Sebastian realised that if all he had to do was to get Jeffrey out of police custody then it would not be needed but in Russia you could never be sure. The police had been notorious for being corrupt but most of this was ended with the reforms of several years before. He knew that Andrey was sure that the corruption had ceased and Sebastian had no intention of using it unless he had no other option.

Together they checked in and boarded the flight to Volgograd.

Andrey assured him that the car rental had been agreed and that the hotel was booked in accordance with instructions.

Sebastian asked how the policeman was, whom he had saved several years before on his first trip to Russia.

"Ilyah Ilytch Volkov. He is good, he is promoted, now is senior constable!"

"Ah!" said Sebastian "that's good".

Andrey ventured "You'll remember when we last visited Volgograd to buy local minerals company, we managed to get away for time to look at massive statue to mother Russia, 'Mameyev Kurgan' in honour of one million dead in that war. City was then called Stalingrad of course. It had originally been called Tsaritsyn. Well, in 2013, City decided that on special days it could call itself 'Hero City of Stalingrad'. So yesterday May 9th was such day, it was Victory Day and there was big parade."

Sebastian looked at him. "Andrey you are very proud of your history aren't you and of being Russian? It's confusing for us outsiders you have heroes in amongst the decades of terrible times. I do hope that one day you can live in a better environment where you can extract the immense wealth that lies underground and use those profits for the good of everyone!"

Conversation lapsed for a time. Then Sebastian said "What on earth do you think has happened, Andrey?"

Andrey replied after a hesitation "I do not understand it."

Sebastian then moved to the next phase. Did he know where this other town was, Kotelnikovo? Apparently it was 190 kilometres southwest of Volgograd. And how long would it take to get there?

Apparently all depended on the condition of the roads. So they agreed to start at 8 am on Monday and hope to get there by noon!

They were soon through the Arrivals as they both carried only on flight hand baggage.

On arrival Andrey went straight to the car hire desk and, within minutes, they were on their way to Volgograd City and were soon walking into the Intourist Hotel in the centre. It had been built in the Stalin era and had a massive external frontage and opulent reception area but the rooms had been carefully modernised.

It was midnight.

CHAPTER NINE

They left after a quick breakfast and headed south out of the city over the River Don and away to what seemed a vast empty plain.

The weather had apparently been dry for a couple of days although Andrey suggested that it usually rained every other day in May. The dust soon became a problem and they had to stop en route to wash the windscreen free of dirt.

They chatted about the countryside and the huge reserves of potash which were known to exist in the area.

They turned right off the main road and made towards Kotelnikovo. Further down towards the river they could see an enormous development complex that was being built and about 2 miles further on what appeared to be a modern village with houses of a vaguely Scandinavian style.

Andrey had heard that this was possibly the complex which their own company Siberian Minerals was supplying with various materials.

They arrived in the town at around 11.30 local time and found the police station, a rather modern building with plenty of concrete but not much style. There were several police cars parked in front in their typical livery of white, with blue flashes and markings.

Andrey parked the car alongside these and they went in. Sebastian asked Andrey to make notes of the conversation as a permanent record, as he said "just in case", but to allow Sebastian to take the lead.

The interior was Spartan with fold down seats, some of which were broken, and a big noticeboard with a large number of instructions and pictures of what were probably people wanted for questioning.

There was a reception area in which was a raised desk at which sat a burly policeman in his early 30's. Andrey whispered that the two bars on his epaulets showed he was a police junior sergeant. He was chewing his pencil and was obviously having problems with paperwork he was completing.

Eventually he put that to one side and Andrey introduced them and stated, from what Sebastian could understand, that their mission was to verify the person held known as Jeffrey Pardoe and to take him back with them.

The junior sergeant immediately called back over his shoulder and another person appeared with a thick gold stripe on his epaulette. "Police Starshina – senior sergeant" whispered Andrey. He was larger and fatter and was balding and he snuffled, Sebastian thought to himself, a bit like a pig!

Andrey repeated his introduction but the sergeant simply said "Dokomenti!" which even Sebastian could understand.

Sebastian interrupted and asked Andrey to confirm that they did indeed hold Jeffrey Pardoe. Sebastian told Andrey that he had no intention of going through a lengthy identification process only to be told he was not there. Andrey nodded and asked the question.

The sergeant didn't move just repeated "Dokomenti".

With a shrug they complied and handed over Sebastian's passport and Andrey's identification papers and driving licence.

Without a word the senior sergeant left and the junior sergeant pointed to the chairs.

They sat and waited for what seemed like a good half an hour, hanging their coats on the pegs on the wall.

A door opened and they were both waved through by the sergeant into a corridor with what appeared to be a series of holding cells on either side. Some were left open and they were small and cramped with a bed and toilet, rather dark cubicles smelling of sweat, urine and disinfectant.

They stopped and a door opened. The sergeant suggested they go in.

In the corner was a huddle of what looked like a bag of old clothes but must have been a man sitting in the corner; his face was covered by matted hair, his head was between his knees and his arms hidden under his legs. His top coat and trousers were covered in mud and his trainers were caked in the same material.

The sergeant leaned against the door, watching.

Sebastian called "Jeffrey is that you?"

Slowly the figure raised his head and put his hand up as if to shade the sun from his eyes. "Yes, yes hello! Who is there?"

"It's me, Jeffrey, Sebastian, Sebastian Edwards". "Are you OK?"

"Oh yes! Thanks for coming". He replied weakly. As he raised his head Sebastian could see that he had severe bruising to his right eye, which was almost totally closed, and that dried blood was all over his face. He had several days stubble on his face. His hair was streaked with mineral of some kind. His top coat was torn in several places and his trousers were shredded at one knee exposing several scratches or cuts.

Sebastian rounded on the sergeant "How dare you leave someone in the cells like this – you should know that he is a British subject and must not be treated in this way. Unless you bring a bowl of hot water, a towel and a glass of drinking water within the next minute I will personally see that this is recorded and reported to the Ministry in Moscow." Andrey translated but with less certainty but the message seemed to have worked.

The sergeant suddenly sprung to attention and rushed off.

"Now Jeffrey what on earth's been happening, are you OK?"

"Yes thank you" his voice was trembling and cracking, "I just met up with some rather rough guys and before I knew it I was dumped in here, I couldn't eat the revolting food so I have nothing except bread and water for the last 5 days!"

"Well" said Sebastian "I got the message from the head of HR of RKW and then from Dmitri here in Moscow. What happened? What are you doing here?"

A police private brought in a bowl and towel and a glass of water. Jeffrey gulped it down in one and asked for more. He put one hand in the bowl but it was clear he could hardly move the other. Then with some difficulty he stood up, perched on one leg, and slowly put the other leg down, gingerly transferring his weight, but fell over again almost immediately. He seemed to have broken or sprained his ankle. He now moved the other hand but it was blown up to almost twice the size of the other and he moved it only slowly.

Sebastian helped him to get up and encouraged him to walk.

Jeffrey was clearly coming to his senses, he spoke slowly. "Oh I remember, yes you are Andrey! Well thank you both for coming I am most grateful. Do you think you can get me out?"

Sebastian reassured him "Well that's what we have come here for!"

Jeffrey took another gulp of water. "Oh that's better!"

Sebastian asked Andrey to call for the sergeant which he did; as there was no response he headed back to the reception area.

Jeffrey said in a whisper "Please get me out, it's been terrible here!"

Sebastian reassured him and, putting Jeffrey's arm over his shoulder, began moving him to the door.

The sergeant came rushing down the corridor towards them shouting "Niet, Niet" and motioning them to return to the cell. But Sebastian just pushed passed and, with Andrey behind, came into the reception area. There they were met by what Andrey said was a police major. In a whisper he said "This man is probably chief here at this station please be careful Mr Edwards otherwise we might all also be staying overnight!"

Sebastian forestalled any attempt to reprimand him by speaking to the major through Andrey and immediately apologising. "I am sorry but I was completely taken aback by the sight of my colleague and co-director of our company. I really cannot imagine that anyone would be left in their cell, whatever the case, without water and with their wounds untreated. Such a condition would earn the station sergeant in the UK a severe reprimand. I should not have barged out but I could not accept that his condition was satisfactory."

The major said nothing but showed them all into a side room with a large desk and several chairs.

The major looked at them. It was clear that he was going to make no attempt to speak English.

Andrey translated the major's "Do you validate that this person is Jeffrey Pardoe a director of Siberian Minerals?" "Yes" replied Sebastian.

Similarly "Did you authorise his coming to this area and carrying out some investigation?" there was a pause "Yes" said Sebastian.

More questions through Andrey. "What was he doing within the Russia potash site? Where are his clothes? And how did he get here?" Sebastian was completely flummoxed. "To be honest with you I am not sure but Jeffrey is a respected employee of the company and I have myself known him for several years and I will vouch for him as a reference!"

"You see Mr Edwards" the major continued in Russian "there has been much trouble at that site, dispute with supplier about sub-contractor which is holding up completion of this huge project; there are arguments about employees working for competitors and staff being bribed - it's very tense. It could close work down. Development of factory and borehole is months behind. Into this walks your Mr Pardoe"

"It's not us that roughed him up but the security guards who caught him trying to get out of site down by the river. He refused to say anything except that he worked for you. All he told security guards was that your company had taken over company supplying constructor of buildings and that there had been some problem which he had been sent to resolve. Security guards gave up on him in end and turned him over to us. We tried to check his story with your company in Volgograd but MD there denied any knowledge of any problem with supplier. So we left him for a bit, hoping he would come to his senses. But he didn't, so in end we emailed your company in Moscow. I am sorry he is in mess. One of our doctors did inspect him and assured us that there was nothing broken. But let's put it this way he did not at any time co-operate."

At times Andrey had to hold up his hand in order to restrain the flow of words so that he could interpret.

Sebastian was alarmed by what the major had said but did not show it. "Well will you release him to us and we will write a report for you filling in the gaps. I am sorry that he was unhelpful, that's not our intention as a company, everywhere we work closely with the authorities. Andrey here is a former police driver for the Militsia."

"Thank you Mr Edwards, we are of course aware of your company and indeed we checked on you, we are happy to release him to you. But I have to give files to Ministry of Interior. I understand you stay in

Volgograd in Intourist Hotel? Please stay there and see Interior Ministry there Wednesday. I have made booking for you in afternoon 4 pm you are to see Sergey Strezhnev he is FSB Federal Security Service. You know Volgograd main railway station was bombed in December last killing 16 people, we have to report all incidents with foreigners, we have no option. But we hope to bring this strange visit to end? Here are your papers but I will have keep hold of Mr Pardoe's passport and his pack with sleeping bag and camera — FSB will give them to you."

Sebastian thanked the major, picked up his coat, and walked with Jeffrey to the door and straight to the car.

They sat for a moment and suddenly Jeffrey burst out. "Please get me to a shop immediately."

He refused to talk about anything else but they soon found a shop in the town and, taking some money from Sebastian, he rushed in and five minutes later emerged with fruit, meat, cheese and bread, strawberry juice in a bottle plus a roll of toilet paper. Jeffrey started eating "Famished, fucking famished — I haven't eaten for 5 days, famished!"

They were talking about which direction to leave the town when again Jeffrey burst out, "Those trees over there by the road stop please stop now — its urgent!" He dashed out of the car with the toilet paper and emerged two of three minutes later wiping his hands. "Thanks, sorry about that had to go - it was filthy in prison — bunged up for days - it'll be so good to shower and sleep in a bed!"

They started on their way and Sebastian was about to ask some detailed questions when he noticed that Jeffrey had fallen fast asleep, flat out on the back seat, still holding in his hands a chunk of cheese. Sebastian looked over at Andrey who was driving "Well what do you make of all that?"

Andrey paused "It's confusing but I cannot understand what he was doing, nor that affects Siberian Minerals; he was not resolving problem for us. Take care Mr Edwards."

Sebastian was quiet too. He wondered what on earth was going on. They drove back in silence.

"Well" said Sebastian "I suppose we will have to buy him some new clothes, can you stop at a suitable place, we should still be in time?"

They stopped in Volgograd at a shop but Jeffrey refused to get out saying he was hurt. So they bought Jeffrey a track suit, anorak, shoes, underclothes, some strapping for his ankle and shaving kit and then made it back to the hotel. Sebastian discussed with Andrey what to do next. As Jeffrey had no passport they would be unable to book him a room since for that a passport identification was always required.

Sebastian suggested that for the time being Jeffrey should sleep in the same room as Sebastian. At Jeffrey's insistence Andrey went into the hotel and found the fire escape at the rear and Jeffrey waited till no-one was about and furtively crept into the hotel and went straight to Sebastian's room. There Jeffrey ate the remainder of the food that they had bought earlier. He then slumped onto the bed and fell asleep immediately.

When he awoke Sebastian tried to ask more questions but Jeffrey seemed nervous and confused and refused to elaborate on his capture by the police. He was unwilling to leave the room. Andrey suggested calling a doctor but Jeffrey refused categorically saying there was "No need to fuss and there was nothing that another good night's rest would not put to rights!" But it was clear to Sebastian that he was carrying an injury to his right hand and left ankle. He was nervous and agitated and took great care when opening the hotel doors, as if he was being followed. Before passing out Jeffrey had assured them that they could discuss things tomorrow at 8 am.

Sebastian and Andrey ate dinner alone in the restaurant and discussed the situation. Sebastian confessed that he was confused as to what had happened.

Sebastian decided that he had to confront Jeffrey and find out the truth but they would let him sleep tonight.

Sebastian emailed back to John Avis in RKW from the Hotel reception a short resume of the day's events; that Jeffrey had been found, but was in pretty poor shape, noting that FSB (Ministry of the interior) were now involved to whom they had to report on Wednesday in Volgograd. He suggested that Jeffrey's disappearance did not seem to relate to RKW operations, saying that he was without his passport which had been retained and confirming Wednesday as the likely exit date.

He called his wife Sylvia as he did every night when he was away "It seems odd he refuses to talk about his ordeal and has been badly beaten up. We are seeing the Ministry of Interior Police on Wednesday, I should be back on Thursday, not to worry if I don't contact you before as the phone doesn't always work from here"

He received an email straight back from John Avis in London which he thought very strange.

"Grand job so far, well done, remember your mission is to get him out, he could be a grave embarrassment to us! GET HIM OUT"

Sebastian mumbled "Out? Well of course! He would be out very soon! Why on earth could he be an embarrassment?"

He rolled up some of the bedding on the floor and prepared for an uncomfortable night's sleep.

CHAPTER TEN

At 7.30 am Sebastian awoke and had breakfast with Andrey in the restaurant. He mentioned that Jeffrey seemed to be going to pieces, he had been very reluctant to get out of the car to buy clothes and had insisted on getting into the hotel by the back door. Sebastian thought that maybe he was cracking under the strain or was becoming paranoid from his mistreatment. Andrey just shrugged his shoulders.

They both returned to Sebastian's room where Jeffrey was hiding in the shower when they came in. He was couched in the corner with a fearful look in his eyes. He rushed over to the window and tried to peer out.

"So Jeffrey, what on earth is going on?" Sebastian demanded "It's really about time that you levelled with us!"

"Ok so please sit down whilst I explain!" Just then a door slammed down the corridor and Jeffrey jumped and whimpered and rushed back into the corner in the shower

They persuaded him to come out and they all sat on the bed as the explanation continued.

"They are after me!"

Sebastian said "Who are after you and why?"

Jeffrey began "The Russian Mafia. As you know I have a contract with Siberian Minerals and am a Director of that company and I act for them as you know collecting monthly financial and statistical returns and visiting each unit routinely to make sure everything is OK. Together we have acquired several operations which seem to fit our profile haven't we Sebastian?. Indeed the company is now almost twice the size that it was when I joined and it is quite pro…."

The lift doors clanged and Jeffrey stopped listening intently as the footsteps moved away. "But my contract is with RKW in London and it is not a full time. I can also to carry out other work."

Sebastian said to Andrey "That sounds like a pre-prepared little chat that he would trundle off if questioned? But what he has said so far does not disagree with my view but of course I never saw his contract."

Jeffrey continued more fluently, "Well I was approached by a firm in Lancashire investigating establishing a new potash operation called 'Lancashire Fertilisers', they asked me to carry out some research for them on potash facilities and operations in Russia".

"You mean that you have been operating for them here at the same time as Siberian Minerals, and without telling us?" Sebastian asked clearly astonished by this news.

"Well it was very recently – only since we acquired the company in Volgograd. I came down here some two weeks ago in order to see what was going on at EURO-AGGRO as we had heard that they are using the same technique of freeze drying the mineshafts as they were intending to use at Lancashire Fertilisers in the UK. It's a critical process reducing the costs of access to the mineral by 50%. My mission was to find out if it was working OK"

"But surely that's industrial spying? but did it work?" asked Sebastian.

"I do not know. I didn't get that far! In fact they are months behind programme which will cost them a fortune in missed deliveries. I asked around at the new village they are building but my questions soon raised concerns and eventually I was arrested by the security staff, I had tried to run and would have got away but I fell badly doing something to my leg.. They said there wasn't any Potash in the UK and appeared to be convinced that I am working for the other large potash producer in Russia called Russia Potash, based as you know Andrey, near Perm near your home"

Jeffrey was relaxing a bit and moved to a seat. He winced holding his leg as he sat down. He bent down, pulled up this trousers and revealed an ankle swollen to twice its normal size. He wobbled as if he was about to faint so Sebastian walked over to the wash basin and poured a glass of water and gave it to him.

"Oh thanks" he said and when he put out his hands to take it one hand seemed to be still bruised.

"So they thought I was working for their bitter rival Potash Company, their products and clients are direct competitors for reserves of potash and for customers. We are talking here of sales of both companies being in hundreds of millions and since the cartel ended they can gain or lose £ millions on single contracts. Apparently they raised this directly with their competitor's board challenging them with setting me on as a spy and threatening legal action but they denied any involvement and immediately put a cap on any staff leaving and joining EURO-AGGRO. Within hours accusations were flying about between these rival companies. I was repeatedly questioned about this other company Russian Potash but of course I knew nothing. I suffered a severe beating. In retaliation I refused all meals which in retrospect was a bit of a mistake. After a two days in custody in a very smelly cell, one of the security staff realised that, because of my English passport, they had better do things through the police and despite his colleague's entreaties pass me over to the police major whom you saw.

The police were not satisfied with the answers that I gave and told me they were keeping me in detention because they felt certain that the thugs hired by either Russia Potash or EURO-AGGRO would be after me to find out what was going on."

Jeffrey's whisper went even quieter and they had to bend over closer to catch what he was saying..

"We are talking about delays to bringing this plant into production and potential losses of at least $4M and the rivalry between them and mutual suspicion that they believe that I have something important to tell about the operation. Maybe we were followed from Kotelnikovo I hope not, as you know I lay down on the back seat to be as invisible as possible. I assume they will suspect that you will know where I am Sebastian. They know you are important to this because I gave them your name as referee."

"What why on earth involve me in your private little spying? So you have brought me here all this way on business that is not remotely connected with Siberian Minerals. Why didn't you get Lancashire Hotpot or whatever you call them to act as a referee instead. I think you are f**king nuts to expect me to help you!"

"But didn't you read the email from John Avis of Head Office about getting me out? RKW are involved; they are thinking of taking over the Lancashire Fertilisers and my investigation order came from them!"

"Rats bloods rats" yelled Sebastian "So what do you expect to do now?"

"As you can see I cannot move well, so I'll lie low here till Wednesday and ask for police protection through to the airport in Moscow so I can get out!"

But Sebastian queried "The police have some unanswered question over your actions too!"

Jeffrey quickly responded "No! All they want to do is to clarify who I am. They are always worried about foreigners. So you don't have to do anything but wait. As I am fluent in Russian there's no need for Andrey to hang around – the job is nearly done. All I have to do is to stay here hidden till them!"

They discussed this matter for a few minutes and it was agreed to release Andrey. Sebastian took Andrey aside into the corridor and walked with him to the front door of the hotel.

"Look Andrey, I cannot say that I understand what's going on but I have my clear instruction to get him out and I am committed to going with him to the Interior Police on Wednesday. It seems frankly that he might be a bit paranoid but that's no reason to keep you here. Change your flight back to today and you can drive to the airport and hand in the rental car."

Andrey replied "I am worried Mr Edwards, I do not think Mr Pardoe is saying truth, as police major said, 'where are his clothes and why did he have sleeping bag?' Be careful Mr Edwards! Two Russian potash groups are fighting but it's usually about how to fix selling price to make millions of dollars, not things like this."

"Thanks Andrey, look I want to thank you for coming all this way for me. Here is an envelope with $500 for your assistance and trouble over the weekend; behave as you usually do, OK? Don't bother to check out of the hotel, Jeffrey can move into your room. And if there is anyone following us then they will follow you back to the airport where they will realise their mistake!! So please put your bag on the back seat with a rug over it so it could be mistaken for a person. OK?"

"But Mr Edwards!" he protested but Sebastian had turned on his heel and had gone back into the bedroom.

Sebastian walked across the room to Jeffrey and was surprised to see that he was reading through the European Timetable that Sebastian always carried with him and had lain on his bedside table.

"Andrey has accepted that his part is finished. There are flights every hour or so; he should make it back tonight. So we are holed up here then for the next two days?"

"No, I am afraid not Sebastian". Sebastian looked at him closely, gone was the look of fear and the terrorised darting eyes, everything was suddenly under control; this was the Jeffrey of old.

"Look, you have been very helpful so far but I am in real trouble. What I did not quite explain is that I managed to get hold of some crucial evidence about the deep freeze method of drilling. What they do in simplest terms is to freeze the ground and drill a shaft straight through. That way the ground is kept rigid and is prevented from fissuring around the hole for the shaft, which is then supported by a cement casement. I managed to get some photos of the actual shaft before I was nabbed.

The FSB are the successors to the Checka. You don't mess with them. They are experts at interrogation, they will find out within hours what I have seen and they will charge me with industrial spying. I could be put away for several years and the other potash producers are going to be keen to understand what's going on as well. As I said at the start they really are after me!"

Sebastian was reeling from this further change. "You mean that both the Interior Police and the Oligarch's mafia boys are after you? Come on this is beyond a joke!"

"A joke is it Sebastian, just take a look at this for a joke!" he was almost shouting and he opened up his shirt and took down his trousers to reveal a body covered with raw scratches and wounds and bruising.

"Some bloody joke! And it's your company that got me into this mess and you have to help me get out! Remember what the email said 'Get him out'! So please let's concentrate".

"So tell me this, why should I not just turn you in as any reasonable person would?"

"Why Sebastian, because if I get caught, you get caught and if they are angry they will close down Siberian Minerals and with that goes your big fat bonus – remember that!"

"So why get rid of Andrey he could perhaps have driven us out?"

"No chance Sebastian! You know he reports everything you and I do to the Ministry in Moscow, so anyhow I hope that he will take back a confusing story!"

"You bloody shite you have dragged me into this and I stand to lose everything I have worked for these past few years!"

"Yea right Sebastian and I'm looking forward to three to six years or so in a Russian prison. Now just shut up and let me think how we can get out of this!"

Sebastian could see he was thinking out loud, muttering to himself, but his voice tailed off.

> "Driver gone - good
> Clothes – OK
> Money – OK
> Food – we will need food!
> It's now 11 am Monday we have a head start and we will be listed as missing only at 4 pm Wednesday. So we have two clear days.
> Cannot use planes as identification always asked for
> Cannot use car as driving licences etc needed and we do not have any.
> Has to be by train. Have to leave a false trail? Also book to Moscow!
>
> Sebastian could not hear much more but the muttering continued.

Hmm earliest we can get … 15.14 train… Povorino line 1965 …. in 21.52
Then "'to Liski line 1977 18.40 …. Liski 22.33 it will have to do……
Then bus to Val… then …border… Kupyansk
Kiev say…, hmm well have to see about that"

Jeffrey stood up "Well it's a bit of a trek but it'll have to do!"

"So what is your proposal?" asked Sebastian wearily.

"You have a small bag, get food and water for two days, meat, cheese, biscuits. OK can you do that? Oh and I need strapping for my ankle and a knife?"

"Yes I suppose – we are on the main street here so it should not be difficult!"

"Only what you can carry Sebastian! Here's the bag take it with you!"

"Oh and buy a red scarf please and a collapsible umbrella! OK Sebastian, see you back here in two hours. There's a shopping mall on Komsomolskaya Ulitsa. That's down by the Volga River about half a mile away. Here take the hotel map of the place. Take a taxi if you need! I'll need some time to work things out! In the meantime I'll shower and get ready."

Sebastian hurried about his tasks and continued to swear at himself for several minutes. "F**k, sh*t, how the hell have I got into that mess and why oh why hadn't I taken the bonus from Siberian Minerals when it was first due? I know, I remember now. I had been trying to optimise my own tax, hoping to spread it over two years. £100K that's what it was and I have earned every penny, only to have this bloody idiot come in and ruin everything."

He found the shopping mall and put his purchases in a basket – no time to ask details in his faltering Russia, all he could do anyhow was to look at the labels, just grab and rush to the till.

He walked back with his bag bursting. He had also bought a large plastic multi-coloured fibre bag common throughout Eastern Europe.

He checked in using the hotel email and left a message for his wife. *"I am off for a couple of days bringing Jeffrey back don't be alarmed if I don't call before Thursday. Then contact me through John Avis of RKW. Love you!"*

He reached his hotel room and knocked on the door, Jeffrey asked "Who's there?" and Sebastian replied "It's me you fool! Stop buggering about!"

The room was cleared, Jeffrey was clean but dressed in his old clothes, the bed was made and all the empty packages from last night's food were in the bin. Sebastian opened his purchases and put them on the bed.

"Not bad, not bad" said Jeffrey "although this is a washing powder, maybe you thought it was disinfectant?"

Sebastian noticed there was a note left by the bed.

"What's that? "he asked.

Jeffrey explained "It's a letter in Russian to the reception explaining that we might be away for some time sightseeing but expect to be back on Wednesday! I want to seal it but we need a further $750 can you put it in please, that should cover the hotel costs!"

Sebastian handed it over that made $1250 plus expenses - gone in one morning!

Jeffrey said "OK let's go. I'll try to get out the back way and meet you in front on the street. If I don't make it, I will say I was looking for you and I'll wait in the lobby OK?" Just pop down to Andrey's room and make sure its cleared. OK".

"So where are we going next" asked Sebastian now resigned to more unexplained moves. "To the train station" came the reply. "It's on the other side of the main road. Get a taxi and I'll stand behind you to give instructions. OK?"

CHAPTER ELEVEN

Sebastian did as instructed and hired a taxi through the receptionist then went outside to meet it a few minutes later. Outside Jeffrey appeared as if my magic at his side giving instructions to the driver to go to the station. He appeared to have found a hotel cleaner's broom and, placing his coat over the bristles, use it as a crutch.

They arrived and Sebastian paid the smallest dollar denomination that he had, two tens at which the taxi driver grunted something happily unintelligible to Sebastian as he got out.

"Now, Sebastian, first change $750 into roubles, you'll need your passport for that – the currency desk is over there see! Then go to the kiosk, I'll tell you which one. Put the red scarf around your neck and hold your umbrella open and ask for two tickets for Moscow tomorrow Tuesday. You ask this – here I will write it for you.

"15.14 May 12 2015 to Moscow line 1965 . Two Singles" – *dvah beel'eht dah Moscva pahzhahistah- zahftrah, ahdeennahtsaht migh*. Then put the time on a piece of paper 15.14. Understood?"

"But" Sebastian protested that's tomorrow, I thought you had said we are leaving today?" Damn he thought that's $2,000 gone which he would have to justify to someone!

"We are" Jeffrey replied "but just do it. See you back here in 10 minutes!"

Sebastian had to wait in line for a few minutes and was getting agitated that he was still not at the front of the queue. At last he made it and repeated the words as he had been instructed. The large lady looked at him mystified. So he repeated it more loudly. Eventually she called over another assistant and he paid for the tickets with cash. Sebastian guessed that the large lady was loudly explaining to the crowd behind him that it was the red scarfed man, a foreigner who was causing the delay.

Jeffrey met him. "Well done Sebastian that was really well done! Now come this way we are taking the same train a day earlier so we had better get a shove on, come on!"

Sebastian felt himself almost dragged along. Although Jeffrey was limping badly he was hopping along and he was able to keep pace with Sebastian and with his good hand took hold of the big bag.

They caught the train and sat exhausted in an empty section of the carriage.

"So what the hell was all that about?" asked Sebastian.

"Decoy!"

"Decoy? Oh I get you red scarfed, foreigner, with umbrella, needs staff to help, creates attention so will be remembered. In other words I have set the decoy running! Well thank you! Meanwhile you nipped in elsewhere and in your perfect Russian get two similar tickets for today. I note you are wearing your torn and dirty clothes. I suppose that's intended to make you look like a Russian workman?!"

"Yes, well you have nearly got it right but we are only going to Povorino. That's about half way!"

"So what then?" Asked Sebastian.

"We will probably take a train to Liski!"

"Probably – well that's a comfort. At least we are off. Let's hope we have two days start on them. I have had enough right now, I'll just read my book if you don't mind?"

"By the way this train is an inter-city and has toilets", offered Jeffrey.

"Well thanks for small mercies!"

"You can jest, Sebastian, but some local trains do not have them!"

Sebastian rummaged around for his pills; to date they were working and he hadn't felt the need to rush to the loo for the past few days. It was like a mini miracle he thought!

Jeffrey said "This is the 15.14 train to Povorino line 1965 gets in 21.52. I suggest you get some sleep". It was clear to Sebastian that the leg was still hurting him although he seemed to be able to use his arm more freely. He used some of the strapping that Sebastian had bought to wind around the upper part and cut the shoe with the knife to ease the pressure on the foot.

Sebastian read his books and then dozed.

He was shaken awake by Jeffrey. They arrived on time.

Sebastian said "What next then?"

Geffrey said "To a bar if possible and maybe get something to eat, then I am afraid it's in the open tonight! We will head over to the railway sidings to see if we can get some cover there but it's a pleasant night we should be OK!"

Sebastian was so far out of his comfort zone he was lost for words and shuffled on behind, occasionally helping him over fences. It was now clear that his ankle was very badly sprained as he was in some pain if he walked without support, but the hand was now improved and the marks on the face less swollen, his black eye was less blue more yellow.

They slept under a railway truck. They managed to evade the local police by blending in with the locals, Jeffrey's dirty coat and torn trousers made them appear like Russian manual workers. Sebastian had changed into his walking kit.

He tried to use his mobile to call home but by now the battery was flat so he could not even get a signal, Sebastian knew that Jeffrey had no phone himself. For the night Sebastian had put on all his spare clothes but was aching all over, he had jammed his bag under his head as a pillow but could not settle. The ground, he decided, was really very, very hard! He noticed Jeffrey seemed quite at home with this state of affairs and lay snoring on his back a few feet away.

When Sebastian awoke Jeffrey had clearly been up some time and was checking the remaining food. They had eaten most of the tinned meat and bread but still had chunks of cheese and the biscuits. They still had the original bottles of water.

Jeffrey explained that the problem was that all regular rail services to Ukraine from Russia had been stopped so they had had to go a circuitous route.

On the following morning they were in luck, there was a local train to Liski near the border with Ukraine and again they managed to find a place to sleep. Using evening or corner bars bars they were able to conserve their food which they ate sparingly.

Sebastian passed the time in reading the two books that he had bought with him.

At 9.01 on Wednesday morning they boarded a bus at Liski for Valuki. There was a five hour stop on the way at a small village. There was a policeman in the square but he seemed intent on finishing his meal rather than checking anything. They arrived in Valuki at 17.00 on Wednesday .By this time Sebastian's nerves had become really frayed. "So what the hell do we now do!"

CHAPTER TWELVE

"Walk!" said Jeffrey "We cannot go any further by public transport. It's not far. In a few hours we will be out of danger and well on our way to Kiev, there we will go straight to the British Embassy".

"Well by this time we will officially be listed as missing and I suppose they will have the equivalent of the 'all points' warning about us and they will be checking no doubt at the frontier so how are we going to get around that Jeffrey? Come on you have done this before haven't you? There's no way that an organised person like yourself would apparently wander about then scurry around playing hide and seek with border guards."

"Sebastian, it's as I told you, if they catch me I will be held for several years and what's more they will almost certainly close down RKW associated company Siberian Minerals. As for you, you will keep to your story that I was deranged and you went to Moscow by rail to seek medical advice where you lost your passport. Look here's your train ticket!".

They walked for a few minutes down a dusty track then Jeffrey said "Now this is what we will do. The Frontier actually lies about a half mile ahead. We are basically going to follow that river; as you can see it's not fast running. There is a track and we will get as far as the bridge. Then we will either go under the bridge or over the road on top. There are sentries about but once we are through we are in Ukraine!

It will be OK you will see. You know I am very grateful for your assistance, although I can make it like this on hard ground my crutch is no good on soggy surfaces. "It's my left ankle so if you get to the right side and prop me up that would help. I will carry the bag in my right hand which is now a bit better and you carry your bag on the left. Is that OK? Right lets go."

"OK let's go we will move along the lane whilst its light OK?"

"They walked along the bank and Jeffrey chatted presumably, Sebastian thought, to keep his mind off the matter in hand. It was getting quite difficult to balance Jeffrey's weight on his shoulder which was getting sore as they continued with the three legged walk. Whenever they stopped it always took them some minutes to get back into rhythm. Jeffrey was chatting.

"You know, until 2003 this border was a joke. It was actually agreed decades ago but it was not until about 2000 that it was enforced.

There's a tale of one old man in a village near Rostov on Don, that's further south, whose house lay actually on the border. Whilst ever the USSR was in being it didn't matter but ever since he has had problems. For example their one cow lives in Ukraine but grazes in Russia. Now they have to carry passports day and night when moving to different parts of the village and the border guards frequently demand money. So the village is split in two with the shop and school in one country and the cemetery and railway station in another. They live by Russian time which is an hour ahead of Ukrainian. He and his wife even got different pensions, his from Russia, hers from Ukraine. But their biggest complaint is that there are no longer any smugglers who also used to sell them goods on the way through, which were of a better selection than in their small shop. Understandably they don't much care for the border! So it was for decades until the problems in Ukraine".

They continued along the right bank of the river. "It's the River Oskil" he explained "In some areas it's quite wide but in others its just 20 feet or so across and in summer time it is quite possible to ford it!"

"So from here on in act naturally, just stroll along as if we are locals, we will be at the frontier In a couple of hours or so. Now look up to your right at those a huge chalk escarpments which continue for a few miles. There is plenty of cover, as you see there are many sorts of trees, poplars, silver birch and willows nearer the river and some bushes like hawthorns along the path. There are reed beds along the banks of the river which is quite slow moving and placid at this time of year. The banks sort of merge with the water there's no drop into the river but that means the rim alongside the river will be muddy and probably very smelly. It's best not to risk drinking the water unless we have to, then we should carefully strain it!"

They seemed to Sebastian to be making good headway and they were able to walk quite fast but he was getting rather nervous. Sebastian mused that the worst that he had ever done before was to get on and off a bus without paying, rushing past the ticket collector. He really did not fancy getting held up by some bored guards with rifles and being taken pot shots at. It was not the sort of death he had in mind. He was looking around and jumping at every sound.

It had begun to drizzle, the sort that won't stop but never really pours. It livened up all the smells of the countryside and apart from this creature on his shoulder it might have passed for a stroll by any little river. The pathway they were following was an old cart track and the ruts made by the wheels could be clearly seen, between them the horses' hooves had created hollows which were now filled with water, so their legs in the middle splash splashed.

Sometimes there was a movement in the rushes probably Sebastian thought caused by water voles or similar. Some ducks flew overhead and they could be heard quacking as they crash landed on the water further upstream. There was no wind. Occasionally there was barking from the houses along the path and it set Sebastian's nerves on edge again.

"Hey take it easy! Sebastian, you are doing fine, most dogs will be on chains they will not come near us unless we approach their home! In a minute, when I spot a suitable tree, I'll try to make a walking stick, that might help. So now tell me about those books you were reading on the train, you were engrossed in them for hours?"

"Well are you sure you want to know?" Asked Sebastian, he assumed it was partially therapeutic but decided to go along with the idea anyhow.

"Of course of course – look I have nothing else to do right now. Tell me more! By the way if we see anyone just keep walking straight on and I will start speaking in Russian as if to you, don't worry about it"

The broom head had by now fallen off so they stumbled along the track until they came to a little copse and Jeffrey was able to make a reasonable walking stick which meant they could walk separately and increase their speed. It was still spotting and rain was beginning to dribble into the bags, but the weather was warm and it was a pleasant day.

"So your story? Come on now Sebastian!"

"OK I get it! Alright here goes! But promise you will stop me if you get bored! You know I was standing for Liberal Democrats and that we got heavily thrashed at the elections? This caused me to stop and think what we did wrong. Of course there are a number of theories, the most prevalent is that the floating voters were quite scared of SNP threatening to control Labour in any future coalition, to the extent that the combination would be even more left wing than the existing Labour party. The general public had not forgotten their handling of the economy. That was the fear and Conservatives were able to use to suggest that Lib Dems might even join in if Labour ended up as the largest party. So we were electorally squeezed not to say squashed. So that's the most obvious summary. But.."

Jeffrey interrupted him and began noisily speaking in Russian gesticulating and seeming to argue with Sebastian and then interrupt him before he could reply. In doing so he pointed to the river side where a local man was fishing whom neither of them had seen. Jeffrey gave the man a wave as they passed on.

"Keep going but quieter, all he will hear will be a jumble of sounds - the trees will soon blanket the noise."

As soon as they had moved on, Jeffrey motioned Sebastian to continue speaking whilst he crept back hopping on his good leg and trailing the other to see if the fisherman had moved from his spot.

"Whew! That was a close one" said Jeffrey "but we got out of that OK! Just carry on as if everything is fine, don't look around, indeed if you are nervous just whistle!"

Sebastian tried but nothing came out. "I am not sure that works Jeffrey, I cannot whistle because I am nervous!"

"Never mind. So where had we got to? Are yes the obvious summary? Carry on its most interesting, just keep talking!" encouraged Jeffrey.

"Well" Sebastian continued " it does not explain why we were thrashed in those seats which had accepted our party for 10, 20 or even 30 years. We had always relied on an incumbency benefit, that is of the sitting MP projecting his good work through regular local newsletters and of course in the press and on TV. Nor does it explain why our vote never even got up to one third of the 2010 level, despite the fact we were 'in power' and able to effect some modest changes and had even more media exposure. The previous jibe at us had always been 'you will never get into power so a Lib Dem vote is a wasted vote' even as we helped save the economy, which by common consent we did but we were heavily punished for it!"

"So Sebastian I can understand all that but what has all this to do with those books you have been reading?"

"Well it's like this, if as a soldier you are in a war it's not the best time to sit and read a book about strategy or tactics, you are probably more interested in whether the next shell is going to land on your head on not. So we are a bit like that, there's actually so much to be done and so many people to speak to at election times that it's just very very difficult to tear yourself away, and separate yourself from the day to day fray, and think. These two books are to force me to do that. One of the reasons why I decided to come and help was, frankly, to get away. I can tell you it's a dreadful feeling losing. You wind yourself up for weeks, pumping adrenaline and getting off ready responses in your sleep to use on canvassing. Then suddenly it all finishes, the victory which you have lead yourself to think MIGHT happen fails, you feel you have let down all your workers who have tried hard to fold, or deliver, or write stuff, or canvas for you, explaining why you should be elected and how things would be better if you were to be elected. You convince yourself and so...."

Jeffrey interrupted "There's a dog barking quite close, could be a building nearby but if it appears don't run or anything just carry on regardless. So, you were saying you have come along partly to rethink and re-energise is that it, just carry on?"

"Well partly but also to work out if there is a future for Lib Dems, are we necessary? Am I just wasting my time? Or is what Labour and Conservatives maintain true, that their parties are indeed coalitions of various views ranging from far right to Lib Dem on one side and far left to Lib Dems on the other. In other words the centre ground is already adequately represented!"

"So you have come here to think through if and how you can revive things? Is that it?"

"Yes I suppose so" said Sebastian.

"So how far have you got?"

"Well the first thing that I noticed was that the very holding of power itself completely inhibited our ability to project radical solutions, all we were able to do was to act like a centre party; we were unable to shift the battleground to areas of policy which suited us. We were crowded out and our failures in office were badly handled and not explained."

"So what you are going to do to refresh your party. Come on, we have time!"

Sebastian knew that this was simply a ruse for him to keep going and keep his mind off the looming danger. Looking at his watch Sebastian could see that they had been going for four hours already, that must have made about 15 miles or so. It was 21.00 and still just light.

Sebastian continued to elaborate his plans. He was glad to take his mind off the present situation.

Jeffrey stopped him gently and whispered in his ear. "See that old brick bridge up there, that's in effect the border. The guards are situated in a wooden box at the right side of the bridge. We have to keep on this side and when the river is narrowest cross it, then pass under the bridge. From now on no talking, it's silent mode. Before we go let's lighten the load and eat well, we will have to get rid of the big plastic bag. Stuff the water and the rest of the food in your bag. We will put the other stuff under the roots of the trees and hide it if we can. All being well we will camp on the other side in Ukraine OK? Warning its likely to be very muddy so tie you shoes tightly and in stagnant areas it will smell. Let's go!"

About a hundred yards from the bridge the cart track ended and was replaced by a single footpath.

They found a patch where the ground sloped directly into the water. They were hidden from the sentry box by head high rushes. They made straight for the bridge and they were in luck there was very little water. They crept under and pushed their way through some wire netting. There was no sound from above. Jeffrey motioned Sebastian to stay quite still. In the distance they could hear and see the lights and flashes of a police car approaching on the other side and to their surprise heard some movement right above them. It must have been the border guard walking the bridge above them. They remained motionless for a good 5 minutes. Each time they moved it disturbed the mud which stank. At one point they could plainly hear the guards talking. There was a faint hiss in the water which startled Sebastian, but he saw a cigarette floating in the water and realised that one of the guards had flicked his cigarette into the river not a meter from him. The sound of a car driving off right on the bridge above allowed Sebastian to relax as his feet were stuck in cold, putrid, water.

Jeffrey raised his hand to move and slowly they proceeded upstream round a small bend in the river. Sebastian had to help him as the walking stick simply sank into the mud. He said "Come on now, Sebastian, quicker we are not safe till we are at least 400 yards away".

They gained the path on the left hand side of the river. After a while the path broadened out to a cart track as before. They walked in silence for a further hour until it was completely dark then slid into the trees along the bank. Within seconds there was the clatter of a helicopter overhead as it raced up and down the valley created by the stream. Its search lights were following the path. "Quick get in here" shouted Jeffrey as he hauled Sebastian behind a thick clump of bushes "and don't look up or move a muscle".

They lay like that for half an hour until the tick tack tick tack of the rotor blades died away into the Russian side.

They ate the remainder of the food and drank most of the water. It had stopped raining.

It was now quite dark. Sebastian fell asleep exhausted.

He awoke with a start, Jeffrey was shaking him and motioning him to be silent. He pointed to some figures in uniform probably border guards walking along the pathway on the other side of the river.

They froze and, as soon as the patrol passed, quickly moved off as quietly as they could. Sebastian looked at his watch it was 7 am. The sun was just up and it looked like being a fine day. Funny, he thought, the grass here seems greyish not like the emerald green in England, there were purple flowers and thigh high seeding grasses wet with morning dew. This soon soaked Sebastian's trousers. Damn! He had forgotten to take his pills. He explained to Jeffrey and they halted for a few minutes as he used the last of the water.

They walked on for another hour. Sometimes Jeffrey used the walking stick but in rough areas Sebastian had to prop him up as before.

"So now Jeffrey I think you owe me some sort of an explanation!"

"Yes I agree, " he said "well the reason we are crossing here is that lower down the two oblasts, that's sort of counties to you, are where the full scale civil war is taking place. Of course it's a much shorter route and one that the Russians might think I was using. In fact we cannot go higher up because the Ukrainians are starting to erect their own border wall, as it cuts right across Russian speaking areas the locals are dead against it. You see, very broadly, all of Ukraine to the right or East of the Dnieper is Russian speaking but I could not be sure exactly where the new excavation works and border posts would be. The only safe area seemed to be this area which is also a traditional smugglers route. So we must still be careful. Smugglers will shoot first and rob you afterwards! I hope the border patrol we saw will have frightened them off!. Look I'll draw you a rough plan of our route. Have you got a bit of paper? The fly sheet from one of your books will do!"

He was silent for a time as he drew a plan of the route. As they walked on he pointed out the chalk cliffs to the right.

"Now here we turn left and walk across some fields, away from the river Oskil. No danger here just keep going along the foot path. Just one more hour I assure you. Ah yes there it is." They reached a road. Jeffrey announced "This is the Ukrainian P 79 road, don't worry Sebastian we are all but home and dry now!" and at Sebastian's prompting Jeffrey was hauled over the wooden fence onto the side of the dusty metalled road.

Jeffrey said "If a car comes take the cue from me. We either carry on walking or we flag him down and ask for a lift. Remember if they do take us on we will have to pay, that's the custom here. If you get a lift you pay! So it's best to hold some money ready. It's a pretty convincing argument."

Soon an old tractor lumbered into view and Jeffrey waved it down and from what Sebastian could tell he was giving a pretty good story about falling down and breaking his leg. They were both allowed to travel on the trailer behind carrying new mown hay. Before getting on Sebastian proffered thirty dollars and the man seemed delighted.

In that way they arrived at Kupyansk.

They were dropped off at the railway station where they were able to drink and eat breakfast.

Sebastian persisted with his questioning. "Jeffrey its clear you have been this route before. Presumably this is the way you got in but what were you doing in that place and why did they find you without clothes or other travelling kit except a sleeping bag? How did you get there? Was it by car? Jeffrey! look I have half carried you this far, I think I deserve a bit more of an explanation"

"Sebastian everything I have told you is true. There is a Lancashire Fertiliser company trying to start potash operations. There are two rival companies in Russia at loggerheads. The older Russian based company does indeed have question marks over its management style., They tried to run a cartel to keep the potash price high, but that fell apart because the Belarus Associate wanted out. The chief executive has been arrested for devious practices. The other more recent company headquartered in Switzerland is carrying out a massive new operation in the area where I was found where there are huge potash reserves. They do indeed have problems with freezing the shaft of the mine which is being done under contract. An employee is believed to have given false reports on progress leading to a huge legal and engineering claim. They are intensely nervous about outsiders snooping around, which is what I was doing using Siberian Minerals as cover."

They boarded a bus for Kharkiv as the number of trains was limited.

Sebastian tried again "So where do you come from Jeffrey? I have worked with you now for two years but I realise I know nothing about you at all!"

"Oh a small town in the East Midlands, Loughborough, do you know it?"

"Yes I do, the odd shaped town square in the centre and the University, specialist in sports isn't it!"

"Yes, I went there actually, straight from school, it still operates a steam train doesn't it? At weekends."

"So you'll know 'The Brush' then?"

"No what's that?"

"or 'Morris' or 'Taylors'?"

"No what are they?"

"They are or have been some of the largest employers in the town. The Brush is a very large electrical business, Morris made huge factory cranes and Taylors are still there making bells church bells. Jeffrey it's not possible to have lived there without knowing these firms!"

"Well I do vaguely remember them now that you remind me but I really wasn't interested in business. My father was the local vicar you see, we didn't get involved in all that! In any case you have the email from the board of RKW, they have clearly checked me out, its they whom I have a contract with! If you are not happy why not make contact with them direct when we get back!"

At Kharkiv they took a train at 13.16 and got into Kyiev at 17.53.

They took a taxi to the British Embassy.

Jeffrey introduced himself and they were greeted by the reception who had clearly been warned of their arrival, it was 18.20 and it was obvious to Sebastian that Jeffrey had been expected, but why?.

They were both filthy and bedraggled, their feet were caked in dried mud and their clothing was torn and dirtied. Neither of them had shaved for several days and there was mud, tangled grass and weed intermingled with their hair. They were both exhausted and barely able to walk. Sebastian's shoulder was raw from Jeffrey's weight and it hurt.

 They were surrounded by several staff, within minutes a doctor had arrived who looked at Jeffrey's now very swollen, leg. "Hm!" He said. "It looks like a break to the ankle or bad sprain, we'll get you for an X-ray immediately at hospital, he's a strained hand and black eye." He then turned to Sebastian "Are you alright?" He checked him over. "Hm" he said "this one's OK".

The first thing that Sebastian insisted on was calling his wife. He was right, she had been nearly frantic with worry and he had to spend time explaining that the battery on the phone was totally flat and he had been unable to recharge it. He briefly explained that they were now safe and the mission was completed and that he would be home hopefully on Saturday.

A young foreign office staffer explained he would be taking Sebastian to a separate flat and, as he was leaving, he turned to Jeffrey and waved "Well we made it! See you in an hour or so to tie up a few loose ends before we fly home?"

Jeffrey responded cheerily "Yes we made it, thanks to you" then he turned and was ushered out the door they had come in.

Sebastian turned to the staffer. "How on earth did you know we were coming?"

"Jeffrey called us soon after you passed the frontier. Now my job is to get you changed and give you something to eat. The Ambassador whom you met in London several months ago, is busy right now but I have booked an appointment for him to see you tomorrow morning at 9.30 am when we can sort everything out. Don't worry about Jeffrey he's well taken care of."

Sebastian found himself in a small en-suite one bedroom flatlet, furnished with the heavy wooden furniture typical of most of Eastern Europe. Clunky and solid.

The staffer brought in some tea, sandwiches, an omelette and a slab of cake.

He took a long shower and took pleasure in seeing the grime falling off him. Within five minutes, he slumped back on the bed and fell fast asleep.

CHAPTER THIRTEEN

He was awakened the following morning by a bright light; he had forgotten to draw the curtains and the sunlight was blinding. He pulled the curtains to. He washed and shaved and there was a knock on the door. The staffer entered with a full English breakfast on a tray.

Sebastian looked at the clock on the wall it was already 10 o'clock. He muttered to the staffer that they were already late and received no reply. He quickly dressed into the cleaner kit from his bag. – He started to gobble down the food. 'What' he thought, 'the first hot meal in days!'

A few minutes later an older man appeared. He thought he recognised the face from the FCO meetings but wasn't sure. "Well Mr Edwards, we meet again! How are you? You remember we met in London, the name's Roland Smith?" He proffered his hand.

"I am OK now and thanks for the overnight stay and breakfast. Is this all paid for by her Majesty? Anyhow thanks. As far as the trip is concerned frankly I have never been so shit scared in all my life! Where's Jeffrey?"

"Your friend is OK he went to the hospital but has had to leave for the UK; he gave me this letter for you."

The man whom Sebastian assumed was the UK ambassador to Ukraine sat down and poured himself a cup of tea as Sebastian read the handwritten note.....

Dear Sebastian.

Just a note to thank you for your help in my rescue. It shows your integrity and loyalty that you came to my help. Any other person might well have left me to my fate. Thanks for propping me up on the walk (although I shall never again willingly enter a three legged race!) and being such good company.

I will look forward to reading in the press about your plans for Lib Dem revival, I hope they come off.

The FCO should be able to return the escape $3000, just file a claim for it.

In the circumstances I have already told RKW HR Director John Avis that I will be resigning my post, you can see that was inevitable? I am effectively a marked man in Russia.

Now I have to move on to a new posting so I am afraid it is farewell then!

Don't look for me through any Loughborough contacts as I never lived there and my name isn't Jeffrey Pardoe.

Thanks, it's good to have known you and worked with you.

Your friend

PS the ambassador will explain further but he will need this letter for his files.

It was left unsigned but dated the previous evening.

Sebastian was shaken, he had hoped to find out what the hell had been going on, but now that would never happen. Also he had grown used to lugging Jeffrey about and it didn't seem right walking about without him attached! But how, he wondered, was Jeffrey connected to the Foreign Office which he clearly was because he had phoned ahead and they knew he was coming?

He automatically handed back the letter to the Ambassador.

The Ambassador spoke. "I think I can give you answers to most of the questions you must be thinking!"

He looked at his watch. "Yes I think we are just in time!" He walked over to the TV in the corner and switched it on.

"We can get Sky and BBC TV here if the reception is OK – let's see! Yes here it is! I think there's a newsflash coming."

A picture came onto the screen. There were lines and lines of tanks and other artillery pieces, recovery equipment and rocket launchers.

A voice over stated *"Information has recently been passed to us from a trusted source that several divisions of Russia's elite guards division has been spotted near Rostov on Don about 100 kilometres from the border, apparently in line and ready to move into the Ukraine".*

It then moved on to discussion of the implications of this on the cease fire.

"So was Jeffrey connected with that?"

"Well I want to thank you Mr Edward for bringing home one of our, what we might call 'Assets'.

"You mean he was your agent – so this has been one big lie from start to finish. First the lie about there being a problem in that Siberian Minerals unit at Volgograd - I suppose that was the first cover story? Well, there had been payment difficulties but it was resolved by Jeffrey on an earlier visit. I checked with the MD when I arrived earlier this week that the outstanding amounts due under the contract had been paid by the customer. But his second trip was not authorised was it?

Then the next deception I suppose was about the potash company and the involvement of the mafia gangs. Was this the reserve cover story? I suppose Jeffrey's apparent terror was just a plant to convince our driver Andrey that he was badly disoriented by the treatment of the security guards. I suppose you knew he would report to our Company HQ in Moscow and then to the Russian Security services?

All this subterfuge, it's lies upon lies that I cannot stand. You both drew me into this didn't you?"

The Ambassador replied "You have to understand how these things work. Dealings with other states can be rather baffling! But yes, I had met you and believed that you could be entrusted with this mission, if we had no other option". He continued without allowing Jeffrey to protest, "and we didn't!"

"A key factor in any military conflict is attack by surprise, but let's say you don't want a war you just want to intimidate another country. Actually charging in with tanks means war but threatening war is a different matter. If you wanted to do that you would announce that you were carrying out troop manoeuvres or something but that's not really going to carry much weight because anyone can say what they like.

Another way then is for the country to signal that it is ready to do something. It leaks that it has several divisions ready to act aggressively – to intervene. It then permits photographs of a military build-up to filter through, taken by an independent source, in this case our agent. This if, you like, primes the threat!

As you know NATO has been constantly on guard about Russian incursions and it has called on all its NATO allies to provide what information they can. If all the allies are made aware of the build-up then it becomes the threat, and achieves what the Russians want.

It seems probable that the Russian secret service were already aware of Jeffrey's presence due to his frequent travels in Russia and that they were probably tracking him and allowed him to get near their military base in order to provide him access to verifiable pictures of troop movements.

But unless they had actually tried to captured him it would have sounded like a put up job. He had to believe that he was escaping. Had he attempted to pass through the normal exit points they would have had to capture him, otherwise it would not appear that he had something of importance. Jeffrey himself might not have known that it was more like a game of cat and mouse, he was after all risking his freedom, he was the mouse.

You provided cover for his extraction, which is what they wanted, after all a man with a broken leg could not get very far on his own. It's likely they knew exactly where you were at any time. Last night we searched your belongings."

He held up two small microchips.

"We took this microchip from your coat and another from your phone. Jeffrey might have thought you were 'clean' since you had the coat with you at all times I think? But you were clearly visible to them all the time!

The instruction to the border guard at the frontier to upgrade the security was probably made after they believed you had already passed through.

The use of the helicopter was rather more to make sure you were not harassed by smugglers who use the same route as they have a habit of turning very nasty if surprised.

So there really **was** a Russia troop build-up, which is what Russia wanted us to see, and that they were really serious and, thanks to you, we **did get out** the evidence, which is what NATO wanted. The Americans were suitably impressed with the operation which gave details of the exact troops and numbers of tanks and artillery pieces.

So it's another round in the dangerous game we are playing here.

If you had not managed to get Jeffrey out then they would have had an interest in imprisoning him for several years perhaps. After all if it was a botched job then he would merely have been another foreign agent and they would have had no interest in just releasing him.

Actually we have been forced to move our 'Assets' because it became clear that Edward Snowden, whom you may remember stole several secret files, ended up with them in Russia and may well have compromised our agents in this area."

The Ambassador paused.

Sebastian was astonished but asked. "Well what happens to my directorship of Siberian Minerals, can I go back there without the visa properly stamped for exiting Russia?"

"If you still have your passport then we will ensure that the correct stamps are applied. It's very unlikely they would want to get at you. They could have legitimately killed you at any time in the last 4 days if they had wanted to! We will give you a temporary passport from here!"

Sebastian insisted, he had been duped he was getting angry, "Unlikely, what the hell does that mean? But of course I would be a marked man, wouldn't I? They know, according to you, exactly where I have been and that I was used by the intelligence services. You have demolished my credibility!" He nervously twiddled the ring on his finger.

The ambassador refrained from answering – he looked away out of the window which overlooked a park and then back again. Sebastian continued.

"You understand that you have destroyed all the hard work that I have put in over the years not only to build a commercial link into Russia but also to get to grips with and understand their political viewpoint. You have destroyed and sacrificed all that for your own short term interest.

Is it in the interests of this country? No I don't believe so, it's a silly school kids game of cat and mouse. I have no doubt the CIA could have removed Jeffrey if you asked them but I suppose you wanted to show that we, in the UK, could still be useful and provide 'exclusive' information; but then I have been nothing but honest with you right from the start and all you have repaid me with is cynical deception!"

The Ambassador coughed gently, clearly trying to close down the meeting. "Of course you understand that this meeting never happened! We can never publicly substantiate or acknowledge anything you say about your trip or about Jeffrey Pardoe, nor indeed that we two have ever met."

"Anyhow now let's get you home as quickly as we can eh? Oh yes! We will ensure we repay you the $3,000!

If you want to leave a message for Jeffrey Pardoe I can make sure that he receives it?"

"Nah, it's all been said; he did after all put me at huge risk for his and your advantage!"

"Yes, I am sorry about that, we will try to make it up to you in some way!"

"Yeh! I bet" Sebastian replied.

The Ambassador proffered a handshake but Sebastian refused the offer, the Ambassador stood up and left.

Sebastian spent some time alone in his room trying to comprehend what had happened.

Later that day he was driven to the airport and he arrived back home on Saturday.

He hugged Sylvia and promised to tell her all about it some day. "We just went for a long walk!" She persisted in asking if he had taken the pills as ordered by the doctor but he assured her, much to her relief, that he had and that he had generally felt fine. He was exhausted and sank back into his favourite armchair and was soon asleep.

CHAPTER FOURTEEN

Sebastian discussed his whole future with Sylvia on the Sunday. He agreed that further work in Russia would likely expose him to more serious risks and that he had to 'cut loose'.

On the following Monday Sebastian emailed a brief report to the John Avis Director of the HR function of RKW in London, copy to the MD of the board.

At your request I went to Russia and managed to extract our employee Jeffrey Pardoe with some difficulty. This involved a considerable cross country trek and an unauthorised exit from that country. I now believe that it's in the best interests of Siberian Minerals if I relinquish my interests there. I have done all that can reasonably be expected and can always assist you from here in the UK if you require selective advice. Am prepared to carry on as a on-executive Director for continuity's sake.

Accordingly I offer my resignation from Siberian Minerals. I came in at a time when there was a particular problem which I helped to resolve and, after several years, I think the position has stabilised enough for you to appoint a local person.

I would like to cash in my Share Options or transfer them to another board member at an agreed price. Please advise the values on this.

I would like the bonuses due to me in respect of my contract with Siberian Minerals for 2013/4 and 2014/5 to be paid to my bank account as soon as possible.

I think that, in the long term, a peace treaty will be forthcoming and that access to the huge mineral wealth in Russia will have been worth the while and cost of my assisting the establishment of a successful company there.

Sebastian Edwards.

The MD responded quickly through his PA.

Sebastian

Jeffrey Pardoe is unknown to us. UK employees working abroad are managed through the HR function, usually under specific contracts, but I am glad that you managed to bring him out, presumably he was ill or something?

Yes, Sebastian you have done well in Russia turning it around was largely due to your efforts.

I will await the report of the HR Director but I see no reason why you may not relinquish posts and obtain the bonus entitlement and exchange your options, there are several members of the board that would I am sure be interested in acquiring these. I will instruct the HR directorate accordingly.

Long term of course the future of the Russian operation does depend on the conflict in the Ukraine. We need a stable economic environment before we can invest further!

A manager in the HR function replied.

The HR Director, John Avis, was dealing with this matter personally but is on holiday. I will put your request to him when he returns. John Avis is actually Director of HR for foreign operations. He is employed on a three year contract which, I understand will not be renewed at the end of this month.

We have no files on Jeffrey Pardoe. You could try the Moscow office, he may have been hired from there directly.

CHAPTER FIFTEEN

Later, on the following Monday afternoon, Sebastian sat at his desk in RKW's local offices and looked through the Nottingham and Derby area Yellow Pages. Normally he tried to ensure that he never used the company phone on private business, but on this occasion he decided he didn't care a fig!

He found the section that he was looking for and made a number of quick calls, he explained precisely what he wanted and asked about the cost.

He returned home and after supper turned to his wife.

"Now, Sylvia, you know I have been promising that after my own family past was exposed and meetings arranged, I wanted to do the same for you; to bring about some reconciliation, if I could, between you and your family, or at least try to find a way of discovering if your sisters were still alive and if they wanted to talk to you?

Well, today, I contacted a couple of detective agencies, one is the offshoot of a very famous Indian ladies detective agency and I have received a quotation from them."

Sylvia immediately protested "But you know Seb, my father's last words to me were "if you ever make contact again I will finish you!" How can you be so sure he will not use the agency to find out where we are?"

"I have been through all that with them and am convinced that they know exactly what they are doing, but listen, if we have to we will move or stay in a hotel till the trouble dies down. I am here now and I will not let anything happen to you I promise!"

He continued "I hope to help you to put an end to decades of pain which I know you have felt. I will be by your side, if you wish, for every moment and I will ensure that your father may only be told of your address when we are both sure that he is reconciled with your situation.

But I need you to write down the full details of your family, for example, your sisters, their ages and last school attended. For your parents their places of work and home address and phone numbers, as well as addresses of any family or friends who might be able to help. Will you do this? The costs of the agency are surprisingly modest!"

So began the process of reconciliation which Sebastian thought would take many months, in fact her family was located in weeks. Her father had died several years previously but the others were all alive.

There was a family reunion and a massive outpouring of joy, Sebastian himself was moved to tears and was treated as the new head of the household. Sylvia spent every night for weeks catching up with past news, of extended relatives, of her sisters' new husbands and nephews and nieces. Her mother came to stay.

Sylvia and Sebastian were married in July 2015. Sebastian commented to all who would listen "She looks more radiant than I have ever seen her." They had intended just to invite close family only, but then it was extended to friends, which of course included all the Councillors as well. Both Chris Walmsley of UKIP and Tim Dabbs of the Greens attended. In the end there were hundreds of people; the old District Offices were used, prior to their demolition!

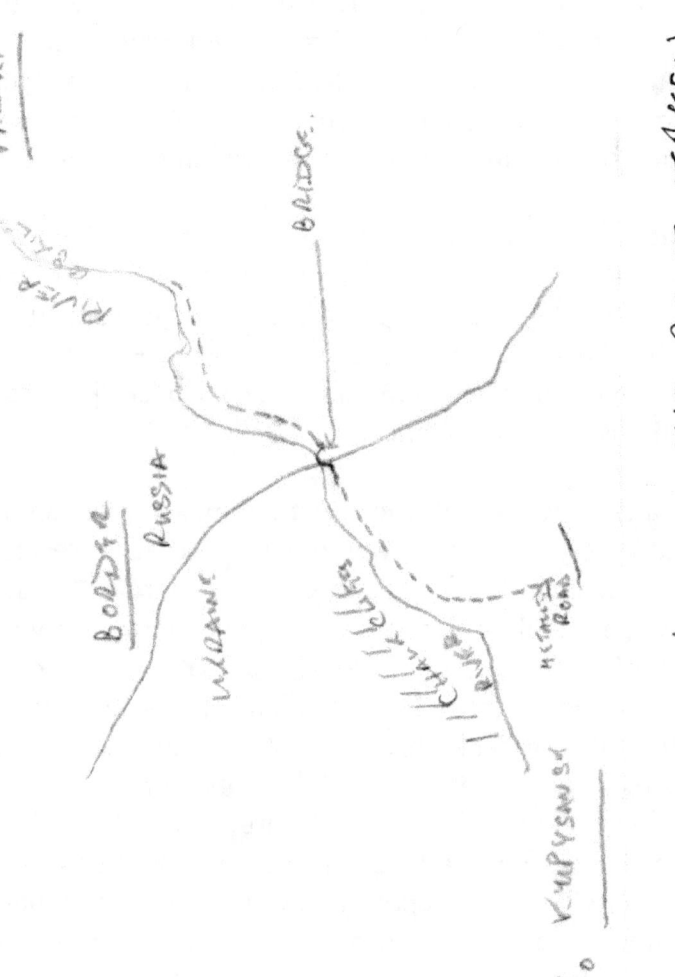

FROM VALUKI

RIVER GORAK

BRIDGE.

BORDER

RUSSIA

WLARNE

CHIN/CLIFFS

RIVER

METALLED ROAD

To KUPYANSK St

JEFFREYS MAP OF THE ROUTE TAKEN

PART SEVEN - Bounce

CHAPTER ONE – July to August 2015

On July 16th a new Lib Dem leader was elected by 56% to 44% in a two horse race- it had been rushed through with few public meetings due to the reduction in the number of LD MPs and, as Sebastian put it, 'the rather muted LD national presence'. The winner was none other than Tim Beaumond whom he had met several times in London.

Edna Leggs had been voted in as Chair of the Middleton Town Council and Sebastian was voted in as chairman of the Constituency Association. The general view was that since his marriage Sebastian had in effect retired from front line politics in that constituency, at least this was the message that Lib Dem members received back from contact with the two UKIP District Councillors.

Within a few weeks of the Election most local Lib Dem members expressed the view at following meetings that, in retrospect, they had achieved considerable successes against the run of play. What on the first view on the night appeared to be a desperate local result was so on the basis of their own internal local expectations. Compared with results in the surrounding areas Sebastian himself was one of the very few Lib Dems to have increased his share of the vote. Sebastian was credited with being the instigator of the key decisions which had made that possible but he himself was not so sure; by a quirk of fortune there had been no UKIP candidate because the Tory candidate was a quasi UKIP and did not wish to see a potential UKIP competitor queer his pitch and furthermore the Greens did not stand a candidate because of Sebastian's deal which effectively had given the Greens a District Council seat.

On a national basis if both those had fought this seat they might have taken 15% between them. Sebastian thought himself lucky to get the vote that he did!.

At work Sebastian had little difficulty in obtaining the bonuses due from Siberian Minerals for prior years' trading and from the sale of the options that he had been granted which were picked up by another member of the board. He had after all secured the amount owing to that company from the largest contract in Volgograd of its most recent acquisition. For a time it had seemed that the Russian Unit could not withstand such a large bad debt, consequently it had looked as though it might force the closure of the newly acquired operation there. But that danger was now passed. It continued to be profitable.

He had asked after John Avis but was told he had returned to his former post at the MOD.

For the time being his employment continued in England with RKW. His exploits in Russia had generally been ignored by the board. It was considered to be a troublesome side show in a troublesome zone at a troublesome time and the board of RKW, the LSE listed mineral extraction company, didn't really know what to do with it. They had got into it by accident and would likely get out of it in the same way. Provided it kept its nose clean and made good money nothing needed to be done, at least that's how the HR director John Avis had explained it to Sebastian. Sooner or later, they thought, the Ukraine problem would go away and it was useful to have a toe-hold in a market with such vast mineral resources.

Sebastian's work continued as a UK Regional Financial Director. The post was reasonably well- paid, he had done the job for many years. Although every year was challenging the work was not difficult as he was accustomed to it.

For the very first time in his life Sebastian was financially stable. He and Sylvia lived frugally, they were both earning, and had no extensive hobbies, except one – his politics; furthermore the house was paid for and there were no other calls on their money. He could, if he chose, spend some of his new found wealth.

At the same time Sebastian was freed from the substantial time he had been obliged to give to his position as a District Councillor where he had been leader of the small Lib Dem group. The main problem had been his role as part of the planning committee which had sucked out, he reckoned, about 20 full days a year. Due to the agreement with his employers they agreed to cover this 50/50, so the company gave him an additional 10 days paid leave but he had to take the other 10 days out of his holiday entitlement. The result was that he had no extensive holidays. After the elections on May 7th he had managed to reposition himself onto less demanding committees cutting his work time to 10 full days, of which only 5 came from his holiday entitlement.

Making use of an internal 'mutiny,' he had himself proposed his Lib Dem erstwhile supporter but now opponent, Tim Holland, as the party leader on the Council and thus managed to avoid that role which otherwise absorbed hours of nervous energy every month. Most of his supporters thought that he would fight to keep hold of that position but he decided he had better things to do and let it go, actually seconding his opponent.

The reduced time on District Council Committees and meetings, together with his reduced commitment to world-wide company operations in Russia meant, that for the first time in years he had been able to seize control over his own timetable. He had much more time to think.

That's exactly what he did. Troubled by the collapse of the Lib Dem vote and the rout of the MPs and Councillors he had determined to at least fully understand the problem before offering proposals to help fix it.

He researched and pondered for several weeks digging into the Lib Dem manifestoes and other published material like copies of Lib Dem speeches and extracts of TV debates.

He had invaded, despite his wife's protests, their small extra bedroom at home, and the walls were papered with extracts of comments from all national and local publications about the Election and the collapse in the vote, with cross references to manifestos.

A big pile of books was wedged between the desk and the wall contained items "Why Vote Liberal Democrat" by Jeremy Browne MP and the earlier "Orange Book – reclaiming Liberalism" and Vince Cable's book on the World Economic Crisis – "The Storm". A map of results by constituencies was blue-tacked onto the back of the door. Piles of the more serious political commentaries such as those of the Economist and New Statesmen were stacked in the only remaining corner of the room.

He had finally come to his conclusion. Lib Dems had fought on the wrong issues and presented themselves in the wrong way.

He had previously suggested to Madge his co-councillor for their ward on May 8th that she might join him in some role looking at the problem of their catastrophic losses and see if they could correct the position here.

So in late July he held a meeting with Madge at his home, downstairs in the little sitting room. Sebastian's wife welcomed her. "Madge I do hope you can help him, he's driving me to distraction, he's hidden himself away every evening for weeks doing his 'research' as he calls it! The whole of our spare bedroom has been taken over – it's a total mess of papers and files and books – I cannot clean anything! And moody? Since the last election he's hardly had a pleasant word to say about anything in the world!"

Sebastian recognised that Madge had played an important part in the election and was now herself a District Councillor elected on May 7th. He knew she was a media student in her final year at the local university working for Lib Dems at evenings and weekends. She was known as having a keen interest in social issues, she had been in charge of the "Focus" production, the Lib Dem local newsletter and had warned

Sebastian about Tim Holland a former lieutenant who had turned against him and who had tried to oust him from his role as leader of the Lib Dems on the District Council. She was lively, dressed informally, was a 'mature student' and not easily put down. Sebastian knew that it had required a lot of imagination and initiative to produce the regular newsletters which was one of her tasks.

Sebastian saw her potential involvement in his project as a reward for her help and loyalty and he assumed that she would enjoy the more academic nature of his suggested research.

At his home, Sebastian ushered his wife out of the small sitting room and explained "I have come to some preliminary findings, Madge, and have written a paper that I can show you. It's taken me weeks longer that I had anticipated. It so happens that the Lib Dem East Midlands Region has proposed a letter of thanks to Nick Clegg for all the good work he has done and I have put my views in an open letter to the Chairman".

He passed her a copy of the letter he had written in response.

She glanced at it, her eyebrows shot up worriedly, "Wow, yes! It looks like a thorough analysis. Do you want me to read it all? Now? You make a lot of points and it's a densely packed critique? It'll take time to go through it and see if I accept what you say, presumably the idea is that we form a little group to make a difference in some way?".

"Well something like that. You see Madge, for the first time I have the time and funds to devote to getting to grips with some of the key issues. The idea is to set up a little local research unit on local matters that we can affect. Basically it has occurred to me that we have nearby three Universities. At each of them there will be Degree Courses on Politics or linked topic like PPE. I intend to offer minor research positions, or internships as they are often called, to a few students based on paid research on an estimated hours at a standard rate. A zero hours contract is all that I could afford I am afraid, but it might be a useful supplement to offset some of their costs being at Uni? I would ensure that they are properly treated, visits to Lib Dem HQ, the House of Commons and maybe EU to do their research. I would get them proper accreditation for that purpose."

"That sounds expensive Sebastian can you raise the funds for it?"

"Well" Said Sebastian" Since I have finished with the Russian side of the business, I have the time and funds and I would try to obtain additional funding to cover these costs from those companies and people that supported me over the last election. Well, it'll be steady as she goes to begin with but I am prepared to commit funds. It is, as it were, my only hobby! Maybe I can later get funding from Lib Dem HQ."

"But Seb you are not expecting me to contribute because I have no savings at all?" she interjected.

"No, No! indeed you could be one of the paid researchers!"

"Paid?" Madge sounded impressed and just to be sure "Paid you say?"

"Yes that's right – not much I mean minimum wage, on time spent, on zero hours contract, not more than £2000 a year. I could afford say three people like that maybe £5000 to £6000 per annum!"

"So how long could that go on for? Seb you aren't made of money!" He could see she was amazed.

"Minimum 2 years maximum 4 years depends on other income and how many people we have working on it!!"

"Seb you are nuts? Why not buy yourself an expensive car like your son's and take your wife on holiday?"

"Because that's not the person I am". Sebastian kept pushing his letter towards her, anxious to get the matter back on track. "Now here's the letter – consider it and let me know what you think! Basically it analyses the failures of the Lib Dem campaign. If you don't want to go into detail you'll get the sense of it by just looking at the headings underlined.

In my opinion the emblems we fought on; 'Stronger Economy, Fairer Society' were neither different enough nor appealing enough nor radical enough. When caught in the headlights the Tories put over a simple message 'Lets finish the job! The alternative is a wobbly Labour leader with SNPs determined to undo all the hard work we have done!' and that bulldozed a century of radical political involvement into the hedgerows.

It's my view that we ourselves had discounted Lib Dems out of the picture by then. We had actually lost the election before the campaign started! What we thought we had established by being in power was credibility and experience, the lack of which had been flung at us for 50 years. In the event the voters couldn't care a fig about either.

So why don't you give me a call and we can meet here tomorrow afternoon when I can put together some ideas and how such a unit might work?"

"Ok I'll do that!"

Sebastian's wife returned with a cup of tea. "I do hope you will help him Madge, I have tried but I couldn't understand all the detail of the policies and besides I now have my own little venture!"

Madge asked "What's that?"

Sylvia replied, "I have decided with the help of one my sisters who has a University degree in Sociology to raise the profile of Asian Women here in the UK. There are little units across the UK dealing with battered women and those damaged by the mediaeval treatment of Asian women; but there is no overall co-ordination, no nationwide action group. We need to help people before they are abused! So I am hoping to use my example to set up and publicise such a group – it's the only way that ultimately we can prevent the abuse happening to the next generation. We all have to stand up to be counted!"

Madge sounded encouraging, "Well, it sounds a very good cause!"

Sylvia emphasised, "After all I am a British Citizen and I am entitled to protection by law as is every other British woman of Asian descent. We have been slow to articulate these views or protect ourselves, mainly because the cultural ethos is to respect a parent's view and further to respect the man as the head of the household. If we are to take our place as full citizens we will have to organise and claim our rights as every generation of Britons has done before us. That's what I am going to try to do!"

"Wow!" said Madge "That's terrific, well done, if I can help in any way please let me know – I may be able to help in PR work and you'll need to set up a charity a get it registered properly?!"

"That's all very well!" interjected Sebastian who had been hovering about taking out the used tea cups and remaining biscuits. "But I am, I hope, first in the queue?" He asked quizzically.

Madge nodded. "So see you tomorrow Madge!"

CHAPTER TWO – A critique of the Lib Dem campaign

The letter given to Madge read as follows:-

To the members of Liberal Democrat East Midlands Regional Party.

Members

It is suggested that we write a letter of thanks to Nick Clegg. I don't agree with that.

Would you thank King Harold for his performance at the battle of Hastings?

You seem to imagine that nothing much happened on May 7th 2015.

What has occurred is the most significant collapse of any party ever at Westminster.

The leadership totally failed to understand or connect with the voters.

I do not see how wasting time praising Nick Clegg will make anything better!

The Lib Dem Campaign group failed to 'sell' the Lib Dem message - which isn't Tory light - that will not sell, nor will the floppy centre ground. So Tories right here! and Labour left there! and LD where? Where else but in the middle? If you present a middle ground position and voters are pushed they will go with what appears to be the strongest position to get the job done. Why vote for a woolly Tory when you can vote for a real one! What we needed was <u>aggressive differentiation</u> – not trying to be 'too-goody shoes' but posing radical questions on broader policies. What we got was largely <u>equi-distance.</u> Or the politics of 'middle for diddle'.

*They failed to deliver a dramatic structural change to Parliament which successive generations of Lib Dem voters had been promised since the 1960's. The key was that they never obtained the support of Cameron to the constitutional changes which they should have within the initial coalition agreement. Merely to **allow** a referendum on AV which was never a Lib Dem policy was never going to be enough and, once Tories actively campaigned against it, the cause was lost! In his book 'A House Divided' David Steel wrote of the Lib Lab Pact and coalition; page 157. 'there is no doubt that a full coalition would exert Liberal influence on policy and events at a crucially earlier stage and that provided we can obtain commitment to electoral reform the Liberal party should be eager to operate on the inside of future government rather than on the fringes'. There was never any Tory commitment. Worse still there was no reform of the House of Lords. It was Aristotle who observed (The Politics V1 iii) that "it is always the weaker who go in search of justice and equality: the strong reck nothing of them". The injustice does not stop because you lost a vote? Lib Dems should have been hammering away at the basic political unfairness and the creaking nature of the UK Constitution. Where was the shout at the election for constitutional reform?.*

They failed to attack the Tory and Labour Achilles' heel of bungled foreign wars. Mr Clegg wrote in a 'very nice' letter to Sir John Chilcot in January 'if the findings are not published with a sense of urgency there is a real danger the public will assume the report is being 'sexed down' by individuals rebutting criticisms put to them by the Inquiry whether that is the case or not'... no wonder Chilcot remained unmoved Clegg never looked like he would use it so the myth of WMD, (remember them), has never been explained. Lib Dems ought to have raised Cain. The failure of the Iraq and Afghanistan wars are not even mentioned in the election campaign! These escapades are becoming a joke even to our allies. Bruce Reidel an adviser to Obama in 2009 said "The US has a better appreciation after the war in Afghanistan of the limits of British power, it will be interesting to see if Afghanistan marks the end of Britain as a global military power!" Not an issue apparently worrying the Lib Dem; will they still contemplate intervention?

They failed to attack the Tory Military policy - where the armed forces are now so small as to be in all practical terms useless, with aircraft carriers we cannot use and a Trident force we cannot send to sea in case they get worn out and against an enemy which no longer exists. Exactly whom would we despatch a nuclear missile to on our own? Our military might is something like 50% of its strength in 1984 and the trouble is that there is a hopeless miss-match between what we are equipped for and these mini wars. We ape being a nuclear power without any defined enemies in a basic foreign policy unchanged since the end of the cold war. We have global military ambitions without equipment or finance to support it. We get into wars on the coat tails of the US that we cannot sustain, we hopelessly underestimate the difficulty of changing regimes where cultures are at variance with our own. The Commander of the British forces in Helmund said "We were under-prepared, we were under resourced and most importantly we didn't have a clear and achievable strategy to deliver success." The cost of these two Wars - £29bn and, of course, there's the small matter of 453 lives.

Labour and Tories should have been horsewhipped for these deficiencies – we let them off Scott free!

They failed to add anything to the discussion on the NHS core service. Everyone says "Hands off the NHS!" "Don't privatise the NHS" but nobody thinks the NHS is well run. In desperation just before the final week the Tories suddenly proposed an extra £8bn for the NHS without saying how it would be supported. Lib Dems matched that with £4bn for Mental Health and there we were! As if it was some sort of bidding war, the NHS could be taken over by the highest bidder. That was a joke! But there was no rational assessment of the latest changes made or whether the NHS was correctly structured. The Tory Government almost to its own surprise initiated in 2012 a changed structure. Clinical Commissioning Groups (CCG) were created of Groups of GPs practices working together each servicing perhaps 60,000 people or so. These groups were to commission services from the basic suppliers which were the NHS hospitals and similar institutions. The whole idea was to encourage hospitals to bid for these charges initially so putting pressure on their charges. They have to balance this income against their costs of running the hospital. The rather strange result is that these CCGs, with about 5% or less of the total costs, are responsible for 100% of the NHS hospital costs. Their primary purpose was to drive costs down and also at the same time, provide a link between hospitals and treatment at home. Huge claims were made for the ability of the CCGs to 'save £10bn'. Not one political party seems to have been aware of this nor attempted to see if it is a successful change or put forward any alternative structure. Instead we sit on the outside and throw around £32bn snowballs at the problem. There has been a total failure to research or to radically challenge how it could be structured more efficiently.

They failed to initiate Legal or even a Public Enquiry into the various Banking scandals which caused thousands of job losses throughout the country, passing off batches of junk mortgages as if good, squeezing small businesses into bankruptcy, swaps, selling inappropriate policies on the back of mortgages, Libor swindle. allowing savings banks to ape international banks for which they were not fitted. Having boards of banks like the Co-op with totally inappropriate directors. It was in short a shambles! The least we should have gone for was a public enquiry to weed out the culprits and restore some sort of prestige to a fully cleaned up financial sector. What are the people to think who lost their jobs because of this largely self-inflicted fiasco caused as someone stated by "A little housing problem in the USA"? Unfortunately it threw up massive inadequacies in the financial and monitoring review of the Banking sector and showed that, unrestrained, the leaders of these 'Banks' were little better than robber barons making money at whoever's expense. No one has been brought to book yet but if you make a wrong benefits claim of a few thousand you could end up in jail. It's a criminal offence for a benefit seeker with income of say £15K to obtain accommodation worth maybe £5K per annum using false information. It is apparently quite OK for a City Banker earning £300K p.a to sign off false information selling dubious blocks of mortgages as if they were good ultimately costing £billions. No political party apparently sees the moral dichotomy that this presents   It leads to a profound cynicism when guilty bankers continue their lives without a hiccup! It's not just a question of separating out Casino Banks from the rest as Vince Cable suggests. It's about perceived moral justice and equality before the law.

They failed to add anything to the Devolution debate of powers from Westminster - dropping regionalisation but succumbing to the cherry picking notion that the 'Strongest city/town Grouping would do – to put in a bid' – but who cares about the not-so-pushing-areas? Do they get nothing? It's apparently the law of first to the trough! How can that result in equality across the UK? The idea seems to be to stick on top of elected councils a single elected mayor, so why bother with the councils at all? Let's just be governed by 12 super mayors? The Independent called the British Constitution a 'Creaking Mechanism'. "We have gone from it being one of the great unwritten miracles of the world... to being the hotchpot of today.. we have different voting systems at every level of government... we have asymmetric devolution across regions and nations". But Lib Dems in Government in practice initiated nothing. Despite being a key driver for 30 years on this matter at Westminster of Scottish devolution Lib Dems were unable to add anything to the Scottish debate and made themselves irrelevant!

They failed to drive home that there was a desperate need for more cheaper affordable housing since it's almost impossible for youngsters to get 'on the ladder'. We should have been much bolder than 'what about a garden city?' We still don't rate this as the huge problem that it is! We needed something like a new Housebuilding Development Agency committed to building a minimum of 50,000 new Council houses a year. We are in a crisis. Governments have behaved as if there is a self-correcting factor but there is no 'free market' in housing because developers can only build where the planning system says. Selling off Council housing has resulted in massive queues for cheaper housing. In the 60 odd years from 1955 whilst inflation has climbed 100% or so the price of housing has increased by 700% to 900%. The lending multiple was 3 times the main earner now its 6 times both. The increase has not been caused by the increase in materials but in the cost of land and the excess profit caused by supplies in demand for which there is a shortage. We, as a nation, invest too much in housing but the resulting gap at the bottom means the creation of an underclass who can neither afford to rent privately nor to buy. These are the new poverty zones made up of benefit seekers, untrained, badly educated people who live a hopeless life often delaying marriage and living with their families until their mid-30's. No generation has had it this bad since the 1930's. Their plight is desperate, we Lib Dems merely say its 'in danger of becoming a crisis!' That's wrong it's here already! Poor immigrants seeking housing merely make the situation worse.

The Student Grant was a fiasco we lost the lead we had in the Student World electorally at a stroke. Where before we were getting 40% of the student vote we have lost that for a generation. Students had been in past years key workers for Lib Dems at elections . Not only that but our failure annoyed to a point of hatred all the parents who had been explaining to their young 'Don't get out of your financial limit - don't buy on credit.' We now say that's fine equivalently 'Get well out of your depth! - it really doesn't matter because there is a 50% chance you will not earn enough to pay it back'. It wasn't a U turn but a somersault which the 'dear leader' embellished with a jokey song. There's a terrible mismatch between the need for some degrees like Engineering, Languages, Maths and Sciences where we appear to be behind other nations and a massive surplus of Legal courses and other hobby type degree courses and all the while complaining about the mythical Polish Plumber because we can't train people in the basic trades that we need.! There seems to be no matching of the country's skills needs with educational facilities and courses provided. There are about 375,000 new graduates chasing 200,000 job. Each of the additional graduates bears a cost of £27,000 for no job. If we had the land we couldn't build the houses we need because lawyers don't make good builders! Basic necessary degrees and trades courses should, be free but now we get the skills that people prefer to learn and not what the nation needs.

Finally there's the EU- Our strongest card but we blew it! Nick lost the debates with Nigel Farage because he accepted a position of trying to defend the EU but he must have had an increasing awareness that the Greek negotiations showed one matter more clearly than anything else. There was simply no way that any UK Government would put itself in a position of being bullied like the Greeks, so membership of the Eurozone is out for perhaps a decade. It was he who had written of the 'lopsided nature' of the EU. As a former MEP he was in a unique position to expose Cameron's ridiculous assumption that he could bring back anything substantive from his short term negotiations. On Immigration, the blunt fact is that Cameron can change anything he likes in so far as it affects equally UK and non UK EU residents – what he cannot do is to prefer UK residents. On a wider range he cannot bring any change in the basic rules affecting powers to Westminster without a treaty change affecting every one of the existing members. That cannot reasonably happen before 2017. Nick Clegg was uniquely placed to expose this flaw. One of Cameron's weakest positions was re UKIP. We failed to even dent his position. His 100,000 limit had become 300,000 actual immigrants.

<u>We were badly beaten – it wasn't a misunderstanding by the voter, it's just that we failed to understand what was going on.</u>

Nick Clegg has a notion that it was all caused by last minute swing voters frightened of the SNP!

Chairman, your letter to King Harold about his disappointing results at Hastings is interesting and of course he tried his best, the problem for us all is that it was not good enough.

We had dozens of major issues available to use as ammunition – indeed we were almost buried by them but we managed to allow the Tories to hold the electoral ground of the Financial Management of the country, as if it were their own.

As to the benefits of helping the country? …… Great! Whoopee! but we have driven ourselves into a position where we cannot do it in the future as we are now irrelevant. Rather like the manager of a local food bank who distributes his wares only to find himself hungry!

If you believe that Lib Dems have a logical place in the political spectrum then their first job before all others is to preserve themselves in being. They failed to do this.

A big defeat ought to shatter old ways of thinking. Repeating the old messages and ways of operating is not good enough!

It was always said before the coalition started that the Lib Dems would be beguiled by the 'ministerial car' well they were, but not quite in the way most people thought. It was not the perks of office but the sense of power and the running of departments on a day to day basis that robbed them of their objectivity and perspective of the problems. It gave them a false sense of security. Ministers were, of course, household names with acres of newspaper and hours of TV exposure; they lost the ability radically to question what has always been at the heart of Radical Liberalism. They failed to develop the meritocracy which the policies implied.

The selling of the virtues of the centre ground the so called 'equi-distance' policies slap bang in between the other two main parties, and of saving the country did not rate. Indeed the only way that the Lib Dem Electoral campaign, as put in place, could ever have worked was if there already was PR.

We now know it is suicidal to play the 'equi-distance' strategy in a first past the post scenario.

In power the Lib Dems lost a sense of direction. They relied on the 'soft centre ground' voting for them.

Indeed the business of being in power was itself a distraction: as Shirley Williams wrote in her book 'Politics is for people, 'For four of the past 6 years I have been engulfed in the work of government. Anyone who has ever been a minister or leader of a large local authority knows that the job leaves little time for thought. One lives on the dwindling resources of past reading and past thinking. But if one doesn't think much one does learn a good deal about the difficulties of governing.'

Perhaps and read in its kindest light the very business of government blinded them to the key issues and how the voters would react at an election?

Sebastian Edwards

CHAPTER THREE - Later August 2015

Madge phoned on the following day and agreed to meet at Sebastian's house again. They sat in the same front room which was big enough for a sofa and two arm chairs and a small table. They used the dining table in the alcove to the right.

Madge started, "I follow the gist of what you are saying but it's not a very popular stance at present is it? It's a bit rough to call Nick, King Harold? It seems unlikely that the Lib Dem hierarchy are going to change quickly! Also we face the same problem as any other party, the tiny membership and even smaller number of activists to whom you are writing are not representative of the voters whom we would like to appeal to vote for us? So who exactly is your audience?

By the way did the Regional Chairman pass on your letter Sebastian?"

"Err well no!" Sebastian replied lamely.

"Well I am not altogether surprised," said Madge apparently not surprised at all. "Maybe one thing that I can do is to try to make your points less densely packed and more.. err – understandable. I mean that in a nice way but your letter is something you have to read through at least twice before you can get the full sense of it. Now you know, Sebastian, I am not as aware as you of all the policies and stuff, but I have a mind of my own, so I will not act as some sort of secretary, it's your show but I do expect to be listened to and the points that I raise to be taken seriously, otherwise I will not be able to work with you!"

"Understood, I have no problems with that! – I need a sounding board, a reviewer who will stand her ground!"

"But you must understand Seb that we are different characters and are constructed in completely different ways. I am not sure exactly how well you know yourself? I have been studying you for some time.

Maybe I should explain that my first two years at Uni were spent in psychoanalysis? I then switched to media studies because I didn't want to spend my life inside other peoples' brains! Shall I give you a summary of my view?"

"Well" grumped Sebastian "if you really must?" He sat back in his chair checking his watch and twiddling his ring.

Madge continued and clearly was not going to be stopped "I see you are a person who has considerable drive and initiative, you are very much a 'shaper' who provides the direction and impetus in the group, but you can also at times be arrogant if you think you are being questioned too closely. So you expect others to read every word of your long emails but tend to overlook details in replies to you? You are a good debater and you challenge when you don't like what people say. You are honest to the point of rudeness and you are direct.

That directness, openness and honesty are what people like you for and they will forgive minor slights and bullying from you since they know you are pressing points and not attacking them personally. You have a good political brain and have pulled off several key scoops here like, Moslem integration, Europhiles and with the Greens. All these deals work, because others believe that you mean it and are not cynically changing your tack to suit others' opinions. Despite your rough exterior you are in fact easily wounded, particularly if your Integrity is doubted. You can be stubborn to the point of being totally infuriating, but you can give way. You are imaginative which seems to contrast with your daily routine as an accountant, which perhaps calls more for accuracy!

You are a person around whom things happen, you engender loyalty and support and hard work, but you equally can ignore people like Tim Holland and Edna Leggs for weeks if they are not in your spectrum at the time. This causes unnecessary friction because they all like you and admire you. You could for example have headed off the 'mutiny' by Tim; the argument that you had with him about devolution was pointless because neither of you could affect the outcome? Similarly you did fine with ' Auntie Edna,' as we call her, when you had regular meetings with her, but you stopped these and suddenly she had no idea what you were doing. You lost her trust when you no longer confided in her.

You seem to fear close relationships, you prefer to keep people at a distance, this is often mistaken for you being offhand."

Madge suddenly stopped, Sebastian had not moved, he froze, he remained silent for a full minute.

In truth he was quite taken aback, he had not expected to be analysed in this way. She was right of course! He thought 'I do keep people at a distance, maybe that's back to school days. As a young vulnerable boarder you quickly learned that to show any weakness would be instantly jumped on and mercilessly exposed. One boy occasionally used to sniff probably having catarrh or something but for the rest of his school career he was derisively known as 'Sniffy White'. Another boy was so demoralised by persistent teasing, that, on leaving school, he had a nervous breakdown and spent a year with a psychologist trying to sort himself out. Others had melted under pressure. Best was to say nothing, offer nothing. Whom could he have confided in anyhow? His parents were then 2000 miles away in Nigeria. He had learned to protect himself by not exposing his inner thoughts. Later he had reckoned that for every career success from that school there had been an equal number of terrible failures.

"Seb, Seb are you alright?" Sebastian shuddered as he bought himself back to the present.

"Hem! Well yes, I am fine, I suppose you have pretty much got it but what that does not include is the reason why I do all this? I know sometimes that I can overdo points and to receive informed criticism is really what I need!

No!" He raised his hand to shut her off. "Let me explain.

Many voters question why people become politicians in the first place. I think they do it for a variety of reasons:

One you might call a 'professional politician'. Some just appear to slide into it, doing secondment with a junior politician in a party HQ, becoming PA, carrying out research, then writing speeches for an MP, then applying for some electable position and finally becoming an MP. You can find these kind of people in every party and provided the PR they exude is within a general framework they may well succeed in getting to the top of their tree. I have difficulty working with these people because I feel they are prepared to change the whole meaning of a text by simply inserting a word or comma, they obtain consensus by drafting and redrafting proposals to render everything mush. They can appear to be devious. Perhaps both Cameron and Clegg were examples. Maybe Blair was originally of this kind convincing a large Labour majority to put into practice, what was, in effect, a conservative regime. Such people can be cynical because to them gaining power or staying in power is the main reason for being in politics and they can shift their ground to accommodate that. To many voters they look shifty."

"Seb, I understand that but does this get us anywhere?" But Sebastian continued

"At the opposite end is the 'conviction politician', something in his or her past background or experience compels him to take an interest. They act on instinct and they win provided they can convince others of the strength of their argument. Both Thatcher and Nigel Farage are these kind of people. I have no problem with working with them because they are easy to understand and they are not devious, their objectives are clear even as I disagree with them. However they need to dominate their parties because the personal conviction cannot easily withstand competition from the use of other different strategies.

Personal conviction can cross apparent political boundaries. Ed Milliband looked as though he fell in this group but his own conviction never shone through and ultimately he was seen as just another professional politician. I think Jeremy Corbyn is clearly a conviction politician but his victory with 60% is not necessarily a victory for the left wing so much as a reaction to the Blair years of 'Bland Politics', PR stuff, policies which aim to commit to nothing but sound really great, the politics of holding power rather than of really achieving something! During the Blair years the Labour party was 'hollowed out' of any meaning. Jeremy Corbyn's problem is that his solutions are a generation out of date. Conviction politicians by their nature acquire a following of people who believe that their leader is right; they can have a following across all parties because they offer a certainty, an apparent clear vision.

I am a conviction politician. My background, my whole life, pushes me to stand up for justice and tolerance!

So what the hell am I doing? I strongly believe that there are always new and better ways of doing things. The treatment of the NHS in the last election was a case in point. All that parties appeared capable of doing was to outbid each other for the amount of the extra £bn commitment. What was needed, in my opinion, was a plan to improve the organisation and its efficiency. The actual public discussion on it was little better than what you could put on the back of a 'fag packet', little better than bar-room chat.

I have come to the conclusion that issuing thousands more Focuses and stuffing them through every door will not help us. We have to be more informed and better prepared! Do you understand my motivation?

I see my role and that of the Lib Dems is in primarily acting as a radical filter looking to improve governance across the board, a think tank, a generator of political ideas. I am not even sure that the proposals need be politically coherent one with another because each might fail for different reasons and to withhold one because it was politically incoherent with another might mean losing both."

"Madge I am of the conviction kind. I believe in a meritocracy but I hate those who abuse systems like the Bankers and I believe that the free market has to be watched like a hawk, but I don't believe in grants and pay-outs as too quickly the systems get abused. So I do know myself Madge – what I stand for and what I believe in".

Madge coughed gently but Sebastian continued.

"There are also leaders whom I call 'in-betweeners'. These have a conviction at heart but are quite willing to opportunistically grasp anything going even if it is not coherent with their proclaimed strategy. I put the leaders of the Greens and SNP in that category. Looking at their manifestoes.. How did both end up anti austerity?"

Madge had sat quietly through all this as Sebastian ploughed on regardless but eventually she butted in. "Err Seb I think we can go into that later perhaps?

Err Sebastian I can see that you have thought through this very deeply but can I bring you back to what we are trying to do in your proposed group? There's surely no point in us trying to cover issues which are in the hands of Westminster – really that's up to the MPs unless we are particularly drawn in?"

"Yes that's right, Madge, first of all we should try and aim at what is here at our feet in the East Midlands that is publicly available but mostly unpublished. We could for example have two or three lines of research, maybe firstly the NHS; amassing data on the performance of the CCGs, of hospitals; of associated units like the East Midlands Ambulance service. I know you have a personal interest in Care Homes and how the elderly are treated. We need to look into that as well!

Now I intend to start off very simply and usefully in the research group until we have achieved some prominence. My idea is first to look at three local matters". He handed her a note he had prepared:-

"SUGGESTED TOPICS

a) The performance of the EMAS the East Midlands Ambulance service whose results have been 'chronic' together with the performance of CCG's, the Clinical Commissioning Groups that effectively contract the hospital side of the NHS in the East Midlands and their 'savings'.

b) The performance of each of the Planning Authorities in the East Midlands to provide Affordable housing. Are they applying the rules correctly? Are they doing their jobs and monitoring the right- to-buy even of the Social Housing? Also number of houses built, price, housing waiting lists.

c) The performance of firms exporting to the EC; we need to keep a running record of all major orders because that information will be needed for the Referendum. We can make a start by getting on side with as many businesses that work with the EU and be prepared to speak up when specific EU sales contracts have been won"

Madge said "I get it! Start from two ends, the principles and, the local details? So could I argue for others can we have performance in terms of new apprentices and of unemployment by ward and crime, and immigration in the same way so we can build policies to cope with facts not just emotions?"

"Absolutely my thinking exactly! Let's make that a fourth!"

"So we will stick an advert into the Universities Job Opportunities Board and off we go?"

"Yes! We should open spreadsheets for the facts that we are collecting and should be prepared to issue some PR if we think it's required. We should try to build up an idea of exactly which EU laws are creating annoyance or alarm and work with our remaining Lib Dem MEP to draw some conclusion.

That gives you a flavour of what we would concentrate on – other matters of interest would be education, which schools are doing badly and why and transport as well as the supposed devolution to major cities or whole area, what exactly does it entail and exactly who is losing out? We will have to follow what's happening just to keep in touch with events.

So it's largely going to be about local regional issues. There are no Lib Dem MPs or MEPs to cross swords with and in most cases local Lib Dem branches here would welcome information which they can use to advantage.

In order to give the unit some chance of not being written off for political bias I intend to run it under a neutral name and call it 'Project Daedalus'."

"You mean the father of Icarus who was the lad that flew too near to the sun and fell into the water?"

"Yes the father had engineered the whole thing to escape from Crete – anyhow it sounds non-political?

But would you help me with this Madge? We will need to set on some researchers and get them drilling down! The question really is do you have time to help? Have you been offered a job yet? This was your last year as a Media Student and I assume you got your degree? But are you going to be around?"

"Sebastian, I think I am going to get a good degree and yes I take your point about the Lib Dem fiasco over the student fees. You were right, at Uni nobody even wanted to hear the name Lib Dem, never mind discussing voting that way. Well why I am here now is that I've managed to get a good job with 'Radio City'. Of course I am only a junior but that's going to give me something in both directions. I can maybe gain access to political events going on and maybe, if your research unit comes up with something, introduce it into the media.

We would need a web page with a good index. Of course I would have to disclose any interest, but if it is run as an apolitical unit, I see no reason why I should not help – I couldn't be a director or anything. So it sounds interesting"

They agreed to meet up and hammer out some basic rules and to work on how to retain some researchers.

Sebastian said he would prepare some spreadsheets after doing some research so that they could be easily be completed and used as a reference.

Sebastian was happy that he had been able to persuade Madge, whom he had spotted as the most politically aware of all his group, to help him.

He announced to his wife that evening over supper "The fight back begins from this moment here in this constituency!"

Sylvia replied sharply "But you won't keep her if all you do is to lecture at her and you will have to learn to cope with acolytes, she seems to like you but she will expect some return into the future. You know that?"

He thought for a moment but looked dejected. She continued "No I thought not!. Maybe she herself has ideas about the sort of things that she's looking for in the future?"

"Okay you are right, I'll discuss it with her! Do I detect a note of jealousy creeping in? Yesterday you were almost begging her to take me off your hands?"   ...."Seb she wouldn't dare!"

CHAPTER FOUR - September 2015

At the next meeting Madge herself had suggested new lines of review such as the analysis of the sorts of degrees and correlation with employment.

Sebastian decided that they could no longer work from his home and persuaded Edna Leggs to allow him the use of the upstairs room in the party's offices, that was on condition that the room would be vacated for executive meetings and that it would be reclaimed for any by-elections. No Council elections were pending in the next couple of years and so Sebastian's offer of a rental covering half the outgoings was well received. It meant that local Lib Dems still had a base.

Sebastian had a meeting with both Edna and Tim and explained what he was doing. Tim was concerned as to whether this might conflict with his role as leader of the Lib Dems on the District Council. "Sebastian it sounds OK but what happens if you come up with some data whose interpretation I disagree with?"

Sebastian became suddenly irritated by this line of questioning "Like what? You mean if I find out that the provision of affordable homes is being ignored – then what? You want me not to publish it? That would be silly!"

Edna interrupted "Now you two. Tim, I take Sebastian's point we do not really know enough about what's going on here never mind in the region. Can you tell me for example the number of affordable houses provided in our District Council last year? No? You cannot! and yet you are assuming that such information would somehow undermine you! Look, Sebastian, why don't you let us have a list of the information that you are going to provide on a regular basis through this 'Project Daedalus' and I'll also have a word with the East Midlands Regional Lib Dem office because I am sure it will prove of interest to them as well?"

Tim reluctantly agreed. Sebastian was aware that Tim had designs on succeeding him to being the constituency candidate for the next election, so he could see Tim bristle as the very notion of him providing basic information. Tim was obliged to concede but Sebastian could see that this was but the first round of many if Sebastian wished to seek re-selection.

The plan however worked perfectly. Application Forms for 'Zero Hours' research assistants appeared on notice boards at the three local universities. One applicant was from a second year student in Business Studies who intended to move at the end of the year to fast track degree conversion into NHS Administration. His name was John Blaney a straightforward sort of person who couldn't stand the sight of blood and realised he could never become a medic but was still dedicated to what he saw as the ideals of the Health Service. He quickly grasped what was needed and saw it as providing ideal training for himself. "One thing I ask is that the information is made available publicly and not hidden". Sebastian agreed to that and realised that it could conceivably also be used against the Lib Dems if they were in power, but he thought that it was so far away that it was not of immediate concern.

Other researchers were set on in the same way, one would specialise in planning and another, in education. Madge decided to take on the local EU aspects, Sebastian himself would have to deal with the 'devolution' aspects of any more powers to the counties and cities.

The first task had been to ask the researchers to identify exactly what information they would try to track and to prepare spreadsheets to capture the information on a regular basis.

Thereafter the information came off on a regular basis and, as they knew exactly where to look, the amount of time needed reduced and soon Sebastian was able to set a reasonable cost budget. All information came from publicly available sources. The skill was to know where the data was published and what exactly it meant.

The information was put in a presentable format and a commentary was attached simply highlighting those items getting better or worse. Eventually other statistics were added like unemployment and crime. It was published widely by email from 'Daedalus Project' to all media contacts, local radio, TV and Press and soon became a regular feature. As director, Sebastian was often called upon to introduce and sometimes interpret the information. Earnings from this also came into the project. Recipients soon became dependent on the data and Sebastian found that he was able to charge a yearly fee of £120 to each recipient. Not enough to cover the costs but enough to meet his own budget.

Sebastian was widely acknowledged as having a great deal of information at his fingertips. He aired the project at the National Lib Dem conference on September 23rd at Bournemouth to test interest from other regions and a fuller presentation was made to the Regional Executive at the East Midlands Regional Conference on November 7th 2015.

As Tim had expected, by December Sebastian was able to give him a substantial amount of information for his District. A key matter of interest was 'affordable homes' provision. Tim reported to Sebastian how one day he arrived early at a Planning Meeting to find the Senior Planning Officer and CEO of the Council together with the Chair and Vice Chair of the planning committee. They were looking at a sheet which he recognised as being from the latest Daedalus report with furrowed brows. The cumulative number of affordable houses provided in that District had been abysmal. This was also partly caused by the poor take up by Housing Associations who did not appear to have any targets of houses in mind and sometimes appeared to avoid certain sites where the developers, as a result, had to 'buy out' affordable homes provision.

Tim was able to refer to his original copy and in giving planning assent to another development with much lower provision of these cheaper homes, managed to highlight this deficiency, which was picked up by the press and lead to a major article.

At the next full local Lib Dem meeting Tim selflessly gave credit to the backroom data provided.

Sebastian knew that he had won the first round but that Tim wouldn't give up his quest for a Westminster seat so easily.

Sebastian fed Tim with the cross comparison on the number of Planning staff per Council and costs in the Democratic Services departments. This caused some annoyance with the Senior Financial officer as he had had to justify his higher cost figures against those of neighbouring District Councils. The Leader of the Council had protested about his staff being 'squeezed' whereas in fact his department appeared just to be underperforming. The Conservatives were caught on the hop, divided between trying to support the Council staff and having to acknowledge poor performance.

The Lib Dem regional office also prodded Councillors on all District Councils to ask similar embarrassing questions and for the moment Sebastian's position appeared to have been established.

Sebastian began to take an interest in the Regional Lib Dem council.

He underlined the changes he thought should come. "One thing we can be clear of is that the standard Focus showing the repair of potholes will not get us back to having 57 MP's. What happened was a seismic shift in the political world and we must absorb it and adapt to it! We must be more clear cut!"

Sebastian tried to relaunch the key mantras. "One of these" he said at the Regional Conference "might be a new banner instead of the rather flaccid; 'Stronger Economy, Fairer Society'." He though that it should be firmly planted in one key word. 'Meritocracy' supported by 'Democracy' and 'Equality'.

He explained to a horrified Regional Executive "So that all job promotions everywhere in the UK have to adjudged on merit. That is someone who matches a positional criteria in direct comparison with others. Equally no posts should exist where the person is not either openly selected against published criteria or by being proposed and elected by votes of the appropriate body. This should also cover all quangos and charities.

All organisations should initially sign up to this as an intention but on a voluntary basis. It has a lot of implications and this means no position can claim protection from sexual or ethnic limitation. Tracking this to everything everywhere means change – a big change. Like the House of Lords a creaking shambles of a second chamber and the dozens of odd committees and other placements carried out by an old boys network. There should be a competitive election for all Ombudsmen and for all Government run or sponsored bodies."

He continued...

"But it is ground fully occupied by either Tories or Labour. For the Tories the idea of a meritocracy is totally alien to their idea of pulling society together under their patronage. Whilst Labour's role has been exclusively to promote Union and worker representatives, a bias which had impacted much of their thinking for the past 60 years, albeit somewhat reduced because of the waning level of Union membership".

Sebastian had made a significant impact on the Regional body and he was asked to prepare a paper on these issues and a main motion for the National Lib Dem Spring Conference. His motion was duly selected.

"This Conference believes we should hold to our radical ideals".

Other issues came back like bad pennies.

The planning permission for the new District Council offices had been passed before May 2015 but the associated planning for transport and tram extension had been 'called in' by the Planning Inspectors at the instigation of the Lib Dems and a public enquiry was due. This dealt mostly with the various conflicting opinions concerning whether the extension of the tram system was preferred to an extension of a spur line from the BR tracks. There was also the possibility of extending the Nottingham tram line directly to Derby.

In the background was the failure of the Parkway station designed to service the East Midlands Airport but which ended up being virtually abandoned because it was not near enough to the airport and so had to be serviced by a costly bus service which was gradually withdrawn, leaving the new station virtually unused.

Part of the reason for the public enquiry was that the new HS2 line was also destined to pass nearby. There was considerable irritation expressed by Sebastian and Tim Holland that whilst Central Government were prepared to throw £billions at HS2 being a prestige project they were unwilling to understand local needs. What local businessmen wanted was better transport within the West & East Midlands to encourage more local trading and provide for a more mobile workforce. Sebastian asserted to the Inspectors that his findings suggested that HS2 would not bring more trade to the East Midlands because the time saving for one-off meetings of visitors from London would be very limited. On the other hand, what it would do would be to draw off to London promising graduates using HS2 as a commuter service because the everyday time saving now made daily commuting a possibility to avoid the ever increasing London housing costs.

Sebastian concluded that "HS2 is more about limiting London house prices by increasing the catchment area rather than bout helping East Midlands businesses". Pushing the Conservatives into a corner he added that "Boris Johnson has the right idea, the new London Airport should be sited in the Thames estuary and Heathrow itself laid out as a massive development, only that would assuage the demand for housing in London".

The local press carried verbatim reports of the hearing. The enquiry findings were unlikely to be made public for several months.

CHAPTER FIVE - November 2015

It was now becoming blazingly apparent to Sebastian that Cameron would get nothing at all from the other EU heads of Government which he could use to suggest to the electorate that he had 'done a deal' to repatriate some powers back to the UK, or at least had obtained agreement to halt the flow of EU residents entering the UK for work.

Even the most supportive of the National Press could see no way of even repackaging his renegotiation. His desperate circling of the EU heads became entangled in minor squabbles on other matters. Like 'would the UK take in the flood of migrants from the Middle East that had ended up in Germany?'. Fearful of the UKIP waiting to attack him and mindful of his dreadful promise to reduce the UK immigrants from 300,000 to 100,000. He had initially said "No!" both to Germany and France to any splitting up of the total between member EU states.

In Sebastian's eye most people actually thought Cameron right to take only those from the Syrian camps direct and not from pools of refugees already in Germany. Sebastian thought Merkel's statements 'loopy' by seemingly welcoming all refugees who can make it to Germany. What was the point of encouraging 'swarms' as Cameron put it, of refugees to cross to Greece on rubber dinghies with the danger and risk of illness and death and having to pay off the people smugglers? Why not shut that route and take from the camps? And why on earth undermine the existing agreed procedure that they must register in the first country of entry, by allowing Syrian refugees and whoever travelled with them to register in Germany? The whole feeble EU immigration policy was exposed as a sham.

The East European Countries were quite right, he felt, what was the point of allocating say 5,000 to say Slovakia where they were not welcomed, if they all wanted to go to Germany, where they were. Slovakia would be unable to hold them anyway once registered as a legal migrant in the EU. That would breech their right to go anywhere within the EU (apart from excluded areas like the UK).

Even so Sebastian saw that Mrs Merkle appeared to have lost her previously sure political footing, for which she was renowned, and 800,000 migrants looked like a mess! Then Cameron had not done himself any favours turning down the Merkel's allocation but similarly Sebastian noted that Cameron refused to co-ordinate his views with the Eastern Europeans.

He hadn't added voice to the logical concerns of Eastern European heads, perhaps because somewhere couched in rhetoric such as 'we only want Christians here!' was a view he found distasteful. But he had simply excluded himself. Cameron had failed to understand yet again how the EU worked. He had failed to collect allies and had annoyed his only friend, Germany.

Cameron was presented by another opportunity at the time of the Paris terrorist attacks. He quickly sided with the French President and offered full support. Although Hollande was loath to admit it, It was obvious to all that the French Secret service had substantially failed but as, they rightly pointed out with no border control and with a neighbour whose reach into the notorious suburb of Molenbeek was extremely weak, their job was much more complex than comparable services in the UK. It was obvious that Cameron was preparing to help in bombing Syria in support. In this way it seemed to Sebastian that he had at least shown he was a 'good European'.

But Cameron was increasingly under pressure to declare exactly where he was going over the referendum.

There was considerable agitation from Euro sceptics in his Cabinet to allow a free vote and free expression for the period of the 60 days leading up to the vote, whenever that came. He was clearly reluctant to do this. It seemed to Sebastian that, if he allowed a Cabinet split, his chances of putting together a credible united performance on the hustings was slim. But he dithered.

The events in the Sinai Desert and the downing of the Russian Passenger plan, plus the horrific events in Paris when, within days, 130 were mown down by terrorists shattered the nervous and strained discussion about allocation of refugees. One of the terrorists at least appeared himself to have been a refugee, others appeared to have used it to return after periods being with ISIS in Syria. No-one wanted to import and be a refuge for terrorists. This coloured the view that all refugees were merely harmless people trying to better themselves.

Immediately the press was full of call for retribution for striking back, to hit ISIS where it seemed to hurt in Aleppo and Raqqa. The French President immediately hit back and ordered air strikes. This apparently raised his standing in the polls. Overnight he jumped from being the worst ever President to being one of the best. It appeared his handling of the case was approved.

Sebastian disagreed and gave a note to his executive committee as such;

Chairman,

I just want to put on record my disappointment with peoples' reactions to these two terrible crimes. It is mostly about hitting back. Unfortunately that's exactly what ISIS want. You may remember that we went through all this over Charley Hebdo? The job of the terrorist is to incite revenge. He hopes by the wild reaction of the victim of the terrorist attack, he will attack the group which surrounds the terrorist. When he does so the victim becomes the aggressor and the group from which the terrorist comes in turn becomes the victims. Those new victims now call on the terrorist to protect them. In this way the whole group becomes infected by support for them.

Clearly whilst it is important to ensure that as far as possible every country is protected, that's not what is important. The key is the millions of Muslims in France, Belgium and the UK. This is the group that ISIS is trying to infiltrate and to claim the moral leadership of.

To sing the praises of French Culture is the exact opposite of what they should be doing. What they ought to do is to engage a huge amount of attention and funds into making sure that every Muslim throughout

France believes that he does indeed have an equal chance of employment, of promotion, of election so that he does see himself as an equal that is the Equality bit, When he feels equal he will feel a sense of Fraternity, when he is no longer viewed with suspicion and is not ridiculed, arrested or looked down on by other Frenchmen then he will know that he is free.

Save the money spent on bombs and spend it in the worst ghettoes in France, the physical and mental ghettoes!

Re-engage with the Russians, do a deal, support the Assad regime as the only credible state structure then remove Assad as part of an overall peace deal.

Sebastian Edwards.

Tim Holland replied by email the same day.

Thanks for your views on this matter but, as the Leader on the District Council, I have to say that I think the message it gives is inappropriate and according I would much prefer it that we just note your opinion but do not publicise it.

Accordingly Sebastian did nothing further.

The Euro sceptics however used the incident yet again to illustrate that we were not in control of our borders and that the terrorist incidents were partly caused by a failure to monitor the flow of people within the EC. The notion that terrorists had used the immigrant trail across Europe to find a way back in undetected simply re-enforced the view that the free flow of populations would never work in the UK context.

In the end on November 27th, The Daily Mail announced in banner headlines:

"TWELVE TORY EURO SCEPTIC MPs TO JOIN UKIP"

but the sub story showed they had insisted on changes to the UKIP constitution, allowing all MP's to select the UKIP leader as part of that deal. The Mail reporter assumed that they wanted to elect their own UKIP Parliamentary Leader rather than working under such a flamboyant and erratic leader as Nigel Farage. That plan had backfired as they were told by the UKIP executive committee that it would not accept that condition.

The press was full of the morality of changing parties so soon after the May elections when those MPs had all accepted the Tory Manifesto. In effect it was trial by press and eventually the media collectively threw out a challenge for them all to resign and stand together in a mini by-election on their revised political positions. Fearful of encouraging a split, Cameron allowed them back in on the basis of their future promised good behaviour. The arguments and counter arguments filled the Press which was left in turmoil since, although most Broadsheets wanted out of Europe, they also wanted the Tories to remain in power to finish the austerity period and then create an easy transition to whatever there was in the future. The defections had been carefully stage-managed by the press who gained millions of £ from the circulation increase in the double Scoop 'OUT' – 'Discussion' – 'BACK IN'. So all they had wanted to do was further scare the Tory Prime Minister into action over the EU. When they realised that the overall loss of majority would cause financial instability the media motor went into reverse quite quickly.

It seemed to Sebastian that for a time the position would hold.

The Labour Party stood by in confusion. They had no view on how to control immigration in any format that sounded half sensible, the left wing of the Labour Party which was assuming control had always been emotionally hostile to the EU which they thought was simply a charter for larger businesses. Even the later changes regarding the EU working time limits failed to motivate positive responses.

Sebastian thought that the same complacency of the Labour Party to UKIP taking second places in Labour seats in the North on May 7th mirrored the complacency to the Labour loss of most of its Scottish seats. They seemed incapable of renewing and representing the party in simple terms to its previous loyal voters. Sebastian thought this presaged a further dramatic collapse in their vote. Meanwhile the Labour MPs had no motivation to force a fight with the Tories in Parliament and were simply forced to watch and wait their opportunity to strike.

By December 2015 Sebastian's three part timers were in place and the production of the 'Project Daedalus' was in full swing.

CHAPTER SIX - Gazetted

Sebastian really was surprised to be accosted at work in his office in early January 2016 with the news that he had been awarded an O.B.E.

It came under the 'Diplomatic Service and Overseas List'.

The citation read:-

'Sebastian Edwards. Former Director Siberian Minerals. For services to British interests in Russia'.

He was pressed by the company office staff but he said it was just in the nature of the work.

He received a congratulatory email from the Board of RKW.

He was questioned by both Tim Holland and Edna Leggs but apart from explaining that on the last trip over there he had managed to help as he termed it a 'consulate official' he could or would add nothing further.

The constituency executive passed a motion of congratulation.

His wife reminded him that she had never heard the full story, he had just kept on putting it off. She decided to tackle him at his moment of least resistance – upstairs in bed!

"Well" he said, "It's like this, I helped a man escaped who never existed and I took him by a secret route to a place I cannot mention and was given an explanation by someone I never met!"

She looked at him blankly and gently tickled him under the bed-clothes. "Come on now Seb"

"OK, OK OK, well it's like this, a British Agent was being held in police custody, I managed to get him out, he feigned illness saying he was being chased by the mafia. He was badly injured and couldn't walk properly. He persuaded me to carry him along a stream across the frontier with Ukraine all the while being chased by the Russian security police, who in fact though I didn't know it at the time sent a helicopter to scare away any smugglers who might attack us. The Ambassador in Ukraine explained that it was all secret and the agent disappeared!"

"Is that it?"

"Yes that's it?"

"Don't be so ridiculous but I suppose one of these days you'll tell me what really happened – I suppose it was just another boring takeover of a Russian company somewhere!"

"Yes that's right dear!" and he leant over, kissed her and switched off the light.

A couple of seconds later she switched it back on, "What is that dreadful looking package in the corner Seb?"

"Oh that's the medal the Russians awarded me!"

"What for you chasing them along the frontier – come on now Seb! I have ways of making you talk! She began prodding him under the sheets. All these ridiculous stories!"

"Sebastian I have the feeling that soon you are going to become a very important person!"

"In your dreams! I suppose!"

CHAPTER SEVEN - January 2016

The Scottish devolution debate was not going well for the Government and although the bill on transfer of powers had been through its first reading, it was clear that the Conservative Government had no idea how to resolve the 'West Lothian Question' – exactly what powers should Scottish MPs have to vote on UK matters.

David Cameron was well aware that if he could remove the SNP MPs from matters relating to English affairs he would carry into the next parliament a working majority but then how should the House of Commons be structured and if this was the case with Scotland should Northern Ireland and even Wales follow suit. In fact an 'Imperial parliament' or UK wide House of Commons was something discussed for over a century in the period leading up to the Irish Rebellion. The Conservatives were otherwise locked into what Sebastian saw as a muddled devolution – a sort of licensed piecemeal cherry picking within the UK. The lack of a written constitution was becoming a nightmare and tampering with it seemed to create even more problems. David Cameron had no majority in the second Chamber 'The Lords' which is made up of retired politicos as well as vestiges of power in the form of 90 peers, bishops, law lords and several dozen non-affiliated cross benchers. What he needed was either a bold plan himself or to hand it over to a Constitutional Commission but, since these often took years to come up with a result, he had simply run out of time. It was generally assumed that he now had no alternative but to force fit or botch it. Like simply, and rather arbitrarily, excluding those MPs not directly affected by the bill in progress.

Sebastian was looking on at all this with increasing dismay and foresaw that the Scottish MSP Election scheduled for 5th May 2016 would centre around the adequacy of such 'Devo Max' to which the SNP thought they were entitled. That is the transfer of even more powers than was originally proposed. If they failed to obtain them it would allow the SNP yet again to feature as the 'victim' punished by Westminster.

Sebastian called together a group of other Constituency Chairmen in the East Midlands and persuaded them to urge the Lib Dem leader to forge a new strategy which they called 'The Scots -Let 'em have it!'

Sebastian was convinced that the only way of stopping the SNP in their tracks was to threaten to give them what they wanted. The price of oil at less than $50 a barrel meant that Scotland had no possible chance under the SNP budget provided at the last referendum of providing a balanced Scottish Independent budget – at least not without a much more savage austerity to Scotland than the Conservatives had applied in the UK through the coalition.

Already there was the notion that the North Sea Oil rigs would become uneconomic so that the number of directly related jobs in that well-paid sector would be greatly reduced. Added to this was the threat of reduction of work by the redeploying of the Nuclear Missile Submarine Fleet to England and final withdrawal of RAF squadrons from their Scottish bases.

Such a picture would give little scope for growth in an independent Scotland, but there was no doubt that their increase in the Scottish Parliament from the current 64 seats to a 2/3rds. majority which needed 86 seats would give SNP an unassailable hold over that Parliament. This would probably allow it to pass its own independence Bills which although theoretically unconstitutional would be almost impossible to negate. They could name it 'The Scottish Provisional Government' and seek international support. In other words sweeping SNP gains there would almost certainly lead to pressure for independence and the most recent polls showed that at least 15% more Labour voters planned to switch to SNP.

Sebastian knew that as a result of the 'Barnet Formula', Scotland received £1700 more funding per head than the average for the UK of £8913. This was supposed to take into account Scotland's greater geographical area and its traditional poverty compared with other areas.

It was obvious to Sebastian that passing over income powers to Scotland also ought to take an adjustment of this Barnet Formula into account

Accordingly Sebastian requested to see the Lib Dem party leader Tim Beaumond for a meeting in London and he put together the following views agreed to by the other constituency chairmen which he had listed and left with the leader.

THE SCOTS - LET 'EM HAVE IT!

1) *That all UK parties need to hammer home that Scottish Independence would lead directly to a disastrous economic position for the Scots based on the current oil price and production forecast being less than a quarter of that projected in 2014. Latest predictions are for a budget deficit of 8.6% of GDP, or without oil a 'Greek style' deficit of 12.2% of GDP. 65,000 jobs had been lost since 2014.*

2) *That the Barnet Formula be adjusted such that the premium should be reduced over 5 years.*

3) *That all the UK Political Parties should agree that only one party (that holding the current constituency MSP seat) would fight that seat as 'National Unionist' with all other parties standing down. The Regional List would be made up of those first now elected. In other words there would be a common anti SNP party.*

4) *That the UK would publish lists of those military contracts, Naval, Land and Air which would be removed from Scotland automatically should SNP gain a majority of seats.*

5) *That all businesses be advised in Scotland that they would have to divide their sales and staff between Scotland and England in view of the potential independence and that all government loans made to industry should be redefined to be repaid in Edinburgh or London and that the Financial Regulatory Authority and all other departments would split all staff over the Scottish elements. In other words business should be prepared to recalibrate itself under an independent Scotland*

Sebastian later heard that the Leader Tim Beaumond had had private discussions with the Labour party. Initially it met with a positive response from the newly elected leader of the Scottish Labour Party, Pamela Brown, who had won a resounding victory 67% against 33%, her stated view was based on the picking up all available 'No!' voters. However this was vetoed by the Labour Shadow Cabinet unwilling to ease up on the hostile approach to Tory austerity. However Pamela Brown reminded the Shadow Cabinet of their earlier acceptance that the Scottish Labour Party could 'reposition' the party in Scotland and produce a different local manifesto giving her much more freedom.

But after two weeks looking at the local polling returns the feedback, through Sebastian, was that although the addition of Tory and Lib Dem voters would assist it would not be all gain; many existing Labour supporters might be switched off by any deal with a Tory and vice versa. However it was eventually agreed that there would be no united party but that all would accept a standard 5 line common policy words. The Union Flag would be used by all 'NO' candidates and that the non SNP party last holding that MSP seat would be entitled to appear as the common candidate all others making way for it.

A joint presentation was then made to Cameron and the details were agreed, UKIP was anxious to agree because of its poor record in Scotland and was glad simply to be amongst the 'top table' for the discussions. The Greens however refused to agree openly, stating that, as the only other party, they would pick up all the voters unhappy with such a 'deal'. By the end of January Sebastian's plan had been taken up.

Sebastian pressed his case. The SNP would realise that this was a make or break decision for them. Support for SNP would then certainly carry them towards independence at a time when economic conditions might leave them bankrupt and dependent on UK handouts from the start.

One of the foremost SNP MPs had had to resign over a financial irregularity although it was not clear if this was a criminal matter.
For once the purity of their case appeared to be disintegrating.

It appeared they would get no help from the EU. It had previously held an ambitious view of 'Europe of the Regions' as it was called, but when there had been an earlier suggestion that the whole of East Germany could be a first new Region so created, Germany was adamant that Reunification of Germany was not an EU matter and would be paid by Germany whatever the cost. That was just 25 years ago.

Since that time no newly divided states had been recognised within the EU (although Slovakia broke off before its split with Czech Lands, and Yugoslavia disintegrated before bits of it acceded to the EU).

Scotland was shown these increasingly dour financial facts and as Sebastian had predicted the polls soon showed that the Scots canny self-interest began to reassert itself. A Scots attachment to the dole and its preservation intact was most easily understood, the benefits of financial independence was less certain..

Sebastian received a formal letter of thanks from the Executive Committee of the Lib Dems but decided against using it in any way to gain publicity. Accordingly his initiative was never commented on locally.

The main reason was that Sebastian was still trying to balance an active political role with his work and he knew that if, at any time he gained national prominence, his employment would be under threat. As a failed Lib Dem would-be-MP, he knew, it would not cause much of a stir but the City press was notoriously right wing and would have had no inhibitions about singling him out for attention if he dared put his head above the parapet. Typically he and possibly his company could be ridiculed even if in something like the 'smart phart' columns such as the Times TMS which positively enjoyed tearing the wings off any political butterfly within reach but not, of course, of the Tory hierarchy.

So his initiative never came to the attention of the press.

CHAPTER EIGHT - February 2016

Sylvia had, with Madge's assistance, created a database of help contacts linking together all similar units across England, so that threatened Asian women could receive immediate support.

At the start of February there was a prominent local case when three schoolgirls went missing from school, luckily they were found before being taken off 'on holiday' to arranged marriages.

Sylvia managed to get onto local TV and said she had opened a register. Any young Asian girls who thought that they might be at risk of an arranged marriage were invited to complete a form. Links were to be established with police such that if any of the girls were absent from school with no explanation, police searches could begin immediately. The form that each sign stated *'I have no intention of entering into an arranged marriage in a foreign country – if therefore I am missing the authorities are asked to take this as an immediate sign that I have been taken against my will!'*

The three girls ended up in the second bedroom at Sebastian's house, only just cleared out of all the statistical data and now full of bunk beds occupied by these girls, pending their return home when the parents had agreed not to continue with their marriages.

Sebastian had had to take second place to all this and although he was delighted that his wife had found at last a means of correcting what Sebastian knew she thought were outmoded cultural habits, Sebastian never-the-less urged caution, but that came at a time when the phone lines were constantly in use by desperate girls trying to register their vulnerability. Sebastian was worried that it had all seemed too easy and yet the culture of honour killings and justice meted out didn't seem likely to him to be solved by a mere form.

Sebastian was horrified when he saw that their home address was on all the letters and leaflets going out.

Their house was in a cul de sac just off a main road so that their small garden backed onto that road. It was big enough to sit out on in a summer's evening but the incessant noise of the traffic was such that they rarely used it.

They awoke one Saturday morning with something that sounded like a bomb going off and then a Woooof and a flash of light.

Sebastian jumped up and sprang to the window something had obviously been flung over the wall and landed plumb in the garden. He called the emergency services and went downstairs first to check the front and then to ensure that the firebomb in the garden had not set the actual building alight.

The flames were quickly doused and the police began making enquiries. They asked about the work that Sylvia did and asked if she might know who could have done it. In reply Sylvia showed them a list of 130 girls who had called her and signed up. "Parents of any of these I suppose!"

The Police asked if they could take the list but Sylvia refused "I am listing down the names of those whom I believe need my help. It would be a breach of my confidence with them if you suddenly began investigating! So no! You may not have the list, but I insist that I am accorded the right of every individual to be protected from thugs like these!"

They tried reasoning with her but she would have none of it. "Look I am doing a job which you, the police, should be doing in my view, but you are just turning a blind eye to this abuse. Please arrange suitable protection for me. At least if you cannot protect the girls you can protect me!"

Sebastian tried to mollify her but she would not listen. "I am a British Citizen and demand my rights!"

Later the following day a large Police Inspector called around. He introduced himself as John Denny the senior policeman in the area. "I wanted to drop by and have a word with you both!"

"Look, my officers report back that you have decided that you are not going to take defensive measures as my officers suggested but that you insist on police protection is that correct?"

"Yes" said Sylvia immediately assuming control, "that's because one of their suggestions was that we should not do this from home which, he said, 'almost invites a personal response'!"

"Just a minute please Mrs Edwards!" He put up his hand as if stopping traffic!

"The problem is for us that however well intended you are, and I am personally sure you are trying to help, you are going about it the wrong way.

Firstly you are, I think, not a registered Charity? Now if you should take in any money your role would be immediately open to question, separating its income and costs from your own.

Secondly you are almost certainly not insured? I can see that you hadn't thought of this, so all damage caused is unlikely to be covered by your regular house insurance. If you are within a charity then everything you do is controlled externally by the Charity Commission; accounts, terms of reference, structure, office holders, reporting etc.

Furthermore you cannot just collect lists of people's personal data and keep files on individuals, that's so even if they wish it and agree to your doing so!. You immediately come within the Data Protection Act created in order to prevent abuse of just this sort of data and, for example, for its onward sale!"

"But I wouldn't do that" said Sylvia somewhat distressed.

The Inspector a big bluff man continued "Of course not but that's not how the world, sees it. Now I understand you have only just started so I do not propose to take this any further, but I do expect you to address these matters within the next 30 days and in the meantime desist from further action! Apart from anything else the Home Office has guidance on forced marriages".

"Yes I know" said Sylvia pulling a leaflet from her pocket and starting to quote out loud the core

'Section 12c of the Matrimonial Causes Act 1973 states that a marriage shall be voidable if "either party to the marriage did not validly consent to it, whether in consequence of duress, mistake, unsoundness of mind or otherwise'.

"Voidable means dah dah dah the court can award a decree of nullity invalidating the marriage etc.etc. Although there is no specific criminal offence of *"forcing someone to marry"* within England and Wales, criminal offences may nevertheless be committed. *"Perpetrators – usually parents or family members – could be prosecuted for offences including threatening behaviour, assault, kidnap, abduction, imprisonment, and murder"*. .. there are 250 cases recorded every year but that's just the tip of the iceberg! Just imagine if there were a 'safe' register so Asian women would be protected!"

"Hm" the Inspector appeared impressed "well at least I can see you have done some homework ! I am happy to meet up with you then to reassess where you are what you are doing and how we can then support you.

Believe me, in my opinion this is a much needed service. We often have referred to us such cases but are drawn in too late to be of effective help!"

Sylvia was crestfallen after he left and was all for giving up the whole venture, but Sebastian disagreed "Look that Molotov cocktail has made the point for you. It's clear you are troubling some entrenched views, but you shouldn't give up now!"

He left the room for a few minutes and returned. "I have booked an appointment with Andrew Laws at his next local surgery on Saturday morning.".

"What?" shouted Sylvia "but he's the Tory MP!"

"Yes I am well aware of that but I think in his earlier years he was a junior minister in the Home Office and I think he might have handled charity cases".

"And??"asked Sylvia.

"Well I think he will be able to find out for you whom to see at the Charity Commissioners and tell you more about the Data Protection Act and finally see how you might apply for grants of some kind. You need an office, locked filing cabinets, a proper recording system for incoming calls, a database of contacts, a meetings room, you know? To put it onto a professional footing."

"But won't it go against me being related to you and fighting it out at the last election?" enquired Sylvia, clearly confused by this referral.

"I shouldn't think so for a moment. When dealing with practical cases which don't appear to have a political bent most politicians these days aim to give a good service, indeed they often take it as a compliment to be trusted in this way by an opponent. Most politicians keep the snarling bit strictly for the public view. I suggest that you take Madge along with you as I am busy at work on that day.

I think that what the Inspector was saying makes sense, you have high ambitions for this Sylvia but it's not suitable to be carried out by one person in an upstairs bedroom. We have, I think, to jump to the next stage of your development quickly."

Sebastian questioned them on their return from the meeting and they indicated how helpful the MP had been. He had asked after him but they had both indicated that for the present Sebastian was 'out of it'.

Within days they were awash with paperwork on the Data Protection Acts, the Charity Commission and further 'Guidance on forced marriages' and how social services people should react and their contact with police services.

Sebastian helped Sylvia complete all the forms and obtain names as directors of the charity, Madge expressly asked to be included and together with former contacts and the directors of those running Sylvia's Asian Women's battered homes Trust, they soon had a formidable list!

Within the month Sylvia called Inspector John Denny and they held a meeting with Sebastian. She explained exactly the processes and registrations, apologising that for the moment, the only place they could afford was home but that they had hopes of obtaining a grant and relocating. John Denny was clearly impressed and agreed to site cameras on the road outside just as a temporary basis!

Sylvia thanked the Inspector and was clearly happy that she could now start.

"Now my next thing is to send leaflets around to all schools in the Midlands with a substantial Asian intake and see what results!"

With the help of Madge the incident was turned into a story and local TV willingly plugged into it. The result was a steady increase in calls asking to be registered. It was not long before another incident occurred.

CHAPTER NINE - Early March - Lib Dem National Conference

Sebastian thought that amongst the goings on at the National Autumn Conference his appearance would scarcely be noticed in the national press.

His motion had been selected for debate but it was loosely enough worded to encourage a certain latitude in the subject matter and Sebastian was determined to press his case for redirection of the party's strategy.

"This Conference believes we should hold to our radical ideals".

Madge helped Sebastian to prepare the case and draft the speech. After introducing the theme of Meritocracy he developed his other theme "Another factor is that we must not be afraid of being radical. If we think that a radical solution is called for, we should hammer it and keep at it, not walk away if at first we do not succeed, like Lords and voting reform. Are SNP worried about not getting independence first time? Not at all, if things don't work properly we shouldn't say 'see you in 20 years for another referendum?'. We have to fight!"

"Get stuck in if you really believe it then keep at it don't just give up!" They gave him a standing ovation at the conference and Sebastian knew then that he was back on track! He could and would succeed!

"Being radical is what Labour and Tories find most difficult and it's where THEY are at THEIR weakest," he said pounding the Lectern to drive home the points. "and this is so for two reasons. Most Governments in office find it very difficult to provide radical solutions, and most of those that are put forward are as surprising for those parties in power as anyone else e.g. the recent Health Service reforms; seemingly no-one had worked it through or knew where it came from. The Governments are like huge liners whose course is set in the Queen's

Speech, any changes are to Civil Servants, who carefully plot the passage of policy to bills, like huge icebergs. In any case there is no mechanism in a party for such abrupt changes if the Minister concerned does not agree. As far as the opposition is concerned they are more interested in crushing the Government's policies, good or bad, than in providing replacement policies unless they also had it in their own manifesto!

The treatment of the NHS in the last election was a case in point. All that political parties appeared capable of doing was to outbid each other for the amount of the extra £bn commitment. What was needed, in my opinion, was a plan to improve the organisation efficiency and performance".

He claimed the discussion was little better than bar-room chat. "We can and must do better than that!"

The light was flashing on the lectern showing time was up. He shouted over the Conference Chairman.

"There's a huge amount of work to be done. We are never going to get back in giving out leaflets on the number of potholes we have filled! We are better than that! We can create better systems of Governance. To do that we have to get inside the 'Beast of Government'. That's where we went wrong, in coalition we lost our radical bite, we became soft Tories or played along as would be Socialists!"

The microphone was switched off but he kept going.

"There is no soft centre ground! We must seize the initiative!"

The rebuke from the chair was drowned out by the cheers from the audience which followed him to his seat.

Luckily, thought Sebastian, he had not had time to read out the separate quote he had in his pocket from the exposed USA 'Clinton email files':

'Clegg has also misplayed almost every turn, presented with big chances and blowing them through a combination of inexperience ... and inbred arrogance (from no less a privileged background than Cameron, though seeming less snobbish because he went to Westminster instead of Eton and has a less pronounced upper class accent).'

'Hm' thought Sebastian 'Possibly a bridge too far!' as he put the note back in his pocket. 'After all at the time I had supported Nick as leader and again, when the question came around the constituencies just before the election, I had decided to persist with him despite his shortcomings'.

Yes in hindsight now it was clear to Sebastian that Nick was always going to lose – 'but' he mused 'who else would we have selected as leader, the whole scenario from the date of the start of the coalition was wrong'. Provided the point was made Sebastian thought, there was no reason to anger and humiliate the Clegg followers.

Humm, he thought 'Madge had been right to tear that bit out of my prepared speech!'

Sebastian hoped that his speech had not been picked up by his employers since they might equate this with 'working politics', he knew that any whiff of being involved with national strategy making would be frowned upon by them and might jeopardise his future as an employee.

CHAPTER TEN - Easter Day March 27th 2016

Sebastian found himself in his usual place on Easter Sunday. At 10 am he was sitting alongside Douglas in chairs on the lawn in front of his old friend's house in Northumberland, whilst his wife cleared away the breakfast she had prepared on the Aga cooker, but things had changed.

His old friend on whom he relied as a sounding board for major decisions in his life, had had a stroke earlier in the year. It had affected his eyesight and restricted the use of his legs. His speech was hesitant as sometimes he searched for words and was annoyed when the correct one would not come to mind. Being an outdoors person he simply could no longer make the hill walks that had been a hall mark and high point of Sebastian's visits there.

His walking was restricted to ambling down the lane to the main road then back up to the cottage again twice a day. The sun was shining as usual and the clouds still floated across the scene creating shadows on the land across the valley but the mood was more serious and concerning.

The expectations were changed, Douglas could no longer drive his car this meant that he and his wife would soon have to decide whether to leave their little paradise or if they were to remain and find ways of obtaining the regular supplies they needed.

He had to work out how they could cope with possibly declining health so far away from all services.

Sebastian was loathe to discuss that matter with his oldest friend. He knew that only he could make that decision, but should Sebastian try to influence that or just wait till his friend recognised the impossibility of his situation?

It was of course technically possible for him to recover fully but for months now his position had plateaued.

Douglas asked softly "So Sebastian what's your next move – retirement like mine?"

"No, Douglas I am thinking quite the opposite, whilst at present everything looks quiet, I do not think it can last. As you know the Prime Minister has officially recognised that the fine idea of actually winning something back from the EC in terms of returning decisions to the UK or repatriation, but it simply cannot be achieved for his own end date of 2017 in time for the In/Out Referendum. He either has to fly with the EC as it is or make proposals for future reform for which he does not have a proven shred of support within the EC.

In short he is going to be massacred, he has nothing to sell. His own party are getting more furious by the day, the pro-EC MPs believe he should have started substantive discussions two years ago and worked through alliances with friendly Euro MPs. It was becoming glaring that his inability to make any change, except withholding benefits from foreign families who do not live here, has devastated their cause and merely highlights his inadequacies and failure to match early rhetoric with any negotiating action.

On the other hand the anti-EC MPs believe that Cameron will try dressing up 'Pigs' Trotters as Ham' exaggerate the gains that he has made and try hoodwinking the voters by using the power of government to claim huge gains of membership from lists produced by individual Ministers.

The Tory Party is at breaking point, I feel that something will happen and that I should be prepared. Andrew Laws the sitting Tory MP is said to be in daily contact with UKIP. The Tory internal coalition cannot hold!

He's falling apart on other matters too such as devolution – this idea of Pick & Mix power by Local areas bidding to take services from Central government provided multiple layers of Local Government are prepared to elect a mayor, simply is seen as lacking any coherence. But the promises made to Local government far outrun the ability of Central government to devolve meaningful powers.

Accordingly I have decided to seek nomination as prospective Parliamentary candidate – again! It will, I think, be my last opportunity because the reduction of MPs from 650 to 600 will likely impact the East Midlands and my constituency is one of those most likely to be affected. So it will never be as easy to get selected for another new Constituency.

So as always when I come to see you, Douglas, I am always on the horns of a dilemma.

This time because of my notoriety and because I stand second in the polls, my employer, RKW, is unlikely to take as relaxed a view. They may ask me to choose between a political life and resign, maybe with a leaving bonus, or stay on as an employee with a changed role. Of course they will not sack me, that would be too obvious, but simply replace me with a new person and appoint me to a meaningless post in London from which they can later declare me redundant due to 'changed operating conditions'. Thus taking me away from the constituency and eventually getting rid of me or at least the problem.

They simply do not want to get embroiled in any controversial statements that I might want to make.

If I take that former choice it's possible that I will end up with no further income. Gambling on being elected has two problems a) It's possible I will not get reselected or that it is overridden by Lib Dem head office who always have the right to appoint their own candidate of choice and we have dozen of former MPs spare!! and b) It's possible even if I am selected that I will not get elected.

To ask for reselection now means that I am trying to book the seat, but this Parliament is likely to last another almost 4 years during which time

I might get no income; but if I leave it and do not apply its likely some other young blood will see the opportunity and jump in and try for my seat, or that one of the defeated MP's will want to try his luck again here!"

"Well, I see," said Douglas, "what does your wife, Sylvia, think?"

"As before she's supportive whatever I do!" Sebastian waited; usually at this stage Douglas would break the decision down into manageable pieces and ask Sebastian to justify each.

But this did not happen and Sebastian turned around and saw Douglas' eyes were full of tears. "I know that I would normally get into the detail but I am afraid I have forgotten the alternatives Sebastian, you know the old brain doesn't work so well anymore."

Sebastian leaned forward and put his arm around his shoulder. "Don't worry Douglas about the detail – the question is do I fight again or not?"

"Well Sebastian I have never known you take the easy option nor, if there's a fight going, to walk away from it and my guess is that you are too old to change now. Your character will not allow you to ignore it, but I think you know that already!"

"Yes, you are right Douglas! Now let's nip over to your church as we normally do for the service this morning.

We can take my car and this afternoon I'll drive you to the coast and we can walk along the beach?

How many attendees do you think there will be for the Easter morning service? Do you remember one year we were down to seven and we didn't even have an organist?

I see your garden looks great this year."

"It's mostly down to my wife I cannot balance well enough to weed properly, so we have a gardener now".

"Well, Douglas, you seem to be improving! Keep at it and I'll let you know what happens at my end OK?"

CHAPTER ELEVEN - April 2016

On return from his Easter break Sebastian had suggested to his Executive Committee that they should initiate the candidate selection, arguing that it was important to start early so that the incumbent could get known locally making press releases, instead of leaving everything till just before the General Election, even if it was still four years away. Edna asked him directly if he wished to stand. "Well" he muttered, "I am considering standing but it depends on persuading my wife and seeing if I can bear the cost of lost income! Anyhow we had better reformulate the appointments committee, just in case!"

There was a new respect for him in the local Executive Committee stemming partly, so Sebastian thought, from his award of the OBE, partly because of his older statesman position and partly the success of his little research unit. Many members were not aware of his role in the changed strategy towards the SNP.

In discussions with Madge he had promised her that if ever he were elected to the House of Commons he would bring her in at his research assistant and secretariat, if that's what she wanted. He had put this in writing to her. Otherwise he said he would give her a reference if she wanted to stand elsewhere. Madge had agreed to second his appointment as Prospective Parliamentary candidate and had agreed to speak for him.

Sebastian talked with Edna Leggs who said immediately. "Well I am not surprised you put your name forward, you have done everything but put your intention as an advert on the local bus!".

Sebastian apologised "I am sorry I have been taken up with the various projects, but I will come to the next Town Council meeting and see if I can help in adding new direction – I understand that the County Council still has not acknowledged the results of the mini-referendum on car parking nor have they carried out any work of their own. I'll try to get over there and discuss it with you!"

Tim's response was more ambivalent but, when asked, he told Sebastian that he knew that Sebastian's profile nationally and regionally was far above his own, but would not yet himself declare either way. He acknowledged he was finding it difficult to make an impact at the District Council. Sebastian had offered to inject new ideas but even as Tim was overstretched being on the Town District and County Councils he said he preferred to work it through himself.

The procedure for adopting the candidate began immediately and was advertised locally in neighbouring constituencies and at the Lib Dem HQ in London. Most local candidates, hearing that Sebastian was standing again, withdrew their applications but Tim left his hat in the ring to be considered and there were additionally two candidates from outside the East Midlands one, a former MP and the other a former MEP.

The Policy Committee of the party sent a brief letter in support explaining that the SNP-directed-strategy had been Sebastian's idea and expressed full confidence in the outcome of the Scottish Election; ending that they would be happy to welcome Sebastian into the Lib Dem benches at Westminster.

So it was that the contest came down to Sebastian and some other excellent candidates. Sebastian was able to draw on a wealth of local knowledge plucked from his 'Daedalus project'. This far outclassed any of his competitors information of the constituency or the East Midlands area.

So all knew that there could only be that one winner. The decision was made on May 10th. Sebastian was congratulated once again by everyone in that little office into which they had all squeezed for the hustings and decision a year before. This time there was no last minute referrals back or questioning of CV's as there had been then.

He was proved correct in that the SNP advance appeared to have been stopped in its tracks on May 5th, there was no urge to tempt fate and run for independence if that meant, they would be running cap in hand to Westminster – much easier to play the victim!

It did not however take long for his company RKW to react when a notice of his selection appeared in the Times.

CHAPTER TWELVE - May 3rd 2016

Although Sebastian had sensed that the political situation was unstable, most people thought that the Tory coalition between the pro and anti-EC wings would last until the referendum; held together by a mutual desire to stay in power. Cameron had been urged by his advisers to hold out for a 'Stay' from his cabinet or at least agreement not to campaign against it. His logic was simple the UKIPpers political influence must end after the referendum. They might win the referendum but there was no room for them to help tidy up the mess and their reason for existence ended right then. They have no mainstream political strategy for continued involvement and no skills in carrying out the huge political load of renegotiation if they did win. Hence what reason would anyone have to leave the Tories? Either way 50% of the UKIPpers would return to the Tory fold. That, at least, was the logic which Sebastian thought the Tories were adopting.

But one of the backbenchers Mr Laws the Tory elected MP for the Middleton Constituency, declared for UKIP on May 1st. With a carefully managed PR, the Leader of UKIP suggested that this would be the first of many defectors fed up with the biased information in the press which they claimed the Government was pushing. Within a day, across England, five other Tory MP's declared for UKIP in a well-co-ordinated press release. This time there were no pre-conditions about the Leadership of UKIP and little doubt that they would be obliged to fight for their seats in by-elections.

Above all they now claimed that the Grexit, the near exit of Greece from the Euro in 2015, was a stark warning to all those who thwarted the EC rules and that the UK would never be willing to subject itself to such internal interference. Eurozone membership was out, as was the notion of ever closer ties within the EC.

The Government gave out a warning of what rejection would mean to employment. UKIP and the 'outers' instantly suggested that this was a biased use of Government power as it was written by Civil Servants and to prove the point pulled in a dozen front line businessmen lead by NEXT PLC the well-known hugely successful clothes chain, saying they wanted OUT!

Within days of the defection however, which was greeted with enthusiasm by the two local Middleton District UKIP Councillors who had won their seats in 2015 May elections, the Tory party was baying for each of the turncoats to prove themselves in fighting a by election.

A little known Bill allowing the local party to deselect a sitting MP had been intended to disbar those MP's who had been found guilty of a criminal offence or unprofessional conduct like receiving money for introductions or questions, some MPs had wanted to include a rule applying the same law in the case of MPs changing party. This was on the basis that the electorate had a right to believe that the MP would try to put into practice the prospectus on which the party was elected but that was clearly impossible if someone changed party. However that Bill had been shelved amidst a failure to agree how it should be worded.

Pressure was applied to each MP by their Conservative Executive Committee to 'come clean and resign'. This followed a well-trodden pattern used in Beaconsfield where the pressure on the sitting MP became so intense that he had eventually resigned.

Andrew Laws was hounded unmercifully by the national press until he agreed to ask for the Chiltern Hundreds and thus resign as an MP, precipitating a by election. The other 5 MPs did the same.

The by-election was scheduled to take place on Thursday June 16th 2016.

There was immediately consternation in the Tory ranks and there was concern that it would precipitate the Referendum scheduled still for 2017.

It was unclear whether Sebastian's apparent withdrawal from standing again was a motivating factor in Andrew Laws reaching his decision.

Certainly UKIP local members had told Lib Dem friends that they had assumed Sebastian had given up on professional politics. They clearly had respected Sebastian's role and knew that his position both on Russia and in reforming the EC meant that he might be an awkward person to fight. Sebastian's agent had heard that they were relieved that he was no longer there and assumed that they would now have to fight a more a 'traditional' Lib Dem like, for example, Tim Holland.

They had not yet picked up that Sebastian had already agreed to stand on May 10th and had in fact put himself forward as a candidate.

The Tories in Middleton were however aware of his position.

Sebastian saw that this election would put the local conservatives in a dilemma. Andrew Laws was a well-known local Tory whom they thought would put up a very tough fight as several of the local executive committee were known to want to support him. By fielding a very weak local candidate they could in effect stand on the current Tory Manifesto of repatriating more powers whilst concentrating on economic issues and leaving the Lib Dem pro Euro candidate to take UKIP head on, on both immigration and EU themes. In this way they hoped to squeeze through making little fuss and concentrate on current financial policies. This they calculated was the most likely way to get rid of Andrew Laws, not to hit him head-on on policy issues.

However a strong Tory candidate would split the pro EC vote and likely leave their candidate humiliated by Andrew Laws as the winner, since direct personal attacks would likely swing voters behind him. So contrary to normal practice they chose an unknown weak local candidate – a district councillor. The Prime Minister acting, so he said out of fairness, and unwilling to provoke the anti EC section of his party into claiming that drawing in Ministers was an unfair advantage for Pro EC campaigners, banned any cabinet minister from mentioning the EC or visiting that constituency during the by-election.

Of course the press were jubilant to have a mini referendum on their hands and the names of the candidates were plastered over the front pages.

Lib Dem HQ always have the last say in agreeing by-election candidates, that's in case there was a very high profile proven Lib Dem character available who would act as an additional draw and tip a losing, into a winnable, seat. The two most likely former Cabinet level ministers likely to want to stand had decided to stand in seats where they thought there was a greater chance of winning.

Accordingly the leader himself, Tim Beaumond, had called giving the constituency the OK to proceed with their choice and asked them to give him possible dates for a visit in order to co-ordinate press releases.

Sebastian's position as candidate was reconfirmed.

As a result Madge took over as the Candidate's Agent and Edna Leggs once more became constituency Chairman, in turn she handed over the Chairmanship of the Town Council to Mohammed Rahmam.

CHAPTER THIRTEEN -May 10th 2016

Sebastian, still adhering to his employer's office hours, received a call from the Chairman of RKW, Sir John Lowdham from London on May 10th.

"Sebastian, I see you are continuing in politics, I had hoped that this had all died down a bit, anyhow, well done with your O.B.E. But you know we cannot go along like this, you are likely to be in the eye of the press for the next 6 weeks much more so in a by-election than in a general election Yeh? Everything you say will be reported and you know what my Board is like? They will all read it in great detail and then bang on about it during the next Board meeting. The Press will give our HR people hell as they go through your Press Release and ask if we agree with your policies on Russia, refugees, minimum wage and whatever else you dig up. In short it might put us in a very embarrassing position. For example I have no idea what the average earnings of our employees are around the world. Am I going to be embarrassed if some wise guy analysing our accounts says by deduction that the average worldwide wage we pay is just £5 per hour and shouldn't we pay a living wage worldwide?

You know that's just not the sort of attention we need?"

"Yes but…." Sebastian tried to intervene and stem the flow of words but it was hopeless, the CEO was not used to staff interrupting him and clearly he was not going to give any leeway here.

"You know at the last General Election you were one in a mass of hundreds of potential MPs but here and now there are less than twenty candidates. Frankly you have had enough time by now to work out what you want to do! We had trouble back then with a Non Exec Director remember that, in the end he resigned – a valuable chap!

I have no problems if you want to set off on a political career and good luck to you but it's not going to work like this is it? You an area Director! Damn it! even if we use it just internally and we call it a mickey mouse directorship, but to the outside world they know it as a Director. Apart from anything else how are you going to get the accounts reviewed and completed for audit?

No – No it's not going to work!" There was a pause and Sebastian jumped in.

"Well, Sir John, the work side is all covered, I now have a deputy. As far as the election is concerned that is how democracy works – we give choices to the people – they elect representatives who in turn select the Government if they are in a majority!

What you seem to be saying is that anyone employed in business, and you know businesses are overwhelmingly conservative, has to stand as a conservative? That's not how things work is it? Only barely a third of people voted conservative! Can you not distinguish the candidate, me, from the company, RKW? There's no reason, surely, why you should be responsible for my views. For example, there are Labour followers in each of the quarries that we work, there might be followers of the Green Party in the offices believing in more wind turbines."

"Well, Sebastian I hear what you say but I am not really very happy. It caused chaos in the board room last time. I do not think we can, as you suggest, 'switch off'. I think you have to make up your mind what to do. I'll talk this through with our HR people, who I think have ideas. Obviously we would be sorry to see you go. Maybe we could find you a staff function somewhere in London without line responsibility and not as a Director, or perhaps you would think of early retirement? It's not far off now is it really? Of course it was good to have this preliminary chat with you. Anyhow think about it and let me know. We will have to resolve it one way or other. And by the way Good Luck!"

There was a click and he was gone.

He had been expecting it but had hoped there would be other options.

He could stand down but he had no intention of doing that.

But it was true the weeks leading up to the by-election would be hell and he would be scrutinised from every angle. He could agree to a London posting which he would take up after the election. In any press discussion they could then assume he was already in place 'Yes he's a head office accountant' sounds sufficiently non-descriptive and bland to head off even the most determined reporter from making an issue of it, but if he lost, then he would have to move to a made-up role doing nothing, until early retirement ended the boredom. He mused the only thing left was to go for a deal involving final salary pension and a leaving package, some of which would be tax free. It would mean a cut in earnings and probably the end of the Daedalus Project which he might have to give up.

On the positive side it would allow him to support Sylvia's project and maybe he could pick up some financial accountancy work. He had faced this before. If he acted quickly there was a chance that the package deal could be considerable whereas if he fought the matter Sir John would get more and more irritable and less likely to be generous. The HR department would cut bits off any deal to prove to Sir John what smart fellows they were!

He went home that night and immediately talked it through with Sylvia; she was furious. "Are they allowed to do things like that? Surely it's like being back in the 1820's. You remember we went through what Gladstone did when he was a Conservative MP in Newark. Did he not have two cottagers kicked out because they had voted for his opponent? This is scandalous! Dreadful! I forbid you to even contemplate it. It's mediaeval! No! No! No!"

"Just a moment!" he said "look it's my life too. Frankly it's not much of a job, had it been so I would never have done all this politics. He's basically right! It's a huge effort every time to drag oneself out of one mode and into another, one's whole attitude and personality changes. At work I am following orders or the financial bloody manual or chasing suppliers' or customers' contracts but in politics it's the opposite; I am leading in areas where there's no precedent, persuading people to do something different, making speeches sometimes where I am not entirely clear myself of the policy, always pushing and trying to make things better for people, like the homeless case.

If he wants me to go to save his embarrassment then I'll go, but at a price. I have a couple of years left and so will try to get the whole two years paid as severance, I'll advise him to amalgamate two regions so that he can declare me redundant and so I'll receive a tax free lump sum, which I can pop into my SIPP and ask for continuance of the minimal health insurance and free use of the car."

"You mean that instead of working for two years and getting paid, you will stop working now and get all the money up front and some of it tax free and some you can stick as a contribution into an enhanced pension scheme?"

"Yep that's it"

"So you will get more net of tax than continuing to work."

"Yep -how clever of you to work that out! It's the tax thing that makes it work!"

"Will he do it?"

"Just depends!" replied Sebastian laconically.

"On what for heaven's sake?" It was clear to Sebastian that she was now buying into the concept!

They went upstairs and went into the bedroom.

"Well I will call him and say that I have thought about it deeply and I am sure that there could well be conflicts of interest. He was actually quite right, the average global wage we pay in RKW is well below the UK minimum wage and I think it's likely to come up as a question for me; 'do you know that RKW is paying much less and you have been with this company and even managed the associated company in Russia and yet you stand by its use selectively only in the UK?' It's likely it will cause embarrassment?

But I will say that I cannot stand down – I hope you realise all that – I have given a commitment now"

"Yes Yes I see "Sir John will say". "Of course! No! once you have committed you have to stand by it!"

"Well then I will suggest the severance package. Saying It could be completed by the weekend and then we could each be free and you could dismiss any question of me as a '**former** Regional Director, no longer employed by us!' as I will disassociate myself from RKW saying it is a '**former** employer company with whom I am no longer associated!'.

"Will he really buy that?"

"Don't know" said Sebastian.

"And is it really so that you are underpaying workers in foreign quarries like you say?"

"I don't know!" It seems likely though – they don't have similar laws in Russia!"

"You mean bastard! So you are an evil, rapacious, business owner just as Karl Marx pointed out?"

"Yep I suppose so! – but at least they have a job because of us!"

"That's no excuse!"

"I know!"

"You know I am beginning to like you less by the minute! You have just demolished my hero Sebastian!"

"Oh yeah you reckon I could turn the whole Russian business world around in 5 years? Oh Yeah!"

"Are the press ever likely to ask the question?"

"No not a chance, there's no employees numbers shown on the Russian published accounts all the quarry workers were paid by subcontractors!"

"You devil!" Sylvia burst out laughing!

"Now stop thumping me with the pillow. I have a reputation to keep up, how would it be if the whole world knew that I faced a battering from my wife like this. Reputation! Remember Reputation!"

Sebastian turned off the light.

"Seb!"

"Yes, you do love me don't you? You are not just sorry for me are you?"

"No"

"No what?"

"Not just sorry for you! And how many times have I told you that?"

There was a pause "I suppose 252 times!"

"How's that?"

"Well I ask you every month and..... that's... let's see how many years?"

"Come here!" whispered Sebastian

"Sebastian we have two Indian girls from my group sharing the twin bunk-bed next door!"

"Oh dear!"

The following day at 9 am, Sebastian phoned Sir John directly and made the points he had practised. He added that of course he could just state that he had been asked to stand down by RKW due to conflicts of interest?

There was a sharp intake of breath at the price of the package but then a sigh.

"Oh well let's get it done – I'll email you and HR and say it's a done deal. We are having a full board meeting this afternoon and I am sure it will receive rapid assent. Well done you have negotiated a smart deal. Only a pity you didn't do that as our employee Eh?"

Sebastian was about so shout "but I did I did!" When he heard the terminal click and knew that was it!

He shouted in frustration, 'Silly old bugger, what the hell did he think I was doing in Russia? Just counting Kopecks!"

CHAPTER FOURTEEN – May 22nd 2016

At the next Local Executive meeting Sebastian announced that, after discussions with Edna Leggs, she had offered the use of her garden for a Lib Dem party. She had a large Victorian era house with ample grounds, bought by her husband who was long departed but it apparently held happy memories for her so, although tempted, she had never sold up.

All the members, officers, councillors and relatives were invited – it was called *'A Retirement & Re-entry party!'* The list also included all those who had financially contributed.

In practice, as Sebastian explained to the assembled people, "it's to announce my retirement from RKW and it's to announce my re-entry into politics"

He said in a little speech "I formally finished with them yesterday having negotiated a generous leaving package. In practice I had mentally left them many years before. I often wonder how many people there are trapped in jobs in which they trundle away. The military are much more aware of deterioration in performance that comes on over a number of years – there they appear to take a 3 year span before moving people on. Most very large firms can do that too but most of those in the middle don't bother.

Never the less it fed and clothed me, starting when I was in a desperate situation which, as you know, came to light last year during my selection process. It enabled me to survive.

However there was a huge strain in trying to do both that company role and this one. At times it almost made me feel schizophrenic and I had to remind myself which role I was in. Each time I had such a role change I found it more difficult to re-adjust, so when the end of my employment came at RKW I just felt an enormous relief and felt that I was really able to relax.

So my first act is to apologise to you all. I was not really the Mr Grumpy that you saw but reacting under strain, often being short tempered and unable to give each of you the attention you deserved and I know that many of you have been hurt by my sudden apparent removal from action from last May till earlier his month!

As you know I have been busy.

But this garden party is to record my thanks for all your efforts over last year's General Election and right up to today.

Now we have a little matter of the by-election. Tomorrow we start! Onward! Let's hope we can win!

So not to put too much stress on you all, any financial contributions will be welcomed!"

For the first time Sylvia was by his side at a formal party gathering.

Tim offered his congratulations.

Sebastian had particularly asked for a group photo of the key players.

Sebastian was standing in the middle, with his wrinkly hair now passing from grey to nearly white, but he still had most of it on top. He was still in good fettle and stood evidently at ease. He usually had a formidable expression so he found it difficult to smile and when he tried it came across as a scowl, so he no longer tried and simply looked serious. He looked straight at the camera as if to say "well here I am". He had a tendency to stoop and his M & S jacket and trousers looked perhaps a little ill-fitting; his face was lined and his broad shoulders were thinner now, but he had a bit of a paunch. He still retained the signet ring on his little finger.

Edna too was showing her years, her greying hair tied with a bun at the back and she wore some Laura Ashley flowered dress. She had a kindly face and her hands were always busy, in the picture she was holding some raffle tickets.

Madge wore her dark hair shoulder length although there was the odd trace of grey here and there. She had an open smiling face, but was slightly taller than the others. She had a firm jaw line as if to suggest that she would hold her ground, she was not beautiful as her mouth seemed slightly too large for her face.

Sylvia, Sebastian's wife, stood next to him and held his right hand tightly in her left, she was not exactly at ease and was looking beyond the lens, she was smiling and dressed in a bright yellow Salwar Kameeze like a coloured silk tailored overshirt. A silk scarf was wound around one hand which covered the scar caused by her father many years ago.

Tim was a tall blonde haired individual, looking older than his 24 years, he appeared uncertain if he really was in the group but never-the-less tagged onto the end of the row, his smile was perhaps rather half-hearted.

At the other end of the line stood Mohammed Rahman who had become a trusted friend and who at a crucial moment had endorsed Sebastian and brought in funds, members and potential council candidates. He was as usual spick and span in a brown suit, he was a smallish man with a serious expression, as one would expect of the recently appointed chairman of the Town Council.

Sebastian kept this photo on his mantelpiece at home. He often later picked it up and sat looking at it for minutes on end; he thought 'maybe this is the highpoint of my political career'.

He thought he would not be unhappy if it were.

At the last election he had had a sense of 'hubris', sometimes he really didn't think he could win but had persuaded himself that he could, and would, and that his energy alone actually justified such a result. The resulting fall had been a terrible agony.

This time he knew the risks, all he could do was to throw his whole effort into it. He would do that for the sake of the team.

CHAPTER FIFTEEN - May 24th 2016

At the local Lib Dem Executive meeting it was agreed at it was 'service as before'. There had been very few changes in helpers and councillors since the General Election in 2015 and each person was asked to draw up their own check lists so that a budget could be prepared and a plan agreed for the by-election.

Sebastian agreed to prepare a draft plan and he sat in the office till 7.30 pm thinking.

The budget, this was the most serious concern Sebastian thought, 'OK we would cut out the local district election stuff but to make an impact across the whole constituency required two or three newsletters across the whole area and that meant reallocating deliverers'. There had been previously a special by-election fund set up by Head Office and Sebastian agreed to call on it, on the grounds that the seat could be won!

Furthermore they had to decide where to canvass. They all knew that their vote was concentrated at one end of the constituency. Here their main enemy was Labour in some neighbouring areas in Middleton and they saw that as ripe to squeeze. The fact that Labour were lying third should be used to squeeze them further, together re-enforcing the local message with stories about Lib Dem activity on the Town Council which had been politically reactivated by the election of six Lib Dem councillors.

In the other 2/3rd of the constituency it looked like being a straight battle between Tories and UKIP. UKIP had only one proven area of strength where the two UKIP District Councillors had won with handsome majorities. Apart from that Sebastian said they had not much to go on.

At the General Election Sebastian had nearly 30% of the vote, Labour 25% and Conservative 44%. Although the UKIP vote nationally had recently dipped he had to assume that it was still a potent force.

Also he was aware that UKIP, although mostly affecting Conservative votes, actually also took from Labour and Lib Dem, maybe in the ratio of 2:1:1, so that if UKIP could achieve 40%, 20% would come from the Tories and 10% from each of Labour and LD.

If that were the case the result would be UKIP 40%, Conservatives 24%, LD 20% and Labour 15%. But try as he might Sebastian could see no way that Tories would defect in droves. This really was not the right sort of territory, there was no great unemployment and indeed there were a large number of exporting small businesses which relied on Asian born labour for the unskilled jobs and there were many second generation Asian born professionals who had made good. There was no noticeable ethnic rivalry or tension as there were in some of UKIP target seats particularly in East Coast port towns. In short this was a seat where the MP himself was UKIP driven but there was no real evidence of support for it across the constituency.

The most Sebastian could see UKIP getting was 20%; this would reduce the Tories to 34%, LD to 25% and Labour to 20%

There was, he felt, a generous amount of guilt still flying around about the harsh treatment of Lib Dem big names who had been so ruthlessly scattered to the winds in 2015; but they would not come on board naturally, that vote had to be identified and cajoled and motivated to vote Lib Dem again.

He would have to switch around 5% of Tory voters to LD and restrain the Labour by fighting in their council wards.

Although he had sympathy with the Jeremy Corbyn style it was, he thought, closer to the views of union officials than District Councillors, many of whom had been elected in the Blair years. Although tied to remaining in the EC, the Labour leadership refused to actively support it as some of the left wing policies were in contradiction of EC rules. The Labour party, Sebastian knew, would present at best an ambivalent position. The local Labour Councillors had been inactive, doing virtually nothing except attending meetings and following specific residents' problems, They had no regular newsletters and no delivery system. Sebastian therefore expected that in areas where Labour held District seats the Labour vote would increase by new left wing voters turning out but that elsewhere their vote would fall away, disillusioned by the infighting.

He therefore concluded that they would need four different leaflets
In LD areas – hold and increase support
In Labour areas – supplant as dominant alternative to Tory
In Tory areas - use the terrible constitutional muddle and crisis they were in, and the 'unfair ticket' - how LD MP's having supported the Coalition were summarily dumped; there was still much goodwill for LDs
In the sole UKIP area - expose the weakness of the UKIP anti-EC policy, expose thinness of their other policies

These themes would cover the one side of the leaflet and the other side would push forward common LD themes, interspersed with alarming statistics from his 'Daedalus Project' on local health, education, crime and employment.

He made contact with the 'by-elections team' at Lib Dem Head Office and tried to find out if there was any suggestion of a co-ordinated approach, but the overheads budget for small national by-election working groups had been hardest hit of all and there was no dedicated staff there any longer, a part time assistant took his name and a note of his enquiry.

Sebastian met with the other members of his executive and ran through the options.

There was basic agreement on most points in terms of tactics and the areas of each leaflet but he was asked to go through the main points.

Sebastian listed these as follows:-

1. For EC, poor Tory negotiation, there really was a case for clarifying a two speed Europe a non-Eurozone EC- one not dedicated to ever-closer ties.
2. Within UK we should demand 50,000, affordable housing, that is Council House replacement for long term cheap rental accommodation. Most of those at the bottom of the pile cannot afford to take up the Frist Time Buyer new Starter Home Scheme brought in under the Autumn Statement 2015 which is more designed to appeal to young professional couples. There is still a fundamental gap at the bottom breeding a new underclass of forgotten people who cannot afford to rent or buy.
3. No additional runway at Heathrow. Airport should be moved to the Thames estuary to allow thousands of new houses in London or one of those new garden cities
4. Keep momentum hostile to SNP using "Let 'em have it!" threat to create a plan for withdrawal from Scotland of UK wide institutions.
5. Devolution Pick & Mix not working. Demand a Constitutional Convention to decide, devolution to regions and mini states, elections to Westminster. Deals to power not even handed.
6. Failure of immigration controls and how to handle immigrants, more funding in countries of origin and renewed political effort to bring the wars to an end
7. Against HS2 but in favour of speeded up local transport between key Midlands' cities
8. Massive reduction in the welfare budget and its damaging impact on the lower paid despite the increase in the living wage

Sebastian stressed. "The main problem as I see it is that there are two very substantial and emotive problems that the euro sceptics will raise, these are the near collapse of the Eurozone and the Immigration policy". He continued with part of his prepared speech.

"But these are mere distractions from an inconvenient truth; the economic argument over Britain's continued membership of the EU has already been convincingly settled. Hardly anyone today questions that participation in the single market is overwhelmingly in Briton's economic interests. The process of harmonisation in most industrial sectors is largely complete, the one-off costs of adaption have passed through. Instead the EU is engaged in an extensive review of all its regulations to get rid of unnecessary rules, which are delightedly picked on by the tabloid press, and reduce the burden on businesses.

At the same time it is pushing hard to extend the single market in areas such as digital services, energy and capital markets in which the UK has significant competitive advantage. Were the UK to be absent from this discussion it might lead to having alien rules imposed on the City by which we might have to work anyhow, even if we left the EC. These new rules could well operate in our favour as the largest single financial centre.

Today it is hard to find a single trade body or industry group that favour Brexit. The only exception is a few high-profile entrepreneurs and some fringe financial institutions who regard any constraints as unacceptable.

But there is a long term problem; British people are unlikely to accept 'ever closer union'. Most thought that Cameron ought to have had negotiations with 'like-minded' EC countries who might also never want full integration, so that process would stop now. This would allow the rest of the EC to proceed at its natural speed without being forever restrained by an unwilling partner. If Romania for example provided a massive potential problem for recipient countries of free movement of people; how much more difficult would this be considering the inclusion of Albania and Serbia and Ukraine. The physical constraints of a small island are simply not suited to accepting all who want to travel here to seek to work. The inclusion of countries with huge wealth disparity is certain to create new waves of immigrants seeking higher pay!"

"The Prime Minster had sought to renegotiate but he had no clear idea what he wanted to achieve, lacked allies and was unaware of the EC bargaining methods. It was quite simply a total disaster!"

Edna Leggs was the first to break the ice "So that's it?"

Madge interjected "Well Sebastian – it's a bit dull perhaps?"

Sebastian replied, "Perhaps that's because chunks of it are taken from 'The Times'! but I will always have up my sleeve what other speakers will not, and that's my secret card! The information I have been putting together in my 'Daedalus Project', has meant that I have literally dozens of examples of successful trading between UK and the EC and can quote the number of new staff employed and new start-ups created by the larger market!"

"Good, well done!" said Edna and Madge added "You could put in about fighting yesterday's wars? I mean the old Britain where you could force people to work more than 48 hours or fire staff on any business company takeovers?"

"Maybe" said Sebastian "but I can save that for the repartee in any debate perhaps?"

"Ok that's good – let's go for it! All agreed?" asked Edna and finally to Sebastian "No need for the inclusion of Ukraine and Putin and the Middle East? We should steer clear of these?"

There was a nodding assent round the table. "OK let's do it!" said Edna.

There were slight ructions to come. The Greens decided to field a candidate against the wishes of the local Greens. Sebastian heard later through his Green Councillor friend that local Greens had assumed that any anti austerity votes were going to be drawn by the local Labour Party and that they did not wish to oppose Sebastian's record locally on green issues. Accordingly the Green National Executive decided to withdraw their candidate. Local Green members put up 'Sebastian' A3 posters which began to sprout around the constituency.

Edna Leggs reported that they were overwhelmed with offers of support from Lib Dems in neighbouring constituencies once the National Press had suggested that this was indeed a winnable seat for the Lib Dems. She was overjoyed and commented frequently "It's like years gone by, the enthusiasm is infectious". They were able to add a daily group of 20 canvassers, many coming from London and even from up in the Borders. In this way Edna reported that they had delivered the first leaflet throughout the entire constituency ahead of schedule.

Sebastian offered all canvassers who had carried out more than 10 hours work a free email copy of the booklet that he intended to write, all they had to do was leave their address and details of their canvassing. This proved a considerable hit. Tim as before was asked to call on likely well-heeled Lib Dems throughout the Region to gain further funds. "Support your First East Midlands Lib Dem MP", they too were promised a free Kindle version of his booklet. The Constituency also received generous financial donations.

Sebastian insisted that they should make as much use as possible of latest techniques. Wherever possible they had obtained email addresses of members, helpers, deliverers and as many supporters as possible. These received a special weekly email update of events both for this by-election and also those held at the same time. Madge was put in charge and soon created an active list of interested parties. There was a special question and answer session with Sebastian, webinars that proved popular particularly the one that was linked into the other parallel by-elections which also had the Party Leader on line. Additional outside help was brought in to test phone canvassing which, it was thought, might work particularly in outlying areas.

Not surprisingly the Press coverage also took a look at his wife's charity and this raised further funds from that connection when the basis of the work was explained.

Of course Sebastian knew that most of the TV and 'the theatrical stuff', as he called it' was going on way above the mundane canvassing level. Nigel Farage of course visited the Constituency as did the Labour Leader. Tim Beaumond visited from the Lib Dems and they put together an afternoon of canvassing for the following Press. This gave good local TV coverage and luckily the doors canvassed turned out to be favourable, or at least not hostile to Sebastian.

A hustings meeting was held by the local vicar. He introduced the candidates and then allowed them 10 minutes speaking time. Sebastian was keen to distinguish the personality from the politics. Andrew Laws was not exactly what one might have expected in a MP of several years' standing, he was rather plump and had on an ill-fitting jacket and black trousers. He favoured a coloured waistcoat which, if anything, accentuated his age, his hair was a grizzled grey but there was a large balding batch in the middle. Although he greeted everyone loudly and openly, with a typical, almost stereotypical "Hello there! I am Andrew!" He was rather hesitant as if he had been rejected by closest colleagues and no longer could distinguish friend from foe. He was clearly nervous and kept wiping his hands on his jacket pocket in a constant movement.

At the hustings he warmly greeted Sebastian who thanked him for helping his wife, "That's OK old boy! Glad to help!"

On making his presentation, Sebastian rather turned on his audience, leaving Madge wincing from a back seat. "You may be surprised but the first thing I am going to do is publically thank Andrew Laws for helping my wife set up her charity recording absentee children. Many of you might think that being political opponents means we have to hate all the other candidates all the time but that's not true. As constituency MP Andrew has worked hard for the people of this town on cases given to him. The problem that I have with him is that I cannot stand the policies he presents, I do understand his obsession with the EC; but I cannot understand any of his other policies which are a rag bag and lack coherency. I do not know why he persists in giving up a perfectly good job for one that might last only till the referendum, even if he is elected!".

Sebastian disposed of the Labour and Conservative candidates who bravely trotted out the required dogmas with no local connectivity, then ended with an impassioned speech for a reformed EC but reform from within and carried out through the proper process. "We shall get most from the EC but putting most effort into it. There is a fund of goodwill for the UK but we have failed to pick it up and use it. That's the measure of the Conservative failure!"

The Labour candidate failed to convince that they could manage the economy given the labour policy of printing money which was openly ridiculed by the audience.

Sebastian's speech, which went out on local TV, was generally regarded as by far the best of all the major parties. Madge had managed to feed cases of EC-UK trade to the press and there was a constant stream of press statements commenting on deficiencies of the local NHS and house-building failures using the Daedalus information.

Two weeks before the election he received a call from his son Andrew "Hey Dad would you need some help? I have a couple of weekends and could nip over?"

"Sure" replied Sebastian "look, Edna is organising the canvassing now. I'll pass you over to her. Give me a call when you have organised something and you can nip over for an evening meal as before. Maybe you would like to meet Sylvia's sisters. You know we found them alive and well, living not too far away?"

Edna reported back to the executive committee that they had what she called "momentum" and "By gum" she averred "if you have ever had it, then you'll know it!"

"It's like selling out of cakes within minutes of opening the stall at a charity event, like phoning to book for the local panto weeks before the event to hear that there are 'only returns' left".

"Everything is going well. We have extra people coming in to help and we have the organisation in place to use them, we have helpers putting up boards because our key man knows where to site them, we have masses of spare leaflets and so can drown any particular locality within a few hours, we have the IT software program giving delivery routes with maps and proper returns for canvassers. Our support in certain areas is soaring. We have offers of funding and at least 30 new members have signed up in areas where we were weak. All the signs are good – but do not stop now. UKIP are failing to get their material out and the Labour Party locally is split on Europe and is only able to move forward on opposition to welfare cuts. The Conservatives are trying in spurts either to ignore UKIP or then hurl 'traitor' at Andrew Laws as they tear at each other's posters each claiming leadership of the conservative flock."

His son Andrew never called back and, in the maelstrom and pandemonium of the party office, Sebastian failed to make a mental note to contact him.

CHAPTER SIXTEEN - June 16th 2016

When it came at midnight the result was greeted with wild enthusiasm by Sebastian's supporters inside the count arena with even many of the Counters themselves clapping furiously.

"It was", said Sebastian "like a phoenix arising, a party which had appeared dead and buried stood up and was alive. We are ALIVE". With a sweep he raised his hands in salute to emphasise the word alive which he shouted at the top of his voice.

That's all he said! It was a phrase picked up again and again by the media. It was splashed as a major headline in virtually all newspapers.

Sebastian had scraped home with 33% of the vote, Conservatives had 29%, Labour 22% and UKIP just 16%.

Overall that night, in what was termed the min-referendum, Lib Dems gained three seats, Labour one and UKIP one, Conservatives held onto just one.

The local Lib Dems were quite literally beside themselves with glee. After the initial outburst they stood around in small groups still unable to take in the news.

Andrew Laws walked over to Sebastian and immediately offered his congratulations "Couldn't happen to a nicer person!"

The Conservative candidate was clearly crestfallen but stayed talking with his agent, it was clear that few supporters offered him any encouragement and they drifted away quickly.

Local Lib Dems went back to their office which was now jammed with supporters and well-wishers and there Sebastian thanked everyone for their hard efforts and made one promise "You think I am going up to London, I am not, or at least mentally I remain here and every week before sundown on Sunday night I will, by email, report to you exactly what I have been doing and will seek your feedback. First of all I invite you to come with me on a special coach trip to the House of Commons as soon as it can be arranged so you can see where I will live and work. My thanks go out particularly to Madge O'Connor and I hope that she will continue as my personal assistant."

The following morning he called his friend Douglas to give him the good news. Douglas himself answered the phone and congratulated him warmly and reported that he had some good news of his own, most of his memory functions had seemed to have returned or at least he had found new ways of linking into old thoughts, and he was well able to walk over 2 miles a day! There were however some remaining limitations in his speech; he often confused left and right, could not remember nearby village names and had taken to striding off across the open fields occupied by herds with bulls, where his wife, to her consternation refused to follow! Still everyone agreed it was an improvement, he was becoming less hesitant, more sure of himself!

CHAPTER SEVENTEEN - June 17th and 20th 2016

After the declaration Sebastian had picked up a package from the returning officer who had called him into a vacant office near the count. "Well congratulations Sebastian! I hope I can call you that? As you know we have always had a close working relationship with our MP and, I think, a mutual respect! I know things have sometimes been difficult between us but I hope I can rely upon you to assist in cases where we need to discuss matters at a Ministerial level? In turn I can keep you informed about the partial devolution of services to Nottinghamshire"

"Of course!" said Sebastian, "You have a package for me concerning working at Westminster and I believe a certificate of my nomination and election that I will need for admittance to the House of Commons? And let me think now – yes happy to increase communication, I know! I would like to hold a monthly 'surgery' in your new offices, I hope that can be arranged?"

"Well Sebastian, er Mr Edwards, that's of a political nature and will lead to complications with the other parties!"

"OK, I'll drop by every so often – just to keep you honest!" and with that he was gone.

As Parliament was still in session Sebastian had to go to London and go through the initial stages of becoming an MP.

He had called LD head office and agreed to be in London by 12 noon on Monday for the photoshoot with the two other newly elected Lib Dem MPs.

He caught the early train from Nottingham, Sylvia waved him off with tears in her eyes "But why are you crying" he asked, "It's because I think that everything is now going to change between us!"

He had booked a second class ticket and spent the trip behind a newspaper hoping to remain unnoticed. But it didn't work and he was soon answering all manner of questions exactly as if it were the continuation of the hustings. Most of the comments were congratulatory.

He was flustered when he arrived in London with a brief case in one hand and an overnight bag in the other and his train ticket between his teeth. He arrived at the House of Commons gates at 11.30 am just in time to meet up with the Leader and the other new LD MPs before being ushered into the building; there was no chance to look around.

Tim Beaumond whispered in his ear as Sebastian's eye was caught by some of the murals, "That comes later, let's get the introduction right first! Until we do that you cannot speak or vote! Look follow me, leave your bags in there and just do what I say OK?"

He was then sponsored by two serving LD MPs who arrived from nowhere and he was pushed from the bar of the House towards the Speaker, the others a pace behind to left and right. He held in his hand a certificate relating to his election from the Public Bill Office. He moved to a Table Clerk at the Despatch Box where he was offered a choice of swearing formats. He chose the affirmation. Sebastian intoned the words:

"I do solemnly, sincerely and truly declare and affirm, that I will be faithful and bear true allegiance to Her Majesty Queen Elizabeth, her heirs and successors, according to law."

'There!' Sebastian thought 'It's now done! I am finally in the most exclusive club in the UK!'

He then moved to the next table and signed the 'Test Roll', a parchment book kept by the Clerk of the House of Commons. Finally he was introduced to the Speaker by the Clerk of the House. There he shook hands and went behind the Speaker's chair where staff took his signature for recognition purposes and ask him to confirm how he wished to be known.

The whole process took about 2 hours. Then they all had to go outside for a photo-shoot for the press and LD magazine!

Tim Beaumond had to leave and so Sebastian was left to his own devices. He got hold of the staff arranging accommodation and was told that it would be a further two weeks before any office for him could be arranged. Staff suggested that he book into an hotel whilst he searched for a suitable flat nearby, which could take months. They had a list of nearby hotels which had agreed to special MP's rates.

Eventually he dumped his bags there and, thoroughly exhausted, fell sound asleep on the bed without undressing.

The rest of the week was a blur of walking around the Palace of Westminster getting used to it, meeting with the LD whips and learning when and how to vote.

Another of the Lib Dem MPs elected at the same time was a man called Bill Bennett, a bald headed individual with a rather stern off-putting look who had worked his area for years and was very much of the doorstep and instant action sort of person, a devout advocate of the newsletter Focus. He and Sebastian immediately fell to comparing notes. They managed to find a flat together and would often use each other to find out what was really going on and where they should be. Sebastian found him a useful foil on Lib Dem politics and their, often opposing, views triggered off lines of thought which Sebastian found interesting. They often referred to each other on which way to vote, how to complete the expenses forms and how to interrupt and catch the Speaker's eye.

The 'Big Middleton Constituency Visit Day' was fixed for a week on Saturday, 28th June, when all his constituency officers, councillors and helpers had hired a bus and intended to descend on the House of Commons for a guided tour at 9 am followed by variously either shopping or a matinee performance at a theatre, before going back at 6 pm.

On a wider scene these by-elections were having major political repercussions.

The immediate result was a shattering of the Conservative Party morale.

It was clear that, with only one of those by-elections as a Tory victory, the Government were at risk of losing control. They had held a majority of 12 even though the working majority was nearer 16. It was now down to two and was thus dependent on rushing in every MP for crucial votes at Westminster.

The Prime Minister, through his whip's office, immediately tried to do a deal with the DUP but this drew them into conflict with the SDLP and Sinn Fein. There were already underlying problems with the introduction in the Welfare cuts in Northern Ireland. Sinn Fein were so incensed at the partisan approach that they determined to do the unthinkable and actually take up their seats in Westminster which they were quite entitled to do but had decided against doing many years ago. This caused the Conservatives to rethink that the acceptance of a deal with the Protestant parties might be a poisoned chalice both in back-tracking on the welfare budget, incurring the wrath and active engagement of Sinn Fein and destabilising Northern Ireland politically.

The Labour party had, as Sebastian had suspected, failed to gather any momentum in England. Although their leader's stance had taken back some MSP seats in Scotland, it was only at the expense of losing two MPs defecting to Lib Dem. They were unwilling to contemplate a permanent shift to the left. They had been encouraged as the Lib Dem's poll rating started to rise once again reaching 15%.

The by-election exposed the myth of the Conservative 'negotiations' with the EC. They were proved as empty as the 'Big Society' had been in 2010, a good idea but then nothing there of substance.

There was a collapse in conservative support shown by the polls and an awareness that they had no political friends, or rather no parties with whom they wanted to make alliances. Any deal with UKIP would destabilise the coalition within the Conservative party between pro- and anti-EU factions.

Amongst all this, the same week, the Labour party proceeded to fall apart in public view. The Labour leader had expected to win several seats in the by-elections but it's poor showing provoked a revolt from which he could not escape. The majority of the party agreed that he was incapable of winning an election. Initially several Shadow Cabinet Ministers resigned and the whips reported that more than half the Labour MPs had signed a letter of no confidence in their leader. Jeremy Corbyn resigned and his deputy Tom Watson took over, but chastened by the growing gap between the Parliamentary Party and the Labour Party membership, he began to seek a change in the rules which gave a better balance between them, the suggestion being that, after election by the members, then such a person must later also win 50% of the votes of the Labour MPs. The Labour Party was thus embroiled in its own internal constitutional problems. It was assumed that it might take months to re-engineer their constitution. There was no other obvious successor amongst the Labour MPs wanting to take over. There appeared to Sebastian to be a power vacuum of an extraordinary kind in the Labour Party.

The Liberal Democrats now stood at 13, not yet a large enough force to forge an alliance with anyone.

The financial collapse happened very quickly.

The initial damage to the £ was done by the recovery of the Euro; slowly the growth in the Eurozone had recovered. Sebastian thought that the funniest things happen in politics. Germany was earlier united in its ferocious demand that Greece should repay everything it owed, like Shylock, and quickly ridiculed the view that what was necessary was a rapid transfer of wealth from the prosperous north to the impoverished south, as it meant giving it's hard earned money away to what they regarded as idle southerners.

Then, in fact, they did something almost identical in taking in 800,000 refugees. This immediately added not only further manpower, meaning that industries short of labour in Germany no longer had to expensively build factories in Eastern Europe, but at last could now build new factories in Germany itself. Soon the additional spending power of the new arrivals would be expected to seep through into the German economy. So the forecast now was of a huge spurt in German growth which was the engine of French and also Polish and Low Countries' growth too. Forecasters now suggested greater growth throughout the Eurozone. In the USA the Fed increased rates by 0.5%.

Under this pressure the £ slumped against the Euro and this forced the Bank of England to raise rates slightly to 1.5 % (up 0.5%) which they did before the Governor had tactically prepared the public. He said that he had had no option, the committee voted for an immediate increase. This emergency hike stunned the market. The short run growth in house build in the UK was forecast to stumble and then go into reverse but the demand for housing saw house price rises in London particularly. Lower priced houses could not be sold because the interest rate increases had again meant that the deposit demanded was several times a person's average salary. At the bottom of the housing market this led to severe tension as there was terrible competition for the available Council or subsidised housing. This was made worse by the 'right to buy' which reduced the affordable housing stock further. One director of an East Coast Council housing department said, "The system is broken – I cannot work it without Government help!"

Several major industry sectors now openly questioned the reason for the referendum stating that they were eyeing up sites in Eastern Europe instead in case the referendum should be for 'out'; there, renewed grants were said to be available. To add to the confusion, in case UK voted NO, the SNP had demanded an additional referendum on independence, since they were determined to remain in the EC themselves.

The Stock Market reacted savagely to all this uncertainty. The FTSE 100 had been riding out the Chinese recession well on the bases of UK dividends on equities being higher than for years.

The Conservative Prime Minister was now openly being called 'the Last Prime Minister of the UK' and appeared to be paralysed, incapable of resolving the constitutional issues as well as the mounting certainty that the UK was heading back into recession.

Many more cautious brokers had advised their clients to sell before the mini-election day, giving new life to the saying "Sell in May and don't come back till St Leger day (September 14th)". Others had also begun to shift back into European Equities on the strength of better trading and possibly increased dividends there.

CHAPTER EIGHTEEN - June 28th to 30th 2016

The Financial Melt Down took place on Thursday June 28th 2016.

Sebastian tried to analyse what was happening.

At first it just seemed like a ripple, there was no further bad news from the USA. It was one of the Groups in the UK representing larger businesses that appeared to set it off. 'The British Federation of Industry' merely, and they thought harmlessly, quoted in their monthly newsletter, from a 'trusted a source', that one of the foreign owned UK car factories was ceasing production in the UK as sales were very sluggish. It was followed by an article about trouble in the mining industry; so long a mainstream part of the FTSE 100. A small FTSE 350 mineral extraction company had collapsed, but some of its shares were also held by an erstwhile predator who had gobbled up 15% of its shares and had intended to float them. This immediately placed that predator also in financial difficulties. They immediately lost their investment credit rating, there was also some suggestion that they had misstated past profits, based on contracted sales which were later revoked. The collapse made 10,000 employees in Africa redundant. But the news of both these unhinged the market dragging down miners' stocks and thus the FTSE100 even though the news from China was upbeat.

This news was quoted in the National News on radio and TV. This seemed to have unnerved the market.

On Friday morning shares went into free-fall as equity holders decided that the uncertainty over Europe 'in or out' would result in further falls until the UK political arena was stabilised in some way.

The £ fell sharply against the Euro and $.

On Friday afternoon, the Chancellor of the Exchequer apparently, so he told Tim later, who repeated this to Sebastian, called on the Chairman of the Stock Exchange and the Bank of England. The Governor thought that any hiking up of interest rates simply to prop up the £ would be counterproductive; until there was a political stability, the pound would be likely to end in free fall as it adjusted to the new conditions.

The Conservative Prime Minister publicly called for calm saying that nothing had actually happened to reduce the value of these companies and that brokers should just advise their clients to sit tight 'Underlying values have not changed!'. The Bank of England did prevail upon futures and derivative traders not to take significant forward positions in the national interest, but this was advisory only.

It was evident that the Conservative Parliamentary majority had crumbled and they could no longer guarantee passing significant bills, especially since the House of Lords, where they held no majority, now insisted on and agitated for its own reform. My Lords had not been impressed by an earlier threat by the Conservatives to create even more Life Peers just to get themselves into a majority position. They were already, in terms of second chambers, second only to China in terms of numbers. They were in no mood to help the Government.

It was clear that politically the Conservatives were in turmoil.

Sebastian had taken Sylvia to a show in London on the Friday night and they had stayed the night at the hotel he was using. He had dropped into LD HQ on the Saturday morning at around 11.30 am. He had been around the House of Commons with a bus load of his supporters at 9 am on the guided tour and had just managed to escape for the rest of the day.

He had called in at HQ just in case there was anything going in such turbulent times and to show Sylvia their 'Head Office'.

He met Tim Beaumond in the corridor outside the leader's office, a tiny room with a desk and two or three chairs, he had left his wife in the reception area. They were all about to set off for lunch together when the on-duty secretary caught them.

"It's the PA to the Prime Minister – he wants to speak to you Mr Beaumond – urgently! He asked for your mobile but I told him you were here and he asked to be put through, I hope that I did OK?"

"Yes! Yes of course put him on!" The secretary left the room and Tim motioned Sebastian to sit across the desk. "Hello are you the PA to the Prime Minister? I have a colleague here, a Mr Sebastian Edwards the new Lib Dem MP you will remember him – is this confidential? Do you think I can put it on the hands free system – there's nobody else here!"

"Yes! Yes!" Sebastian heard the assent as it boomed into life.

"What can I do for you?"

"Let me pass you to the Prime Minister!"

"Prime Minister, before we chat and just to test security, we were together at a ceremony last week and sat next to each other – can you remember what we talked about? You know it's easy to make hoax calls and my lines here are not security tested so we should do elementary tests?"

"Hm! Let me think, yes! It was about Charles Kennedy!"

"OK that's correct. If these are confidential discussions can we refer to them under the code word "Charles"?"

"That's fine" came the voice. "All that I am going to say is strictly confidential. Of course I cannot bind you in any way to keep silent. All that I do ask is that if you have to use this in any way, that you will call me and a least give me the opportunity to dissuade you?"

"This sounds, well, really serious? I suppose it's to do with the financial markets?"

"Yes" there was a pause and he seemed to gather himself as if being forced to speak.

"Well I have just been in discussions with the Chancellor and the Bank of England and the CEO of the Stock Exchange. They present a pretty gloomy view and are worried that Monday will bring chaos. The Bank tells me that of course everyone realises that the pound is supported by thin air and is overvalued. Tells me NOW! For heaven sake! We, in the UK don't balance our trading account budgets, and invisible earnings from financials are nothing like enough to make up the difference, so we have a current account deficit. The result is that the strengthening of the Euro has meant that our position as a sort of reserve currency has been undermined.

In short there's nothing holding up the £. At times yesterday the £ slipped to near parity with the $ and that's really dire. Foreign pension funds which had invested in UK Equities panicked, fearing the value of their investments would collapse and started to get out of the UK. The Stock Market fell 10% on Thursday and a further 20% on Friday to its lowest in 15 years.

We face a possible rout on Monday.

We could stabilise that in the short term by rapidly increasing interest rates say by something like 5% or even 10% but that would send out danger signals, rapidly increase inflation and leave an estimated million homes unable to pay their variable interest rate loans. The stock market would collapse as companies cut back expansion plans, dragging us into recession! However we tried this before at the time of the Exchange Rate Mechanism. We have never beaten the market and even the hiking upwards of interest rates to ridiculous levels failed to stop it.

As I now appear to have nearly lost my majority, I could perhaps step down. The Governor of the Bank warns against it, that's because the Labour party seems to have veered to the left and the SNP has vowed to use every opportunity to embarrass the Government of the day until a second Scottish referendum was agreed. It would cause further uncertainty and financial chaos if I acceded to that demand.

We face having our financial status being downgraded on Monday. The French President is sure to crow about the financial stability we could have got inside Euro. IMF would be likely to call for stable government. We could face the same 'financial troika' as Greece had to endure, and that means months of investigation, whilst they consider a plan and work out what changes they think we must make internally!"

"So Prime Minister how can I help you?"

"In short the Bank says I need a political solution, something that will show that my Government can last out and will not arbitrarily fall. He says it should be with a party in favour of the EC as the market is hostile to a Brexit which they are convinced will bring a further collapse in confidence. I have offered my own resignation but the Bank have told me that it would simply destabilise matters even more! I am told I have to stay and all the Conservative leadership contenders here have accepted that!"

"So Prime Minister exactly what are you proposing?"

"Some sort of a political deal with you to last us through until after the referendum which we can pull forward to October 2016 if necessary. I am told that anything earlier would be quite impossible to introduce all the enabling Bills and to resolve the Scottish devolution problems!"

Tim replied, "You know Prime Minister I was one of the few Lib Dems never to join your coalition and having virtually destroyed our party by your attitude, can you realistically expect us to agree?"

Sebastian interjected "Well if you want that you'll have to pay a very heavy price, you understand that?" "Let us discuss the matter here and perhaps you can call back in half an hour when we have a moment to chat it through!"

"Who is that?" asked the Prime Minister, "Its Sebastian Edwards, Prime Minister, our new MP, he just called in here on the off chance!"

"Yes certainly!" there was a click and he was gone.

Tim turned on Sebastian "You must be mad if you think we can be drawn into another coalition!"

"Tim, he is desperate. A financial collapse might well trigger an economic rout worse than what we have ever seen before, he knows that, the alternative is another General Election but that will take several weeks to organise. The summer months, July to September, are the worst possible months to hold any election. He knows he will face a total defeat, the Tories pride themselves on one thing above everything – management of the financial sector. Failure here could end them for a decade!"

"So what do you suggest Sebastian?"

"Something which, with respect, we should have done in 2010, something like this!..
1) That HMG agrees to put in place immediately a Constitutional Commission to cover the following a) devolution to Scotland of what powers b) devolution to Regions within UK, Wales, NI; powers and voting system c) powers of an overriding National parliament, how to operate different levels of powers and d) reform of the House of Lords, and proposed voting system e) Voting age for all elections/referenda
2) That the Conservatives will go along with such changes as are agreed by the majority of that commission and will commit to supporting the changes needed.

3) Euro referendum brought forward to October 2016.

We could add more stabilising points to calm left wing fears that we are maybe propping up a failing and ailing Tory Party. These might be a) repeal of some of the welfare reforms, particularly for the cuts to the London rates, and b) repeal of the 2015 Trade Union Act particularly clauses on agency labour to replace strikers.

If these were included it would give Labour a reason for supporting it, both of these are very important to them, there's no way they could otherwise be sure of facing the electorate and winning and then putting the Bills in place. In this way they could have an immediate impact on the political scene but not at such a cost as Conservatives could not go along with it. Probably many Conservative MPs would accept those changes anyhow. The other clauses of the Welfare Bill would be left, as would the remainder of the Union Bill. Devolution to Scotland would be halted pending the Constitutional commission.

We would take no Ministerial posts and give the Conservatives a 'supply and maintenance' basis just until the EU referendum is completed. I do not think it's possible to stop that in its tracks, the public expectation is that they would be offered the chance to decide our future and, like it or not, we cannot go against it now.

The brief to the commission is that they should report within one year and that it would be voted on as a package by another national referendum. It may sound like a very short period of time but the UK has been toying with this for well over 150 years since the first Irish troubles and several times since. It's a well-trodden path but one which has to be taken urgently. Our unwritten constitution can no longer take the strain!"

"Hmm Sebastian do you think they will agree, more's the point do you think our MPs and members will agree?"

"If the Conservatives are desperate they will do it. If they don't do it then at least we have responded positively and in the spirit of genuine care for our country."

"Well Sebastian do you want me to put it to him? Like that? Of course we would have to put in caveats about all Lib Dem MPs agreeing and so on and we would have to stress that it's not just a paper agreement. In this case he and the whole of his cabinet have to commit to a reform package of which they do not yet know the details. That's a tough call! Are we ready for this?"

Sebastian asked "How do you think the other LD MPs would take it?"

"Sebastian we are still knocked sideways by the 2015 elections. They would probably take this if it meant the probable long term survival of the party which faces being totally eclipsed!"

Tim thought carefully with his head in his hands, sitting at his desk, he started to scribble notes.

"OK let's do it on a draft basis." said Tim.

Within minutes the Prime Minister was back on the phone. "Code word "Charles"."

Tim went through the proposal in detail, adding that in view of the likely timescale it may not be possible to call in all Tory MPs but that the 1922 committee would also have to give their consent.

There was a long pause then "So no Ministries then?"

"No! No Ministries! Just on a 'Supply and Maintenance basis' to enable you to get through to the Euro referendum."

"Well it may not work – I'll let you know. We are having an emergency cabinet meeting this afternoon, I suggest that you get hold of as many of your MPs as you can OK, We will talk again, anyhow thank you for responding so quickly and positively!"

Sebastian and Tim Beaumond spent the next few hours making contact and recalling all MPs, Peers on committees and all Executive Committee members. In addition staff were recalled whose role was each to make contact with 30 constituency chairman who had been alerted that their vote might be needed by Sunday at 12 noon. As more of the senior LD MPs and Peers arrived Sebastian was able to free himself for a time.

He found Sylvia sitting in the crowded reception area, a tiny enclave near the door. He apologised profusely, "Sylvia I am really sorry, we seem to have a national emergency on our hands – a real crisis".

"I am OK Seb I've been looking at the books on the origins of the party, something that until now I have tried to ignore and I have had 5 cups of coffee and 4 of that dreadful soup from the machine. Ugh! Anyhow I have introduced myself to several of your MPs, it has at least passed the time! Maybe I had better go back to the Hotel?"

"Good idea" said Sebastian, "we booked out this morning but I think it's going to be an all-night job."

"Well Sebastian I did tell you that you were going to be a really important person!"

"So see you when I can!" he went outside and managed to capture a taxi for her which was delivering its load of Lib Dems for the meetings.

By 3 pm on Saturday LD MPs began drifting in and, apart from one in transit, everyone was contacted.

By 4 pm the Prime Minister was back on the phone. "Code "Charles!"". "In principle we agree and these civil service people need to get in on the act?"

Sebastian shook his head in the background "No! We don't want to get argued out of anything particularly the time table. If it warrants it then it will be done in time!"

Tim declined the addition of civil servants, he agreed a joint meeting would take place the following afternoon, Sunday at 5 pm for signing, with a Press and TV release at 6 pm, until then all parties were to observe absolute media silence.

There was great excitement and interest by the press, they had guessed that something had to happen. They were still not aware of the detailed implications but anxious not to miss any opportunity for a scoop. As a result there were numerous probing phone calls – but the silent moratorium held, there was no leak.

The dispersal calls to constituency chairmen worked well, each chairman had been asked to call at least 50 of their members. The message was essentially simple and almost all constituency reports showed a clear 75/25 majority in favour. Of course this was influenced by the news that 14 of the 15 LD MPs were in favour with only one demurring but as he himself said he had no alternatives to offer. "After last time, full coalition was out of the question but so was doing nothing!"

By 5 pm the deal was done even the 1922 Committee had agreed though only by a slim majority.

Sebastian raised the matter of contacting Greens, UKIP and Labour and asked to be allowed, together with the Home Secretary, to make contact and quickly explain the position. The Prime Minister and Tim agreed. Accordingly from 4 pm Sebastian tried desperately to make contact with the other leaders so that they could visit them. They managed to locate the UKIP leader and the Labour Party deputy leader and explain. Sebastian leading off in both cases, "You see we ourselves will get nothing from this, not a single ministerial car!"

All the other party leaders expressed gratitude for being kept informed and to hear at first-hand what was going on. This would allow them to gain feedback from their own parties during the evening before the Stock Exchange re-opened. The Welsh, Northern Ireland and SNP leaders were called by phone at 6 pm from the Prime Minister's Office as the information hit the TV screens. Of course the SNP reacted angrily seeing it as merely a subterfuge to delay granting further powers to Scotland.

The TV and Press release was made as agreed at 6 pm, with the two leaders, Tory and Lib Dem, outside Downing Street. The Prime Minister paid great respect to the help given by the Lib Dems and praised them for once again acting in the best interests of the nation.

Early trading in Far Eastern markets showed that the pressure was off the £ and that the run on the Stock Market was likely to slow abruptly as buyers sought opportunities to buy UK shares on the cheap. The bounce caught several currency traders off balance and one immediately went into liquidation having taken out positions suggesting further losses to the £ and in shares. They were immediately referred for police investigation.

By 5 pm on the following day a full transcript signed by all LD MPs and the Cabinet was presented to the press. During the day all other English political parties represented in Parliament also signed the accord. Welsh, Northern Ireland and even the SNP MPs followed suit.

Tim reminded Sebastian that the procedure that they had used was contrary to the standard triple arm-lock procedure used by Lib Dems previously, "but as it turned out, it was clearly an emergency situation and I felt we had no alternative. The feedback within the party was overwhelmingly positive, never-the-less we will have to formally agree to carry out the procedure even if this makes us look silly, we will have to put up with that and simply risk that everyone in the Lib Dems acknowledges that!"

Members of the Constitutional Commission began to be selected. It was chaired by a leading judge. It included several well-known Constitutional lawyers, a few University boffins, three of the senior-most civil servants and the leaders of all the main English parties with other party leaders as on a call basis. It was to sit full time. The Chairman was a Judge. All parties were asked to make detailed submissions within 4 weeks and it was agreed that the House would be recalled early to prepare Bills to present the Constitutional Commission's report findings to a Constitutional Referendum in November 2017.

The House rose as normal on 19th July 2016 for the summer recess and calm was, by then, fully restored.

The Stock Market had recovered most of the losses although still 10% below the level of before the crisis and interest rates were held at a modest 1.5%, more than the Eurozone rate, although warning was given that the era of cheap money was over and rates would slowly climb to over 2%. It was thought that the £ rate would settle permanently at 20% below the previous level.

To take advantage of the lower value of the £, the Conservative Government began a policy of supporting exports and considered ways of offering cheap export credit, having studied the French system which apparently gave some scope for manoeuvre within the EU rules.

During the summer there was much speculation as to whether Lib Dems or others would enter into a formal coalition with the Conservatives but this was denied by both parties. Tim stressed that this was a temporary measure merely to save the financial meltdown which otherwise looked inescapable.

CHAPTER NINETEEN - July 2016

Sebastian was warmly thanked by the Lib Dem Executive Committee for supporting the leader during the financial crisis.

He sorted out some basic 'housekeeping' matters. First he gave Madge a real contract of employment as his PA based in Middleton. She was delighted and they began to work out what equipment they would need to handle all his constituency affairs in Middleton, leaving ad hoc London work to be done by temps there. A key element was Sebastian's promise of a weekly update of his activities before midnight on every Sunday.

Secondly he belatedly thanked James Smith who had, a couple of years ago, given them rent free use of the shop they used in Middleton as the Lib Dem HQ. "Look you have supported us through thick and thin and I feel that now I am able to return something to you. I am allowed to charge certain expenses for my Constituency Office and, accordingly, I am prepared to pay you for ongoing use at market rates! I hope that at least gives you some reward for your patience?" James Smith said he was well satisfied and was delighted to be part of Sebastian's success.

At the beginning of July Sebastian reminded his leader of the former contact with Russia where he was used as a go-between by the Russians to resolve issues in the Crimea although nothing definitive had come of it.

Sebastian suggested to Tim Beaumond that he should try again to make use of his contacts before time moved on and put those contacts into history. With any luck, he suggested, the Russian contacts were still warm enough to use.

Sebastian outlined a bold plan to Tim that would fundamentally change the whole political environment relating to Russia although he admitted the chances of its coming off were less than, say, one in ten.

He gave Tim an idea of the changes he had in mind. Tim was amazed "Do you think you can do it?"

"I have no idea" said Sebastian "but if I don't try we shall lose the opportunity, of that I am sure! Look if we are to win credibility within the UK we will have to prove we are relevant to making new decisions in new ground not being a pale reflection of other parties. Here we have an opportunity to forge a totally new and ground breaking policy. Of course the key players there know of me but I'll need some validation of my position here. Could you give me a letter of introduction?"

"Well, I'll have a word with the Lib Dem Foreign Affairs Committee Chairman and call you back!"

Tim Beaumond called back the following day. "Yes," said Tim "we are prepared to give you a chance but you must not imply to anyone that you are empowered to change Lib Dem policy on the hoof! I can write you a letter simply stating that you have been asked to open certain lines of enquiry, but on no condition can it be taken as policy unless agreed to by the Lib Dem Foreign Affairs Committee and validated by a Conference motion if it involves a basic change in policy! Is that agreed?"

Sebastian then outlined his intended course of action to which Tim gave his assent.

He received the letter from the leader on formal Liberal Democratic Party notepaper, which identified him, Sebastian Edwards MP, as the person entrusted with the mission.

Sebastian made a phone call direct to the Minister-Counsellor of the Russian Embassy, Sergey Kramrenko, whom he had previously met. Initially he could not get through so he left a messaging saying he, Sebastian, would call at 3 pm that afternoon. He called as indicated and was put through immediately. After some careful questioning Sergey agreed to meet with Sebastian at the Russian Embassy on the following afternoon.

Sergey was a professional diplomat with responsibility for looking at initiatives to resolve the problems in the Ukraine. Sebastian remembered that he was aged about 65 with thinning greying hair. He was smallish and rather plump but had an approachable personality. He had been, so his FCO handlers had earlier claimed, in the diplomatic service for forty years. They had concluded that he was involved with a so-called 'full review', the 360 degree Russian Foreign Policy Plan, which was personally approved by the then President Medvedev in 2008 and discussed the various foreign policy options. In that sense he was senior to the actual Russian Ambassador to the UK who was rather the mouthpiece of the Russian Government and not privy to these secret plans.

They met in the first week of July.

Sebastian was shown into the Embassy and greeted by Sergey as an old friend. "Hello Mr Sebastian, I thought some day we would meet again. Your timing is perfect I have just completed three years' duty here and am due to return soon 'v Dom, to Home". As usual with such diplomats his English was workable even if it was somewhat stilted. "So how is it for you? – I understand that two things have happened since we met last. One, your party has been, how you say, wiped out, but two, you yourself have achieved some miracle in being elected! Is that so?"

"Yes that's about it." said Sebastian as he slumped into a chair in a rather grand office and wondered how he could make himself relevant to the top tier in Russian power politics as he had before when his party the Lib Dems appeared to have the ear of Government in the UK. Now he knew that he had nothing, he was nothing of importance to the Russian Government. Best to get the worst over first.

"Well I suppose you have heard of my escapade getting out Jeffrey Pardoe out through Ukraine?"

"Yes, silly man, he was running away from our security and slipped and fell and broke his ankle or something. Of course we wanted him to escape and take with him the photos which he duly published, so at least he served some purpose, but sleeping rough and walking through water was unnecessary. Sorry to hear you have given up the Directorship of Siberian Minerals, that's pity as company was doing well and we like encourage foreign investment. You know money coming into Russia?"

"So you know all about that?"

"Of course the idea was ours, how otherwise could we get him out? We knew he could not use the Americans as that might lead us to their agents"

"You mean that you were aware of my going from the start?"

"Of course! But that is another story. How can I help you now?"

"Well" started Sebastian slowly "I really believed in the mission of trying to do something to resolve the problems in Ukraine and in Syria."

"Ah" said Sergey "still idealistic politically naïve, how you say 'do-gooding' person. You know you British take how you say 'biscuit'. You treat people in your empire, as in India, like rubbish, kill thousand and hundreds in wars of independence which you still call 'Indian Mutiny' and yet you expect them to vote with you in United Nations and buy your military aircraft and tanks. It doesn't seem to occur to you that just saying 'sorry' is not enough. But as result you now find yourself skilled enough to tell us how we Russians should operate on the world stage."

"Alright, alright!" Sebastian suddenly surprised himself by his own interjection, "and what happened to the Polish Offices in Katyn Forest and what about the Gulags and the forced removal of all the Volga Germans who had lived in Russia for centuries?"

"Humf – khahroshiy – good – I see that you have not lost your what you say.. spark? We are not here to play victim or aggressor in history are we? So you want some sort of trade?"

"In a way yes" said Sebastian. "I'll be frank otherwise there's no point in my misleading you!"

"That's good start, Sebastian, we recognised your honesty which is why we decided we could do business with you!"

"In fact I am seeking nothing less than a political realignment in the global power structure of today." Sebastian announced rather grandly. "Let's ignore the reasons why you are embroiled as you are in Ukraine and Syria. You claim with some justice that in both cases you were supporting the legally elected government of the area.

In Ukraine the Russian culture had been dominant for centuries and the then President looked to Russia for trade and development. You say that the Maidan uprising in Kiev was a mutiny against an elected government even if that was riddled with corruption. Attempts to downgrade the Russian language there were as ham-fisted as would, say the downgrading of English be to second language status in Cardiff or Swansea.

But Mr Putin knew that the takeover of the Crimea was in direct contravention of international law, the downing of the passenger aircraft MH17 and setting up of the independent regimes in Eastern Ukraine could only have happened with direct Russian support.

He is now trapped in a position where sanctions are reducing growth in Russia.

In Syria again an apparently harmless initial support for a worn out legitimate Syria regime by Russia has, instead of securing any sort of victory, drawn itself further and further into a war that it cannot win. Mr Putin may well have formed a useful coalition with Iraq and particularly Iran, but unless he commits ground forces on a long term basis he has no hope of victory. The downing of the Russian holiday plane in Sinai illustrates the potential problems.

Within Russia these apparent strong arm tactics give him a reputation as a strong leader and puts him in an unassailable position. His party the United Russia Party had 49% of the vote in 2011 in the State Duma and 45 million votes in the presidential elections in 2012 out of a total of 71 million votes cast. The nearest opponents were the Communist Party and the Liberal Democrats which, as many have said, is neither Liberal or Democratic but right wing.

There is no democratic party in opposition, there is no credible alternative vote.

But all the while he has become the bogey-man that the USA were always looking for, the reason to increase their military spending.

It has been my hope that Russia could be turned from this position. Some of us would like to see Russia playing a positive role in Europe and the World. As I have proved, bringing UK financial resources and know-how to assist in development of Russia's wealth, could have mutual benefits.

 "So that's your thesis Sebastian? His Excellency Putin listens to you and then follows your advice? Is that likely?"

"My own motivation is clear, and I'll be straightforward, we Lib Dems are a tiny party in the UK struggling for our very survival. Of course magically finding that we have single-handedly managed to 'turn' Putin's idea on its head would be good but very unlikely! One the other hand in Ukraine your position is causing massive damage to your economy and in Syria you are in a position where your surrogate will lose. What harm would there be in talking? It could not make the situation worse?"

"So Sebastian, you try to be miracle worker and change Russian foreign policy all on your own? Hah! It seems ridiculous! Preposterous! Do you have any headings for such peace plan – any details that I could see? Is this for example view of your Military Chiefs? Is this your new party policy? Have you tested this out in Euro Parliament for their views?"

"Well", said Sebastian "I do in fact have a statement that I have prepared, which sets out the salient points." Sebastian pulled a sheet of paper from his pocket and passed it across the large wooden table which was between them.

Sergey read it briefly. "So, it would all depend on some personal meeting I suppose? Well thank you for calling in, I will report this discussion and I am sure we value your support but I cannot think we can use your idea. If we do we will let you know!" Sergey rose from his chair and guided him to the door "But Mr Edwards, take my advice, first thing you have to do is to secure your own seat, these are unstable times in the UK!" Sergey pushed back into his hands the letter of introduction from Lib Dem HQ.

Sebastian was ushered out and as the door of the Embassy closed behind him, he realised how stupid his words must have sounded, he knew his points would be reported back at high level, but he had no hopes that anything would come of it. He sighed. "Well I had to try!" and he returned home by train, thinking that he had after all done his best, but he understood that being an MP didn't necessarily mean anything internationally.

He reported back to party HQ by phone that he had made his pitch but that it had fallen on rocky ground.

Tim Beaumond responded with relief. "Whew! Look I know that you are disappointed but frankly I am neither surprised nor alarmed. What you were proposing was a total change in Party policy. The last thing I want is for you to be seen as some sort of maverick suggesting alternative ad hoc policies. My advice, Sebastian, is to sit on this for a bit, maybe we will find time for a policy discussion at the next conference in the Autumn, that will allow for a more detailed airing of the topic and give you time to prepare a more persuasive case. Something like 'Bringing Russia in from the cold – towards a new realignment of Global Politics'?

"Being an MP Sebastian may give you a greater reach in what you can do here but in international politics it simply does not count, unless these heavyweights themselves want to discuss they will simply ignore you.

You are one of our very few MPs and you have what we lack and that's political momentum. Let's try and use it to wrest back some of the seats we have lost OK?"

"OK" said Sebastian, "point taken, how can I help then? You appreciate that all I wanted to do was to make use of my existing contacts before they moved on?"

"Let's not be naïve though, start off by getting your energy linked in with the Euro Referendum. I would like you to take a leading role as a speaker at events up and down the country – would you do that?"

"Yes." Sebastian agreed.

"Right let's get you plugged into it – you'll have a massive amount to learn and Radio and TV political programmes are interested in having you make guest appearances. We have to gauge this very carefully, some of the interviewers can take even an experienced politician apart in minutes and they enjoy that! So we want to grade your introduction and start off with some easy stuff till you gain confidence? But no more Russia for the time being OK?"

CHAPTER TWENTY - August to October 2016 – Euro Referendum

Sebastian was promoted to the Speakers list for the Lib Dems and immediately he was swamped with urgent calls for events which the 'Staying IN' team organised. His base was within the East and West Midlands where there were no other Lib Dem MPs and he was asked to cover that area.

He immediately sought advice of a Bill Grange who had been a Lib Dem MEP until recently for part of the East Midlands. He spent several days going through the various Acts transferring powers and how Bill thought they might be improved. Then he prepared his case for use in the speech. The key factors Sebastian listed were:

- A very large number of existing jobs would be at risk, employers would prefer being within the EU.
- It would likely initially throw the UK back into recession causing further austerity and cut backs.
- Historically the EU has formed a base for ex-Communist & Fascist regimes ridding us of extremes.
- EU is now one of the most powerful trading blocs which it would be senseless to leave.
- EU can be improved and petty rules eliminated but only from inside.
- Outside the EU as trading partner we would still have to use their standards there'll be no saving leaving.

In addition he was able to quote from a long list of detailed examples of cases of contracts gained by particularly East Midland business leading to hundreds of new jobs and business opportunities.

He tried out his speeches with Madge in the office one day. As his PA she usually tried to write his speeches. On a few occasions it had worked but mostly she found that he had already started and she had to prise from him bits of speeches which he agreed could be horribly boring.

She said "Look it's just very dry, Sebastian, after two or three speeches like this all the front row will nod off and just wake up for question time at 10.30 pm! Can't you say something funny or at least intellectual?"

"OK I get the message! What about this?" *Should Britain be in Europe? I have just checked my Atlas. Yes it should - at the top of the page it says 'Europe'- see its really easy!"*

"No!" said Madge, "Not really funny!"

"Well I don't do funny very well how about this?"

"Europe doesn't grow because of the treaties. It grows from the heart of the citizens, or is doomed to failure".

"But that's serious!" protested Madge.

"I know I know but it's all serious stuff anyhow I then aim to move onto the attack!"

"You mean to attack the EU?" asked Madge by now thoroughly exasperated.

"No No! to attack the handling by the UK Governments of potential UK grant claims. You realise that there has been subsidiarity which effectively means that most UK grants for EC are passed through the UK treasury so are knocked out if such grants are already available in the UK This is one of the reasons why we often read headlines such as."

"British firms miss billions in EU grants"

....SMALL firms are losing out on billions of pounds of European grants because the government is not applying for them, according to a special report by a group of Conservative MEPs...."

And "THE EUROPEAN Community this weekend invited tenders for projects to improve energy technology amid rising concern that British firms are failing to compete and win a fair share of the grants for industry.

The EC's Thermie project, which will dispense 350m euro (£252m) to European industry over the next two years, promotes investment in improved technology in hydrocarbon and coal production and also technology to develop renewable energy, such as wind and solar power.

British industry has won just 12 per cent of Thermie funding for energy-saving projects and only 10 per cent for investment in projects promoting the use of renewable energy. The association reckons that UK firms should be winning 18 per cent of the grants overall.

Andrew Warren, the association's director, said: 'There is a basic belief that the British are not serious about energy and the environment. But UK firms should apply because they can win 40 per cent of the cost of any project."

"So" he said triumphantly warming to his key point" often we have failed to take advantage of the grants that are available and yet we criticise the French, for example, for their keenness in exploiting the grants to the full".

"In another field too UK has been a laggard. There was initially a burst of enthusiasm in the EU, especially for undergraduates to obtain direct access to other European Universities to study their cultures as part of their own degrees. The programme called 'Erasmus' has been running for several years but for example in 2011/2 only 13,662 UK students participated in the scheme compared with Spain at 39,545, Germany 33,363 and France with 33,269. If we are going to trade with the EU in or out we still need managers who can understand different languages and cultures, Don't we?

Wherever you look the UK has at best been a hesitant member of the EC and its failure to 'get stuck in' and embrace the methods used by the EC can be directly traced to the current British PM's inability to coherently say what he wants to change within the EC and how he wants to do it. Indeed his methods are so far removed from the EC mechanisms that it comes over as a massive rant similar but with no greater intelligence applied than the front pages of the UK tabloids.

If we are not seen to be serious about our interest in the EC why do you expect that they would even bother to discuss possible changes to a constitution, when they cannot even understand your point of view!!"

Madge shouted out, "OK, OK! That's better! You come over much better when you have something concrete to say! That's good! Use that in your speech OK?"

Sebastian was drawn into the formal set piece speeches across the Midlands and he became a popular visitor on TV and radio shows for political analysis often debating with UKIP leaders.

As the referendum drew closer the views became more strident and entrenched. The Government had intended to set out its case in a special booklet to be delivered to every household, but a minority of cabinet ministers had revolted insisting that this was taking advantage of the less well funded getting out campaign.

The Labour party seemed to freeze in the spotlights. It was unwilling to 'rescue' the Conservatives from their obvious split and were unwilling to push their own members to take positions. On the one hand they thought the EU an organisation set up for the advancement of big business and suspected that the EU would try to prevent renationalisation, on the other hand they accepted that there were advances in the treatment of employees and were unwilling to see these thrown away.

The papers were generally split with broadsheets voting to stay in but the tabloids to get out.

Factually the 'staying in' group seemed to have won the day but within minutes of Nigel Farage, who appeared to be a successful average 'bloke', starting one of his well-publicised speeches, the emotions had swung around to support 'exit'.

It seemed that he only had to comment on a) Dreadful Eurozone mess b) Being ruled by faceless EU bureaucrats c) Strong enough in the world to negotiate revised trading agreements and d) Allusions to a proud military past, and whole audiences would be swayed.

Sebastian noted that each side taunted the other with variously "What after the exit then!" and conversely "Nothing the Prime Minister said will stop one more immigrant – 100,000 remember that comment of his? *"No if's and no but's!"*

After one enormous 'exit' rally the opinion polls registered 40% for exit, 35% for in and 25% don't knows.

Parliament was in a state of turmoil. It had become clear that, apart from virtually the same 60 Tory backbenchers who had made noises all along, plus a few Northern Ireland followers, the few UK MPs and some 20 hard-left Labour who wished to implement re-nationalisation, in total there were barely 75 MPs certainly in favour of exit.

This left the situation in a further constitutional crisis. The Referendum Bill was about holding the referendum, there would still be a need for dozens of enabling Acts both to extract the UK from the EU and to prepare any replacement trade agreement or even negotiate the legislative changes needed to extract the UK from the EU itself. But it was clear in this Parliament there would be no majority for any such moves.

It was clear even to the 60, whom at the time of Maastricht, Prime Minister Major had called 'bastards' that, if a General Election followed, it would certainly split the Tory Party wide open.

Sebastian thought the Lib Dems lucky that there was no disagreement within their own ranks.

Just before the referendum the TV screens came up with 'breaking news'. The immigrants in the 'Jungle' at Calais now numbering more than 5,000, fearing that a 'No!' vote would end for ever their hope of gaining asylum in the UK, had surged through the wire netting pushing aside the French police, then entered the tunnel and began running towards England. The UK police were alerted and a pitched battle took place at the exit near Dover. Several trains, one with Cars and passengers on board, were destroyed by fire. Luckily all the travellers were brought out safely. But in the confusion several hundred immigrants managed to escape at the UK end. Although most of these were hunted down by police within hours, causing a man hunt in the surrounding area, a handful eventually made it as far as London to claim asylum.

Some 20 immigrants had died from fumes inhaled in the first 'battle ' in the tunnel itself but a further 5 died from later confrontation with French police on their return from the English end as they tried to resist arrest, even as they were choking on the fumes pouring from the tunnel. It was a terrible scene of fighting but the French police alleged that some immigrants had been armed with knives and two were shot and killed.

The damage put the Channel Tunnel out of action for two weeks and exporters' container trucks backed up the motorways to the M25 and to the outskirts of London.

It became so bad that additional ferries were put on at East Coast ports. These were in turn invaded by immigrants and one ferry had to stay at sea until all the immigrants had been rounded up, before returning to France. In desperation one immigrant flung himself into the sea to evade capture and was drowned.

The Press was full of the pictures of the event. The public appeared to be shocked by the whole episode.

The BBC TV news team had an often repeated clip of one desperate immigrant shouting "Why you do this to me, all I want is to live free and work in England, you good people Yes?" As he was hit by a police truncheon.

Rival 'in' and 'out' speakers re-interpreted these events in their own ways but as Sebastian observed it reminded everyone of the seriousness of the situation. As he later wrote in his weekend email update to members. "It makes you think, what do we do? Can we shut out the world and live a privileged existence inside our magic kingdom, but if all those that want to come do so, how could we possible cope?"

The tabloids fearful, so it seemed to Sebastian, of being blamed for the chaos that would ensue in the event of a NO! vote quickly began to back-pedal and suddenly shut off the cheer leader role they had won for themselves from UKIP supporters.

On the evening of the referendum the pollsters had it 42% against, 38% staying in and 10% undecided, it appeared that Scotland were marginally in favour of staying in, as were Wales and Northern Ireland the latter probably, Sebastian assumed, because of the Irish link, but virtually the whole of the Eastern Coastal Towns and a majority of the Midlands and North East and West were against. In the South East it was too close to call.

In the event it was a bright sunny autumn day. The turnout was one of the highest recorded at 70%.

Sebastian was sitting in the Lib Dem local offices surrounded by the councillors and helpers who had just, as at any normal election, been handing out 'staying in' literature. The count was due at midnight on a constituency basis.

It was almost impossible to trace what was happening, some areas were for, other neighbouring areas were against.

The result sent shock waves through out every conversation in every politically aware household in the land.

The 'Out' had won by the narrowest of margins; 50.2% to 49.8% a difference of some 130,000 votes.

There was a horrible stunned silence in every TV and radio station across the country.

There was a collective "Oh my God!" in the room from the Lib Dems in the Middleton constituency office.

Nigel Farage appeared and expressed himself delighted but wondered if "all the votes were in yet?"

The Conservative Prime Minister made a very brief appearance acknowledging that the 'in' vote was less than he had hoped and said that "A further statement will be forthcoming later on that morning!"

The Stock Market was closed on instructions from the Prime Minister but that could not stop trading in the far East where UK shares were already tumbling.

Nigel Farage was again drawn into the BBC for a substantive discussion

"So Mr Farage, you believe that you have won your case? What do you intend to do now?"

"Yes it was a victory! Over 50% that's a democratic result! For now? Well that's clear, we have to begin negotiations to get out of the EU!"

"But how are you going to do that?" asked the BBC reporter, "There's no parliamentary majority to do anything of the kind is there?"

"But" Nigel Farage insisted "We have had a referendum and the people have spoken, the answer is OUT!

"Do you expect the Prime Minister to call an election? Why should he do that if he can still muster a majority?"

"You mean if he still gets the support of the Lib Dems? I think that's unlikely, don't you? They have been gabbled up and spat out once before"

"But Mr Farage you have just 3 MPs now. Even if the Tories were prepared to agree some sort of a deal with you that would still not be enough to create a working majority. So what exactly are you proposing?"

"Well, we will just have to wait and see what happens" and with that he concluded the BBC interview.

It was 2 am when Sebastian's phone rang at home.

He rolled over in bed and sat up, waking up his wife in the process "Got to go to London, right now it's an emergency again, got to be there by 6.00 am, going by car right now, straight to the House of Commons!"

It was after 4 am when he arrived and parked his car. He walked towards the Lib Dem leader's office.

It was already bursting with MP's and Peers. At 6.00 the Leader, Tim Beaumond speaking from notes, made several points which he said he would then open the meeting for discussion and eventually to a vote.

"You all know the result. I had a call from the PM at 12.30 am. He made certain points over the phone which he confirmed by written message which I will read for you, and he made a proposal.

1) The loss is a tiny one, sure it's a loss but just as likely if it were done again right now the result might be different. It's not a significant loss, indeed it's so finely balanced as not to be clear across the country.

2) Had there been a small loss in every area it might be different but that's not the case. Scotland voted to stay in by a significant majority as did Northern Ireland. If we are to move to get out we would have to decide if we mean the whole of the UK or just bits.

3) East & West Midlands and the North all voted to exit as did the whole of the East Coast and East Anglia all by a margin of 10%. The South East and South West were delicately balanced whilst London was for staying in by 10% (probably after assurances by the EU last week on the special relationship of the City to the EU one of the very few of the PM's demands which the EU conceded).

4) With barely 75 MP's in favour of an 'exit', there is currently in practice no majority in Parliament to untangle the exit with the EU and renegotiate. If the PM called a General Election he is clear that it would split the Tory party, the gainers would be UKIP who appear to have no idea what to do next! But unless he can concoct another coalition he will have no other alternative. The 'out' people have no skilled negotiators in their group so who would do it?

5) Several of the Tories who supported 'exit' are shocked by the result. They had expected to see a clear message but they privately acknowledged that the margin is just too small to begin a such a massive upheaval, indeed exit will cause very considerable anger and hostility amongst certain groups which is

likely to rebound against those MPs. Accordingly they are prepared to keep up the appearances of unity provided a) that the result is used to seriously renegotiate with the EU or else EU should face the UK withdrawal and that the referendum should be held again at the time of the Constitutional Referendum and b) there is a formal coalition.

6) What they want is now clear a) Immigration to be controlled by an Australian type system limited to net inward migration of 200,000 maximum. This is to be applied immediately across all comers, the only concession to the EU is that all new jobs will be advertised by email across the EU b) Special recognition of London being the primary Banking and Finance Centre is acknowledged giving it in effect a veto over certain changes c) Special provision being made within the EU agreements that a non-Eurozone part of the EU is created in some way perhaps on an associated basis but yet with a full say in the EU development d) Separated function of UK's military not ever to be under EU control e) Exclusion from freedom of movement of labour to the UK for all future new EC countries like Ukraine and Turkey because they would exacerbate the problem in the UK.

Tim concluded "Thank you for listening to all this and I am sorry it has taken so long. So he wants a formal coalition with us!

The points as far as we are concerned are relatively simple a) We all believe that it's right to remain in the EU? And b) We now desperately need the constitutional referendum to succeed?

To hover around between success and oblivion – I must tell you is almost driving me nuts. I tell you I have nightmares about being the last Lib Dem MP in the Country explaining to Beveridge and Keynes what we did wrong! It's like walking a tightrope. In short we cannot be sure of surviving as a Party without PR".

The discussion was muted. Several survivor MP's re-visited the earlier failed formal Coalition but Tim reminded them "This time we are doing it for us, for the Lib Dems, and also saving the Country from possible financial meltdown but that calamity cannot be put at our door this time, he could surely at a price go with SNP this time we are not in the firing line!"

There was additional discussion about the format of the coalition, numbers of ministers, how it would be made public etc.

By 7 am it was all agreed and the Prime Minister was informed by phone using code word "Charles".

In the House of Commons the following day, Nigel Farage introduced a new MP from an earlier by election then called for a vote of confidence in the Government, "In view of the vote last night!"

Although he knew he could not win, he had expected all the 'out' MP's to vote against. That combined with all opposition MPs should give him the majority he was seeking. They didn't, the Tory body remained intact. The opposition MP's refused to be drawn. He mustered scarcely 40 votes.

Shortly afterwards the Prime Minister issued a press release which gave details of the Lib Dem second formal coalition to run until the Constitutional Referendum in 2017 and that the intervening period would be used by the coalition to enshrine further changes into EU treaties which were now quite specific but which, If not accepted, would lead automatically to the UK exit at that time. If changes were forthcoming they would be subject to another referendum on the same day along with the other constitutional matters.

If no changes were forthcoming the UK would formally exit the EU.

In the Commons the Prime Minister put the matter succinctly.

"Imagine that the referendum had been about hanging, it might well have got a similar result to this EC referendum, but knowing the view of most MPs, it would be almost impossible to find more than 50 to 100 MPs who would support it. The country might have been persuaded but the individual MPs are not. We are a Parliamentary Democracy and in that light I, as Prime Minister, have to make difficult decisions.

I do not believe that the case has been made overwhelmingly for such a dramatic change!"

"What we have agreed however is this;

The referendum drew out quite clearly the key issues. We, in the new coalition, will therefore make one last attempt to persuade the EC of the need for changes formally ratified in the treaties, if they do not then they, and we, will have to face the consequences of a No! and de-activate our agreement accordingly. I do not personally believe that a margin of 130,000 votes is enough, on its own, to begin such a huge and dangerous change to our existing commercial and social contacts.

In the interval steps will be taken to introduce laws which will revoke membership of the EU and these will be made available at the time of and depending on the second EU referendum which will take place at the same time as the Constitutional Referendum. The Conservatives remain committed to accepting the findings of the Constitutional Commission."

There was a general agreement even from UKIP that this was a considered response. Their Leader stated that "We will accept that if those those changes are enshrined in EC treaties we will withdraw support for 'exit'. Although we would have preferred a further strengthening of the UK position to be able to ignore some of the bizarre and stupid rules coming out of the EC. At least in this way we would more or less control our own boarders!"

The second Conservative and Lib Dem coalition began work. It was part of the agreement that certain past Acts would be changed and a programme of forward Parliamentary work was agreed. All Lib Dem MPs were awarded Junior Ministries. They held no Cabinet positions.

The £ and the Stock Market wobbled but then recovered.

Sebastian was asked to take on a junior ministerial role in the Ministry of Health. This was Parliamentary Under Secretary of State for NHS Productivity, this position was responsible for NHS England, economic regulation, finance and efficiency. It was a post previously held by Lord Prior.

CHAPTER TWENTY-ONE - October 2016 to May 2017

– at the Ministry of Health

As he had been involved in the EC referendum he was also asked to be on the UK renegotiating committee on an ad hoc basis but for the most part he had to carry out his ministerial duties.

The chat with Tim Beaumond had been very brief. "In recognition of your hard work in the EU referendum we would like you to take over a role as Junior Minister in the Health Ministry. It's a huge department much in need of your radical review. Would you please take over as soon as possible and keep me updated particularly with any conflicts with the other Ministers so that I can quickly move to diffuse any problems. OK? Good luck Sebastian with your first ministerial posting!"

He wondered why he had been given this position. Of course he had got to know details of the NHS in the East Midlands and had openly questioned the lack of debate over the future of the NHS. He had therefore in a way set himself up as being interested and knowledgeable on the subject. It was a chunky portfolio with a huge budget involving considerable work because the NHS never sleeps and there's always a pot-boiler somewhere waiting to explode in the neatest of kitchens. The NHS was also considered to be such an amorphous mass, that, outlandish comments apart, such as Kenneth Clarke's well remembered comment 'Ambulance drivers being merely taxi drivers' or at least that's what legend now suggests he said, they thought Sebastian couldn't surely get himself into much trouble?

He was untried Lib Dem material considered to be something of a maverick. Sebastian ruefully concluded that he was put in this position more to tame and control him and use his undoubted energy rather than to expect a useable contribution to new Lib Dem policies from him.

For the first time Sebastian was allocated a Ministerial car and driver, partly it seems because of his expected frequent visits to hospitals. It caused some surprise in the cul de sac where he lived. The local police politely told him that his house was indefensible from attack and he must therefore move. Sebastian refused. In the end some compromise was reached when a next door neighbour moved away and the Notts County Council agreed to buy it and lease it to the police who then used it as their base. Inspector John Denny with whom they had crossed swords barely six months ago was responsible for working out that package.

Sylvia's charity had by then grown considerably and she was much in demand from schools in the East and West Midlands, particularly visiting and lecturing, and maintaining a database of the addresses of those girls who believed they were under threat. Sylvia had frequently to rush away at any time of the day or night to talk with girls and their parents to try to resolve their difficulties.

Sebastian realised that they each would spend so much time away that their marriage was in real danger of collapsing; their lifestyle had become a hectic game of musical chairs. Sylvia became agitated every time Sebastian praised Madge for the work she was doing. Sebastian tried to explain what he was doing on a daily basis but it was unintelligible even to his most avid supporter. Sometimes Sebastian did not get back till after midnight on Friday, but weekends were often the busiest time for Sylvia because that's when most parents took their children for holidays back home in India or Pakistan.

They tried hard to keep certain days free and managed to get away for three brief holidays each year one over Christmas, which they usually spent at a posh hotel somewhere where they could just, if they chose, go to ground for a couple of days. Another around Easter with his old friend Douglas in Northumberland and finally a two week holiday either in Paradours in Spain or Pousadas in Portugal where they thought they could get away unnoticed. They spent three or four nights at each place and created their own tour. So far the plans had worked and they were still together.

In Russia the legislative elections took place in October 2016 and the United Russia Party was returned as before with a massive majority achieving again 50% of the vote and 54% of the seats. The Presidential elections were not due till 2018. Sebastian saw no means to bring to bear his experience of that country.

Sebastian did what he always did in such circumstances where he felt he was under threat, he just buried his head in his work and kept up such a remorseless tempo that his senior Civil Servants were run off their feet.

Sebastian realised that he had a huge amount to learn and that although, as a patient he had seen hospitals, he had no idea of the huge amount of back-up that was required both to keep the 'beast' supplied and to manage and monitor it's performance. He managed to persuade his senior Civil Servant, John Stewart, to stop any forward meetings until he had carried out his own research into all the material. Apart from two one day visits to a regular hospital and to a teaching hospital, he managed to ward off any detailed plans for himself for the first two weeks, arguing that it was important that he didn't go into meetings misinformed. He was granted that time.

He began his research.

A year or so before his appointment there had been several changes in the Ministry of Health both of these directly impacted on Sebastian's work and role. He realised that he had quickly to bring himself up to speed on the existing background material or otherwise he might simply be ignored by his civil service staff!

The first and little-commented-upon-change was that there was, in effect, the beginnings of a merger within the units under Sebastian's ministerial brief. A new joint chair position had been created covering the work of both Monitor and the NHS Trust Development Authority -

TDA.

Hospital Foundation Trusts had been created by Alan Millburn following on from a trip to Spain, there the hospital that he had seen was exempt from many of the rules normally imposed on State run hospitals. The governance of those hospitals included local government, trade unions, health workers and community groups. He hoped to set up such units in the UK and he thought that this might blur the issue between private and public if they could trade without restrictions. They were supposed to be financially autonomous. By 2015 there were some 145 such Foundation Trusts in the UK. 'Monitor', an NHS Consultancy body, had oversight of these units and actually consolidated their accounts on a yearly basis. The financial results varied from unit to unit and several were clearly not financially autonomous.

The award of a Foundation Trusts was usually only given after a detailed review of their operations. It was thought of as a hallmark of success. Unfortunately Sebastian saw that three matters rather took away the shine from what was seen as a radical new way to democratise hospitals.

The first was that Mid Staffs after a number of complaints was revealed to be less good quality wise; in fact a terrible mess and needed to be put into special measures, thus blotting the copybook that the Foundation Trust was some sort of quality mark.

Secondly these Foundation Trusts had amassed a huge amount of cash about £4.3bn in 2014. Whilst on the one hand the NHS appeared to be desperate for funding, one portion of it was literally rolling in money. Although all but few hospitals in London traded exclusively as NHS units and were funded as such for ordinary residents, the ownership of each hospital was technically different.

Thirdly as expressed by the Nuffield Trust 'The dilemma for the NHS is that hospital trusts operate autonomously there is a very fine line between trusts using their marketing power and moving towards a standardised approach which can create a huge state bureaucracy that is inflexible to change'. Sebastian saw that Foundation Trusts certainly muddied the lines of authority within the NHS and didn't necessarily respond to direction from above. For example this impacts on the ability of units to make the suggested increased saving of £2bn per annum.

In other words technically the Foundation Hospitals were not exactly directly under state control.

The rump of those not enrolled as Foundation Hospitals, some 90 units, came under the NHS Trust Development Authority called TDA, the obvious intention in drawing the review of both sides together was to draw together experiences and to improve efficiencies.

All hospitals were run to the same very detailed performance metric; like times for waiting, referral in cases of cancer, 2 weeks standard, and also ambulance call outs and response times for Red 1 calls within 8 minutes 75% standard, and could be compared exactly one with another despite regional and local differences in patient profiles and skills.

This represented a huge flow of information which was analysed in detail and then either acted upon locally or special measures taken to manage the problem.

Of course the NHS traditionally had a rather weak buying function, partly because staff were trained up using one type of equipment or medication or supply and were reluctant to change from something that they knew. In order to begin the task of really digging into these supply costs the NHS had its own Price Comparison Website created in 2013, after studies by the National Audit office showed that as much as 10% could be saved by better procurement. They found that for 5,000 items the difference in amount paid was more than 50%. The price of blankets for example varied from £47 to £120.

Sebastian could see that there were a number of problems and there was a huge amount to get stuck into and that the gains could be considerable.

The other main change was that in October 2014 there had been published 'NHS Five Year Forward Review'. This was agreed to by the five other big NHS organisations, these were Monitor, NHS TDA, Care Quality Commission, Public Health England and Health Education England. As if that were not enough it was prepared by NHS's new boss Simon Stevens, the author, who was regarded almost as a messiah, a man who had come back into the fold after 10 years in US private healthcare.

Sebastian was told in no uncertain terms that this was the bible to which he should subscribe and help to implement. He read it through several times but with a sense of increasing horror. It, for him, was simply the sort of report which he most disliked.

It's true he thought that many treated it as a 'Strategic Direction' rather than 'The Plan'. The problem for Sebastian was that there was depressingly little detail, as if someone had written a larger report then stripped out all the figures, finances and action lists.

Sebastian had been incensed at the stupidity of the level of discussion and debate on the NHS during the General Election in 2015. The debate was literally summed up in three figures.

NHS faces £30bn of increased pressures and funding to provide the services indicated over the 5 years to 2021, that there are savings expected of £22bn, so that £8bn will be required in additional funding.

So now he knew exactly why the discussion had been so banal with each party seeming to outbid the other. The £8bn had been quickly subscribed to by each of the political parties. Review and Job Done – just like that!

This 'NHS Five Year Forward Review' was a tour de force by a person who was himself a master politician. He had played a brilliant game and had won hands down. There was simply nothing that an opponent could grab hold of, it was substantially a wish list of all the good things which all parts of the NHS agreed and there was literally the one Big Figure at the end of £30bn. It was a take it or leave it approach delivered by the 'expert' in the dying days of the old coalition, there was no time for MPs to discuss and debate and consider options. There were no options, there was no debate. Take it or leave it.

Sebastian remembered the same sort of wish lists exactly on setting up the original Clinical Commissioning Groups 4 years before. However, in that case those CCGs had had to provide a budget and details of expected savings and spend. Sebastian laughed to himself, 'perhaps they have the same civil servant whose exclusive skill is to think up the wish lists and link them together!

Sebastian had seen papers like this before, full of fluff and good intentions which could never be compared with reality. Worse still it meant that only he, the CEO, could implement it because it was so open to interpretation. Who, for example, was to adjudicate whether hospitals should take over CCG's or medical practices ? Or in some cases, if CCG's should take over smaller hospitals? There were several formats for care but there were no guidelines as to which should be preferred. It seemed to Sebastian that this assumed that within the average medical practice there was a budding manager willing to grow ever bigger and anxious to take over other units. Whilst it sounded like a war cry "Go for it try it!" and might encourage some in the medical profession, he thought that most would be offended. The most avaricious might build medical empires but Sebastian could not see what advantage there would be for the average patient. Everything seemed to depend upon the leadership within the NHS as it says in the Review 'To support these changes the national leadership of the NHS will need to act clearly together, and make sure that the rules and ways for working are able to be flexible to local needs. We will support local leadership with new ideas.'

Much of the wish list was made up of changing human behaviour which would take well beyond the period of this Review. To fight obesity and secure good health for the population was a mission requiring national support in dozens of ways.

Alongside the Review Sebastian knew that there were huge questions over the existing Health Service which had simply been overlooked. The NHS itself seemed to have been incapable of training and supplying the number of Doctors and Staff that were needed. He looked at some negative comments; Rachel Sylvester noted in the Times that the NHS seemed to incur huge costs for locums. According to her in 2014 the NHS received 52,000 applications from potential students for nursing courses, more than 30,000 were turned away because of a lack of places. Part of the problem appeared to be the high dropout rate of 20%, but the situation was likely to get worse as 45% of the workforce was aged 45 or over. It costs over £70K to train a nurse, so the NHS preferred apparently to hire from abroad; at least 9,000 had been hired in this way in 2015. The cost for that was a mere £3K each.

That's not the picture that most people had in mind. Sebastian was surprised, it turns out that far from being an employer obliged to hire from abroad because there was no local talent, it appeared to be simply either sloppy UK staff planning and recruitment or buying in outside foreign trained staff because they were cheaper?

It suggested an NHS unable to plan ahead in a meaningful way. In the Forward Review there was no plan of staff merely stating that 'The number of GP's in training needs to be increased as fast as possible, with new options to help them want to stay working as GPs'. No figures, no acknowledgement of large losses as UK trained staff leach away elsewhere. No apparent problems with Doctor morale.

There had been an extraordinary intervention by Monitor and TDA jointly in October 2015 giving direct instructions to all unit to cap the amount paid per hour for temporary Agency staff. The 'Mirror' of

September 1st 2015 suggested that temporary workers cost a staggering £3.3bn in 2014. Yet it says nothing for the internal management of each unit's strength that the capping instruction came about as a direct instruction from above by central diktat.

The Nuffield Trust of 9th October 2015 suggested that the chances of giving effect to the improvement needs would take much longer that the Review suggested, 'Given the scale of these deficits there appears to be an extraordinary absence of the sort of urgency one might expect from those in charge of the NHS.' They also found that '67% of social care leaders were not confident their local area had a credible plan to achieve the savings they require in that financial year!'

The accountants professional body most closely associated with the NHS, the CIPFA, suggested that they were unable to review the financial projections because none were quoted, it was not even certain that the increase to 7 day 24 hour hospital working was taken into account to eliminate excessive weekend deaths. They concluded that whilst, 'It seems likely that £30bn is a fair assessment of the pressures faced over the coming five years', but 'It seems UNLIKELY that the £22bn of savings planned for will be delivered at a pace to match the developing pressures.

In other words, thought Sebastian 'The £8bn coming as extra funding is likely to be exceeded'.

Some of the problem was that part of the savings could only result from the integration with Care Services administered by Local Authorities, largely County Councils, which would require their active support; but they themselves have been under pressure to reduce costs even further, under their own cuts programme. Under new schemes of devolution to some cities, it appeared that services were moving from NHS control so how was that to be calculated, monitored or controlled? The promise under the Autumn Statement 2015 that councils could add 2% to the precept to re-engage this care responsibility was good news but it was of course important that this care function was integrated with the NHS. How would that be done and at what level this was still unclear.

After the first two weeks in post and having read the material, he knew that this was a posting that he would regret. He held his head in his hands over the weekend.

Sebastian decided to consult with his intern John Blaney on some technical matters and such help proved very valuable but he was unable to show him information not in the public domain such as the financial justification.

At home Sylvia was concerned as he refused either to talk or to eat. It seemed his system had just gone on strike. Eventually he broke his silence.

"Sylvia, for me this is a disaster, it's a political nightmare. The Civil Service has taken the politicians by the balls, they were offered a take it or leave it way of running the NHS with almost no justification and lacking even a modicum of logic and finances. There's no plan – it's a wish list. All recognised NHS senior management units have bought into it. There is indeed no political input, there's no linking targeted achievements no dateline. We have in effect given the NHS the biggest blank cheque in the history of the country amounting to a chunk of GDP and there seems nothing we can do about it, we can argue about pay deals but that's it. I have seen nothing like it since the Generals in WW1 determined that they wanted 'More troops, ever more troops.'

There's no chance of me succeeding in changing that mentality. Every political Party says 'Yes' to the NHS and this is the payoff. We have virtually passed over some 8.5% of the UK GDP to this one body, one man on the basis of a wish list.

Everything really hinges on the NHS CEO.   Even if he assumes the virtual dictatorial powers to needs to make the changes and achieve the objectives, it seems unlikely that the existing formats and structures will survive.

I have no confidence in the achievement of his review, but being in the 'Health Team' I cannot actively speak against it. The objective of junior ministers is to assist, not to challenge, the existing policies which they are pursuing. To do that I would have to go through my own party leader Tim Beaumond but as yet I have no credible alternative!"

"Well, Seb, can't you run on neutral? You had years of experience at RKW playing lip service to Head Office, but you managed to do your own thing despite all that? Can't you find a niche and concentrate on that and make it your own. If you resigned you would simply disappoint all your supporters and discount yourself from any future political role?"

"Sylvia, you are right of course – I have to stay and work my way through it! Thanks for your advice! But it means that for the first time in my life I am going to have to be two-faced and I always prided myself on my moral integrity and honesty, I could have done that years ago and been two faced enough to tell the Directors in RKW what they wanted to hear, I always resisted that but now it seems it goes with the patch, I'll have to become someone that I always resented."

Sebastian gave an upbeat report of his new role to Madge for inclusion in the weekly email bulletin to local Lib Dem members.

He finally arranged a planning meeting with his top Civil Servants and the Head of NHS during the following week and he began to devise a plan to at least allow him to work. He told the assembled meeting which included all heads of departments under him: "I am very proud to be your Minister for the NHS, proud to be entrusted by the current government with what has been rightfully described as the first service which all residents see as important. It has a proud tradition of selfless services.

I have read and was delighted by the 5 Year Forward Review and hope to work closely with the CEO as well as with the now joined up Monitor and TDA. There is a huge amount of work to do and I hope that I can support you in that. I clearly don't want to get in the way of the bodies whose efforts have been laid down in the Review".

Sebastian continued:

"In my opinion therefore I would like initially to look at two matters which are not directly involved in that review, I will be as it were working my way into the NHS work. The first of these is the comparability of our service with others in the EU, here I can use my emerging contacts within the EC to see if there's anything we can learn from them. The second is the knotty problem of transfer price of drugs within the EC, you will appreciate that there is a potential here for saving millions if we can buy our drugs more cheaply."

There was a general applause and warm handshakes from the CEO "We, didn't know what you were doing for the past two weeks Sebastian, but I am glad to hear that you are onside now. I think what you say makes good sense I'll have a word with the Ministry officials and see if we can get a plan together."

John Stewart was his senior Civil Servant and Sebastian immediately apologised for just asking for information and for not discussing matters previously. John Stewart opened up, "Well Mr Edwards we all thought that you were about to resign when we heard nothing from you day after day."

"Guessing that as an accountant you would need some financial data to start with, I have compiled a dossier such as it is, you understand that we are not privy to the calculations of the £30bn and the £22bn but I hope these will be forthcoming when we convert the review into a full implementation plan."

"Well Mr Stewart, you are correct I was and still am very concerned by the lack of finances something I have pushed for all my working life, and to be frank I am also concerned by let's call it the 'democratic deficit', I don't think we need to go into that further right now. So can we plan the EC comparisons, I would like to make contact with political heads of the Health Services in France, Germany and Poland and perhaps one or two others. Please can you put together a pack containing the NHS processes, budgets and of course the '5 Year Forward Review'? I want to persuade the other EC countries to offer me the same information on the same basis; what the USA Government Contractors call, I believe, 'Equality of Information' and at the same depth. So the more detailed you can make it the more benefit will accrue to us!

I also need a list please of all the major drug manufacturers and branches of suppliers of world-wide drugs together with the drugs acquired and the price paid by the NHS"

John Stewart replied "it'll obviously take some time to collect all this and work out a programme of visits, shall we say one month?"

Sebastian nodded assent and added "In the meantime I would like to visit at least 3 hospitals a week, I'll give you a suggested visit plan and how I would like it to work in a couple of days".

"I'll need a meeting with the Lib Dem leader as I need clearance for a pairing if it involves visits to MP's territory of other parties"

Sebastian requested an early meeting with the Lib Dem leader this was quickly granted "So how is it coming on Sebastian. I heard rumours last week that you might even resign but I now understand that everything is back on track?"

"Yes that's right Tim. I did have second thoughts. It's really all about the stresses on family life of being a Minister even a junior one. I understand that I'll be run off my feet!"

He then outlined his plan of visits to the EC and also to the hospitals in the UK over the next few weeks and described that he wanted a pairing "I feel very strongly that we should do all we can to keep Labour on side, I see nothing wrong at all in taking one of their MPs with me to the next hospital visit and sharing information!"

Tim agreed, "Seems positive" he said.

On November 8th 2016, Hillary Clinton won the USA Presidential Elections and vowed to start a new chapter of relations with Russia. She had made a point of continuing with the USA Healthcare changes initiated by President Obama.

In the sense that the Five Year Review moved the debate in terms of what resources were likely to be on offer, Sebastian could see a lot of merit if it was viewed simply as a mechanism of understanding that a fundamental shift was required in health service provision With ever increasing medical costs and increasing longevity, a person at home might have a medical attendant of some kind for say 1 hour but, transfer that into a hospital setting and using the average number of patients per nurse of 6 per day and 8 per night -, as used by Royal College of nursing suggested staffing levels, - this would give 3.5 hours equivalent per day to that 1 hour at home. This is irrespective of the costs of the doctors and other specialists which would surely build it to more than 5 hours. So shifting care from hospitals to home sounded much cheaper and in terms of medical time it might be 5 times more efficient. So care at home is much, much cheaper, although there are clearly limitations on services that can be provided at home.

But Sebastian thought, to carry that out in full would need a whole army of helpers and carers to support vulnerable ill people at home whilst recovering. Was that support problem properly addressed? Each CCG was supposed to have by now invisible 'virtual wards' staffed by such home visitor-nurses but where were they? But it also meant more non-medical support, where was that? There was nothing in the report about this!

Sebastian could see that costs would force a move towards homecare which would be unstoppable.

Sebastian noted for himself that he wanted answers to the following questions within six months. Whatever the success of the Review he didn't believe in principle that the democratic deficit could be supported.

a) **Was the idea of Foundation Hospitals a success or a failure?** Technically these were independent and supposedly answerable to local influences. Had they worked or not? Was there any indication that they were successful as units? We they more efficient? Most of them drew more than 95% from NHS but what of those that did substantially less than 95% did they operate differently?

b) **Were CCGs a good innovation or not?** How many had been able to make the savings expected when they were set up. How many of them were successful and how many were failures and what distinguished one from the other? The concept was that CCGs could control hospital movements and direct patients to more efficient hospital, was that working or not? What was the impact of that on hospital costs?

c) **Was there any evidence that the separation of Health Services to Wales and Scotland meant that the services were less efficient?** Would it be possible similarly to devolve Health Service to Regions of the UK? In smaller portions perhaps the costs, saving and efficiencies would be easier to identify?

d) **Staff Planning.** Locum costs. It seems that such costs are often at 200% to 300% of normal costs. Sebastian needed to know why it had not proved possible to plan the number of doctors and nurses ahead and train up the number that seemed to be required. Part of the problem appears to have been self-inflicted as the relatively frequent changes to manning and hours of work impacted thousands of skilled staff. This appeared to be a political overlay. But morale seems low in places?

Sebastian anyhow determined to press ahead with his European visits.

A plan was agreed with the Ministries of Germany France and Poland. Each country was anxious to see the details of the others Health Services and Sebastian's initiative achieved considerable publicity. He took a small team of staff with him which helped to unravel different international interpretations of illness and treatment.

The result was 3 huge dossiers of comparable information a summary of which was issued to all senior UK managers.

The Polish Ministry was slightly embarrassed as they realised that their spend of Health Services at around 6.5% of GDP was way behind that of the UK 8.5% which was in turn way behind that of France and Germany of around 11% of GDP.

Sebastian explained to the Polish Minister that he was also working on a plan of co-operation with Poland in two ways.

First was to open up NHS procurement to Polish equipment suppliers once they were taken as being accredited suppliers to the Polish Ministry of Health.

Secondly he wanted the Polish authorities to consider a joint venture for the supply of locums to the NHS. Whilst at first sight it seemed simply a method of draining off skilled Polish medical staff to the UK it was in fact something much deeper. Polish medical staff were paid much less than UK NHS staff. Sebastian's idea was that an NHS training ward be established in Poland. All interested Polish staff would take a 4 week 'conversion' course covering the English language used in medicine, use of NHS systems like IT and entry to CT scans, pharmacy, typical medical operations etc. They would then be placed on a register which could be matched with vacancies as they became known. The idea would be to eliminate the UK agencies' mark up for locums and share such gains with the Polish Health Service. The individual on locum would be paid the UK going staff rate and the agency fee would be paid to the Polish Health Service. If the Polish person was eventually taken on then a capitation fee would be paid by the NHS to the Polish Authorities allowing them to train up replacements.

Sebastian explained that he thought this would give value both ways. The Polish staff would be trained onto more modern equipment and gain experience working under different systems. These would possibly provide Poland with future Health Service leaders. It would provide the Polish Health Service with useful income from staff who might leave anyhow but in this case they would retain them on their books for recall to Poland. When he stated that Agency staff had cost the NHS £3.3bn there was a sharp intake of breath.

Sebastian was not sure if this wasn't seen as simply the UK wanting to get their hands on skilled staff at a cheaper price than what the NHS could train them for.

Never-the-less the Polish Health Minister thanked Sebastian for making the offers saying "It's a pity that the UK is only now realising the potential benefit of being in the EC!"

France and Germany which use the Insurance refund model, also welcomed the initiative, although their systems appeared more efficient than the so-called 'single-payer' model used in the UK, their costs were substantially more than the UK and that provoked considerable interest. Private healthcare was much more extensive in Germany where nearly 60% of hospital beds are 'not for profit' and also privately funded. The French of course were always willing to show off their advances in medical treatments so the visit there took several days longer than expected!

Sebastian acknowledged that various bodies gave different interpretations as to the efficacy and efficiency of the various health services but the UK ranked as one of the most cost effective.

At the same time Sebastian launched an enquiry into the transfer pricing of drugs EC wide.

Sebastian's attention was drawn to this by the Astra Zeneca Settlement which was a claim first started by the UK government in 2002 and finally settled in 2015 for £505M. It was common knowledge that whilst the sales income generated in each country was relatively clear cut, the derivation of the costs were not. A product could be researched in one country, manufactured in another, be tested in another and have a sales force in another. This gave ample opportunity for deliberate manipulation and transfer of profits from one country to another. Accordingly some companies tended to move costs by the means of fictitious internal transfers so that the most profit was made by the country with the lowest tax rate. Thus with the USA corporate tax rate being nearly twice some of the EC rates, it was common practice to attempt to transfer costs to the USA. Incidentally this had led to the so-called 'inversion take overs' where USA companies would be taken over by foreign companies which would then incur much lower corporate tax. The divergence in corporate rates within the EC had become considerable with smaller countries, like Ireland, particularly offering special packages of very low corporate tax rates to encourage companies to set up there.

Sebastian boldly asked the EC commission to look at and recommend changes to the basis of transfers. He stated that his concern was that the selling price of the same drugs was different in different countries. Sebastian's case was that this disadvantaged certain countries from acquiring what were much needed and sometimes essential pharmaceuticals. According to an earlier OECD report the European share of global pharmaceutical production was 36%, with Ireland making 11%. The market was dominated by a few enormous firms. In 2006 the top 10 firms produced nearly 50% of global sales. Sebastian asked for clarity in terms of defining exactly what the relevant costs were and how they could be transferred to avoid tax gained by manipulation. He was also concerned that sometimes research which had been started was often held in abeyance and he sought a ruling on whether costs should be permitted to be written off. Instead, registered new research should be subject to a 'use it or lose it' rule to speed up the rate of supply of new drugs.

Sebastian drew attention from several EC members, here at last was another example of UK using the EC rules to advantage.

After several months working on both these foreign initiatives he could not much longer avoid the eventual confrontation in the UK which he knew must soon come.

He managed to 'escape' on his own up to Northumberland for the Easter break on April 16th 2017. His friend Douglas Finlay was proud of his success and Sebastian related to him what it was like actually being in office. Sebastian did not bother him with his concerns. He feared that his friend might not be able to see that he had any reason to resign. Together they walked up to the Hareshaw Linn waterfall, Bellingham. It was a beautiful day and the sun sparkled through the trees overhead playing onto the little stream below. The water was stained brown due to the peat. Over centuries it had created this little gorge and various trees, predominantly ash and hazel had gained a foothold. The ground was covered in mosses and ferns and in amongst them were emerging bluebells. At the end of the walk was a fine little rainbow created by the water vapour. Sebastian exhaled and took a deep breath as if he was a whale needing oxygen about to plunge into the political depths for another year.

His friend seemed in good spirits and it appeared to Sebastian that slowly and surely he was regaining his faculties.

On his return, the next day the new, recently appointed CEO of the NHS bumped into Sebastian in the corridor in the Ministry and whilst he commended him for the EC initiatives, asked him to call around for a chat.

This Sebastian did on the following day.

They sat in the CEO's large office. Sebastian was in the visitor's chair, the desk in front of the CEO was crammed with screens and files which Sebastian had to peer through to see him. Aides were dismissed.

"Look here Sebastian!"

'Humpf' thought Sebastian 'this is trouble coming – look here means 'you have to listen to and agree with me!''

"Whilst I appreciate the work you have been doing – I wonder if we are travelling the same path? You know the NHS is the jewel in any Government's crown, the public is behind it, if anyone speaks against it, it ultimately will damage them. You understand that?"

Sebastian quickly replied "Well I hope that I have given no reason for anyone to doubt my loyalty to the NHS, are you making some sort of a case?"

"No!, No! Of course not! But you have not been exactly verbally behind the Five Year Forward Review, for example I note that you were not at the recent update!" In fact Sebastian had deliberately avoided that meeting as he felt unable to contain himself and thus showing his concern at some points. He had spent the time instead completing the e-booklet on his by election success which he had promised all his helpers. It was long overdue!

Sebastian parried "Yes that's right, I was busy that day but remember I still don't have the modelled figures and criteria for the £30bn and the £22bn yet despite requests – I just have the summaries. I am looking for numbers of staff, of hospitals and CCG savings plus current actual NHS 2014/15 costs?"

"Yes I remember your interest, it's because of your accounting training I suppose, you need the figures!"

"No! not really" retorted Sebastian "I found it symptomatic of the dreadful lack of figures throughout and lack of acknowledgement of earlier failures and difficulties within the NHS. The Review was in my view little more than a wish list!"

The CEO jumped in leaning forward in his chair; "You know comments like that rather irritate me, it was approved by the Ministers, by the leaders of all political parties, by Monitor, by Nuffield, by just about all the senior management and you Sebastian question it?"

"Yes that's right!" said Sebastian standing his ground, "and what's more I am aghast at the Democratic Deficit within all this. You are responsible for a good chunk of the UK GDP and yet you manage to avoid all democratic oversight. You plonk the figures down and dare the politicians to take it or leave it! No wonder the public debate on the matter is so inane. I don't buy into that nor your wish list which, of course, is exactly what we OUGHT to be doing but are we? Where are the detailed implementation plans, where are the timelines for action, where are the other parties responding in areas where you cannot yourself control?"

"Sebastian, let me stop you there of course it's a wish list, though I call it a strategic vision, we have to start somewhere. I had only one opportunity to engage with the last coalition in October 2014. Of course I could have started off with all the mistakes that were made and how we will correct those, but that wasn't the brief. I was asked to prepare a strategic vision and give approximate costs. This I have done. I have shown people that the NHS is workable, that it can achieve what the country is looking for and that it can do its job – but only with more funding and more political support, like the need to make the whole population healthier!"

"Yes" said Sebastian "I suppose that's the difference between us, you are looking at it hoping that you will achieve all that you set out to do. If you do then it's true, the country and residents will gain enormously, but I don't see that happening, you are not making the savings suggested, you could be £2bn short of expectations. I do not believe that you have within the NHS the leadership skills to achieve what you want to do. I feel that you are not going to achieve the turnaround which everyone wants to see you do because mostly you just ignore all the failures and concentrate only on the successes. Basically the NHS now is what it was before; in offering alternative care models and encouraging local initiatives you are making it more not less difficult to control and lead!"

The CEO asked "Is there any meeting ground between us, Sebastian? Because we seem to be on different planets here!"

"Well", Sebastian replied cautiously. "there could be. I have three main problems, the democratic deficit, the failure to acknowledge problem areas and therefore to correct them and the detailed financials which require regular updating."

"What do you mean by Democratic Deficit?"

"The whole amorphous mass of the NHS is almost impossible to understand and lead. In my opinion it should be cut into geographical regions with responsibility for all NHS activities. The report on the separate bits of the NHS under Scotland, Wales and Northern Ireland, showed quite clearly that there was no catastrophic fall off of services, rather the contrary, they were able to adjust to local needs. Consider just one point, diet and healthy living is very much a regional thing, failing statistics do appear to encourage later improvement. So I would cut it up into 9 regions and get them under the control of elected regional bodies apply local pressure to change local diets."

"And the other matters, Sebastian?"

"Well that's much more simple. I want to see an update of the Review on a yearly basis, looking at the failures and how these were addressed. It's not good enough just to ignore the chaos in staff planning which you and I know exists, how does that improve anything? And finally I want the Review modelled figures to be revealed and updated together with achievement targets every year."

"Those are the missing bits!" Sebastian stopped suddenly.

"Well thank you Sebastian, at least I now know why you failed to give the Review the ringing endorsement that I had hoped for. You know, Sebastian, if you are trying to pull a deadweight oil tanker behind you, even the intrusion of a minor problem obliges me to take my eyes off the chart. It's a distraction. If I get too many distractions then I certainly will fail in the task. Let's talk again!"

Sebastian went back to his own office, he knew he had unable to keep up the pretence for long and he felt a sense of relief that it was out in the open. At least he had been true to himself. He thought he had no chance at all of changing the CEO's views and that he had just provoked a row for which there could be only one result.

Over the following week the Lib Dems held their Spring Conference and Sebastian's motion on Russia was finally accepted as a main motion. In other words if it was successful, the idea that 'Russia must be brought in out of the cold' would become established Lib Dem Party policy.

He carefully prepared his speech with Madge, it covered briefly the break-up of the Soviet Union and how neither Russia nor the west had really attempted to invest in better relations, how the Putin/Medvedev, 'boxing and coxing' of the Presidency led observers to believe that a dangerous personality cult was emerging. Sebastian made the point that both in Ukraine and Syria Putin had supported the lawfully elected governments, in no way was he imposing his military strength on other countries. The Crimea was 90% Russian ethnic and was 'given by Stalin' to Ukraine without consulting the residents. He suggested that it was time to end the cold war and the sanctions and get down to talking. A priority must be to encourage in Russia the concept of Democracy which had hardly taken root there. There was immense wealth in Russia but it needed finance and access to markets to unlock that treasure. The key he said, was getting Russia to acknowledge its responsibility for the airline disaster. Sebastian ended "It was most likely caused by dissidents under the control of Russia for which it must be prepared to openly offer an apology, it was clear that the equipment was Russian and would have needed extensive training to operate."

The motion was passed and according became Lib Dem policy.

During the following day Sebastian met with Tim Beaumont in the corridor outside the conference hall. "Hey Sebastian good to meet with you! See you did manage in the end to change policy! But how are you getting on?"

"Hmm in the Ministry of Health not so well actually!"

"Yes so I hear, democratic deficit, past mistakes and missing calculation of the £30bn. Was that about it?"

"Except that I think he's going to ask for way over £8bn I suspect the savings are nothing like expectations!"

"Yes but the PM seems to agree with you, or at least the Treasury Boys do. He has already put on record to the constitutional commission that the NHS could be regionalised with no harm to quality but it would improve its Democratic Deficit. The NHS must be brought into full and detailed review. The NHS CEO doesn't yet know this but the Commission is likely to agree, also the Treasury agree that he is likely to overrun his costs.

So you have a basic disagreement with the CEO? I can see it's going to make it difficult for you to continue working there!"

"However I just had a call from the Foreign Office, apparently Moscow is preparing to shift its position to end sanctions over the Ukraine. Sergey what's 'is name whom you met last has asked for a meeting with you prior to some sort of statement. Of course we cannot have junior

Ministers of Health trotting off for Foreign meetings, so I have persuaded the PM to have a mini-shuffle with you moving to the Foreign Office as Junior Minister with responsibility for Europe outside the EC. Would you accept that?"

"Why yes that's perfect!" Sebastian was relieved both that his analysis of the Ministry of Health was supported elsewhere and that he was moving from a position that he had found tested his self-control to the limit.

He spent his last day at the Ministry of Health and met with the CEO who asked him in for a final chat. "So they have found you another post then? I am sorry about all that, I am sure you will do well in a smaller department!"

"No don't worry about it, it's all for the best, at least this change is, now please don't forget I have done some considerable work on Regionalisation what to include and if you need help then let me know. I am as convinced as you are that we need an efficient NHS."

"So you had a talk with Tim Beaumond? I hardly think I'll need help on Regionalisation" he paused "so was the Democratic deficit mentioned then? Hm! I see. Well good luck Sebastian and thank you for the work you did here!"

CHAPTER TWENTY-TWO - May to November 2017

at the Foreign Office.

Within a few days of his arrival at the Foreign Office he was fully briefed on the impending change in Russian policy. He also asked some detailed penetrating questions like;

"What exactly is the EU doing to ensure that Russian speakers in the former Baltic States have full language and legal rights?" Sebastian insisted that if he was to present a case of no further movement of the Russian boundaries West, it was equally important that they should know and understand the frustration of seeing their kin treated as second class citizens in EU territory.

Also he asked "What's the position over Belarus? We know the Russians are hyper-sensitive about bits of the former USSR being added to the EC. To avoid another Ukraine we shall have to give a green light that we would not interfere over a Russian takeover of Belarus provided it was endorsed by a genuine referendum."

Unfortunately Peter Williams, the permanent Under Secretary, whom he had met and for whom he had high regard, was away on vacation.

He was assigned a person new to the post who was more cautious "We cannot say much more now except that we will consider them, the whole point is to get the discussions moving!"

"Well" said Sebastian, "I am sure he will ask, I shall just wave my hands in your direction when the point comes up! He is a special envoy of Mr Medvedev, you understand that?"

The first meeting was at the Russian Embassy in London called at the request of Minister-Counsellor Sergey Kramrenko.

On arrival Sebastian was greeted by Sergey with a great bear hug as if he were a long lost brother much to the amusement and dismay of the two FO staffers who had accompanied him.

"Ah Sebastian how are you, now Minister in coalition! So things change and change about?"

"And you Sergey, I thought you said you were finishing your UK posting?"

"Well so I have, so I have, I am here for special meeting with you! On express wishes of his excellency Prime Minister Medvedev! So "Bringing Russia in from cold? Please explain?"

Sebastian started "We are thinking beyond a solution to the Ukraine problem, which as you know requires that, as evidence of your seriousness in wanting to do a lasting deal with the West, you acknowledge responsibility for the Airline disaster. It was, we think, carried out by dissidents claiming affinity to Russia, so whether or not Russia pressed the button it was carried out in your name. It was a Russian-made guided weapon, launched from an area controlled by dissidents, it was sophisticated requiring training which probably came from Russian soldiers. What is the alternative? That Ukraine forces, from within the dissident area shot down a plane but most planes would have been Ukraine supply planes and helicopters, so far we have no motive why Ukraine forces would want to do that?"

Sergey merely grunted and asked "Is there more?"

"Yes, in addition to the clauses that we have already discussed in the Ukraine negotiations nearly two years ago we are keen to promote political and cultural exchanges. We want to see the end to sanctions. But we also have on offer some scholarships to Business Schools in the UK, student exchanges, cultural exchanges, ballets and plays and perhaps most importantly a major UK fund has been persuaded to offer a £500K grant, the largest in its history to encourage and promote democracy at all levels in Russia! We will facilitate Russia's access to capital by opening a branch of the Stock Exchange in Moscow as a joint venture with you.

You know, Sergey, we are well aware here of the problems of introducing pure democracy in Russia. For example there are, are there not, over 200 company towns in Russia, often in inhospitable locations? That is where the residents are dependent on just one manufacturing company, that's not an ideal situation to start a democratic debate. It's a legacy from the past which you cannot change, clearly everyone is an employee and everyone wants the business to stay, there is no alternative employment as the nearest town might be 800 kilometres or 500 miles away. So you have much more difficulty than we do in devising political options. We are aware of some of your problems, but you have to try harder otherwise you will always be open to some putsch or other!"

"Well, Sebastian, at least you learn something about us!" Sergey grunted, "still lecturing us I see!"

"But what about Belarus, what about Russians in Baltic States with no vote! Is this democracy?"

Sebastian turned to the FO staffer at his side who rather lamely added, "We shall, I assure you, take steps to improve matters in the Baltic States and we will have to discuss Belarus with our allies".

"Good" said Sergey "so when you have done this then let me know for next discussion Yes? And you can list out the scholarships and exchanges in letter, yes?"

"Well thank you for the meeting" said Sebastian, "shall we meet in 2 weeks yes?"

"Yes" Sergey grunted.

Out of earshot walking back to the FO Sebastian lost no time in turning on the staffer. "What did I tell you for heaven's sake? It's all really about the Baltic States and Belarus. If he thinks that, should the existing dictator (for that's what he really is) in Belarus be swept aside by a bunch of 'Maidan' type of people as there were in Ukraine, the same chaos would arise on his doorstep he will never ever agree to anything!"

The staffer was unfazed and unapologetic "These sorts of things take time, we now have to use the EC to negotiate a deal for the Russians in the Baltic States and discuss with the USA the NATO position on Belarus".

Sebastian researched the position further and was convinced that the position was hopeless in the short term. All the Baltic States were members of NATO and hence could just stubbornly hide behind that defensive line. The EU apparently had few powers to compel individual states to change their legislation. The treatment of Russian minorities in the Baltic States, depended from country to country. Basically there was little problem in Lithuania because Russians provided a small proportion, just 5% and posed no threat politically. But in Latvia 27% are Russian ethnic and 24% in Estonia. The problem is that a large % of Russians in Latvia and Estonia have non-citizen or alien status.

As Sebastian ruefully noted. 'Once again the 'Enlargement Group' of the EC have let through another terrible problem, after undisclosed weak finances in Greece, half negotiation on unification in Cyprus, bribery and corruption in Rumania and alien status in the Baltic States. They seem incapable of actually finding out problems that are likely to arise and make sure the matters are resolved before EU status is granted. How bloody stupid can you get? A Union based on Democracies allows second class status in a member state!'

As far as Belarus was concerned he could see no way in which Russia could publicly be given a free hand in that country.

On his return to the Foreign Office he immediately called the Foreign Minister himself and lodged a formal complaint. "My contact and reputation with the Russians is based on my honesty and integrity. There's no point in using me on this type of mission if you immediately negate my best position."

"OK, so Sebastian, what's your option? If we told them the truth that we can do nothing in either case they might just walk away!"

"Well the problem with your system is that they already know that. They know the UK has zero ability to change either of them. So they are testing out your honesty! Are you really keen to bring Russia in from the cold or are you simply continuing to play Foreign Office games? I would like to tell Sergey immediately that whilst we are looking at Russians in the Baltic States and Belarus we are not at all hopeful of achieving anything but we would still like to meet and continue the discussion!

"Sebastian that's not how the Foreign Office works, they don't reveal their hand like that! But OK this is your lead so I will instruct them to follow your instructions. Look I am happy to leave this in the hands of Peter Williams. You know him of course!"

At the following meeting with Sergey the Permanent Under Secretary was also in attendance but told Sergey that he was happy for Sebastian to take the lead.

Sebastian started "Sergey, I have discussed these matters here at the Foreign Office and, although we can try, we see no realistic prospect of achieving what you want for the Baltic States or Belarus!" He looked despondent "but what I can tell you is that I am prepared, if you are serious, to visit each of the member states myself to see if I can find supporters for bringing Russia in from the cold and starting a real dialogue! That's all I can offer!"

"Thank you Sebastian, if it were someone else I would not believe them but if you say so we accept it. Accordingly I will recommend that Russia accepts responsibility for the MH 17 crash"

On the way back Peter Williams, "Well Sebastian I think that's a first! Let's see what happens next?" Sebastian in turn thanked Peter Williams for giving him his head in this! They shook hands!

They need not have worried, a press release from the Russian Embassy in London was syndicated throughout the world. Russia had accepted responsibility, although emphasising that no Russia troops were involved, Russia accepted that the likelihood was that it came from those dissidents in the Lukhansk area. Russia apologised that there was huge loss of life and accepted the convention of paying for human life loss at typical rates. They also pointed out that several other planes had been downed in Ukraine and that it was surely the responsibility of Ukrainian flight control to have re-routed all flights away from that zone.

The Dutch in particular were impressed by the Russian press release because many passengers were from Holland and Sebastian made a bee-line for their foreign office to try to persuade them to reconsider their views on Russian sanctions, in fact the Ukraine peace agreement seemed to have held and there had of course been no further incursions into former USSR territory which the Baltic State in particular had feared.

The British Foreign Office encouraged Sebastian to himself speak out on the issue of the 'alien' residents in the Baltic States and he persuaded the Prime Minister to raise this as an issue. In this way Sebastian put continued pressure for improvement calling it an "Outrageous Injustice for people to be treated in that way!"

The German Chancellor was also moved by the progress on the Ukrainian Agreement and the press release and openly argued for the removal of sanctions which, as she said, did more damage to the EU than Russia who literally floated on oil and gas and simply could not be bankrupted into changing their policies as they had hoped. The Germans were of course interested in the huge Russian wealth in minerals which they were well placed to extract and use in their own industries.

Sebastian continued at the Foreign Office. As part of a team he helped prepare a trade deal with Russia and supervised the discussions with the charity to introduce democracy there.

He managed to live a normal life working a 5 day week, and usually got home at weekends, relieving pressure on his marriage. But he himself was still regarded as a 'bit of a maverick'. He had managed to irritate the Party's important Foreign Affairs and Health Committees, mostly filled by former MPs.

After several months the EC attitude began to change and by October 2017 the sanctions were removed and trading began with the EC as before. The UK highlighted the benefits of the UK trade agreement. This lead to a boost in Russia's trade and good economic growth. Under British pressure the USA agreed that it would not encourage any proposal for Belarus to join NATO.

CHAPTER TWENTY-THREE - July 2016 to October 26th 2017

the Constitutional Referendum

Sebastian became involved with the Lib Dem presentation to the Constitutional Commission. He had prepared his own paper on behalf of his constituency for consideration when requested. This was done within the 30 days' time-frame in July 2016.

He and Madge researched as far as they could into possible structures.

At first they took the oldest and most referred to of all constitutional commentaries, Walter Bagehot's 'The English Constitution'. The problem with it was that Bagehot himself had not contemplated any devolution. He was just describing how the constitution worked at a specific time, it was published in 1867. Indeed he did not even distinguish between a 'British' and 'English' constitution and the words are used interchangeably; in the first couple of pages referring to it as 'English' Constitution 8 times but 'British' 3 times.

However Bagehot's comments were important in that he centred on two key matters. The first of these is nowadays seen as a permanent fixture whatever the constitutional proposals. He suggested that the Monarchy was in fact a 'Disguised Republic' in the sense that all its powers have been devolved leaving only the pomp and visual impact. Probably most would still agree with that even in 2016.

The second was the *'efficient secret' of the English Constitution.*
...'which maybe described as the close union, the nearly complete fusion, of the executive and legislative powers'.

As R H Crossman commented:

"In departmental matters ministers are individually responsible to Parliament and play the role vis-à-vis their permanent civil servants. But on all the great decisions of state the Cabinet takes its decisions and acts collectively. In the secrecy of this committee each member is free to express his views. But once the decision has been taken they are all automatically committed by the doctrine of Cabinet responsibility, to support it in public". (Pages 20 & 21 Introduction to 'The English Constitution') This he says sharply reduces the interference by the Commons in this committee. The Civil Service works to that Cabinet brief.

Sebastian suggested "The problem with a constitutional change is not to find alternative structures, but to make sure that these key points are not overlooked, I think we can take the first one as agreed?" Madge agreed.

"Now let's say we go with a federal type structure where at least Scotland, Wales, Northern Ireland and possibly other strong UK Regions like London have some legislative powers but due to changes in circumstances the political parties in those devolved assemblies are not the same as in the Main Governing body as for example in Scotland with the SNP and Northern Ireland. The close knit agreement of the current UK Cabinet must either permanently exclude the power representation of those areas replaced by a parachuted in Minister responsible, or else their representatives must be drawn into a cabinet. But they may be unable to accept Cabinet responsibility. Indeed this would likely have been the case had in 2015 the Conservative Government attempted to draw in the SNP to any coalition because of its stated hatred of austerity".

Sebastian added "It looks as though we had an accident on our hands waiting to happen? Is it realistic to suggest that you can devolve significant powers to Scotland under say Devo Max but exclude representatives of that Assembly from a national cabinet? The first thing that any federal type unit will demand is that the powers given to it, whatever they are, can never be withdrawn, otherwise the federal unit would always be in fear of losing its powers, perhaps arbitrarily, at the whim of the governing party of the National Government. How can any National UK parliament operate in the current sense of being all powerful if it is incapable of changes in one of the lower Assemblies? Any future National UK Parliament then, if it is to be representative of the that area, cannot operate the traditional Cabinet System and has to acknowledge that it cannot upset the legislative powers already devolved."

"That suggests that any over-arching National Parliament and Government has to evolve in a different way. Probably that the individual federated units have a right to being represented in that National Government in some way. This may prevent the close knit Cabinet Committee structure which Bagehot thought so much about. Although that could operate at the level of an England Parliament

The problem with the current crisis of the British Constitution is that each of the Assemblies and indeed the regions within the UK, appear to be at different points in their travel along the road to greater devolution, any constitutional change has to allow for this. It's clearly no longer possible to suggest the same powers to say Devon & Cornwall as it is to Scotland although 40 years ago that might have been acceptable to both parties".

They researched further, there were other views on the matter:

David Steel the former Liberal leader suggested a test 'No scheme of devolution will ever win public enthusiasm unless it 1. Involves genuine decentralisation from Westminster, 2. Genuine reduction in local government patterns to one tier, 3. Reasonable financial independence and responsibility, 4. An electoral system which avoids domination by any one party or region of the country.' (partners in one nation page 87 as reported by Richard Holme).

Others have suggested different criteria for the choice of a system. A) Which system will provide the greatest degree of popular participation *and thus satisfy the feelings of provincial allegiance? B) Which system would produce the optimal balance of financial independence with the maintenance of an acceptable equalisation of economic conditions among the provinces) C) Which system would provide the most reliable safeguards for the human rights of individuals and minority groups within the provinces. D) Which system is more likely to preserve the coherence of the UK. E) Which system will be the most simple to administer avoiding bureaucracy if a further tier is introduced* (Burrows & Denton –'Devolution or Federalism' pages 14 & 15).

Madge held up a map of the UK from a former devolution study, "There's very little argument about the structure of new provinces, the UK naturally falls into certain regions and these have tended to be used over the years. They are North East, North West, Yorkshire, East Midlands, West Midlands, East Anglia, South West, South East and London. Maybe certain individual county sized units might prefer to be in a neighbouring province, but these could be subjected to a local referendum to settle that issue- but whatever, it's not like starting from scratch, most of the work is already done!"

They concluded "Considering all these points it would seem logical if there were to be devolution to the English Regions that, to prevent over-democratisation, unitary councils should be adopted throughout, eliminating District Councils. Probably adopting county wide single tier councils responsible for all regulatory issues like planning, registering of gaming, pubs and all other establishments plus waste collect and road cleaning. Then there would be a new Regional Assembly responsible for devolved services; health, education, local and regional transport, fire services, policing, housing development. It's likely that initially they would have devolved, not legislative, powers."

An English Parliament would be needed to legislate on the sum of the regional units as well as to cover non devolved (or retained) powers such as military, tertiary education, major motorway planning, rail and airport installations and services, justice, prison services, foreign affairs and foreign aid.

They both saw that the difficulty came with what happens above that level.

They agreed that it was most likely that the number of English MPs would be reduced and equalised on a per head basis with the MPs of the federated units like Scotland, Wales and Northern Ireland. So those same MPs meeting for the National Federated units, would meet again at specific times of the year to deal with 'all UK legislation' which would deal specifically with retained powers. All MPs would therefore have a double role.

"OK" Madge interjected "Then just explain who decides on the Trident replacement? Can a National Government over-rule a Regional Government? Can I say 'Not here!'? We are so used in the UK to seeing the all-powerful parliament in Westminster, we cannot, as yet, imagine it constrained in any way!"

They also submitted an appendix on House of Lords reform. There were two lines of thought.

On the one hand Sebastian realised that the House of Lords should be comprised of the most experienced and knowledgeable people in the country so that these could be brought to bear when reviewing, amending and improving Bills. On finance Bills for example who better to review the Bill than the Head of the Accountancy bodies. However although this would lead to a broader based house in terms of experience it would mean that they would have to accept indirect elections so that each person would be elected from their own body.

They prepared a list of such indirect elections that might be needed on the 'best brains basis'; they started off with Law Lords (perhaps 5 - essential for adjudicating on Constitutional matters), Bishops (5 plus other faith representatives another 5 – these would allow religions to be heard on important matters as a right), Trade Union representatives (5 – again to bind them into the legislative process). Chancellors of top universities (5 to ensure that there is a route to 'best brains'). Leaders of Business Groups (5 representing FTSE100 companies as well as Small businesses). Ombudsmen (7 to ensure that the results of cases requiring improvement can be fed directly back into the law-making process. Then we would add, the head of the Law Society, Head of Accountancy bodies and other leading professions such as Barristers, Doctors, Nurses, Architects, Surveyors and so on. Perhaps also adding the mayors of the top 10 Cities. There might even be a place for the election of a token number say 10 of the Peers to add continuity – the sense of show that Bagehot thought important. Perhaps to that might be added some 30 members selected by this chamber as having given meritorious service to the UK.

In the Constituency discussion most acknowledged the problem with such a list was that it was likely to be impossible to get acceptance of which posts should be included. For example, maybe the former Head of Scotland Yard should be included and the former Chief of the Military, but then why not the former Head of Prisons and why universities and not schools or technical colleges. Representation by occupation or skill risked unbalancing politics that were based on class, since those selected by position are more likely to be successful and therefore more wealthy and more likely to be unrepresentative of the working class and biased against the Labour Party.

On the other hand, opponents thought that this detail was unnecessary and that The House of Lords ought to be directly elected by the people. Few were able then to decide if, for example, they were make up seats from a PR system, how the powers of the House of Lords might possibly directly conflict with the House of Commons.

A final view was that perhaps a second chamber was not necessary following the New Zealand example.

The method of election to parliaments would present little emotional problems, the constitutional referendum has been called because the existing constitution is no longer fit for purpose. The electorate itself is changing in its loyalties and willingness to change votes, it's no longer good enough to avoid the chances of coalitions, the electorate itself appears to understand this. Whenever any review committees have made constitutional proposals they are always the same, none have ever accepted the first past the post as a fair electoral system. All systems should use proportional representation PR, preferably by STV which gives statistically the most accurate representation of peoples' votes. However its major problem is that it required huge constituencies making it much more difficult for the MP to relate to individuals. Hotspot canvassing swamping an area would no longer be possible.

Madge and Sebastian mused over their submission, they both clearly thought that all of these proposals would have a dramatic and permanent impact on the political scene. Madge was brutally frank to the Executive Committee " I don't think we have done a very good job with our submission, I just hope that the Constitutional Commission will do better!"

They doubted if one single Commission would tackle all these issues.

Anyhow they prepared a full version and issued this within the constituency for review and then passed this to LD Headquarters where it was incorporated within the Liberal Democrat submission.

They then filed the papers and sat and waited.

The draft report on the Constitutional proposals was published on Bank Holiday August 28th 2017.

It was impressive in its simplicity.

Regional Assemblies will be accepted in all areas of the England subject to a simple majority in the referendum. These will have powers similar to Wales covering, health, transport, education, fire, police and culture. Income will be allowed from Road Fund Tax, a proportion of the tax on motor petrol and diesel, all business rates, all registration fees. Regional Assembly members will be elected on STV with agreed ratio of Councillors per 1000 of the population

Unitary Councils below that will be based on County Councils with the abolition of District Councils and enhanced powers for Parish Councils still with unpaid Parish Councillors. They will cover all physical maintenance in their areas.

Scotland will receive additional income from North Sea oil tax on a basis to be agreed but the Bennett formula would will be adjusted to reflect their new financial income.

There will be an English Parliament run under the existing Cabinet system

There will be a UK Parliament made up of the Representatives of MPs from England and proportionately of Wales, Scotland and Northern Ireland. Its decision making powers to be determined by legal experts.

The House of Lords, it will number not more than 200 and will be agreed by the first UK Parliament as representing the widest cross section of the population as possible with sufficient experience. Peers will be limited to two terms.

It was, in effect, much as Sebastian had thought likely, though there were still enough problem areas to worry constitutional lawyers, particularly the numerous possible political combinations of parties. The proposals acknowledged that parties will strive to take the Constitution apart at the seams if it suited their purpose and to hold to ransom or frustrate a legally elected government. A new Supreme Court of Justice will adjudicate.

There were a large number of TV programmes to explain the impact of the changes and as all English parties had agreed to support the proposals there was little formal opposition. There was however considerable public disquiet and most of the public realised that however bad the previous system was, it was at least understood and had survived for hundreds of years. Sebastian was active as speaker. He was regularly on TV.

The fear that the UK would exit the EC eventually managed to concentrate the minds of the EU leaders and several meetings were held in early 2017 to discuss the detailed implications, at the first one the leaders decided that they would agree to the renegotiated points but each had to be referred back to their own national parliament.

At the same time the EC was subject to other individual nations in the EC wanting minor modifications to their treaties but many of these were fobbed off by the EC because of the lack of time for detailed discussions, but a new agreement was reached on immigrants such that all EC External Border Guards services were to be manned, funded and managed by an EC department, except in Schengen excluded areas. No immigrants were permitted unless registered outside the EC, all illegal immigrants were in future to be returned to external holding camps.

However certain countries including Denmark and Sweden took the opportunity to join with the UK in the detailed discussions and particularly in registering the rejection the clause of 'ever closer ties' and limited the EC movement of people and thus carried out a full treaty renegotiation alongside the UK. This in effect created the two stage Europe for which many pundits had been aiming for several years.

All the treaty changes were put up for referenda in each of the EC countries on the same day October 26th 2017. Sebastian worked tirelessly on the EC renegotiation when not needed by the Foreign Office.

CHAPTER TWENTY-FOUR - up to December 7th 2017

The Referendum was won by a 66/33 majority on most issues though less on the establishment of Regional Assemblies where the results varied considerably.

The Re-referendum on the EC was won by an overwhelming majority of 75/25

Sebastian arrived home on Friday after the Constitutional Referendum. He was exhausted and Sylvia immediately proscribed five working days off and called the Foreign Office and Lib Dem party to explain his absence.

He slept for a full 24 hours like a log and when he awoke he told Sylvia that the whole of the last 6 months had been a blur of meetings and lectures and talks and TV shows.

However to Sylvia's amazement by Monday he had already typed out, with Madge's help, the normal weekly report for constituents which was sent out by email. That night he attended the regular Lib Dem executive meeting. He was cheered on his entry to the room though he was quite clearly tired he also looked happy. "Well we at last have the Constitution that we want!"

On Tuesday he received an urgent call from Lib Dem Headquarters

The press had leaked a story that Government was about to go to the Country.

Tim Beaumond phoned, "Sebastian, I had a call from the PM, he said in view of the circumstances he did not see how he could continue since the basis on which he was elected had been jettisoned".

On the day following the Prime Minister announced his retirement and resignation.

He stated *"I made it clear tha I would reserve my position pending the outcome of this Commission and I believe that this is now an appropriate time to withdraw. The new proposed Electoral voting system chosen by the Constitutional Commission is STV the single transferable vote. Since that is likely to throw up a totally different mix of parties in different proportions, I feel that it is no longer appropriate to attempt to drag out the existing system by a day longer than is necessary as it clearly now lacks moral authority.*

Accordingly I aim to call a General Election at the earliest convenient date"

Another press release emerged later on that day giving further details.

"This Government accepted the Fixed-term Parliaments Act 2011. This specified that General Elections would be held on the first Thursday in May every fifth year after 7th May 2015. Earlier elections may only be held if a) a motion is agreed by two thirds of the whole house or b) if a motion of no confidence is passed and no alternative government is confirmed within 14 days. I have today had discussions with the other party leaders and I believe that the necessary number of members of two thirds of the house will assent. A General Election will be called for Thursday December 7th 2017. I would like to thank the members of the Commission for their work in achieving this workable constitution so quickly and to thank all my colleagues for their loyalty and dedication who have borne some difficult periods in this administration in good heart."

CHAPTER TWENTY-FIVE - December 7th to 22nd 2017

This notification plunged each of the parties into a period of intense activity all complaining that they didn't have enough time to re-organise their political support or structure from the smaller existing constituencies to the larger ones covering generally 4 times the area, 5 in city areas. There was also some quibbling about individual constituencies being in another area. None of the Regional Assemblies was yet elected, the dates of those were yet to be fixed.

In practice all political parties had begun to address the problem when the draft report was first issued a month before.

Within the Liberal Democrat camp there was a scene of chaos as the overloaded staff tried to react to current demands. The most difficult problem was sorting out the larger constituencies and calculating how many candidates to run. Under PR there's a golden rule 'the number of seats you expect to win, plus one'. This meant looking at the past returns of actual votes in 2015 and estimating the future voting pattern then add one just in case your vote is higher.

They knew the new rules of the game. Pitch the number of candidates too high and you risk spreading the votes too thinly so that none of the candidates reaches the minimum number, so all get eliminated before they can pass on their second votes. Pitch the number too low and all your candidates get elected but there's a surplus of party votes which simply goes nowhere. Luckily some bright spark had developed software taking the candidates actual voting returns in 2010 and 2015 and averaging them and then adapting to current circumstances.

Within each new larger constituency a 'pecking order' had to be established so that the lists were agreed as to which candidate was named as 'No 1 preference Mr S Smith', 'No 2 Mrs Brown', etc. etc.

All parties agreed that in this initial election each party would be likely to make mistakes but accepted that it was better than limping along using a now discredited voting system.

Important decisions would be needed to be made quickly on the exact composition of the House of Lords and settling dates for the number of Regional Assemblies.

It appeared from the results that the introduction of devolved health services and the reduction to unitary councils below that had done the trick and all regions had agreed to move ahead even though in some regions there was a very slim majority for this change, but London, East Anglia and the South West the approval rating was well over 60%.

It was expected that the impact on the District Councils would be delayed for a year to allow for the replacing and amalgamation of these councils and the run down of the existing structure. The biggest complainants of all were the parties who had established their own little District Council power bases for the past two decades, which they saw as now being completely destroyed. The CEO and Leader of Middleton Council both tried to persuade Sebastian to write to the Minister responsible to delay the changes, but he said he would not do that.

Tim Beaumond himself complained to his executive committee that the pressure on him was intense as each of the disagreements over the new constituencies was expected to get his personal approval on appeal and he was spending all his time on internal matters rather than prepare for the General Election campaign. Unlike other main political parties the Lib Dems did not have an elected Deputy Leader but had instead elected a Deputy Leader of the Parliamentary Lib Dem Party who was sometimes used in that role. The fourteen members agreed that it was time to resurrect that Deputy Leader position which had remained dormant since 2015.

Sebastian's work-rate was acknowledged as 'fantastic'. He was put forward for that position with the brief of taking all internal decisions concerning candidates off the shoulders of the Leader. He was enthusiastically supported by his colleague Bill Bennett.

Sebastian realised what was in effect happening was that each of the other Lib Dem MPs were positioning themselves for the imminent General Election for a major role as expert speakers for the 'Major Offices of State', Foreign, Home, Chancellor, Military, Health and Education, so that the 12 remaining Lib Dem MPs split those fronting roles between themselves. They would be expected to present the Party on TV and at set piece debates.

Sebastian realised that it was a logical progression in several ways. He had worked well with Tim and had considerable respect for him, his own knowledge of Lib Dem policies on several of the 'Major Offices' was nothing like as detailed as those who had been full Ministers in the last coalition. His new position would, however, bring him into contact with a large number of potential new Lib Dem MP's, though many would be former MPs, Sebastian reckoned that making contacts at this stage would be likely to yield returns in the future. He was assiduous in racing around the country resolving smaller issues relating to the candidates and raising party morale at constituency level.

Sebastian found it hard to reconnect with his constituency but he had supported both Tim Holland and Madge O'Connor as Parliamentary Candidates for the enlarged constituency seat and had hoped for their active support. In view of his commitment on the national scene Sebastian had had to leave the details of the constituency battle to his two allies. They would have to lead the larger constituency election planning.

Trouble arose at the first meeting. Tim Holland felt that as Leader of the Lib Dems on the District Council he ought to be in No 2 position after Sebastian but he had already indicated to Madge over a year ago that he would support her, so she expected to be in the No 2 preference position on any lists given to the voters covering the Middleton area. However, Tim called for a vote from members, an emergency meeting was held and he won narrowly. Sebastian was concerned that he had let Madge down but managed to find a Number 2 position at the Constituency covering Lincoln with which she had some connection because it was her home town. Sebastian hoped that, with her excellent ability to write speeches, she would succeed in that area. No number 3 was recruited for Sebastian's area as the view was that 2 would be the maximum likely to be elected.

It was a nervous time, the Lib Dems were incapable of canvassing such a huge new extended area because their supporters were not concentrated in other nearby old constituencies. Everything therefore depended on the leaflet which was delivered for free.

Sebastian was more worried than on any previous election and he knew that he had not spent enough time 'pressing the flesh' in the wider constituency. Moving Madge to another constituency further reduced the number of local activists. Most of his time was still spent sorting out boundary matters and it was only in the last two weeks that he was able to base himself at home and work exclusively in his constituency.

Sebastian gloomily was reviewing the canvassing returns in the constituency office when Edna Leggs came in "How's it going Sebastian?" she enquired in a matter of fact way. Sebastian threw down some papers from one of the chairs so she could sit down. The office was a cluttered as at every election time with all sorts of mess from old fish & chip papers to pizza boxes, empty coffee mugs and cans of coke with piles of leaflets either waiting to go out or surpluses from a previous run. Madge was a good deal more tidy than the other workers and her departure was quickly felt.

"Well", he said "nothing like as positive as I had hoped! As you will remember before my by-election we were regularly getting opinion polls in the upper teens from 13% to 17% and we assumed that would continue, but that's not the case. Once again a period in coalition appears to have reduced it to between 10% and 13%. Whilst in the total number of votes that's fine, but if it's equally spread evenly across the country we might not get the full benefit of PR, that's because we are probably putting up too many candidates. Everything therefore depends on the discipline of the voters in putting the Lib Dem candidates in the same priority order. If, for example, one third of Lib Dems in one constituency give first preference to candidate A, if another third gives their first preference vote to B and the final third gives in first to candidate C, there's a possibility that all candidates fall off the bottom before being able to activate the rest of the preference votes. It's a real worry! I have already pointed this out to Tim Beaumond but in some areas where there were several former MP's it proved very difficult to get one to stand down and to prioritise preferences 1,2 etc."

He began twiddling the signet ring on his finger, Edna noticed this and the fear in his voice. Edna Leggs talked quietly. "Is there anything we can do here?"

"No not really, I am well enough known here to be given the No 1 preference. But in this larger constituency we are a Lib Dem island within a largely Tory area, the natural majority would be Conservative, but of course we have no UKIP candidate standing here. One or two of them remain, for example over in Lincoln, but it depends how their vote splits back. Winning my by-election was only possible by the split of the Tory vote and incompetence of Labour but they have already elected a more winnable leader. Logically we might not even be able to win if the by-election was re-run without UKIP. I am sorry to say so but my own chances of election are remote!"

"How are you going to use your time then? And surely we can help in some way?" Edna was clearly increasingly concerned.

"Well I am due to take part in the National TV political advert and am likely to be on one of the local radio stations, apart from that the only thing we can do is to do as much canvassing in likely Lib Dem areas. As we have little voter information and no canvassing records for the two constituencies on either side of us, we are playing in the dark. We shall have to fix on several estates and just run with those, then finally do an evening-before-the-vote leaflet and spread it as far as we can. I can try to work out a programme for all our helpers; luckily our membership has continued to increase, so we should get more helpers for delivery."

"Come on Sebastian don't give up yet, we didn't all of us put all that effort into getting you elected just to lose everything now! Think of the work you have done, of the need to address the Democratic Deficit in the NHS and bringing Russia in from the cold. These were your ideas, don't give up on them and your supporters now!"

"Yes you are right Edna, dear Edna you have always been motivated by the best of feelings, for which I am permanently grateful. Yes I must shake myself and get into canvassing mode. I will do whatever I can, I promise you! It's just that the central Deputy role has temporarily worn me out, drained me of energy. But OK from tomorrow we go on again!!! Thanks for this chat, let's call a meeting for tomorrow; we still have two weeks!!"

With that Sebastian geared up for action over the last two weeks, at least he had the satisfaction of knowing that the freely delivered leaflet was ready to go and he had hopes that the other political parties would be in at least as much of a muddle as Lib Dems were locally.

Many voters pointed out that to have a new electoral system deployed for an election just before Christmas was not the smartest of moves and there was some hostility, but it had been an all-party accord which meant that the complaint was never taken seriously enough to force any change to the timetable.

What happened in practice was that many areas were not canvassed at all and much depended on the TV debates which, as their length in minutes depended on a mixture of current polls and last time's election results, scarcely favoured the Lib Dems.

When the results came through it was clear that there was again no overall majority.

What in effect had happened was that Lib Dems had gained more seats but were now at 30 seats still a long way short of the hope of returning to former levels of 50 plus MPs. Still there were wins in the South West, South East and London and one or two more in Scotland, North East and North West. Sebastian himself was re-elected on the slimmest of margins using the final transferred preference votes. Most of the gains were from Conservatives.

Labour had regained some of the seats in Scotland from SNP, the Greens gained 5 seats and the rump of UKIP also won 2 seats. Conservatives remained the largest party but fell short of a majority.

There was a pause of a couple of days as the Parties began to absorb the output of the new system and its results.

A week or so before Christmas 2017 Edna Leggs died after a very short illness. Sebastian phoned one of her friends whom he had met at the garden party over a year before, and asked about the circumstances. He was told that she had been poorly for some time and, by the time she had visited the doctor, it was too late, the cancer was unstoppable. Sebastian mulled over the last words that he had had with her and realised how much he had valued her common sense. Had he even asked how she was? Typically her last comments were about supporting him not about herself.

On the same day he was called by Lib Dem HQ and asked to come quickly.

He arrived that same afternoon. Tim Beaumont was addressing the MPs as he arrived. He first went through the results and congratulated the Lib Dem winners then he said...

"Remember we are now on an STV system so whereas previously we could swing from 8 to 65 MPs this method makes that less likely, so we are in a much stronger position. It's likely we will form a coalition with one 'side' or the other, or possibly with several parties.

Accordingly I intend to form an interim steering committee to conduct all Coalition discussions. In order to do that we need first to elect members to these roles. As you know we chose several MPs during the election as spokesmen for the major offices and I intend to take 4 of these plus 2 representatives from those newly elected, the Leader in the House of Lords and the Chief Whip. Because of his exceptional work during the last election I have proposed Sebastian Edwards as Chief Whip, he's a man of exceptional organising ability in whom I have complete faith. The team will comprise 8 people."

Since the work of this group is likely to start very soon, it's not really practical to have an open vote since many of you have never worked with each other before, nor is it possible to seek a vote on a wider basis and involve members because we simply do not have the time. I hope members will realise that what I am doing is to try to blend experience of older heads with the enthusiasm of newer members. I intend to seek formal approval by all paid-up members at a later stage, but anyhow within 3 months."

Accordingly all MPs were asked to discuss and then vote for a named list.

Bill Bennett spoke up for Sebastian and this was given nodding assent by several of those whom Sebastian had helped during the campaign. There was considerable discussion about whom to select to represent the new members but it was thought advisable to ensure that there was a representative in-so-far as possible from each of the Regions. This whittled down the possible candidates to 4 and two of those withdrew.

Sebastian was confirmed as the chief whip.

Tim Beaumond called for an immediate meeting of those named, all other MP's were invited to attend this initial meeting.

They discussed first the criteria for any coalition, but then was the inevitable question. If a combination was required for a majority Government which would include Lib Dems. Then whom would they favour?

There were, it was agreed, several ways of looking at it a) Follow the lead of the largest party b) Consider the matter open and listen to any other combinations proposed c) Consider the total votes cast – a coalition ought to try to have a majority of votes d) Consider the programmes of all the parties and attempt first to work with those who have similar programmes and are likely to support our key policies e) Consider those parties who have different or objectionable policies with whom Lib Dems would find it difficult to work – crossing so called 'red lines.'

They all agreed that this was going to be much more complex than many had thought since the choice of criteria might result in different combinations.

Tim suggested a way out of this dilemma. "First I would like all members apart from the Chief Whip to identify Policy differences and similarities. Sebastian, I intend to use you as the access to the MP's who are not on our committee and be their mouthpiece on the committee. Does everyone understand?

Central Lib Dem staff were given the task of going through each parties manifesto and listing down key policies. These were then to be circulated Monday before Christmas with a view to meeting up later in the week.

Sebastian arrived back home on Friday night December 15th.

Sylvia welcomed him home and he briefed her on his new role "There you are I told you you were going to be a very important person!" as she produced a bottle of champagne but she was interrupted by a call from a new nervous MP wondering about what he should tell his constituents; another called saying his constituency demanded that their MP carry out a vote of all members before any coalition agreement. Sebastian tried to resolve these issues.

Of course as he was leaving Lib Dem HQ someone jammed a file of CVs of all Lib Dem MP's with Tim's note "Could you spot please any possible Junior ministers here?" Another file related to all the other Party's' Manifestos. So as he commented to Sylvia "I do have some light reading – no need to give me a novel for Christmas I have two here!" All of the Steering Committee members were given notes on 'Red Lines' and 'Priority Policies'.

He was called again on Saturday morning "Come quickly the discussions on forming a new Government will begin soon". Apparently the Conservatives first thoughts were to form a minority Government and they had been talking with Northern Ireland Parties but that had fallen apart. At the same time Labour were in discussions with the SNP. At Lib Dem HQ the steering group completed their analysis but no call came. They were all told to be within reach of a phone over the Christmas period, leaving mobile phones if they wandered off for a Boxing Day walk. They spent the rest of the week carrying out 'Game theory - managing tactics!'

Accordingly they each returned home on December 22nd along with the remaining 50% of the population who hadn't been able to get away earlier. He thought that it might be a 'White Christmas' it was cold enough!

It was late when he arrived home. They dined alone and Sebastian began to relax, he knew the bedlam would start again but for the moment he was beyond recall, he would not budge till after Boxing Day. That was four whole days off.

He was sitting by the fire in his father's old wooden swivel chair. It was Christmas Eve and Sylvia had already gone upstairs. He picked up from the mantelpiece the framed photo of those key people at the Garden Party on May 22nd 2016. Some of those had gone of course; Edna Leggs, dead, and he had heard nothing from Tim Holland and Madge O'Connor but he worried that they both would have felt he had let them down.

'He mused perhaps it was right? What was the saying? "To travel hopefully is a better thing than to arrive"

Now who on earth said that – Ah yes Robert Lewis Stevenson – was he right – I wonder?' Sebastian thought that he would never again recreate the same camaraderie, the same teamwork, the same hope.

His son Rupert called him on Christmas Day "So what are you now Kingmakers? I see you have got a peg up! A bit different from being shown as in the pocket of the Conservative Prime Minister? Anyhow good luck!"

The call that mattered came at noon on Boxing Day "Come immediately!"

He knew his life would change for ever! But how and when would it end? He had no idea, nor any career plan, up to now it had been just an instinct for survival that had carried him through.

People in this Story   Relationship to story

Douglas Finlay	Close Friend & Confidant lives in Northumberland
Sarah Edwards	Sebastian's first wife
Alexander Edwards	Sebastian's elder son
Rupert Edwards	Sebastian's younger son
Jenny Jefferies	Sebastian's mother-in-law
William Jefferies	Sebastian's father-in-law
Sylvia Edwards	Sebastian's secretary then second wife
Andrew Steel	MD of N. Ireland Communications Co, Sebastian's boss.
Roy Booth	Operations Director & MD of Sebastian's Belfast Co.
William Bartlet	Union representative at Co. in Northern Ireland
Manuel Diago	California Electronics, Sebastian's employer Scotland
Elizabeth Trickett	Dishonest employee in Scotland.
RKW	His employer a FTSE listed Mineral Extraction co in UK
John Avis	HR Director of RKW
Sir John Lowdham	Chairman of RKW
Siberian Minerals	The Russian offshoot saved by Sebastian
Gennady Badurin	Rogue investor in Siberian Minerals
Jeffrey Pardoe	Sebastian's Assistant & Dir in Russia did acquisitions
Dmitri Davidoff	The Russian MD of Siberian Minerals based in Moscow
Andrey Petrov	Part-time translator and driver for Sebastian in Russia
Dr Singh	Sebastian's GP who introduced him to his charity
Dr Cottee	Sebastian's consultant for stomach ailments
Edna Leggs	Sebastian's mentor and Chair of local Lib Dems
Tim Holland	Lib Dem rival, District & County Councillor, Middleton
Madge O'Connor	Lib Dem activist for Focus, Councillor, PA to Sebastian
Mohammed Rahmam	Lib Dem, dentist crucial supporter & District Councillor
Dallat Ahmed	Lib Dem supporter and later Councillor
Will Jenkins	Lib Dem former councillor, ill part of the time
John Laver	Lib Dem Councillor, limited time on Council work
Norman Dodgson	Lib Dem local Treasurer
Sally Jones	Lib Dem Activist & Helper – Focus Routes
Rod James	Lib Dem helper – Posters and signs
Tim Beaumond MP	Lib Dem Foreign Affairs spokesman later leader of LDs
Bill Bennett MP	Lib Dem MP, Sebastian's friend elected at same time
David Liffington MP	Minister for Europe in the Coalition 2010-2015
Roland Smith	British Ambassador to Ukraine

Keith Williams	Permanent Under Secretary at the Foreign Office
Sergey Kramrenko	Special Envoy, Minister Counsellor at London Embassy
Andrew Laws MP	Conservative MP for Middleton
John Clark	Leader of Labour Group on Council, contested seat.
Tim Dabbs	Green Councillor with whom Sebastian does a deal
Chris Walmsley	UKIP District Councillor former Conservative
Pamela Brown	Leader of the Labour Party in Scotland
Jim Hannah	Police Sergeant in Cultra Northern Ireland
William (Billy) Stewart	Policeman in Cultra Northern Ireland
James Stewart	Police Sergeant in Glasgow
Ilya Ilyitch Volkov	Policeman near Perm in Russia saved by Sebastian
John Denny	Police Inspector in Middleton